Small Prices

Small Prices

Justice Hawk

iUniverse, Inc.
New York Lincoln Shanghai

Small Prices

iUniverse, Inc.

For information address:
iUniverse, Inc.
2021 Pine Lake Road, Suite 100
Lincoln, NE 68512
www.iuniverse.com

ISBN: 0-595-30774-4

Printed in the United States of America

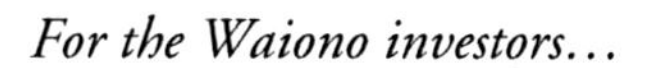

For the Waiono investors…

Acknowledgments

There are many people who helped in the production of this story. First is the production staff: Renee Szeligas and her associates in Chicago. Second is the publisher. Third are the informants who desire to remain anonymous. There are others who assisted with the production of this novel who also have desired to remain anonymous.

Preface

In the three decades following statehood, the state of Hawai'i struggled to control a lawlessness of tropical exuberance. In the first decade, following a period of easy money from the enormous buildup of troops in the Pacific Theater for World War II and the Korean Conflict, Hawai'i arose as a vacation paradise. Land reclamation commenced in earnest in order to sate the tremendous demand for resort hotels. A chicken farm surrounded by swamp was converted into Waikiki Beach. Hotels sprung up like palm trees. Every form of celebrity and charlatan imaginable flocked into the islands. There was money to be made...easy money...in entertainment, real estate, tourism, human trafficking, drugs, and robberies.

During this first decade, the political landscape changed, as well. The Democratic Party slowly eroded the dominance of the Republican Party. By the end of first decade after statehood, the Democratic Party had taken over political control of the City & County of Honolulu, the Governorship of the state of Hawai'i, and most of the representation to the United States Congress. With the incoming Democrats came a more *laissez faire* and relationship related form of governance. The ancient regime of the huge corporations, plantations and the prominent law firms had given way to a more laborer class oriented leadership. Although there was an effort to curb the lawlessness of big time era spenders, Hawai'i remained a popular tourist spot that encouraged laxer law enforcement.

In the second decade following statehood, the Democratic Party solidified their political stronghold over the state. *Laissez faire* and relationship-type governance permeated every corridor of the state bureaucracy. Businesses with good political ties flourished, whereas, businesses without political ties took a backseat. This scenario repeated itself in the criminal element of Hawai'i, as well. Criminals with strong ties with powerful politicians and bureaucrats essentially went about their affairs with near immunity.

During this second decade, horizontal real estate development diminished as more lands were taken up. Slowly, some of the huge plantations were parceled up to provide more land with which to feed the expanding housing demand, providing opportunities for windfall profits by politicians and senior bureaucrats with cognizance over these land areas. Children of plantation workers who rose into the bureaucratic or political ranks amassed fortunes form these opportunities. Vertical real estate in the form of condominiums began to displace horizontal real estate developments. Air space became a marketable commodity, as real estate development rose above ground level. A middle class established itself for the first time in the state of Hawai'i and controlled its politics. Unions flourished in support of the middle class and aligned themselves firmly with the Democratic Party.

The new middle class, basking in good living, demanded a reduction in the lawlessness of the prior decades. Good living equated with peaceful existence. Slowly, law enforcement began to eradicate the wilder elements of society.

As the third decade after statehood commenced the population began to realize that their resources were limited. First, it was land. Second, the ocean resources began to dwindle. Third, overseas competition pressured the huge sugar and fruit plantations.

By the middle of the third decade after statehood, Hawai'i only has tourism and military presence accommodating for most of the state revenues. Honolulu never becomes a boomtown. The unions, via the dominant Democratic Party, have relinquished their middle-of-the-Pacific-Ocean strategic location to the Mainland ports of Los Angeles and Oakland. International trade for Honolulu becomes subservient to Los Angeles and Oakland. The days of easy money begin to dwindle rapidly. Honolulu witnesses a business climate collapsing upon itself. As plantations lose their competitiveness, the military undergoes reduction in numbers and other Pacific Basin locations begin to rival Hawai'i as a vacation destination, the coffers of the state dwindle. With less money in the state treasury, the huge bureaucracy created in the earlier decades by the Democratic Party experiences pressure to reduce its numbers. Likewise, the unions see a slip in work demand, compelling them to reduce their numbers. By the end of the third decade, the financial status of the state of Hawai'i is in a tailspin. Increased taxation and borrowing maintain the Democratic Party in power, as they consolidate their hold on all the major City & County and State elected offices.

This story takes place during the later part of the second decade after statehood, before the middle class effectively can influence a reduction in lawlessness. The story traces the lives of an assortment of characters, as they navigate this troublesome time. Most of the characters in this novel are based upon real life individuals. Most of the events depicted in the novel are based upon real events that have been compressed and molded to fit the story. This novel penetrates deeply into the underworld of Hawai'i. The names of the characters have been changed to protect the innocent and the guilty. Most are guilty!

Caution: This novel contains passages of unsavory practices and violence.

CHAPTER 1

It is lunchtime in Downtown Honolulu. As Easy Eddie makes my way down Fort Street Mall to the Mattoon Financial Center, he smiles at the little groups clustering at the rest benches enjoying their snacks. A cosmopolitan crowd frequents the Mall. We have Northern Europeans sitting under a covered area outside a Mexican restaurant, Southern Europeans emerging from a Vietnamese restaurant, East Asians chatting in a booth of a local Subway sandwich shop, South Asians enjoying a mini-pizza, Africans and Pacific Islanders stuffing into a hamburger stand, and everywhere locals and college students milling about and chatting away. Some even join in singing to a ukulele being strummed by a local musician. Life is that way in Honolulu for the leisure crowd. Absent from the pressures of competition and survival, life can be full of meaningless enterprises, affirmations toward a better world and short-lived rejoicing. I suppose that is what it is like on the surface of any large city. Why would it not be? It does not cost anything.

This is Easy Eddie's town. His family has been here since the Portuguese settled in the islands. There is a little Chinese blood in him as well. He plays that up to enable himself to make connections in Hawai'i's jewelry trade. Jewelry is his business. He even carries a business card to prove it.

Today, Easy Eddie is on my way to meet a couple of hotheads with acid in their veins that are in need of his collateral services. He promised a family connection he would assist them. He knows it is a bad idea, but a promise is a promise.

As Easy Eddie waits for the light to change to cross Honolulu's main east-west running thoroughfare, King Street, he notices two characters seated on the cement wall next to the Mattoon Financial Center, the business heart of Honolulu. Both are locals of Hawai'ian descent, the typical Hawai'ian Reservation rat variety. From their facial expressions, they have been waiting for Easy Eddie a while. They seem impatient. How does Easy Eddie get myself into these situations? These two Mokes look dangerous.

Moke is a derogatory term for a Hawai'ian male.

Easy Eddie "Good to see you guys. Sorry I am late. I got tied up with a client."

Bosco obviously angry with Easy Eddie's tardiness, "We gonna do this, or what?"

Bosco is a long, frizzy-haired weirdo that looks like he just climbed down from a jungle tree. He is a 200-pound, dark-skinned, local with a rough looking face. The sooner he is incarcerated the better. His partner, Keno, looks like a scrawny, sewer rat. Thank God, they wore Aloha shirts! At least they will be presentable when Easy Eddie takes them into the vault area.

Easy Eddie "Hey, your cousin asked me to do you a favor. I like your cousin, so don't get excited. Calm down. Shall we get on with this?"

Keno "You better be OK, Eddie, or you'll find yourself face up in a sugar cane field as food for the mongooses."

Easy Eddie disturbingly shakes off the threat, "It's fine, Keno. Let's get this done."

Easy Eddie mumbles, "If these two Mokes weren't my cousin's friends, I would shoot them myself, right now."

Easy Eddie and the two Mokes enter the Mattoon Financial Center's main office area and take the elevator down to the vault area.

As they enter the vault, the staff greets Easy Eddie, "Hey, Eddie, got any good things for us, today?"

Easy Eddie laughs, "I might have something next week."

Vault manager, after he appraises the two Mokes, smiles at Easy Eddie, "You've been slow lately, Eddie. I hope business picks up for you."

The vault manager suspects these are two of Easy Eddie's boys. Easy Eddie has known the vault manager for a long time. The vault manager knows what Easy Eddie does in the vault.

Easy Eddie fakes a smile that conveys what the vault manager suspects, "Things might be better this next week."

The vault manager presents Easy Eddie a vault access slip to sign. Easy Eddie signs it Ed Sone. Easy Eddie keeps all his safe deposit boxes under that name. The vault manager knows it is a fake name. But, given the contents of the safe deposit boxes, it is better for everyone that no one knows the identity of the owner.

The vault manager opens the vault access door. Easy Eddie and the two Mokes are allowed to enter the inner vault area. The vault manager escorts the group to one of Easy Eddie's safe deposit boxes. Easy Eddie motions the vault manager to another area of bank of boxes. The vault manager smiles at Easy Eddie, as he enters his key into the safe deposit lock. Easy Eddie returns the smile, as he enters his key into the adjoining lock. The vault manager opens the outer door and removes a large safe deposit box. He hands the box to Easy Eddie and then escorts the group to a private booth in the rear of the vault area. Easy Eddie reminds the vault manager that he will need a few moments alone. The vault manager assures Easy Eddie that no one will disturb him.

After the vault manager leaves us, Easy Eddie locks the booth door and opens the safe deposit box. In the box is a cache of guns wrapped in sealed, cellophane-like material.

Bosco elated, "My cousin was right, Keno. He does have the guns!"

Both the Mokes smile approvingly.

Easy Eddie "Be quiet while we do this."

Bosco cups his mouth, "OK, sorry."

The amplitude of the conversation lowers into a whisper.

Easy Eddie "These guns are clean. They are in these bags, because my good friend has cleaned them of any fingerprints. When you are done with what you need to do, return the guns to me, so I can have them wiped clean of your fingerprints. My good friend will keep the guns in a safe place, so no one can find them. Do you understand?"

Bosco "My cousin said you could dispose of any dead bodies as well."

Easy Eddie "That can be arranged, depending on the circumstances. If someone sees you kill the guy, then I can't help you with that. You've got my private number."

The two Mokes pick out two guns. They choose low caliber .32s.

Easy Eddie "Those are good choices. They are light and easy to handle. Make sure you are close to the target when you use them."

Bosco "Thanks, Eddie."

The two Mokes stuff the weapons into their waistline under their shirts. The weapons are still in their cellophane-like containers.

Easy Eddie calls for the vault manager. He escorts the group to the vault where Easy Eddie reinserts the safe deposit box. Easy Eddie and the two Mokes leave the Mattoon Financial Center area, shake hands and go our separate ways.

Lunchtime is about over, Easy Eddie needs to run over to the Main Post Office and check his jewelry business' mail.

The Main Post Office is a few blocks in the direction of Diamond Head from the Mattoon Financial Center. Diamond Head is the landmark inactive volcano on the east end of the Koolau Mountain Range of O'ahu. The walk is an easy stroll down King Street. Easy Eddie takes his time on the first block to check out the *wahines* (Hawai'ian for female) in a park area set up for lunchtime entertainment. Easy Eddie thanks God that he is a jeweler; otherwise, he could never have a chance to hustle some of those young babes. The next block consists of a number of little sandwich and *saimin* shops. They always seem busy at this time of day. Easy Eddie has never understood why someone would leave his high-rise, condo office to order just a half of a sandwich then take the half sandwich back to his office. It must be the pretty *wahines* doing the same thing that lures them.

As Easy Eddie walks through the second block, he always smiles when he passes the South Pacific Title Building. There are some secrets worth smiling about in that company's archives. If the general public only knew!

The Main Post Office of Honolulu complex straddles King and Merchant streets. Its Spanish design is stark in comparison with the surrounding architecture, and it looks old. Easy Eddie's store has a large post office box that he checks. His store has had this box since the 1950s when his uncle took over the business after the war. Honolulu has sure changed since the war, but this post office and this box have remained essentially the same.

As Easy Eddie opens the box, he hears over my shoulder, "Hey, Eddie, how are you?"

Easy Eddie turns to see his old friend from the Big Island, "Good to see you! How are you?"

The Big Island is the local expression for the island of Hawai'i, the largest of the Hawai'ian islands.

Old friend "Your uncle said I might catch you here. I was just up at your store."

The old friend is a 250 lbs., 6'3", local of Hawai'ian and Portuguese ancestry.

Easy Eddie "Yes, I check this box everyday during the lunch hour. It's a good walk for me. I have to keep in shape, you know."

Old friend "Listen Eddie, I need a favor. Can you help me?"

Easy Eddie "Of course, what are old friends for?"

Old friend "My son is getting married, and he needs a good ring for his bride."

Easy Eddie "Is he looking for a Hawai'ian wedding band or a diamond?"

Old friend "He would like a nice diamond, but he can't afford one."

Easy Eddie "If he can afford a thousand dollars, I can get him a near investment-grade, one carat diamond."

Diamonds are rated according to the four Cs: carat, clarity, color and cut. Investment grade refer to clarity greater than very slightly included and color better than H. Clarity ranges from flawless down through very, very slightly included (VVS) to very slightly included (VS). D, E, F and G are clearly investment-grade colors. H is a borderline color that is sometimes accepted as investment grade when the clarity exceeds the lowest very slightly included clarity grade (VS2).

Old friend pleasantly surprised, "One thousand dollars? Eddie, my jeweler friend in Hilo quoted him six thousand dollars for a one-carat diamond. I doubt it was investment grade even. That's wonderful!"

Hilo is a large city on the Big Island.

Easy Eddie "For you, old friend, I'll even mount the stone for him in a white or yellow gold ring. I'll even get him GIA papers, authenticating its quality and value."

GIA refers to the Gemologist Institute of America, the most reliable in precious gem certification.

Old friend "Really! How soon can you get this done?"

Easy Eddie rubbing his chin with his right hand, "When does he get married?"

Old friend "The wedding is set for five weeks from now."

Easy Eddie "Stop by the store in three weeks. I'll have the ring and papers ready for you. Just fax or phone me the bride's ring size as soon as you can."

Old friend "Eddie, you amaze me. How can you get such good deals?"

Easy Eddie "I'm in the business, and for old friends, I can slash my profit margin."

Old friend "I hadn't realized that jewelers make such a profit."

Easy Eddie smiles, "If the public only knew how much they actually make, they would be shocked. But, you have to keep this price to yourself. It is a one-time deal. Do you understand? I cannot do this for everyone; otherwise, I make no money, and I would anger the jewelry industry."

Easy Eddie shakes hands with the Big Island friend. His friend seems content. People always seem content when they get a good deal. It is strange how they never do the numbers in order to realize that Easy Eddie could not possibly have deals that good. They never want to know. They get a deal, and they just shut up. This old friend is even a police officer on the Big Island. They just do not want to know.

God! If his friend quoted him six thousand dollars for a one-carat diamond, then that must have been a near wholesale price. It was probably somewhere near sixty percent of value. That means the DeBeers New York price would be around three thousand dollars. Even if we consider his jeweler friend could be operating on triple-key pricing, the cheapest that diamond could be in New York is two thousand dollars plus security and shipping costs.

Triple key pricing refers to tripling the wholesale price rather than the normal doubling. How can Easy Eddie offer a diamond for half the New York price? It is not like Easy Eddie has his own diamond mine right here in Hawai'i. People just do not ask!

There was not much mail in the post office box, today. Easy Eddie needs to get back to the store. An easy stroll through the park area crossing though Union Mall and Fort Street Mall gets him back quickly enough. He gets to check out all the *wahines* on the way back, too.

Fort Street and Union Mall run perpendicular to King Street in Downtown Honolulu.

Easy Eddie's store is on the third floor of the old O'ahu Mercantile Building on Cornish Street. Cornish Street is just west of and runs parallel to Fort Street Mall. The O'ahu Mercantile Building is an old building located right in the center of Honolulu. The landlords have changed often during the past thirty years. Easy Eddie has been told the rental potential for the building is attractive when viewed from a market analysis standpoint. However, despite the increase in amenities that each succeeding landlord has applied to the building to improve its aesthetic appearance, rental rates have remained stubbornly at the same low level over the past decade. The building has not been able to attract "anchor" tenants. Some people have teased that it is because of Easy Eddie's presence in the building. Some reputations are always good.

As Easy Eddie enters the store, he hears, "It's about time you came back! Did you stop to play craps?"

That is Uncle Jacob scolding Easy Eddie. He is the major partner in the store. If it were not for him, Easy Eddie would not have a job here.

Uncle Jacob is a slender built, 6'2" tall Chinese local with a receding hairline.

Easy Eddie "No, I came right back. Are there any deliveries I need to make?"

Jacob furious, "One guy has been screaming all morning for his delivery."

As Jacob hands Easy Eddie the package, "Silver Teal Jewelry wants this, right now."

Easy Eddie "Were there any calls for me?"

Jacob obviously upset, "Damn the calls, Eddie, get that delivery to Silver Teal."

Sensing Uncle Jacob's displeasure, Easy Eddie grabs the package and heads down the elevator to the parking garage.

Silver Teal Jewelry is near Waikiki. It will be a good drive; besides, Easy Eddie has not stopped for lunch. His Uncle Jacob is right, Easy Eddie did take a long lunch hour. Easy Eddie left the shop around 9:30 AM. It is what, 2:00 PM now? Oh well, it is another day in paradise.

As Easy Eddie pulls up to the Silver Teal Jewelry and parks his car in front, the owner, a short, overfed, Chinese immigrant, comes running out of the store yelling in poor English and waving his finger, "You no can park there! You no can park there!"

The Silver Teal Jewelry, like most business locations along this street, is a converted garage or summerhouse that has been upgraded to resemble a jewelry outlet. The rent is cheap here. It has to be to make ends meat. This company specializes in jewelry manufacturing and repair. They are true jewelers. Silver Teal Jewelry, like many other jewelry stores owned by Chinese immigrants, are the sweatshops of Honolulu's jewelry industry. The big name jewelers in Honolulu actually get all their alterations, designs and repairs done in places like these.

Easy Eddie exits the vehicle, obviously illegally parked, and says, "How are you, Mr. Lau? I have your delivery."

Mr. Lau "Eddie, I tell you, you cannot park here. The policeman will tow you away."

Easy Eddie just smiles at Mr. Lau.

Easy Eddie "Calm down, Mr. Lau. If the policeman tows me, I just pay the fine, OK. You no need worry so much."

Mr. Lau "Policeman bug me so much about this parking. He should have other things to do beside bother me."

Easy Eddie gets his signature for the delivery. He is a credit customer.

Mr. Lau still excited, "How come you so late?"

Easy Eddie smiling, "We are so busy nowadays. I came here as soon as I could, Mr. Lau."

As Easy Eddie is leaving, Mr. Lau says in broken English, "Eddie, my son trying for real estate license. He fail exam twice. Can you help him out?"

Easy Eddie pauses to consider this request, "Has he got all his other requirements completed?"

Mr. Lau "Yes, I think so. He take exam twice and fail."

Easy Eddie "OK, tell you what, Mr. Lau. You have him come see me. I'll hook him up with my good friend. Now, you understand that my good friend will want some money to help him."

Mr. Lau all smiles, "Yes, I know."

Easy Eddie "He might want...say...two thousand dollars."

Mr. Lau pats Easy Eddie on the shoulder, "Two thousand cash, I can no do. It too much!"

Easy Eddie "Mr. Lau, it's my good friend. He will demand that much. He will be risking his job to help your son. Do you understand?"

Mr. Lau thinking, "Eddie, do your good friend play golf?"

Easy Eddie "Yes, I believe he does. Why?"

Mr. Lau whispers, "Eddie, I know golf manager at Ala Wai Golf Course. I tell you what. I give you one thousand dollars and golf membership at Ala Wai for you and your friend."

Easy Eddie aloud and chuckling, "Ala Wai is a public golf course. There are no memberships."

Mr. Lau still whispering, "Eddie, listen to me, I get you 'play anytime membership' at Ala Wai for you and your good friend. Honest!"

Easy Eddie still chuckling, "Mr. Lau, it's near impossible to even get a tee time at Ala Wai. It is booked, always. How can you do this?"

Mr. Lau very seriously whispers and hands Easy Eddie a note with a telephone number on it, "I can do. This Saturday, you call this number. You ask for Mr. Wo. You tell him you play for Silver Teal, and you get tee time on Sunday guaranteed. Now, if you get tee time on Sunday, you help my son get real estate license for one thousand dollars, OK."

Easy Eddie somewhat amazed, "I will talk to my good friend. Are you sure you can do this?"

Mr. Lau slowly nodding his head, "My side guaranteed, Eddie. What about your side?"

Easy Eddie nodding his head and thinking, "Yes, my good friend can get your son a real estate license, guaranteed."

Mr. Lau "Good, you enjoy golf Sunday. When my son get license, you and your good friend get golf anytime, guaranteed."

Easy Eddie shakes hands with Mr. Lau and then leaves the store only to find a parking ticket on his car.

Late That Evening

Bosco is picking up Keno at his work place in Waikiki. Waikiki is that stretch of beach between Honolulu and Diamond Head. Keno works at Goofy Greg's Guard Pigs. Greg Steimann, the owner of Goofy Greg's, lost his liquor license when FBI Agents caught his bartender shortchanging overseas customers and a few of the strippers performing casual sex inside the establishment. After the tenth or so violation, the Liquor Commission revoked his liquor license. So, Greg Steimann operated the establishment without serving any alcoholic beverages. When the girls were caught in similar compromising conditions (…sipping 7 Up), the authorities ordered Steimann to "open" his establishment to the public view. Parts of the walls had to be removed in order to allow the public to view the interior of his establishment. Regrettably, this action did not deter some of his girls from their intimate performances. The outrage at providing a ringside seat for teenagers to observe fellatio was too much for the authorities, and they ordered Steimann to cease and desist all beverage sales on the premises. Being stuck with three years remaining on his five-year commercial lease, Steimann decided to retaliate against the City & County of Honolulu. He commenced a guard pig business and began keeping half a dozen filthy pigs on the premises. He kept the critters enclosed with a wide-open, barnyard-variety fence. Since the fence allowed open viewing within his premises, he complied completely with the directives of the authorities. Hence, in the center of the most popular tourist area of Hawai'i, Waikiki, we have some half dozen pigs in residence, marked with a huge sign: Goofy Greg's Guard Pigs.

Keno works the swing shift from 2:00 to 10:00 PM. There is not much to do with the pigs. They kind of just snort and lay around all day until someone yells "soowee." Keno manages to light up at least one joint each shift. It relaxes him from the tensions of the day and his overbearing responsibilities.

Bosco pulls up in an island-variety jalopy, as Keno is turning over the establishment to the night shift manager. The jalopy is an old, patch-painted, Tercell-like vehicle with the roof shoddily cut off. It is great for transporting surfboards.

Bosco anxiously, "You ready, brah?"

Brah is a local, slang term for man.

Keno hops over the door into the shotgun seat. The door has been welded shut.

Keno "Yeah, man, I'm ready. Where we going?"

As he drives out of the parking area of Goofy Greg's into the main traffic lane of Waikiki, Kalakaua Avenue, "We got a tip! Your main man is sipping some brews at Bobby's in Chinatown."

Chinatown covers an area six blocks by three blocks just west of the Mattoon Financial Center in Downtown Honolulu. Bobby's Cocktail Lounge is at the far west end of Chinatown.

Keno "He's in Bobby's Cocktail Lounge. Isn't that right across from that *mahou* place that peddles heroin?"

Mahou is the Hawai'ian word for female impersonator.

Bosco "That's' the place, brah."

Keno "Let's go. You got your heat, brah?"

Bosco lifting his aloha shirt, "Right here, brah."

Keno flashing his piece and smiling approvingly, "Let's get this asshole."

Bosco driving down Beretania Street to Chinatown, "You betcha. We gonna get this asshole tonight."

Keno "I waited a long time for this asshole. I know he gonna comeback here. Tonight, I avenge my papa's murder."

As the jalopy approaches Chinatown, Bosco says, "Let's park on River Street. That way, it won't be far for us to run after we pop this asshole."

River Street comprises the far western boundary of Chinatown.

Keno "Sure thing, brah."

Bosco illegally parks the jalopy on River Street, less than a block from Bobby's Cocktail Lounge. River Street is the anus of Downtown Honolulu. The lowest forms of existence thrive here: drug addicts, *mahous,* felons on the lamb, loonies, and street bums. Bosco and Keno blend right in. They don't even get hustled by the *mahous* and street bums, as they make their way toward Bobby's.

Keno fondling his gun on his waist, "You cover the door, brah, while I go in and pop this asshole."

Bosco nods in acknowledgment.

Bosco reaches the entrance to Bobby's Cocktail Lounge first. He eases back the nailed-up, horse blanket and sites the asshole in the center booth, sipping a draft beer with a friend. The friend's back is turned toward the entrance. Bosco does not recognize the asshole's friend. There are a half-dozen customers and a bartender inside. Bobby's Cocktail Lounge consists of three booths, a music box, a pool table and a four-stool bar. Tonight, two booths are taken. The asshole and his friend have the center booth. A passed out customer has the near booth. The far booth is empty. Three of the four barstools are taken: an old prostitute is sponging up to two old, drunken sailors. The bartender seems occupied filling the beer chests behind the bar. It is perfect. It is about 11:00 PM, and nothing is happening in lower Chinatown.

Bosco "It's prime, brah. Your man is in the center booth, facing the entrance."

Keno "Good, he doesn't know me. I was ten years old when he killed my papa."

Bosco "Make it quick, brah. Just do that asshole good, and get out of there."

Bosco and Keno make one last survey of the Chinatown street area. The street traffic is normal. Everyone on the street seems occupied with his or her affairs.

Bosco nods to Keno and says, "It's good. Make it quick."

Keno steps quickly inside Bobby's Cocktail Lounge. He walks slowly between the pool table and the bar, as if going to the far booth.

Bartender "Can I get you a beer?"

Keno motioning his intention to take a seat in the far booth, "Sure, Budweiser."

Bartender "Coming right up."

The occupants of Bobby's Cocktail Lounge take little notice of Keno. With the exception of the bartender, the asshole and his friend, the rest of the customers are drunk.

As Keno walks around the far end of the pool table, he reaches under his aloha shirt and firmly grips his revolver. He takes two more steps and rushes the center booth, drawing the revolver from his waist. He grabs the asshole by the hair, jams the revolver against the back of his head and squeezes the trigger. The sudden explosion from the snub nose revolver awakens everyone in the lounge.

The bartender drops the beer he just poured for Keno.

The old prostitute starts screaming like someone is trying to rape her. One of the drunken sailors drops immediately to the floor, a war habit no doubt. The other sailor just freezes on his stool.

The asshole's friend, shocked by the sudden appearance of the asshole's brains on his shirt and splattered on his face, begins fondling his left side.

The drunk in the other booth is so intoxicated he stands up quickly and passes out, collapsing on the booth table.

Keno shouts, "That's for me papa, asshole." He fires another round into the asshole's back.

As Keno begins to run out, the bartender confronts him with a sawed-off shotgun that he grabbed from behind the bar. Keno fires a round from his hip at the bartender. The bartender's shoulder erupts with blood and the mirror behind him shatters. As the bartender is hit, he fires the shotgun, expending it into the head of the sailor still sitting on his stool. The percussion from the blast dislodges the shotgun from the bartender's hand, and it falls to the floor. The bartender, grabbing his shoulder, cries out in pain and falls to his knees behind the bar. Another shot is heard. Keno stiffens, as he feels something quickly pass through his chest. The asshole's friend has just fired on Keno. Keno gasps to inhale a breath, staggers a few steps and collapses to the floor.

Hearing the commotion inside, Bosco slips past the horse blanket with his revolver drawn. He sees the asshole's friend pointing a gun at Keno. He sees Keno is obviously in pain, staggering. Bosco fires three point blank rounds into the asshole's friend. One bullet embeds itself deep into the friend's chest. Another bullet tears off a portion of his right shoulder blade. The other bullet apparently misses. The asshole's friend turns towards the entrance and commences firing at Bosco. The two exchange two rounds each and collapse to the floor. Bosco fires his last round, as he hits the floor. It hits the screaming prostitute in the leg. She falls off her barstool and craws toward the entrance.

By now the commotion from inside Bobby's Cocktail Lounge has attracted the attention of the Chinatown street traffic. After the sounds of gunfire and the muzzle flashes have extinguished, the street traffic sees a woman, obviously in much pain, crawling out from under the nailed-up horse blanket onto the sidewalk. She continues to crawl down the sidewalk. No one comes to her aid until she has cleared the cocktail lounge by two establishments.

Three police cars, sirens wailing, skid up in front of Bobby's Cocktail Lounge. Policemen exit the vehicles quickly, draw their weapons and take up containment positions.

A voice is heard from inside the establishment, "Don't shoot! Don't shoot! I'm unarmed. I'm coming out with my hands up. Don't shoot!"

One policeman responds, "OK, come out with your hands up."

The surviving drunken sailor emerges from behind the horse blanket.

The policemen frisk the drunken sailor. After getting the drunken sailor's story of what happened, the police decide to enter the establishment. They find six dead bodies and a critically injured bartender. Five died by bullet wounds while a sixth, the drunk that passed out in the near booth, succumbed to a heart attack.

The story reported by the surviving, drunken sailor and prostitute was that a young guy came in, ordered a beer and the whole place erupted in gunfire.

Next Afternoon Easy Eddie's Store

Easy Eddie's store is basically a two-room area. The entrance area, or showroom, contains cluster after cluster of jewelry-part, storage cabinets. These cabinets stand about five feet in height. Each cabinet contains some twenty drawers. Each drawer is packed with jewelry and watch parts. Surrounding the islands of clustered cabinets are display cases of precision, jewelry equipment, such as, electronic gold testers, engraving tools, microscopes, etc. Easy Eddie's staff spends most of their time around the display cases serving customers. Most customers just enter, request a particular jewelry part and wait for the staff to locate the part in one of the cabinets.

The rear room acts as an office and a storage area. It contains the bulkier items that would take up too much space in the showroom, such as investment, gift boxes, filters, and large machinery. After incoming shipments, the rear room is quite crowded with inventory. Passage has to be navigated delicately in order to enter or exit the room. The secretary/accountant's desk is located in the rear room, as is Easy Eddie's private, partitioned office.

The entire store is well ventilated by the building's air conditioning system, making Easy Eddie's place a cool sanctuary from the tropical humidity of the islands. Easy Eddie smiles when the trade winds subside in the morning, for he can expect a store full of jewelers trying to escape the humidity by noontime.

This afternoon, Easy Eddie gets an unexpected guest.

Jacob yelling from the showroom, "Eddie, your friend is here."

Easy Eddie replies as he maneuvers his way out from the rear room, "Which friend is that?"

Jacob in a little lower voice, "He's waiting for you."

Easy Eddie surprised, as he emerges from the storeroom, "Oh, what can I do for you, Detective Green Tree?"

It is Detective Aoki, a middle-aged, Japanese-American of average height and weight.

Aoki means green tree in Japanese.

Easy Eddie and Detective Aoki were karate students in the same dojo as kids. Their friendship goes way back. They kept in touch after Easy Eddie's parents enlisted him into a Chinese martial arts school, Kung Fu.

Detective Aoki motioning with his head to go into the back room, "Can we talk in private, Eddie?"

Easy Eddie "Of course, let's go into my office."

Easy Eddie navigates their way back into Easy Eddie's partitioned office area that is reminiscent of a World War II era military cubicle. The partitions are a split-level design with thin metal on the lower half and corrugated, fiberglass on the upper half. The office area provides tight seating for two: Easy Eddie behind his desk and one chair squeezed between his desk and the near side partition.

After the two have settled in, Detective Aoki says, "Eddie, the reason I stopped by is to let you know that two of our guns were found in Bobby's Cocktail Lounge after the shootout."

Easy Eddie feeling uncomfortable, "Are we in trouble?"

Detective Aoki pressing his lips together and moving his head from side to side, "No, we can cover it up. Our boys do the fingerprinting and filing, so we can sweep it under the rug. They will choose not to investigate the guns. That's not the main reason I came over."

Easy Eddie relieved, "That's good."

Detective Aoki leaning forward to speak softly, "Eddie, one of the guys killed in the shootout was a federal agent working undercover trying to bust a drug dealer. You can appreciate the situation, if one of our guns was used to kill him."

Easy Eddie suddenly feeling tense again, "No shit, one of the dead guys was a federal agent!"

Detective Aoki "That's right, Eddie. He was there meeting with a major drug trafficker from the Big Island to arrange a large purchase and schedule a shipment of marijuana. The Feds have been trying to locate the source of the huge marijuana shipments coming into O'ahu from the Big Island."

Easy Eddie, "I don't know anything about this marijuana."

Detective Aoki "Did you know the guys carrying our guns were going to do someone in Bobby's Cocktail Lounge that night?"

Easy Eddie "No, Fat Willie just asked me to do these guys a favor."

Detective Aoki "Fat Willie Wong knew these two cowboys, is that right?"

Fat Willie Wong is the underworld boss on the island of O'ahu.

Easy Eddie "I can't say how well he knew them, but he's the one that asked me to pack them as a favor to him."

Detective Aoki "Did you know who their target was going to be?"

Easy Eddie "No, I had no idea. And, that's not something I would ask or like to hear, do you understand?"

Detective Aoki nods his head approvingly and smiles, "Do you have any idea how they knew their target would be in Bobby's?"

Easy Eddie "No, I don't. I was just doing Fat Willie a favor."

Detective Aoki "Well, I think when the word gets out that Fat Willie had something to do with this, sparks will be flying. You see, Eddie, the guy the shooter murdered was a lieutenant for Vince Nene."

Vince Nene is reportedly the godfather of organized crime in Hawai'i. He resides on the Big Island.

Easy Eddie really uncomfortable now, "Listen, I doubt Fat Willie knew that. What I heard is that it was a revenge killing. This Vince Nene lieutenant had assassinated the kid's father some ten years ago. The kid was doing him as revenge. I doubt that there was anything else to this. It was just bad timing."

Detective Aoki "Eddie, you and I both know that neither Vince nor Fat Willie would conclude that this shootout was a stroke of bad timing. For that matter, I doubt the Feds will see it that way either. To the Feds, their guy was killed attempting to bust a drug trafficking organization related to Vince Nene."

Easy Eddie tapping his desk "Wow, Vince will be taking some real heat for killing a Fed. This is terrible."

Detective Aoki "Yes, it is terrible. What I need to find out is how the kids knew the lieutenant and the Fed were in Bobby's that night. Knowing that, I can unravel how all this played out. Someone had to tip off these two novices. They had never been seen in Bobby's before that night. They were tipped off, Eddie."

Easy Eddie "All I can say is that they never mentioned anything to me. When I met them, I got the impression that they were just getting the guns to plan a hit. I didn't get the impression that these two guys had anything planned beyond getting guns."

Detective Aoki "So, first they get the guns, then they plan. Not bad, they hit the guy that evening in a part of town that they were not known to frequent. If I can reach this puzzling state of inquiry, you know the Feds and Vince Nene have already come to the conclusion that Fat Willie had something to do with the demise of their people."

Easy Eddie "It's hard to imagine otherwise, isn't it?"

Detective Aoki getting up to leave, "I just thought I'd drop by to see if you had any other insights into this shooting. Not to worry about the guns, my guys cleaned it up, nicely. No one will know it was our guns."

The two shake hands. Easy Eddie escorts the detective out the back door.

CHAPTER 2

Fat Willie Wong has asked Easy Eddie to visit him at his Maunekea Street location. That location houses the Downtown Honolulu gambling house on the corner of Maunekea and Pauahi Streets. It is only about three blocks west from Easy Eddie's store. When Fat Willie Wong requests that someone stop by, it means stop by or else. Eddie is not uncomfortable at the request. He expected some communication from Fat Willie Wong, given the fiasco that has unfolded as a result of the shootout in Bobby's Cocktail Lounge.

After work one late afternoon, Easy Eddie wanders down Pauahi Street to Fat Willie's place. He nods his acknowledgment to the street sentry, sitting in a rattan chair that is propped up against the building, and knocks on the main entranceway door. A familiar face greets him. It is his friend Billy. Billy, a local, Chinese-Filipino character with a rugged, 150 lbs., 5'7", athletic build, runs the muscle in the lower Chinatown area for Fat Willie Wong.

Billy smiles, "Good to see you, Eddie! Fat Willie has been expecting you."

Easy Eddie, "Billy, how long has it been since we got together?"

Billy as he lets Eddie into the vestibule of the establishment, "It's been a while, Eddie."

As Eddie enters the vestibule, a lovely hostess greets him, "Can I get you something?"

The hostess is a 5'6", 120-lbs., longhaired, brown-eyed, gorgeous brunette. Easy Eddie's mouth fills with saliva. Her large breasts and small waist and hips make her incredibly desirable.

Easy Eddie sizing up this desirable creature up, "Do you have any apple juice?"

Hostess seductively responds, "I think I can find some."

As the hostess leaves to get the apple juice, Billy remarks, "She kinda gets you going, doesn't she?"

Easy Eddie as he watches the hostess walk away, "She sure does. What's her name?"

Billy "That's Candace. She's from Nebraska. She was a cheerleader for the football team."

Easy Eddie surprised, "No shit! What's she doing here with Fat Willie?"

Billy "She dropped out of college and decided to check out our overseas employment."

Easy Eddie "Do you plan to ship that gorgeous creature off to Japan?"

Billy, as he escorts Easy Eddie into Fat Willie's private chamber, exclaims, "That's the plan Eddie. That's the plan."

Both Eddie and Billy shake their heads in disgust.

Easy Eddie "What a waste!"

Billy agrees as he opens the chamber door, "I agree with you."

As the door opens fully Fat Willie shouts, "Eddie, so good of you to stop by."

Easy Eddie noticing that Fat Willie has a few of his people with him busy counting money and receipts from the numbers racket, "Did I come at a bad time, Fat Willie?"

Fat Willie "No, not at all, Eddie. You know what we do here. I don't have to hide my business from you. Come, just take a seat."

Fat Willie, Billy and Easy Eddie take seats around an isolated table in the rear of the room.

The room is large and serves as an extension to the main gambling room on busy days. A good month of dust buildup clings to the upper surfaces of the unused furniture. A dark shade reeks from the room's décor, making it ideal for drinking and discussing underworld maters. Prior to police raids Fat Willie's boys replace the room's 25-watt light bulbs with 100-watt light bulbs to remove the room's clandestine, aesthetic appearance.

Fat Willie to Eddie, "The reason I called you here is that I've run into some trouble with Vince over the killing of his man at Bobby's."

Easy Eddie "A detective came by and told me about the screw up, Fat Willie."

Fat Willie "Do you mean Green Tree?"

Easy Eddie nods, "Yes, he's the one."

Billy interjects, "He's no detective. He's too busy pushing drugs to do any police work."

Fat Willie bursts into in laughter.

Fat Willie after he stops laughing, "Eddie, I told Vince I would cover his drug shipments to O'ahu until he found a replacement for his man. That's why I called you here, Eddie. I want you to do that for me."

Easy Eddie shocked, "Fat Willie, you know I hate drugs."

Fat Willie "I know, I know, Billy kept telling me, but Vince wants me to cover this. Since we killed his man, I can't say, no. Since you gave the guns to the assassins, you can't say, no, either, Eddie."

Easy Eddie more shocked, "Do you mean we either do what Vince wants or he comes after us?"

Fat Willie "I'm afraid so, Eddie. If we don't cover this, then we will have a war on our hands. Besides, Eddie, it's a small price."

Easy Eddie acquiescing, "What do I have to do?"

Fat Willie motions to Billy to explain.

Billy "Eddie, every other week, you will fly to Kona. In Kona, you will meet with Vince's boys. They will provide you with four or five large cardboard boxes. These boxes will be loaded aboard a helicopter at the Grand Beach Resort. Once loaded, you will accompany the pilot on the flight to O'ahu. Once you touchdown on O'ahu at the West Waianae Resort, my boys will unload the helicopter. Once unloaded and checked, you are free to go."

Kona is a major city on the opposite end of the island of Hawai'i (Big Island) from Hilo.

Easy Eddie somewhat hesitant, "Fat Willie, I've never flown in a helicopter?"

Fat Willie smiles, "Think of the adventure!"

Easy Eddie puzzled, "What's in the cardboard boxes, Fat Willie?"

Fat Willie "High grade marijuana, Eddie."

Easy Eddie "I never realized they brought marijuana in by helicopter."

Billy "Well, just make sure you don't mention it to anyone."

Easy Eddie "You can trust me, guys. I won't say a word."

Billy "So, I take it, you will do this for us, Eddie."

Easy Eddie nodding his head, "I suppose I can do that. How long do you think I will be doing this?"

Billy rubbing his chin and glancing over at Fat Willie, "I would suspect a few weeks, maybe as long as a couple months. Unless, you find you would like to do it, permanently. Vince would like that."

As Easy Eddie mulls over the proposition, the hostess, Candace, enters the chamber with his apple juice.

The three men eye her over. She delivers the apple juice, smiles seductively and leaves the room.

Billy exhales, "My that is one fine woman."

Easy Eddie likewise exhales, "You can say that again. Is she available?"

Fat Willie shaking his head, "No guys, I have to deliver her to Guam in a few weeks. The boys in Japan want her in good condition. They got this guy in Mainland China, Shanghai, I think, that's willing to pay us $100,000.00 for her."

Easy Eddie surprised, "Does she know she is being sold?"

Fat Willie laughs and pats Easy Eddie on the shoulder, "Of course not, Eddie."

Billy to Fat Willie, "Tell Eddie about her friend, the redhead, Fat Willie."

Fat Willie smiles, "She has a friend, Eddie. A large breasted redhead named Angie who we can get $250,000.00 for from a guy in Xinjiang Province in Mainland China."

Easy Eddie "Where's that?"

Fat Willie "It's the province furthest away from the coast in China. So, we are taking special care of these two girls."

Easy Eddie surprised, "Don't these gals even suspect anything?"

Billy "No, we treat them with respect. We pay them good money just to hostess. They get great tips. None of us touch them. What is there to suspect?"

Easy Eddie "How long have you been in the white slave trade business?"

Fat Willie "Maybe ten years now, maybe longer."

Easy Eddie "How do you convince them? Don't they ask questions?"

Billy chuckles, "We pay Judas goats to tell these girls about all the money they made overseas."

Easy Eddie puzzled, "Judas goats?"

Billy "We have girls on our staff reassure them of the easy money overseas. These girls speak to them from experience."

Easy Eddie "Well, what about when they realize they have been had?"

Billy "Once they leave the USA, their civil rights are less. Employment overseas places them under the rights of the company that hired them. They sign on with contracts to fulfill. Until those contracts are fulfilled, they can be held overseas. They are second-class citizens overseas. They have fewer rights than permanent residents, so they are bound by their contractual obligations. While overseas, we expose them to money and all the other inducements to go beyond hostess duties. They soon succumb to the temptation to do more than hostess. We persuade most of them to stay overseas."

Easy Eddie "What about selling them?"

Billy "Once in Japan, they are either shanghaied directly from Tokyo or we encourage them to take a free trip to Hong Kong to check out opportunities there. Once in Hong Kong, we shanghai them into Mainland China. Once in Mainland China, they disappear forever."

Easy Eddie somewhat saddened, "I hate to see such a beautiful girl, like Candace, go that way."

Billy reassuring, "Eddie, it's just business. It's not like we are killing them."

Easy Eddie "Do you move a lot of girls this way?"

Billy looking over at Fat Willie, "Yes, Eddie, we do. The buyers see their pictures before the girls leave Hawai'i. In many cases, the buyer comes to Honolulu to see them in person, without the girl's knowledge. If he likes the girl, funds are exchanged via bank-to-bank transfers. Once we have the funds, the girl is on her way."

Easy Eddie with a surprised look on his face, "The girls never even know that they are being sold?"

Fat Willie "No, Eddie, they never even suspect it. It's best that way."

All three settle into more pleasant conversation. Then, Billy informs Eddie that his first trip to Kona is tomorrow!

Next Morning Honolulu International Airport, Inter-Island Terminal

Easy Eddie manages to sweet talk some local gal into allowing him to park in the airport security area for the day. He knows his vehicle will be safe there, because it is right next to the consulate-designated areas. Plenty of customs people traverse that area at all hours of the day and night.

Wearing the latest in fashion island Aloha shirts and boasting a million dollar smile, Easy Eddie makes his way to the Inter-Island check in area. His ticket is waiting for him, as is his plane. Easy Eddie never enjoys waiting for anything. The Inter-Island attendant grumbles a little as Easy Eddie passes him on his way to the ramp. He will be last to board.

Gate Attendant "Eddie, I knew it had to be you. Who else would hold up the flight for five minutes?"

Easy Eddie "Parking here is terrible. That's why I'm late."

Gate Attendant disgusted, "Sure thing Eddie, sure thing, just climb aboard."

Easy Eddie smiling and waving his boarding pass, "Don't you even want to check my boarding pass?"

Gate Attendant shaking his head, "No, Eddie, with my luck, you would have the wrong ticket."

They both laugh as Eddie boards the plane.

The first seat after he enters the cabin is his. The flight attendant reserved it for him. She even has a glass of apple juice waiting to present him.

Easy Eddie smiles approvingly, "Why thank you pretty lady! If I were only ten years younger!"

Flight attendant chuckles to herself, "How about if you were twenty years younger?"

Easy Eddie sizes her up and mumbles, "She's right. Wow, am I getting old!"

Easy Eddie no sooner gets settled into his seat, and the plane taxis to the runway. The plane is a prop jet design that can carry some twenty passengers. Estimated flight time to Kona is about forty-five minutes. Easy Eddie settles in, sips his apple juice and relaxes. His seat has no side seat, so his trip is quiet. He has an excellent view of the islands, as the plane propels its way to the Big Island.

Easy Eddie reminisces his boyhood days in Honolulu. He was nine years old when the attack on Pearl Harbor occurred. He remembers playing basketball in the heights overlooking the naval base and watching the planes strafe the ships at anchor. From the altitude of the prop plane, Easy Eddie imagines that the Japanese fighter pilots attacking Pearl Harbor must have had a similar view of endless, blue ocean. That was a long time ago, he says to himself.

In the middle of Easy Eddie's daydreaming, the pilot announces his intention to land at Kona. Those were a fast forty-five minutes. Time always seems to go faster when you are anxious. The landing is easy. The taxi to the disembarkation point is even easier.

Kona Airport consists of short runway and a poorly constructed sandstone building that acts as a terminal. There is no umbilical ramp with which passengers can enter the terminal building. Disembarkation occurs on the runway, and passengers walk to the terminal. The terminal operators and passengers dread rainy days.

As Easy Eddie is exiting the cabin, he notices his old friend, Ralph, waiting for him near the terminal building. Ralph is leaning on a new luxury car.

Ralph notices Easy Eddie and begins to wave about furiously. Easy Eddie waves back in acknowledgment. The two meet half way between the plane and the car. They exchange hugs.

Ralph is a heavy-set, 5'10" Hawai'ian who always seems to be smiling.

Ralph smiling, "I couldn't believe my ears when I heard it would be you that I would be picking up. It's been a long time, brah."

Easy Eddie surprised, "Are you involved in this deal?"

Ralph pats Easy Eddie on the shoulder, "Of course, I am, brah. Come on, I'll show you around. By the way, you bring any bags?"

Easy Eddie "No, I'm just here for the day."

Ralph puzzled, "No, brah you don't leave until tomorrow morning. I got a place for you at the resort for tonight."

Easy Eddie shocked, "You're kidding, right?"

Ralph "No, Eddie, I'm serious. Today, they pack everything. You fly out first thing tomorrow morning. Besides, we got lots to talk about."

Easy Eddie as he settles into the car, "This is a nice car. Is it yours?"

Ralph smiles and says, "Yes, it's mine. I got it with my tax refund."

Easy Eddie laughs, "Have you ever paid taxes?"

Ralph "Sure, I pay taxes. When I bought gas this morning to come here to pick you up, I paid taxes on the gas."

They both laugh.

Ralph continues, "Besides, Eddie, what am I going to claim as my employment? I can't tell the IRS how I got the money. Since I can't say how I make my money, I guess it's OK if I don't tell them anything. But, Eddie, I would. Truly, I would, but no one, I mean, no one, ever gives me a receipt. And, sure as shit, if I claimed they gave me money, I suspect that they would deny it."

Easy Eddie laughs, "You're right, Ralph. It is best you do not call anyone a liar in this business."

Ralph moving his head up and down, "There you go Eddie. Calling someone a liar in this business is down right unhealthy."

The conversation drifts to their boyhood days on O'ahu for a while. Suddenly, Ralph interrupts and says, "Eddie, how about I show you the works over here?"

Easy Eddie nods, "OK, Ralph, let's see what you got cooking over here."

Ralph turns the vehicle up a dirt road and pulls up to a farmhouse.

Easy Eddie looking around, "Are you growing papaya in your spare time, Ralph?"

Ralph chuckles, "We do grow papaya here. We store them in the barn back there."

Ralph turns off the ignition and motions Easy Eddie to follow him to the barn. The barn is an old wooden structure that has not seen paint in at least the last decade. Ralph opens a side, squeaky door and invites Easy Eddie in.

Easy Eddie as he scopes out the barn, "Where are the papayas? I see plenty of loading boxes, but I don't see any papayas."

Ralph walks further into the barn where a lone, horse stable remains. He opens the stable gate and motions with his arm for Easy Eddie to follow.

Easy Eddie confused, "Do you keep a horse here?"

Ralph laughs, "No, Eddie, just follow me."

Ralph moves away some straw on the floor with his sandals. A wooden door in the floor appears. It resembles an old trap door. Ralph finds the rope-latch and opens the door. Like the cover of an old chest opening, an unlit void begins to appear. Ralph fumbles about and finally finds the light. Once the light is on, Ralph invites Easy Eddie to go down into the void with him. Easy Eddie makes certain of his footing with each step down the ladder to the base of the void. Once at the bottom of the ladder, Ralph knocks on the wall four times. Suddenly, an unlatching sound is heard, and a portion of the wall folds inward and opens up into a huge, lighted chamber. It is a huge area, at least an acre in size, filled with marijuana plants.

Easy Eddie in awe, "My God, Ralph, you have a gold mine down here!"

Ralph "I thought you'd be impressed, Eddie."

Ralph introduces Easy Eddie to the botanical staff, as they tour the entire underground marijuana farm.

Easy Eddie still in awe, "Ralph, it's all underground, too!"

Ralph "That's the beauty of it all, Eddie. No one knows it is here. We never get spotted by aerial surveillance."

Easy Eddie admiring the engineering, "Are you using special lights to make up for the sunlight?"

Ralph "Yes, we are. We experimented a lot before we got the right lighting to produce a good quality marijuana plant."

Easy Eddie looking around, "I see you have a backup generator in case you lose power."

Ralph "Yes, Eddie, this place is totally self-sufficient. We even have a backup water supply from a well that is piped in here. We even have runway tunnels for the workers to walk to their homes in the area. People seldom see us come and go from the barn above."

Easy Eddie "It must have taken a long a time to build all this?"

Ralph looking around the space, "We built it in sections, actually. As we needed to expand, we added on."

Easy Eddie nodding approvingly, "I'm impressed."

Ralph motioning to Eddie to return upstairs, "Come, I'll show you how we prepare everything upstairs."

Eddie follows Ralph out of the lower chamber. One of the workers closes the folding door behind them as they walk into the void containing to the ladder, leading back into the barn upstairs. The distinct sound of a pressure seal latch is heard as the folding door is closed behind them.

Easy Eddie responding to the sound of the pressure seal, "This place is secure, isn't it?"

Ralph acknowledging, "You bet it is. There's millions of dollars growing in there."

Easy Eddie follows Ralph up the ladder into the stable. After Easy Eddie has cleared the ladder, Ralph closes the trap door and moves straw over the access latch with his feet.

Ralph makes a hand signal to leave the stable area. As Ralph closes the stable gate, he points to a mound on the near side of the stable area covered by a tarp. Ralph removes the tarp and exposes a mechanized assembly apparatus. Ralph walks Easy Eddie through the process by which the marijuana is compressed and contained within the cardboard boxes and prepared for air shipment. Easy Eddie is awed by the sophistication.

Easy Eddie "How often do you ship?"

Ralph pauses, counts aloud then says, "We ship about a half dozen cardboard boxes every two weeks to O'ahu. We do one shipment of a half dozen boxes every two months to Maui. And, to Kauai, we do one shipment of a half dozen boxes about every six months. That pretty much sums up our air shipments. We also have a booming sea trade, as well."

Easy Eddie surprised, "This is big operation, then, isn't it?"

Ralph nodding his head, "Well, I suppose that it is. It is so routine now, that we seldom acknowledge the volume of marijuana that leaves this place."

Easy Eddie "Can the space downstairs sustain that much volume?"

Ralph "No, the downstairs operation just covers the air shipments. The sea trade comes from another location."

Easy Eddie "Do you have more than one location like this?"

Ralph "Of course, Eddie, but I don't have the OK to show you the other locations. You will be handling the goods from this site only."

Easy Eddie looks over the cardboard containers. They are about three feet long by one foot wide by one foot high. Each cardboard box contains three cubic feet of pressed marijuana. Easy Eddie calculates that some thirty-six cubic feet of pressed marijuana is shipped to O'ahu each month.

As Easy Eddie is calculating the amount of marijuana, two local fellows pull up in a Jeep. Ralph informs Easy Eddie that they are the operators of the mechanized assembly apparatus.

Ralph motioning that it is time to let the men do their work, "We best be going, Eddie. These guys insist on working undisturbed."

Easy Eddie "OK, I understand. This is impressive, Ralph. It is very impressive."

As Ralph passes the two men, they exchange nods.

Ralph to Easy Eddie, "We will meet these guys again tomorrow morning at the resort helipad at about 5:00 AM. They will have the copter loaded with six cardboard boxes for you."

Easy Eddie "What will we do until then?"

Ralph "First, I'll get you settled into your room at the resort. We'll have some chow at about 8:00 PM. I'll introduce you to a few more people. After which, you can catch some rest, and I'll wake you at 4:00 AM to prepare you for your return trip to O'ahu."

Easy Eddie "That sounds good to me. What time will I be back on O'ahu?"

Ralph looking skyward, "I think the flight takes about an hour and ten minutes. You should land at the resort on O'ahu easily by 6:30 AM. Don't worry about the goods; there will be guys there to greet you upon landing. They will take care of everything and give you a lift to your car."

Easy Eddie seems satisfied that everything is in order. He eases into the luxury car.

Easy Eddie "Great! I guess I'm all yours tonight, then. I'm ready to be entertained."

Ralph smiling, "That's my Eddie!"

Ralph starts the ignition, and they are off to the resort.

At Dinner

Ralph has set up dinner in a gazebo. We will be alone at an exclusive plantation restaurant. Evenings in the islands are generally calm. This evening, we have a slight breeze that just manages to move the palm leaves.

As Ralph holds the mosquito net back for Easy Eddie to enter the gazebo, two local guys who have been sampling cocktails for a while greet us. They will be joining Ralph and Easy Eddie for dinner. Ralph identifies the large one as a lieutenant for Vince Nene. The other guy, a slender, athletic Polynesian, is a local attorney associated with the Big Island police department.

Lieutenant "Ralph, I thought you told us 7:00 PM. We have been drinking this place out of booze."

Ralph chuckles, "Is there any booze left?"

Lieutenant "I think so. What are you two having?"

Ralph turns to Easy Eddie, "It's Budweiser, right?"

Easy Eddie "Sure, I can handle a Budweiser."

The lieutenant tells the waiter to bring two Buds.

We exchange pleasantries. Our beers arrive with frosted mugs. There is nothing like a cold beer in the evening on a tropical island.

Lieutenant to Easy Eddie, "Ralph tells me you are our new man."

Easy Eddie uncertain as to how to respond, "I suppose I am. Whatever that means?"

Attorney "What the lieutenant means is that you are the new escort for our shipments to O'ahu."

Ralph "It's OK, Eddie. These guys are part of the team."

Easy Eddie "Yes, I take my first trip in the morning. Although, I should add I am just temporary."

Lieutenant chuckling, "And, here I was ready to offer you full time employment."

The attorney and Ralph both start laughing.

Easy Eddie puzzled, "Was it something I said?"

Lieutenant sipping his beer, "No, Eddie, it was nothing you said. We understand. You can hurt my feelings if you like."

The attorney and Ralph break out in laughter, once again.

Easy Eddie to the group, "I have a job in Honolulu. I can't be doing this too long."

Attorney trying to hold back a smile, "We understand, Eddie. We really do."

Waiter makes his way through the mosquito net. He pauses near the lieutenant and begins reciting the specials for the evening. We all chose the rainbow trout.

Most of the evening conversation concerns deep-sea fishing off the Kona Coast. That area is considered one of the best in the world for game fish. The attorney recounts a few of his spectacular marlin catches. The attorney gets Easy Eddie to promise to join him one Sunday afternoon for a go at marlin fishing.

Interestingly, there are few questions about Easy Eddie's work in Honolulu or his involvement with Fat Willie Wong. The dinner was more of a get-acquainted affair. Easy Eddie could sense that he was being interviewed for something. He maintained his best demeanor. After all, this was merely a favor to Fat Willie that he was here at all. He had no intention of getting involved in Hawai'i's drug trafficking.

Just after we had ordered dessert, a local guy, wearing the latest design in Aloha attire, disturbs the lieutenant. He whispers something in his ear. The lieutenant nods in approval and extends a smile to the attorney. The lieutenant excuses the local guy. Once the local guy has left the gazebo, the lieutenant leans forward and motions for us to all do likewise.

Lieutenant speaking softly, "I was just informed that Fat Willie Wong was gunned down on Maunakea Street earlier this evening."

Easy Eddie shocked, "Was he hit bad?"

Lieutenant to Easy Eddie, "They machine gunned him down, Eddie, right outside Canton Chop Suey restaurant. Fat Willie Wong is dead."

Easy Eddie is overcome with fear. He could be gunned down right here and now.

Attorney to Easy Eddie, "Relax, Eddie, if we wanted you dead, we wouldn't have let you order the rainbow trout."

Easy Eddie somewhat relieved. Ralph and the lieutenant laugh at the attorney's statement.

Lieutenant to Easy Eddie, "But, we do have one question to resolve: Would you reconsider doing this escort service more permanently for us?"

Easy Eddie stuttering, "I do have a job in Honolulu that takes up a good deal of my time."

Lieutenant moving his head up and down, "I see. Well, I should tell you then that the brother of the guy that was murdered in Bobby's Cocktail Lounge has volunteered to take you back to your room, tonight."

Easy Eddie with an immense sense of fear welling up in his tummy, "You know, I could escort your merchandise a little longer, I suppose."

Lieutenant "That's good to hear. Then, I guess Ralph could take you back to your room. If you don't mind putting up with his lousy manners?"

Easy Eddie "Ralph will be just fine."

That was close!

4:00 AM

Ring, ring…

Easy Eddie fumbles around for the phone. In the air-conditioned room, Easy Eddie is hesitant to brave an arm outside the warmth of the blankets. A red flashing light accompanies the ringing sound. Even if you can muffle the sound, the light annoys you too much to ignore it.

Easy Eddie still asleep, "Good morning."

A loud "ALOHA" blasts through the receiver.

Easy Eddie "Is that you Ralph?"

Ralph laughing, "Get up you lazy bugger, it's time to go to work."

Easy Eddie mumbling to himself, "OK, OK, I'll be right down."

Ralph still laughing, "I'll have some breakfast waiting for you."

Easy Eddie falls out of bed trying to wake up and stand up. He makes his way to the bathroom, bumping into furniture. He curses that he should have found the light before he sacked out. With the bathroom light on, he relieves himself, staggering still. As he depresses the flushing valve, a jet engine roar shocks him into full consciousness.

Easy Eddie stunned, "My God! What was that?"

It takes Easy Eddie a while to collect himself. Finally, he realizes that it was the sound of the toilet flushing. For a moment, he felt his room was being impacted by a stray jetliner.

Next is the shower, Easy Eddie has not learned yet to allow the shower to flow a while before you step in. The icy, cold, spring water of the Big Island halts his heartbeat. He is awake now. Life has new meaning!

In the lobby, Ralph greets Easy Eddie by handing him a bland-looking, plastic cup, and says, "It was apple juice, right?"

Easy Eddie surprised, "Yes, I do like apple juice, thank you."

Ralph motions for Easy Eddie to follow him to the car. It is a short drive to the helipad. The helicopter is revved up and ready. Easy Eddie has to gulp down his apple juice. Ralph introduces the pilot. Ralph hurries Easy Eddie into the copter passenger seat.

Easy Eddie awed by the pace, "Good morning. Are we ready to go already?"

Before Easy Eddie can say another word, the copter is airborne. All he sees is the ground distancing from the copter. Suddenly, the copter swings away. Only ocean lies below. It remains that way for the next hour. The noise inside the copter is so loud it discourages conversation. Looking around the interior of the copter, Easy Eddie identifies six "papaya" boxes in the rear area.

Easy Eddie speaks loudly to the pilot, "Do you make this trip often?"

The pilot just smiles at him. He does not say a word. He just keeps smiling.

Easy Eddie acquiesces, "I know, I know. I better just keep my mouth shut."

The helicopter bypasses the Diamond Head portion of O'ahu and continues onward along the North Shore. From the ocean, his seat in the copter provides a spectacular view of the Koolau Mountain Range. The Koolaus were formed by lava flows. They extend some one thousand feet straight up from sea level. Many have rated the view from the lookout on the Koolaus, at Pali that overlooks the bay at Kaneohe, to be the most spectacular view in the world. Easy Eddie concludes that the view does not rate any less from the other direction either.

As we approach the end of the Koolau Mountain Range, the pilot turns the copter inland until we fly over the Waianae Mountain Range. It seems we just barely clear a mountain peak, and the helicopter descends quickly onto a helipad. Easy Eddie knows this area. He plays golf here at this resort. The isolated location of this resort was chosen to provide secrecy for the delivery of the marijuana.

As the copter descends onto the pad, two men come rushing out of a nearby building to unload the cargo. They nod to the pilot. He nods back. Before Easy Eddie can disembark, the cargo has been unloaded. As Easy Eddie sets his second foot on the helipad, he is greeted by, "You're under arrest. Turn around, and face the helicopter."

Easy Eddie mumbles, "This is just great."

Suddenly, the group around him starts laughing. Easy Eddie feels a pat on his back. A familiar voice says, "It's OK, Eddie. We're all friends here."

Easy Eddie turns around to see four people bending over laughing.

Easy Eddie stunned, "Is that you, Detective Aoki?"

Detective Aoki smiling, "Well, Eddie, who else would it be? This is narcotics, isn't it?"

Easy Eddie still stunned "Yes, I suppose that it is."

Detective Aoki "Well, don't you think the people of Hawai'i would want their most experienced man on the job, here?"

Easy Eddie in disbelief, "Are you involved in this?"

Detective Aoki raises his arms as if to hug Easy Eddie, "Of course not Eddie, I came all the way out here this morning to arrest you. Come on, I'll give a ride to your car at the Inter-Island Terminal."

The Inter-Island Terminal abuts Honolulu International Airport in the center of the South shore of O'ahu. From the West coast of O'ahu, the drive to the Inter-Island Terminal takes about a twenty minutes on the island's main central highway, H-1.

The designation H-1 is used instead of I-1 for interstate highway, because the state of Hawai'i does not connect to any other state.

Easy Eddie notices that he has not been handcuffed. He just follows Detective Aoki to his car.

Detective Aoki to Easy Eddie as they approach the car, "Go on, get in. I'm in a hurry this morning."

Easy Eddie still unsure how to take all this, "What's going on here?"

Detective Aoki "Welcome to organized crime, Eddie. How do you like burning money?"

Burning money is the underworld code for marijuana trafficking.

Easy Eddie stunned but manages to exhale, "OK."

As Detective Aoki drives down the highway, "Did you hear about Fat Willie Wong?"

Easy Eddie "Yes, I got the word on the Big Island."

Detective Aoki chuckles, "Did you know that they waited for that slob to finish ten courses at Canton's before they gunned him down? Talk about a last meal. I heard one of the gunmen feel asleep waiting for Fat Willie to stop stuffing his face."

Easy Eddie "Really?"

Detective Aoki moving his head up and down, "That's right! Then, as soon as Fat Willie emerged from the restaurant and stepped onto Maunekea Street, they opened up with three machineguns on him. Most of the bullets hit Fat Willie in the belly too!"

Easy Eddie "Well, at least he ate well before he died."

Detective Aoki "You and Fat Willie were close, weren't you?"

Easy Eddie shaking his head, "No, we weren't close, at all. I won't miss him. By the way, who's the new boss?"

Detective Aoki "That would be Frank Kealoha."

Easy Eddie "What about Joshua Puna?"

Detective Aoki grins, "Well, there are a few wrinkles to iron out before Honolulu is calm again."

Easy Eddie as the car turns into the Inter-Island terminal parking area, "My car is over there near the consulate parking area."

Detective Aoki smiling, "I know where your car is, Eddie."

Easy Eddie nods his head up and down. Detective Aoki has been in on this all along.

As they part, Detective Aoki says, "See you in a couple of weeks, Eddie. It's good to have you along."

Easy Eddie nodding, "See you in a couple of weeks."

Life changes so quickly when things go haywire. I had better keep that in mind if I am going to survive with these characters. Joshua Puna has been left out of the leadership role on O'ahu. That will not go over well with that character. There will be much more bloodshed. Joshua is too crazy anyway. I can see why the big boss did not select him.

The traffic into Honolulu is atrocious this morning. Easy Eddie has never taken this route at this time before. Now, for the first time, he appreciates the comments made by the traffic monitors on the radio in the morning. When he arrives at the O'ahu Mercantile Building parking area, Billy is waiting to greet him.

Easy Eddie surprised, "Billy, I'm glad you are here."

Billy smoking a cigarette and sipping coffee, "It's good to see you too, Eddie. How did everything go?"

Easy Eddie parks his car. Billy and he talk in the refuge of the private, underground, parking garage of the O'ahu Mercantile Building.

Easy Eddie shrugging his shoulders, "It went OK, I guess. It got tense when they told me what happened to Fat Willie."

Billy surprised, "Do you know what happened to Fat Willie, already?"

Easy Eddie "Yes, one of Vince's lieutenants told me during dinner last night. And, Detective Aoki filled me in a little more this morning when I delivered the merchandise."

Billy shaking his head, "Eddie, I was there. I was paying the tab in Canton's when I heard the gunfire. By the time I got outside, Fat Willie was bleeding all over Maunekea Street. They took a few shots at me as well."

Easy Eddie surprised, "Do you think, they want to hit you too, Billy?"

Billy "I'm not sure. Maybe they just shot at me as a precaution, last night. I'm not going around like I used to, just in case."

Easy Eddie "Listen, why don't you stay with me until this cools down?"

Billy nodding his head up and down, "We go back a long way, Eddie, don't we?"

Easy Eddie "Yes, we do, Billy."

Billy "They will expect me to come to you, eventually. So, if they are after me, they will be watching your place."

Easy Eddie "You're right, Billy. They would be watching my place. How about I fix you up at my girlfriend's place? Nobody knows about her."

Billy "Is this a new girlfriend, Eddie?"

Easy Eddie "Yes, we've been seeing each other on the side for a few months. I can ask her to take you in for a while."

Billy "Can you trust her, Eddie?"

Easy Eddie "Yes, I can."

Billy suspicious, "What does she do?"

Easy Eddie "She works at the bank. She's a teller."

Billy "Tellers are entry level positions. Isn't a teller a little young for you?"

Easy Eddie "Hey, Billy, young women make you feel younger."

Billy laughs, "I see. Are you helping her out?"

Easy Eddie somewhat embarrassed, "Well, you could say that."

Billy moves his head up and down, "She'll do."

Easy Eddie motions for them to go upstairs to his office. Billy and Easy Eddie walk to the elevator and make their way to his third floor store. Once in the store, Easy Eddie calls his girlfriend. Since it is only 8:00 AM, she had not left for work yet. She agrees to let Billy stay in the extra room. Easy Eddie tells her that he will let Billy into the apartment.

As soon as Easy Eddie sets the phone handset in the cradle, Jacob enters the store. He spots Easy Eddie immediately.

Jacob bellows out, "Well, a good morning to you, Eddie. I trust you made all the deliveries yesterday, especially, since no one saw you yesterday. Where in the hell have you been?"

Easy Eddie embarrassed, "I had some emergency business to handle. I couldn't make it in yesterday."

Jacob still speaking loudly, "Urgent business, was it? What was it? You have to get one of your girlfriends an abortion again?"

Easy Eddie has a reputation for those kinds of emergencies.

Suddenly, a loud laugh is heard emanating from Eddie's office area. Billy is all too familiar with Easy Eddie's constant female problems.

Jacob surprised, "Is there someone in there with you? Are you getting it on back there, Eddie?"

Easy Eddie smiles, "No, it's just a friend of mine that I haven't seen in a while?"

Jacob still probing, "What, does she want palimony?"

Billy steps out from behind Easy Eddie's office partition. The sight of Billy shuts Jacob up immediate.

Easy Eddie to Jacob, "I have to take Billy some place. I'll be right back."

Jacob just nods. He does not utter a word. He knows who Billy is. Given Fat Willie's recent demise, Jacob understands the seriousness of having Billy in the office.

Easy Eddie and Billy make their way out of the office, down the elevator and into the parking garage.

Billy breaks the silence, "Eddie, you really should wear a rubber."

Easy Eddie shaking his head, "I know, but it spoils my performance."

Billy "Eddie, Hawai'i and the Mainland have gained in population because of your performance concerns."

Easy Eddie laughs, "Yes, I know, I know. I wish these young women would take the pill."

Billy "Eddie, the girls you knock up are barely out of high school. Weren't a few of them still in high school?"

Easy Eddie staring at Billy, "They had dropped out of high school."

Billy as Easy Eddie unlocks the car door for him, "Sorry, I was just commenting that they were under eighteen. By the way, how old is this gal?"

Easy Eddie "She's twenty-three, I think"

Billy "Wonderful, I'm looking forward to meeting her. How'd you meet her?"

Easy Eddie starts the ignition and begins to pull out of his parking stall, "I met her at the bank. We talked friendly for a year or so. She was having boyfriend problems, so I asked her out. We've been seeing each other on and off since then."

Billy lighting up a cigarette, "Would any of our people have seen you take her out?"

Easy Eddie "No, we just go to movies at the university. I bring dinner to the apartment. Since our ages are so far apart, we don't go out."

Billy "It sounds like you have things well arranged. What's her name?"

Easy Eddie "Patricia."

Billy "What mix is she?"

Easy Eddie as he pulls into the Patricia's apartment complex, "Let's sees she looks Spanish. I think she said she was Spanish, Chinese and Filipina."

Billy "That's a nice combination. She must make you quite happy."

Easy Eddie smiles, "That she does."

Easy Eddie gets Billy settled into the apartment. Patricia had left for work already. Easy Eddie gives Billy his door key.

Easy Eddie "I'll stop back by at lunch to see how you are doing."

Billy as Easy Eddie is leaving the apartment, "That's fine. Do you mind if I use the phone?"

Easy Eddie "No, help yourself, Billy."

Lunchtime

Easy Eddie decided to stop by the Yantse Dream restaurant to pick up some Chinese food. The Yantse Dream is ideal, because he can order prior to leaving his store. He knows Billy adores boneless chicken with vegetables. With a couple of illegal, parking situations, Easy Eddie has kept the food warm as he knocks on the door to the apartment. The sound of someone inside the apartment being cautious to respond to his knocking can be heard from the hallway. Easy Eddie hears the faint, but distinctive, sound of a revolver cylinder being turned and a hammer cocking.

Finally, he hears Billy in a muffled voice, "Who's there?"

Easy Eddie "It's food time, Billy, open up."

Easy Eddie hears the security latch being operated then the door opens.

Billy smiling, "Good to see you. What did you get for lunch?"

Easy Eddie enters the apartment, "I stopped off along the way and got some Chinese food. You like Chinese, right?"

Billy anxious, "Yes, I like Chinese. Anything would be fine right now. I'm starving."

Easy Eddie maneuvers the food bags to the kitchen table. He hands Billy some chopsticks and a cup of Chinese mustard and soy sauce.

During Billy's feeding frenzy, Easy Eddie asks what he did all morning. Billy replies that he made some calls to get a sense of what was coming down. From Billy's rendition, it does not appear that anyone is looking for Billy, so long as he does not interfere with the new arrangements being planned.

Easy Eddie "Do you think you'll be fine walking about freely? What about going to your place?"

Billy "Yes, I do. Right now, everyone is concentrating on the rift developing between Joshua Puna and Frank Kealoha. Kealoha is the new big boss. Joshua doesn't like it. Either way, I've been assured of Chinatown."

Easy Eddie "Will you get to take over all of Fat Willie Wong's downtown stuff?"

Billy "That's what they are telling me. I get nothing from the other areas, but I get the lion's share of the downtown gambling, prostitution, and drugs."

Easy Eddie "How will you like working for Kealoha?"

Billy "Kealoha is a strange character. He does more muscle stuff than anything else. Have you heard of his company: 'The Collector?'"

Easy Eddie "Of course, he collects bad debts for people."

Billy "That collection is not restricted to underworld debts, Eddie. He'll collect anything for a cut of what he gets."

Easy Eddie "So, you really don't see any problem working under Kealoha, do you?"

Billy "Not really, he seems pretty straight. He ventures into drugs and prostitution in Waikiki. Waikiki is his stomping grounds. He operates out of a penthouse on Martin Street in the jungle area."

The jungle refers to the a six city block area encompassing everything from the Waikiki beach up to Kalani Street then inward to the Ala Wai Canal and then in the Diamond Head direction to the zoo.

Easy Eddie "That's 250 Martin Street, right? I've seen a lot of great looking *wahines* go into that building."

Billy smiling, "Those *wahines* were probably part of his high-class stables. He has a handful of $1000-a-night hookers."

Easy Eddie whispering, "Do you think he'll let you sample the stable?"

Billy surprised by Easy Eddie's interests, "Tell you what, Eddie. If he does, I'll be sure to include you into the sampling. How's that?"

Easy Eddie with an uncontrollable smile, "You got it!"

Billy continues to manipulate his chopsticks. The extra large portion of boneless chicken sates him.

After mouthing the last piece of chicken, Billy says, "What concerns me is this character, Joshua. I think he is too far gone on drugs to listen to anyone. And, he being the leader in the murder for hire gang, he could cause a lot trouble for all of us. That Joshua is crazy."

Easy Eddie "Didn't you know Joshua when you two were younger?"

Billy "Oh yes, I knew him as well as you did. He's crazy now. He runs drugs and chicken fights on the islands. The only good thing is that he seldom ventures into Waikiki."

Easy Eddie "Can't you talk to him, Billy?"

Billy "If I am asked, then I will. Until then though, I'm staying clear of that character. I think we'll see a lot of killings with him running loose. If anyone could talk to Joshua, it would be you, Eddie. You aren't involved in the rackets."

Easy Eddie redirecting the question, "How did Fat Willie keep him in control?"

Billy "Eddie, Joshua was Fat Willie's cousin. They were family. Fat Willie made Joshua what he is today."

Easy Eddie surprised, "Wow, we are in for a lot of trouble. Fat Willie and Joshua were family, is that right?"

Billy nodding his head and exhales, "That's right. They were family."

Easy Eddie "By the way, Billy, do you know who killed Fat Willie?"

Billy "Well, I hear Vince Nene ordered it in retaliation for the killing of his drug escort. As it turns out, Vince was protecting the drug escort. It embarrassed Vince when the guy was gunned down in a hit-like fashion in Fat Willie's backyard."

Easy Eddie "It probably embarrassed him more when the gunmen's trail led to Fat Willie."

Billy "That it did. I'm sure when Vince realized Fat Willie was implicated, he had no choice."

Easy Eddie as he sees Billy finish the meal, "Can I get you something else?"

Billy patting his belly, "That was great, Eddie. I'm fine. Matter of fact, why don't you take me to my place. I think I will be OK now."

They toss the food bags and wooden utensils into the trash and make their way out of the apartment to Easy Eddie's car.

As they approach Easy Eddie's car, Billy notices some papers flapping on the windshield. He starts laughing.

Easy Eddie "What's so funny?"

Billy "How long have you been parked here?"

Easy Eddie "I parked here when I brought the food, why?"

Billy "Do the police follow you around, or what? Look at this street. It looks more like a widened alley than a street. I'm surprised a police car even attempts going down it. And, there's a ticket on your car?"

Easy Eddie surprised and angry, "No shit. I got another ticket!"

Billy in uncontrollable laughter, "Eddie, I swear, you must be going for some city record. I bet I can count the number of times that I have rode with you in which you did not get a ticket for something or other."

Easy Eddie disturbed and shaking his head, "Man! Have these guys got nothing better to do? Gangsters getting gun downed and multiple shootouts in Honolulu, and all they got to do is follow me around and give out parking tickets."

Billy still laughing, "Hey, Eddie, that's our boys in blue at work."

Easy Eddie tossing the ticket to the ground, "Go on and get in, let's go. If I stand here any longer, I might get another ticket."

As they drive away, Billy says, "Eddie, how do you beat all these tickets?"

Easy Eddie still shaking his head, "Well, after I get fifty or so, I go see one of my good friends. They fix me up."

Billy "Do they clear your record as well?"

Easy Eddie "Of course, all this data goes into a computer. They have the girls erase the data, so it appears that I have no tickets at all."

Billy "Is that for all tickets?"

Easy Eddie "Oh yes, they clear all tickets: parking, speeding, improper turns, etc."

Billy "Would they do that for drunk driving as well?"

Easy Eddie "I suppose they could; although, I don't drink and drive."

Billy "How do you get them to do this?"

Easy Eddie "I'm a businessman, Billy. Sometimes they need things, and I can provide them."

Billy smiling. "Do you mean like expensive jewelry?"

Easy Eddie smiling back, "Yes, I mean, exactly, like expensive jewelry."

Billy chuckles, "How many of these cops are on the take?"

Easy Eddie "What do you mean 'how many'? They all are. Well, at least, all the ones that I know."

Billy "I guess they would be. They don't make the kind of money to buy the goodies that you could provide."

Easy Eddie as he pulls into Billy's condo complex, "No, they don't. So, I make life more equitable for them. It's a small price, Billy."

As Easy Eddie parks the car, Billy smiles and says, "Don't they even help you out in your business?"

Easy Eddie "Yes, they provide a most impressive service that greatly enhances the success of my business."

They both break out in laughter.

Billy manages to squeeze out a few words among his laughs, "If the public only knew!"

Easy Eddie stops the car, "Shall I go up with you?"

Billy as he gets out of the car, "No, it's fine. Besides, I want to spare you another parking ticket."

Billy makes his way to the elevator. Easy Eddie waits for Billy to enter the elevator before he pulls away and returns to his store. As he is making the turn to enter the underground parking garage of his store's building, a policeman waves to him. He recognizes the policeman. He motions for the policeman to meet him in the underground garage.

Easy Eddie "What's up?"

Policeman "Sorry to hold you up, Eddie, I was just checking on how my wife's ring is coming."

Easy Eddie "It should be ready by next week. I haven't had a chance to see the jeweler this week, but it should be ready next week."

Policeman "Great! That was all."

Easy Eddie parks in the underground garage. He and the policeman take the elevator up to his store. They discuss the manufacture of his wife's marquis-shape ruby ring. Easy Eddie discusses the difficulty of surrounding marquis-shaped rubies with one point diamonds.

There are one hundred one-point diamonds in a carat.

At the entrance to Easy Eddie's store, the policeman bids him farewell.

As Easy Eddie enters his store, Jacob bellows out, "Jiminy Christmas look who's here! I didn't expect you back this week."

Easy Eddie somewhat embarrassed, "Sorry, I got tied up. Are there any pressing deliveries?"

Jacob "What, do you need to run some more errands?"

Easy Eddie "No, I was just checking. I know I have some catching up to do."

Jacob "Eddie, I'm afraid to give you a delivery. You might decide to go to Las Vegas again for the weekend."

Easy Eddie says nothing and makes his way into his office. Jacob is referring to the number of times that Easy Eddie has left on a delivery on a Wednesday morning only to return from the delivery on the following Monday, after spending four days in Las Vegas. Wednesdays make Jacob nervous. Easy Eddie knows this.

As Easy Eddie enters his office, he notices three messages on his desk. One is from Patricia. One is from Detective Aoki. The last message concerns some real estate deal on the North Shore. The North Shore deal can make Easy Eddie lots of money. Money is what he needs right now. The last three trips to Las Vegas cost him plenty. He needs salvation.

Easy Eddie decides to call Hans Hoffman concerning the North Shore land deal. Hans and he developed the limited partnership that assembled the partners for the multi-million dollar enterprise. With the partners, the group purchased a huge 99-acre lot with a spectacular view of the North Shore. Though the lot is zoned for agriculture and preservation, the agricultural portion can be subdivided easily into some thirty, one-acre, residential estates with the preservation portion reserved for recreation. Furthermore, the deal gets sweeter in that the property contains some one million cubic yards of fill material that can be relocated to areas closer to the ocean in order to elevate those lots above sea level. At the bottom of the hill from the 99-acre lot is a fifty-acre lot that needs to be elevated some six feet in order to comply with requirements for subdivision. At over $2.00 per cubic yard for fill material, the 99-acre lot would bring the partnership over $2 million, less the cost of relocating the fill material, in profits. That is well over the price the partnership paid for the 99-acres initially. Since the 99-acre lot requires terracing in order to provide spectacular views for the proposed thirty residential estates anyway, the selling of fill material is a bonus. Easy Eddie is quite excited about the North Shore project.

Easy Eddie as Hans answers the phone, "Well, good afternoon, Hans, I'm returning your call."

Hans "I'm glad you called, Eddie. I spoke with Erik earlier today. He reported that an inspection of the Bishop Estate property in the Hauula Forest Reserve below our lot discovered marijuana and cocaine plants. Erik said that Bishop Estate commanded a closer inspection after discovering the drug plants and uncovered long runs of PVC piping stretching all over the flatland of Waiono Valley. One estimate had the over all length of pipe at over two miles."

Bishop Estate is the entity that holds in trust all the property contained in the estate of the late Princess Bernice Pauahi Bishop. Bishop Estate manages the entrusted property for the benefit of the Hawai'ian people. The trust has been estimated to be worth over US $6 Billion.

Waiono Valley also is referred to as Punaluu or Green Valley. It is located on O'ahu's North Shore just inland of Punaluu Beach.

Easy Eddie "Are you kidding? Two miles! That valley was a major drug harvesting area."

Hans "Yes, that's the same conclusion Bishop Estate came to as well. So, Eddie, we have some questionable neighbors whose agricultural exploits have gone undetected by the real estate industry."

Easy Eddie "Does Erik predict trouble?"

Hans "Yes, Bishop Estate told him that the people who ran that PVC piping intended Waiono Valley to remain undeveloped. Since we have the only high ground, those PVC people would try to oppose any development ideas we might try to promote in the valley."

Easy Eddie "Amazing, we have a sweet deal, and we run into a bunch of drug dealers."

Hans "Eddie, they could not have run over two miles of PVC piping unnoticed. Many of the landowners in the valley must be aware of it, if not in cahoots with these drug dealers. I would suspect the true strength of that infamous community association out there as being these drug dealers."

Easy Eddie "It has to be. How can that infamous community association that only seems to piss everyone off get so many contributions to keep it going? They have to be in with the drug dealers. Besides, as strict as they are to movement in the valley, they would have noticed all that PVC piping come in."

Hans "You got that right. Two miles of PVC piping had to come in via truck. They know it, and they support it."

Easy Eddie "So, now, we are confronted with drug dealers."

Hans "Yes, Eddie, Erik wanted me to relay that information to you. Amongst our other problems, we have to confront O'ahu's major drug lords."

Easy Eddie "Any idea as to who they might be?"

Hans "No, Erik is looking into it right now with Bishop Estate. Good news is Bishop Estate has ordered all the PVC piping removed form Waiono Valley."

Easy Eddie "Whoever installed that piping is going to be pissed off."

Hans "I bet. Two miles of PVC piping doesn't come cheap. The labor used in installing it is another cost."

Easy Eddie "It must have taken them months to lay all that pipe."

Hans "Bishop Estate estimated a few months as well. Since it is gravity fed from Punaluu Stream, it required a precise layout and some landscaping to insure a proper slope for the water to flow. They certainly put some time into laying all that pipe."

Easy Eddie "My, my, we are going to have some pissed off drug traffickers."

Hans "Eddie, Erik asked if you could ask around as to whom these drug traffickers might be. Can you do that for him?"

Easy Eddie "Sure, I'll pass the word around."

Hans "There's another thing to this that is puzzling Erik. Are you familiar with Green Valley Road?"

Easy Eddie "Do you mean the access road to the valley?"

Hans "Yes, the one we drive down to get into the valley."

Easy Eddie "Yes, I use it to get into the valley."

Hans "Well, Erik has discovered that at least two lots extend their boundaries across that road."

Easy Eddie "How can that be? That's a road."

Hans "Eddie, Erik is going to look into that. If what he discovered is true about those two lots, then the Green Valley Road is not a road at all."

Easy Eddie "As a licensed real estate broker, I can tell you that it has to be a road; otherwise, all those house lots in the valley could not have acquired a building permit."

Hans "It does seem strange, doesn't it? But, that's what Erik said. I'm trained in real estate, as well, as you know, so I find it hard to believe that any of those lots in the valley could have been subdivided, much less developed, if there were no access road into the valley."

Subdivision rules require vehicular access routes suitable to City & Country development standards. For most of these properties in the Waiono Valley, that translates into forty-four-foot wide roads. For development, water and sewage are additional requirements.

Easy Eddie "That's right! Green Valley Road would have to be a road in order for the lots to be subdivided. Erik must have read the tax map keys wrong. Otherwise, there must be some easement recorded to enable people to pass over the effected portion of those two lots."

Hans chuckling, "You're right, Eddie. Erik must have read it wrong. He doesn't share our real estate training. Anyway, can you check on who the drug dealers could be for us?"

Easy Eddie "Of course, I know a few guys out there that can enlighten us. I'll catch up with them this weekend."

The conversation ends with a run down of the Fat Willie Wong incident. Easy Eddie amazes Hans with his grasp of the ongoings of the underworld in Hawai'i. If anything goes down in Hawai'i, it seems Easy Eddie knows some of the culprits, personally. Hans enjoys listening to Easy Eddie's crime tales.

Next call, Easy Eddie decides to contact Patricia. Ah yes, the lovely Patricia should be home by now. Easy Eddie eases back into his office chair. It is one of those therapeutically-designed models with thick, leather padding that provides the impression of relaxation as one reclines. Easy Eddie tells everyone that the chair simply "fell off a truck." That is a common expression in the Hawai'ian underworld when one receives a sweet deal.

Easy Eddie listens to the phone ring, as he fantasizes about a wonderful evening with Patricia. After about ten rings, he concludes that she must be in the shower. He drools of being there in the shower with her. To Easy Eddie, showering with young twenty-year-olds is truly a heavenly experience. He envies the Chinese nobility that surrounded themselves with these sensuous concubines with their glistening dark hair and moist lips. As Easy Eddie hangs up the phone, Jacob informs him that he has a call on the other line.

Easy Eddie "Good afternoon, Eddie speaking."

A soft, sexy female voice says, "Hey, when are you getting off work?"

Easy Eddie surprised, "I was just trying to call you."

Patricia "Really! Sorry! I stopped off on Fort Street Mall for an ice coffee with a few of the gals from work. I can wait here for you, if you like. When are you free?"

Easy Eddie anxious, "OK, I can be right down there. It's quitting time anyway."

Patricia worried, "Won't your uncle be upset, if you just up and leave?"

Easy Eddie "Well, he's always upset anyway. Besides, I seldom get to meet you in town."

Patricia responds with her characteristic little giggle that never fails to arouse Easy Eddie. It does not take long for Easy Eddie to make an excuse to leave early. Actually, this time, he tells Jacob that he is in need of sex, and an opportunity worth death has presented itself. Jacob understands perfectly and even encourages Easy Eddie out of the office, reminding him to use a rubber, even, as he clears the door. Since the hallway is packed with people leaving for home at this time of day, Easy Eddie attempts to hide his embarrassment. Jacob was quite loud. Easy Eddie is certain everyone heard the comment. It is a long ride down the elevator, as the middle-aged gals just give Easy Eddie that knowing smile.

It does not take a minute for Easy Eddie to clear the elevator on the ground floor and make his way onto Fort Street Mall. Sure enough, Patricia is seated alone at one of the outdoor coffee tables. He rushes up to her table.

Easy Eddie out of breath, "I got here as quick as I could."

Patricia sensing his urgency, "I can see that. Did your uncle give you any trouble?"

Easy Eddie shaking his head, "No, actually, he urged me along. It was a slow day anyway. There was no need to hang around the store."

Patricia smiling, "That's good, then I suppose I have you for the entire evening."

Easy Eddie nodding, "That you do, sweetie."

Patricia "You've been very busy, lately. I was getting the impression you had forgotten me."

Easy Eddie "I would never forget you, sweetie. I just got called away on business. That's all. Sometimes, I have to travel, and I get tied up with clients."

Patricia looks incredibly sexy this afternoon. She can sense Easy Eddie's urgency to get home. She better get him home, before he is too embarrassed to walk down the Mall.

Patricia has a way of rubbing her knees onto Easy Eddie's knees in order to convey her intentions to get home and play. Easy Eddie seizes on the gesture, immediately. He will run for the car while Patricia makes her way to the end of the Mall to wait for him. Honolulu has many one-way streets, so Easy Eddie has to drive around a few blocks in order to meet up with Patricia at the far mountain end of the Mall. He does the task with ease. When Easy Eddie is primed, he makes the difficult look easy. And, this afternoon, he is primed!

As Easy Eddie pulls up to the curb, "Can I offer you a ride, Pretty Lady?"

Patricia smiles, "You know, kind sir, my momma told me never to accept a ride from a sweet talking stranger. She warned me that all they wanted to do was to separate me from my panties. Is that what you have in mind, sir?"

Easy Eddie chuckles, "The thought never crossed my mind, Pretty Lady?"

Patricia pressing her lips together firmly and stomps her foot, "Well, in that case, I better wait for another who does have those intentions. If I ever listened to my momma, I'd never get any sex at all."

Easy Eddie laughs, "Come on, get in. You don't have wait for anyone. I've changed my mind!"

Patricia sensually eases herself into Easy Eddie's car, intentionally offering him a glimpse of her breasts. She knows Easy Eddie is a breast man. She loves to tease him. It is the way his eyeballs seem to float when he looks at her breasts that encourages her.

It is a quick ride to Patricia's apartment. Easy Eddie even manages to open the door for her. As they begin to walk to her apartment from the parking garage, Patricia runs her hand slowly and deliberately over the fender of a Cadillac.

Patricia musing, "Don't you just admire this fender, Eddie?"

Easy Eddie stuttering a bit, "Yes, Cadillac makes a wonderful automobile."

Patricia smiles, "I was referring to how cool it feels."

Easy Eddie puzzled, "Why is that?"

Patricia realizes that some men are just too dense to catch onto anything. How she would adore being stretched over this fender. She wishes Easy Eddie would be a bit more daring.

Patricia shaking off a missed moment of sheer excitement, "Nothing!"

Easy Eddie is too occupied with getting Patricia into her apartment to realize how ready she actually is for him. The little head truly controls the big head right now. Eventually, they get into her apartment. Patricia, sensing his urgency, takes her time changing into something more comfortable. She enjoys being handled firmly. Easy Eddie's main fault is his delicate mannerisms when being intimate. So, to compensate, Patricia teases Easy Eddie into a fury. She even presses him back when he attempts to get close to her too gently. And, the curse of it is that Easy Eddie never learns. He never adjusts his tactics to please Patricia. For the next thirty minutes, providing Easy Eddie does not ejaculate prematurely, Patricia orchestrates him into a sexual frenzy.

First, she changes into a see-through nightgown. It is one that accentuates her breasts to the point that her breasts completely captivate his awareness. She moves deliberately, offering her breasts, to slow his breath. She brings him to that point where he would offer her anything to quench his sexual appetite. Patricia is a teaser.

Patricia drives Easy Eddie over the brink by reaching down between her thighs, sampling herself with two fingers and then rubbing her moisture across his lips. It only requires Easy Eddie to inhale her fragrance once, and Patricia has the man she desires for the evening. How she adores the way his rump muscles contract so firmly and the sensation of his hot breath gasping against the side of her neck. She even forgets about the Cadillac's fender.

CHAPTER 3

Next Day Easy Eddie's Office

Following Jacob's routine, debasing, morning greetings, Easy Eddie returns to his office and thumbs through his incoming calls' file. He realizes that in his haste to meet Patricia, he forgot to return Detective Aoki's call. It is 9:00 AM right now. Detective Aoki should be in his office still sipping coffee.

Easy Eddie as a voice answers the phone, "Detective Aoki, please."

Detective Aoki "This is Detective Aoki. Is this you, Eddie?"

Easy Eddie "I couldn't make out your voice, Detective Aoki. Do you have a cold?"

Detective Aoki clearing his throat, "It's worse than that, Eddie. I think I caught a case of strep throat."

Easy Eddie "Is it from anyone I know?"

Detective Aoki still clearing his throat, "As a matter of fact, do you know that Japanese gal that works for Frank Kealoha?"

Easy Eddie "That really fine looking one in Waikiki?"

Detective Aoki "Yes, that's the very one."

Easy Eddie "Do you think she gave it to you?"

Detective Aoki still clearing his throat, "Yup, I bet it was her."

Easy Eddie breathing out some air, "I hope she don't give it to Frank. He'll toss her in the ocean."

Detective Aoki clears his throat vehemently, "She is a real babe though, Eddie."

Easy Eddie "What's up? I'm returning your call?"

Detective Aoki "Eddie, I called because I need some help with Joshua. He's getting crazy."

Easy Eddie "Hey, Joshua's been crazy for long time."

Detective Aoki clears his throat again, "Well, this time he's talking about killing Frank to take over the gangs."

Easy Eddie "Like I said, he's crazy."

Detective Aoki "Listen, Eddie, we need someone to go over and talk to Joshua. We need someone to calm him down before he starts shooting people all over Honolulu."

Easy Eddie "Why did you pick me?"

Detective Aoki clears his throat again, "Eddie, you know Joshua. He will listen to you."

Easy Eddie "Joshua is so crazy he might shoot me."

Detective Aoki clears his throat again, "I doubt that. You and Billy grew up with him."

Easy Eddie "Why not ask Billy to go see Joshua?"

Detective Aoki "It's political, Eddie. Billy was too close to Fat Willie. The feeling is that he might team up with Joshua and create a war."

Easy Eddie laughs, "That's true. Billy was close to Fat Willie."

Detective Aoki "Frank feels that you would be the right person to make a truce."

Easy Eddie "Did Frank recommend me?"

Detective Aoki clears his throat yet again, "As a matter of fact, he did."

Easy Eddie "OK, tell you what, Detective. How about you get Frank to send the Japanese gal with me when I go see Joshua?"

Detective Aoki chuckles and coughs, "I think I could get Frank to go along with that. She is a looker, Eddie."

Easy Eddie "Joshua won't shoot me, if I'm with a good looking woman."

Detective Aoki "OK. I'll get back to you."

Easy Eddie "Before you hang up, I have a question to ask."

Detective Aoki clears his throat, "OK, what is it?"

Easy Eddie "What do you know about the drug operation in Waiono Valley?"

Detective Aoki clearing his throat, "Do you mean Green Valley behind Punaluu Beach?"

Easy Eddie "That's the one."

Detective Aoki clears his throat, "That's not a topic for the telephone, Eddie. Why are you interested?"

Easy Eddie "I'm involved in a land deal out there, and I want to know the score in the valley."

Detective Aoki clearing his throat, "Well, first, there is a strong Mormon community association out there. They are 60s-throwback protesters. They object to any development whatsoever. Personally, I think they smoke way too much marijuana to be connected with the Mormons."

Easy Eddie "Are they a religious group?"

Detective Aoki clearing his throat, "Well, they claim to be. But, whatever they claim, they will give you a hard time, if you try to develop anything in Punaluu. They are connected with the two politicians from the area. For some odd reason, the politicians don't mind being associated with them. They get good press with the newspapers, as well."

Easy Eddie "Are they the biggest stumbling block out there?"

Detective Aoki clears his throat, "No, I'll talk to you in person about it."

Easy Eddie "OK, get back to me on the Japanese gal."

Jacob bellows out from the main showroom, "Hey, Eddie, are you working today or what?"

Easy Eddie yells back, "I'll be right there."

As Eddie enters the showroom, he quickly identifies two individuals in need of assistance, "Yes, sir. What can I do for you gentlemen, this morning?"

Jacob is shaking his head. Easy Eddie always seems to be able to bounce right back into the business environment. To Jacob, Easy Eddie has the right talents to make this a successful business and to become a premier businessman. Regrettably, Easy Eddie is more like the rabbit that skirts about in every which direction. He needs to become a turtle and keep his attention on the business. It has been the same with Easy Eddie for the last fifteen years. He just has too many distractions. Jacob feels remorse for having brought Easy Eddie into the business. He should have left him alone as a bartender's assistant in Waikiki. Soon, Jacob and his World War II era partners will be retiring. There will be no one to carry on the business. Jacob predicts the business will fold in a few years with Easy Eddie at the helm. It is such a sad future for a business with so much promise.

The two customers to Easy Eddie, "What we are looking for is a machine to make silver molds. The people in Waikiki told us that your firm carried them."

Easy Eddie "Yes, we usually carry them, but we don't have one in stock right now."

One of the customers, "When will you have one in stock?"

Easy Eddie shrugging his shoulders, "I'm not sure."

The two customers thank Easy Eddie and leave. Jacob is in total disbelief. Easy Eddie made no attempt whatsoever to sell them a unit. From where Easy Eddie waited on the customers, there were two catalogs on the counter top that contained write-ups about those units. What is more, there was a unit exactly like what they wanted in the storage area waiting for repair? Easy Eddie could have showed them that one and got an order for a sale. Yet, he made no effort at all to sell them. He just does not understand how to make sales. He is just too lazy. The other two partners having observed Easy Eddie's lackluster performance just look over at Jacob in disgust. Jacob is embarrassed. If he had not asked Easy Eddie to come into the showroom to help out, those two customers would have waited for one of the other partners to get free, and they would have made a sale. The profit from that one sale would have meant one month's salary for one of the partners.

After Easy Eddie leaves the showroom, one of the partners whispers to Jacob, "He's too busy making easy money selling stolen jewelry."

Jacob shakes off the comment, "We don't know that for sure. Besides, he's my sister's son. I have to take care of him. You know that. What can I do?"

The partner still whispering, "Jacob, he's going to get us into trouble with all his antics. Some of the customers are talking. They say he arranges for discounts on our merchandise after hours."

Jacob "OK, OK, I'll talk to him again."

The partner "Make sure you bring up his tardiness and recurrent absences. These four-day trips to Las Vegas have to stop."

Jacob "I know. I can't believe this guy. He thinks I owe him a living just because he's my older sister's son."

The partner "Jacob, I admire what you are doing for your family, but this guy is too much. Do you know how bad business would be for us, if word got out that he was fencing stolen jewelry, or worse, involved in robberies?"

Jacob disgusted, "I'll talk to him again."

Easy Eddie makes himself look busy by rearranging the storage area for the rest of the morning. By lunchtime, he has moved every item in the storage area at least twice. From the results, one would get the impression that the items in the storage area merely were relocated sixty degrees to their left of their original position. What a way for a middle-aged man to pass the morning!

Easy Eddie had thought of going to the Chinese restaurant nearby for lunch, but when he overheard Jacob taking orders from the other two partners for Chinese food, he decided to walk a little further to the Chinese Cultural Center to have lunch there. He takes enough abuse from Jacob during the workday to endure even more at lunchtime.

It is a nice walk to the Chinese Cultural Center from Cornish Street. The walk cannot be more than six blocks through the historical area of Chinatown. He will avoid Canton Chop Suey on Maunakea Street. Somehow, the sense of being impaled by burning, lead bullets does not sit well in his tummy. He feels sorry for Fat Willie Wong. By hugging the outer walkway of Beretania Street that runs perpendicular to Maunakea Street, the gangster hot spots can be circumvented. Today, Easy Eddie chooses the serene comfort of the outer walkway. So far, this week has brought him too much excitement. A little Zen-like tranquility is just what a Chinese therapist would prescribe.

The Chinese Cultural Center is located on the corner of Maunakea and Beretania Streets. It is about ten years old. The facility covers about two acres and contains a variety of Chinese shops. Mainly, it was designed as a tourist destination. Busloads of tourists are dropped off there twice a week. Today is one of the off days. So, the Center is quiet. It is easy to find a table in the restaurant.

While Easy Eddie waits for his entrée, an old friend enters and notices Easy Eddie right away.

Friend waving as he approaches Easy Eddie's table, "Hey, Eddie, I thought you were dead. So, good to see you!"

Easy Eddie dropping his head in disbelief, "I can't believe this."

Friend pulling out a chair to join Easy Eddie, "How are you? I'm so glad you are OK."

Easy Eddie manages to say, "Please join me, take a seat."

Friend leaning across the table, "Eddie, we got a job. I want to run it by you."

Easy Eddie sipping his hot tea, "What kind of job is this?"

Friend "Do you know the jewelry store in your basement?"

Easy Eddie nodding, "Yes, I know the owner, why?"

Friend smiling, "Good, we plan to hit him."

Easy Eddie "Well, I'm glad you spoke to me first. He doesn't have much in the form of easy-to-move jewelry in his store. He does more repair work."

Friend "We hear his store has lots of silver coins that are worth a mint and easy to move."

Easy Eddie nodding, "You're right. He is a coin collector. As a matter of fact, he showed me his collection a few months ago."

Friend "That's beautiful! You even know where it is."

Easy Eddie, drawing a map of the store on a table napkin, points out the location of the safe that contains the coins.

Friend overlooking the map, "How big is this safe?"

Easy Eddie "I would say it weighs a few hundred pounds. It's not on rollers, so it will be bulky to move."

Friend "Can we open it in the store?"

Easy Eddie pointing out partitions that would make the removal of the safe difficult, "Well, you could open it there, but that would make a lot of noise. And, it would take some time."

Friend "What kind of security system does he have installed?"

Easy Eddie "He used to have a good one with a call alert to a local dispatcher. Since he has reduced his jewelry stock, he relies only on the two-door barrier to discourage unauthorized entry. And, he has this heavy safe."

Friend nodding his head, "So, all we need is time and to be quiet."

Easy Eddie "Yes, an early Sunday morning would be ideal. There are no security personnel in the building after midnight. After 3:00 AM Sunday, there is no traffic around that area at all. From 3:00 to 5:00 AM Sunday morning would be the ideal time."

Friend "Can you get us a pass key to the underground garage gate and a master key to his store entrance door?"

Easy Eddie smiling, "You know I can. I can let you in the underground garage gate and stand lookout for you."

Friend "There's no need for you to stand lookout. We can have the area police patrol car do that for us. Besides, they can even keep people away from the area."

Easy Eddie "That's a good idea. I've used those guys before too. They are dependable."

Friend "I know you did."

The waitress brings Easy Eddie his entrée, Almond Duck. She asks if his friend would like anything. He orders a bowl of Ox tail soup.

After the waitress leaves the friend says, "When can I pick up the keys?"

Easy Eddie "Stop by the store next Wednesday afternoon. Remember, we close at noon. I'll hang around an hour or so. You knock on my private door between 1:00 and 2:00 PM. I'll have the keys for you."

Friend "That's great! We'll do the usual arrangement with you for the fencing."

Easy Eddie manipulating his wooden chopsticks to smooth them, "That will be fine. We can meet the following Wednesday afternoon in my private office. We work a half day on Wednesdays, so we will be alone."

Easy Eddie and the friend reminisce old jobs, as they enjoy their lunch. Easy Eddie's friend is a cat burglar from way back. He could have been someone important in life, yet the money was just too easy and too good in his after-hours profession. He does one cat burglary, and he is set for five or six months.

After Easy Eddie finishes sipping his tea, the friend asks if he can walk back to the store with him. Easy Eddie sees no problem with that request. Besides, given the recent shootouts, he would prefer the company. All this talk about past capers has gotten Easy Eddie excited again. Easy Eddie expresses the few words that he has mastered in Cantonese as he exits the restaurant. They make their way up Beretania Street towards his store.

It is warm today. The warmth from the sun in paradise has a way of slowing you down. A slight, trade wind breeze keeps the two men cool enough to prevent perspiration. As they cross Maunakea Street, the friend presents Easy Eddie with the idea of forming a group to hit jewelry stores on a regular basis. The friend feels that Easy Eddie could check out the jewelry stores ahead of time. After all, Easy Eddie is in the business. He could use the excuse of generating sales to visit potential target stores ahead of time to get the current layout and location of the loot. The idea has appeal to Easy Eddie. He could use that same excuse with his Uncle Jacob to get out of the store. Jacob has always wanted him to build the business, anyway.

For the remaining five blocks, Easy Eddie and his friend discuss possible stores to hit. Easy Eddie provides the friend with six names of jewelry stores that are plump with precious inventory. Easy Eddie identifies their most vulnerable times to robberies. He knows when workers arrive, their break times, and those days of the week when the owners are distracted with incoming shipments. It does not take long for Easy Eddie to realize that he has been sitting on a gold mine all the time. He just has to set up his customers for his friend's group. Most of the robberies will be burglaries; although, Easy Eddie envisions a couple of promising cowboy-style stickups.

There are seven in the friend's group. One in the group is a woman. Only two men in the group have prior arrests. Those two men will work in the background so as not to alert undercover police. Easy Eddie will case out all the stores then provide detailed layouts of the stores to the group. Each job will be meticulously planned. The friend estimates that they can hit a store a month without raising any concerns. He considers a-hit-a-month an acceptable tax on the jewelry community. If they vary their entry patterns, the group will remain undetected by the police. Both the friend and Easy Eddie concur that cowboy-style robberies and cat burglaries should be alternated so as to create the appearance of excess time between the robberies. Also, a different member of the group will be used each time in the cowboy-style stickups. Easy Eddie will provide different guns for each robbery. That way, the police will be hindered in concluding that a group of criminals is involved. The two men part with the promise to get together one evening and introduce the team members.

It is just a block down Cornish Street to Easy Eddie's store. During the walk, he makes the decision that given this new business, he will need to acquire a few more safe deposit boxes. Two more large safe deposit boxes in the vault should do it. The more he thinks it over, the more he realizes that he may need more boxes. He cannot get too many; otherwise, he will surely arouse the suspicion of the vault staff. He has four safe deposit boxes already. With eight boxes and the type of business they will generate for him, he practically would be living in the vault just to keep up. He concludes that he will start with two more large boxes and see how it goes

As he enters the showroom, Jacob says, "Jiminy Christmas, Eddie, you actually came back on time."

Easy Eddie "Well, I realized that I better start shaping up. I know you count on me, Uncle Jacob."

Jacob smiles, "Yes, Eddie, we all do. It is good to see that you have come to your senses."

Easy Eddie nodding, "Yes, I realize that I will inherit this business from all you guys, so I'm going to start working to build it up."

Jacob all smiles, "That's fantastic, Eddie."

Easy Eddie leaning over to speak softly to Jacob, "I'll even start going out to the stores to generate more sales. A few times a week when the business is slow, I will go out and drum up some business. I'll check with you before I go, so you'll know where I'm going and when, OK."

Jacob pats Easy Eddie on the back, "I like that idea, Eddie."

Easy Eddie looked so sincere when he told that to Jacob that none of the partners doubted that he had any other agenda in mind. Sometimes, when you get so hopeful of someone, you cheer any movement by that person in the direction of those aspirations.

As Easy Eddie is about the leave the showroom for his office, Jacob mentions to him, "Did you hear that fellow Kealoha is planning on running for governor?"

Easy Eddie surprised, "Do you mean Frank Kealoha?"

Jacob looks over at the partners then back at Easy Eddie, "I'm not sure. All I heard at the restaurant was the name Kealoha. I think it's the same guy. How many Kealohas are there that could run for governor?"

Easy Eddie "Frank would be the only one I know."

One of the partners inquires, "Isn't he a gangster?"

Easy Eddie with a little laugh, "Are you kidding? He's one of Honolulu's biggest gangsters."

Jacob joins in on the laughter, "I'll be, a gangster running for public office."

Easy Eddie smirking, "Well, he's not so bad. Most of these politicians are low level crooks anyway. What difference could it make to have a big crook in charge?"

The same partner adds, "Would you vote for the guy, Eddie?"

Easy Eddie somewhat uncomfortable with the question, "Well, I'd have to think about it. I suppose I would depending on what he offered."

Jacob "What the group was saying at lunch was that this Kealoha character held a meeting to gather up signatures for his nomination. Apparently, he already has the number of signatures required from Hawai'i residents to run for the office. One guy in the group said he got over 2,000 signatures."

Easy Eddie "I didn't realize that anyone needed that many signatures to run for an office."

Jacob "He's running for governor, Eddie. He just can't put an ad in the newspaper."

Easy Eddie laughing, "I suppose you're right."

Jacob nodding in affirmation, "And, get this. At the meeting, this one guy at the table said that Kealoha outlined his 'Draino Strategy.'"

Easy Eddie laughing, "Draino Strategy! What the hell is that?"

Jacob laughing too, "Well, according to this guy at the table, Kealoha plans to get on top and, like 'Draino,' flow down through the bureaucracy cleaning out the waste."

Easy Eddie "Is that it?"

Jacob nodding his head up and down, "Yes, that was it. And, he acquired all those signatures with that plan."

Easy Eddie in disbelief, "You have to be kidding?"

Jacob shaking his head, "No, I'm not. That's what the guy at the table said. It's Kealoha's 'Draino Strategy.'"

The whole showroom is in laughter now.

One of the partners "Isn't there some of our tax dollars involved in this, if Kealoha runs for governor?"

The other partner "That's right! If he acquires some minuscule amount of the votes, he gets so many million dollars to reimburse his campaign."

Easy Eddie stunned, "Are you kidding? The government would give Kealoha money to run for governor?"

The other partner "Yes, it's a law passed to compensate *bona fide* candidates who lack the financial resources to run for an office."

Easy Eddie "How do they determine who is a *bona fide* candidate?"

The other partner "If the candidate acquires the minimum number of signatures attesting to his character and accumulates a certain number of votes based on the percentage of the votes cast in the election, then the candidate gets awarded the funds."

Jacob "So, if this gangster gets a certain percentage of the vote, he can dip into our tax moneys, is that right?"

The other partner "That's right. I believe he gets a few million dollars of our tax money for his campaign."

Jacob "Do you mean he would get this money even if he has absolutely no chance to win?"

The other partner "Yes, that's right. He only needs to get something like one percent of the votes cast to get the money."

Easy Eddie "So, if 200,000 people vote, and he gets only 2,000 of the votes, then he gets the money. That can't be right."

The other partner "That's right, Eddie. It's only one percent of the vote."

Jacob "With his 2,000 signatures, he assures himself of the money, assuming those 2,000 people vote for him."

The other partner "You got it, Jacob. This gangster just used our candidacy laws to enrich himself. Think of it, he can't possibly believe that the people of the state would elect him. He must be running to get those funds. What does he spend? He gets his goons to go around sizing people up. Hell, it might be good business for his goons. They get to case the neighborhoods doing a legitimate campaign. If Kealoha loses, the goons go around burglarizing those same neighborhoods."

Easy Eddie laughing and shaking his head, "This is unbelievable."

Jacob laughing, "This is one smart gangster, this Kealoha character. He's got balls to run for governor."

After the group gets a good, but disgusting, laugh, Jacob reminds them all that they still have a half-day of work left to do. The group returns to their assignments. Easy Eddie wanders back into his office.

By mid-afternoon, as Easy Eddie is rearranging the storeroom, once again, he receives an unexpected phone call.

Soft female voice, "Is this Eddie?"

Easy Eddie "Yes, what can I do for you, miss?"

From the sound of her voice, the woman is very young. Her mannerisms are not those of someone in the jewelry business.

Soft female voice, "Eddie, a friend asked me to call you. This is Hatsue Yanage."

Easy Eddie puzzled, "OK, do I know you?"

Hatsue "My friend Frank told me that you wanted to know me."

Easy Eddie now really confused, "I'm sorry, when did Frank tell you this?"

Hatsue "At lunch, Frank said he got the word from a detective."

Easy Eddie, suspecting whom this is, senses his voice become a little softer, "Was that Detective Aoki?"

Hatsue "I'm not sure, Eddie. It was some detective. Anyway, I'm calling to tell you I'll be available when you need to go and see Joshua."

Easy Eddie, somewhat lost for words, fumbles about getting her phone number and address. The sound of her soft voice excites him. He never dreamed getting a date with this gorgeous creature would be so easy. The thought that Joshua Puna might kill the girl and him never crosses his mind. Besides, he is drooling too much to worry about being murdered right now.

Easy Eddie "I'll try to get an evening meeting time with Joshua."

Hatsue with an incredibly soft voice that seems to ooze with moisture, "I like evenings, Eddie."

Easy Eddie's tummy feels like 10,000 butterflies suddenly took flight inside it. He can hear every movement Hatsue's chest makes as she breathes. What a fine woman!

Easy Eddie talking just to hear her breathe, "Good, I'll try to set something up for this week."

Hatsue speaking seductively soft, "The sooner the better, Eddie. Besides, I know Joshua. He will want me to dress provocatively. I'll be ready, Eddie. I'll just need a couple hours notice."

Easy Eddie enjoying this conversation immensely, "I'll give you at least that much time, I promise."

Hatsue in one soft breathe, "Good!"

Easy Eddie "Thank you for the call."

Hatsue "*Sayonara,* Eddie"

Sayonara means "see you again" in Japanese.

The rest of the afternoon, Easy Eddie battles a developing erection. He adores this woman! Once, he saw her in a royal blue silk dress at a wedding reception for one of Kealoha's cousins. When she walked, it was as if her dress was a gently, flowing stream. Her long, shinny dark hair rippled with each step she took. Her hair was particular sensuous to watch as it moved over her shoulders. Easy Eddie could imagine his hands moving her hair over her bare shoulders. Sensuous visions like that last a lifetime. Like portraits hanging at the *Louvre* in Paris, they etch themselves into your mind. They are cherished forever. Hatsue Yanage is like that. What a gorgeous woman! If she were Eve in the Garden of Eden, Easy Eddie would eat all the apples not just the one being offered in her hand to quench his appetite for this woman. Today, for Easy Eddie, it was wonderful to be alive.

When the minute hand lines up vertically with the twelve-position on the clock, signifying it is 5:00 PM, Easy Eddie scurries out the door of the store. Jacob does not see him leave. Presto! Easy Eddie is gone. He needs to walk up the next block to the oldest tavern in Honolulu. This place, affectionately referred to as the "Old Tavern," is a popular hangout for underworld characters at this time of day.

The Old Tavern looks unimpressive from the outside. Actually, one would be hard pressed to identify it as a bar at all. The façade gives the impression that the inside of the semi-black-painted windows contains an acupuncture or Chinese herbal medicine establishment. Once inside, the dark interior confronts the visitor. Everything is dark. Even the felt on the pool tables is a dark green. Hanging on the wall above the ten-stool bar is a mounted moose head. That is right! In the heart of Honolulu, a huge moose head is mounted on a bar wall. It is one of those Canadian wilderness moose with some 20 points on its antlers. Given its size and the amount of dust build up on the upper surfaces of the moose head, the creature was taken in the 19th Century. The Old Tavern dates back to the 1880s, so the moose head was probably the centerpiece when the bar originally commenced serving customers.

Easy Eddie spots a few of the Hawai'ian wise guys clustered around a table in the rear of the establishment. Since it has been a decade or more that he was in the Old Tavern, everyone sizes him up as he makes his way past the bar to the wise guys' table. It is a strange feeling, like being a runway model performing for the customers.

Easy Eddie says as approaches the table, "Hey guys, how are you doing?"

One of the wise guys, sensing trouble, rests his right hand near the bulge on his waist and begins to lean to his left to make whatever is under that bulge accessible to his right hand.

Easy Eddie noticing this wise guy's movement raises both his hands palms open away from his chest, "Hey, there's no need to get excited."

One of the other wise guys says, "What do you want?"

There is a sudden silence at the table. None of these wise guys appear to know Easy Eddie.

Easy Eddie with his hands still raised, "I'm looking for Joshua Puna. Can someone tell me where to find him?"

Upon hearing Joshua's name, all the wise guys bring their hands to their waists. One even manages to take his gun out of its holster and point it at Easy Eddie from under the table.

This is a tense situation for Easy Eddie. These wise guys could start shooting any second.

The wise guy closest to Easy Eddie says, "Who are you, and what do you want with Joshua?"

From the wise guys mannerism, these are Joshua Puna's boys. Easy Eddie came to the right place. Now, he just needs to leave alive.

Easy Eddie somewhat nervously responds, "I'm Eddie. I'm an old schoolmate of Joshua's. I just want to talk to him."

Finally, one of the older wise guys says, "Are you the Eddie from Kalihi Heights?"

Kalihi is the first, western-direction suburb outside of Honolulu. Kalihi Heights is that part of Kalihi that extends up to the Koolau Mountain Range. The Heights have a spectacular view of Honolulu and Pearl Harbor.

Easy Eddie nodding, "Yes, I live in Kalihi Heights."

Same wise guy "Don't you own a jewelry store on the next block?"

Easy Eddie "Yes, I do."

Same wise guy to the other wise guys, "He's OK. He's a close friend of Joshua's."

All the wise guys relax their trigger hands and continue enjoying their whiskey and waters.

Same wise guy to Eddie, "Joshua's not here. He won't be in here tonight. Actually, he seldom comes into town. I may see him later tonight, can I give him a message for you?"

Easy Eddie "I can give you my business card. You can ask him to call me. It is very important that I meet with him."

Easy Eddie motions that he is going to reach for his wallet in his back pocket. He waits until the wise guys gesture to him that it is OK to reach around behind his back and get his wallet. He pulls out his wallet slowly and hands the wise guy who knows him a business card.

Easy Eddie as he hands the business card to the wise guy, "Have Joshua call me as soon as he can."

The wise guy takes the business card and says, "OK, I'll get this to Joshua for you."

As Easy Eddie is about to walk away, the wise guy who knows him says, "Guys, if you want a good deal on jewelry, you can talk to this guy."

One of the other wise guys "That's where I've seen this guy before."

Another wise guy to Easy Eddie, "Oh yes, you work with the cat burglars, right?"

Easy Eddie chuckles, "Yes, that's me."

All the wise guys start chuckling, "OK, OK, we know who you are now. You grew up with Joshua."

Easy Eddie nodding in agreement, "Yes, Joshua and I went to school together as kids."

The wise guy who knows Easy Eddie says, "We'll make sure Joshua gets this tonight, Eddie."

Easy Eddie thanks them then makes his way back down the runway and out of the Old Tavern. As Easy Eddie emerges onto Cornish Street he says to himself, "What a shit hole!"

Next Afternoon Easy Eddie's Store

As Easy Eddie is assisting a customer in the showroom, one of the partners hands him a telephone memo. The memo requests that he return a call from a person named Kahele. After Easy Eddie finishes with his customer, he makes his way into his office and calls the number on the memo.

A heavy Hawai'ian voice answers, "Aloha!"

Easy Eddie somewhat apprehensive, "I'm returning a call from a Mr. Kahele."

Heavy Hawai'ian voice, "This is Kahele."

Easy Eddie expecting more of a response, "This is Eddie. You just left this message for me in my store about five minutes ago."

There is no response from Kahele. The phone line seems dead.

Easy Eddie "Hello, is there anyone there?"

Kahele clearing his throat, "Yeah, brah, I'm still here. What do you want?"

Easy Eddie sensing someone with a serious drug problem on the other end, "I'm returning your call, Mr. Kahele."

There is another long pause of silence. Finally, the heavy Hawai'ian voice responds, "Oh yeah, you wanted to speak to Joshua. Isn't that right? I've got your business card here."

Easy Eddie "Yes, I'm looking for Joshua Puna. Is he there?"

Another long silent pause follows. Easy Eddie can hear what appears to be someone sniffing something. Snorting would be closer to the sound that he is hearing.

Finally, Easy Eddie says, "If I'm calling at a bad time, I can call back later."

Kahele "No, brah, you're calling at the right time. Listen, Joshua will meet you at your other office at 4:30 PM this afternoon."

Easy Eddie "What do you mean my other office?"

Kahele "You know, the one you do your other business...the one on the other floor."

Easy Eddie thinks then realizes that Kahele means the second floor card game. He responds, "OK, I'll be there at 4:30 PM sharp."

There is no response just more snorting sounds, so Easy Eddie hangs up. He immediately calls Hatsue to let her know. She says that she will come to his office around 4:00 PM.

Easy Eddie is called to the showroom to wait on another customer. It is busy today. The jewelers are coming in droves to stock up on their supplies. With only a few exceptions, the jewelers are buying consumable items anticipating future work. That is good news for the jewelry industry in Hawai'i.

At 4:00 PM, Hatsue Yanage enters the showroom. Easy Eddie is still with a customer. One of the other partners attempts to wait on Hatsue, but she defers for Easy Eddie. As Easy Eddie finishes with his customer, he greets Hatsue. From the look in his eyes, he does not have to mention to her how great she looks. She has on a tight dress. The dress is as close fitting as aerobics class attire. She has great cleavage. There is something about Japanese-American women, like Hatsue Yanage, that seems to scream out at Easy Eddie: take me; take me now!

Hatsue Yanage is an athletically built, 5'2", 100-lb., gorgeous, Japanese-American with long, silky, dark hair.

Easy Eddie "Are you ready to go?"

Hatsue nods, "Of course, Eddie, I'm always ready."

Easy Eddie turns toward Jacob, "I'll be right back. I have to do something important."

Jacob drooling at the sight of Hatsue, "OK."

Easy Eddie expected a scolding, but this time, all Jacob could manage was an "OK."

Easy Eddie and Hatsue make their way to the second floor. As they emerge from the elevator, Easy Eddie gestures that the card room is just around the corner.

Hatsue noticing the beauty salon sign above the entrance says, "Eddie, if I'd known it was a beauty parlor, I would have waited to have my hair done."

Easy Eddie and Hatsue enter the beauty parlor, walk past the two revolving seats towards the rear. At the rear, Easy Eddie parts two hanging drapes. He holds one up for Hatsue. After they clear the drapes, Easy Eddie scans the back room for Joshua. The back room contains a felt, six-seat poker table in the center close to the near wall, a crap table close to the rear wall, and some Asian betting game against the far wall. There are probably fifteen people in the room. Most of the occupants are engaged in gambling; however, one table against the far wall has two Hawai'ians seated with their backs turned away from Easy Eddie. Easy Eddie immediately identifies one of them as Joshua Puna. Hatsue recognizes Joshua at the same time and motions to Easy Eddie for them to join Joshua.

As Easy Eddie approaches Joshua's table, Joshua's partner gets up to greet them. He frisks Easy Eddie. He just looks at Hatsue's tight dress, seductively smiles and motions for the two of them to sit down.

Joshua Puna is a 5'3", scrawny Hawai'ian with long, bushy hair. He looks like something that escaped from a zoo or research laboratory. He has a revolver tucked into the waistline of his trousers. It looks like a .38 caliber.

Joshua as he admires Hatsue, "Eddie, how long has it been, brah?"

Easy Eddie offers his hand, "It's been years, Joshua."

Hatsue just gives Joshua a seductive stare as she slowly settles herself into her seat at the table.

Joshua still admiring Hatsue and allowing her to seduce him with her eyes, "What can I do for you, Eddie? I heard that you wanted to talk to me."

Easy Eddie sensing Joshua's distraction with Hatsue, "Joshua, this is Hatsue."

Joshua breathes in deeply, "You got yourself one fine woman here, Eddie. I never realized the cat burglary business would be so rewarding."

Hatsue just smiles at Joshua and leans forward so he can admire her cleavage.

Easy Eddie trying to steer the conversation to more pressing matters, "Joshua, some of the boys asked me to speak to you about the problems developing between Frank and you."

Joshua turns to Easy Eddie, "Frank! I'll kill that bastard. You just go back and tell him, I'll kill him."

Easy Eddie shocked, "Joshua, you don't mean that. Frank and we go back a long way. He wants to be your friend."

Joshua getting angry removes his revolver from his waist and points it at Easy Eddie, "Frank ain't no friend of mine no more. I'm going to kill that bastard."

Hatsue sensing an altercation coming says, "Joshua, Eddie forgot to introduce me, properly. I'm Frank's main squeeze."

Joshua lowers the revolver and looks over at Hatsue, "What?"

Hatsue licking her lips, "That's right, Joshua. Frank does me everyday."

Joshua in total disbelief, "What's a gorgeous creature like you doing with a chump like Frank?"

Hatsue smiles, "Frank asked me the same thing today. He thought maybe I would like to try on a real man…like you, Joshua. Frank thought I might be able to cool some of that hot blood pumping in your veins. Do you think I can do that, Joshua?"

Hatsue puts the tip of her thumb in her mouth and runs her tongue over the top, as she waits for Joshua's response.

Joshua turns to Easy Eddie, "Is she for real, Eddie?"

Easy Eddie, as stunned by Hatsue's forwardness as Joshua, says as he bites his lip, "She's for real, Joshua."

Joshua "Eddie, is she really Frank's girl?"

Easy Eddie still stunned, "Yes, Joshua, she is. I swear she is."

Joshua smiles at Easy Eddie, "Is Frank offering me this fine piece of ass to cool me off and be friends again?"

Easy Eddie looks over at Hatsue. Hatsue nods approvingly.

Easy Eddie says, "Yes, he is, Joshua."

Joshua sizes up Hatsue one more time then turns back to Easy Eddie and says, "OK, tell him I accept."

Easy Eddie looks over at Hatsue. She just smiles and says, "You can leave now, Eddie. I'll be in good hands."

Easy Eddie just sits there in disbelief.

Joshua looks at Easy Eddie, "Well, get out here, Eddie. Can't you see I'm going to be busy?"

Easy Eddie stands up to leave and offers his hand to Joshua. Joshua just ignores him. Joshua's partner just gestures for Easy Eddie to get out of there, quickly.

CHAPTER 4

Next Week Monday, lunchtime at Canton Chop Suey Chinese Restaurant

Canton Chop Suey Chinese Restaurant resembles a cupboard shelf that opens up and pours its contents onto Mauankea Street. The entrance is a wide, garage door that is pulled up by a chain and locked into position. Anyone walking past can observe all the patrons scooping from their rice bowls. Five, circular, ten-seat tables fill out the center area of the restaurant while a series of four-person booths line the two side walls. The kitchen resides beyond the far wall. The front of the far wall displays the dessert options in enclosed glass cases. A lone cash register anchors the dessert displays. Each table setting contains a Chinese teacup, chopsticks, a Chinese spoon, a thumb-size saucer, and one bland, white napkin.

Walk-ins, usually tourists, are assigned seating at one of the ten-seat tables. In so doing, the management creates a family environment. Rather than the preferred, secluded, four-seat tables of the Mainlanders, Canton's arrangement promotes a friendly, large-family-style atmosphere. Tourists usually boast of this dining experience more than any other dining experience that they encounter on their trip to the islands. At Canton's, Mainland tourists actually get to sit down and dine with Asian and Pacific Island people. They get to hear their strange languages and observe their strange, eating mannerisms.

When Easy Eddie arrives, the main waiter recognizes him immediately. He is escorted to one of the side booths where Detective Aoki is waiting for him.

Detective Aoki as Easy Eddie takes a seat, "I'm glad you could make it, Eddie. Can I order you a beer?"

Easy Eddie stops to consider the beer then shakes his head slightly back and forth, "No, thanks, Chinese tea will be fine."

The waiter knows Easy Eddie's special, "Shall I bring your special, Eddie?"

Easy Eddie to the waiter, "Please, and bring some wooden chopsticks, too."

Easy Eddie prefers wooden chopsticks. Wooden chopsticks provide a better grip on the slipperier items. Easy Eddie's special is marinated in a slippery sauce. On more than one occasion, the smaller items in his special have soiled his Aloha shirt when he used the semi-plastic chopsticks.

Detective Aoki pouring Easy Eddie his first cup of tea, "Eddie, I've been told that you met with Joshua Puna last week, is that right?"

Easy Eddie takes a sip of his warm tea then responds, "Yes, I did."

Detective Aoki notices that Easy Eddie is not alarmed by the inquiry, "Who was there at the meeting with you?"

Easy Eddie responds quickly, "Well, there was Joshua, one of his bodyguards, Hatsue Yanage and me."

Detective Aoki "Did Hatsue Yanage leave with you, Eddie?"

Easy Eddie nodding his head, "No, she stayed with Joshua."

Detective Aoki "Have you heard from Hatsue Yanage since you last saw her with Joshua?"

Easy Eddie "No, I haven't; actually, when I met with Joshua that was the first time that I ever talked to her in person."

Detective Aoki "OK, I was just wondering if you heard how things went between Joshua and her."

Easy Eddie "Well, before I left the table, Joshua said that he accepted Frank's offer for peace."

Detective Aoki surprised, "Did Joshua actually say that?"

Easy Eddie nodding, "Yes, those were his words exactly. He accepted Frank's offer."

Detective Aoki nodding, "That is so good to hear."

The main waiter sets Easy Eddie's special and Detective Aoki's order on the table and says, "Be careful the plates are hot."

The main waiter's presence at the table silences the conversation. Easy Eddie busies himself mixing some Chinese mustard with soy sauce in the thumb-size saucer to create a dipping plate. The conversation drifts to the expected performance of the Oakland Raiders football team this season.

A few minutes after the main waiter leaves, Detective Aoki reminds Easy Eddie of the question he had asked him concerning the property in the Punaluu area.

Detective Aoki "Do you remember that property you wanted to know about earlier?"

Easy Eddie stops fiddling with his chopsticks, "Oh yes, what did you find out about that?"

Detective Aoki sips some tea then responds, "OK, the area in Punaluu that abuts the Koolaus often is referred to as Green Valley. The US Army used that area to practice war games during World War II. On the other side of the Koolaus was called Red Valley where the opposing forces of the war games were located. Anyway, Green Valley was originally sugar cane land being cultivated by Kahuku Sugar Company. The US Army seized the land during World War II and turned it into a military training area. After the war, the US Army released the land back to the sugar company. The sugar company never recultivated that land, so it remained inactive. Now, sugar cane was still being cultivated in other parts of the valley, so the train still made runs into that area to pick up the harvested cane. In 1974, Kahuku Sugar Company went out of business; at which time, the properties previously under lease for sugar cane cultivation returned to their rightful owners, mostly the Mormon Church and ultimately Blackwater Holdings. An enterprising, young real estate broker, named Kai Svensen, decided to sell off these new parcels of land for Blackwater Holdings.

Let me retrace the events that took place here in the real estate industry over the past 150 years. When Kakuhu Sugar Company commenced leasing the lands in Punaluu Valley or Green Valley, the land was owned by the Kingdom of Hawai'i. Lands were divided radially from the mountaintops into what was called *apuaha*. These *apuahas* resembled pie slices that started at a tip on the mountaintops and ended broadly at the shoreline. Within an *apuaha,* properties were divided into lots called *kuleanas.*"

Easy Eddie injects, "Yes, I've heard someone use the word *kuleana* to describe some of the lots in Punaluu Valley."

Detective Aoki "OK, good, since the time of the Kingdom of Hawai'i, a lot has happened. In the 1850s, there were no cars. There were no roads like we have today. City and Country requirements for house lots have changed dramatically. Regrettably, when this enterprising real estate broker embarked on his land sales in the late 1970s, he never thought twice about what changes had taken place in the real estate laws over the past 120 years. He sold lots without any concern for access to them, water to them, or if they met with real estate codes of the time."

Easy Eddie putting down his chopsticks, "I have a real estate salesman license and I know you have to check all these things. How could he overlook that?"

Detective Aoki raising his hands like to hold a melon, "Well, he didn't overlook it, he presumably just sidestepped the issue by maintaining the notion that these *kuleanas* were granted access and water by the Kingdom of Hawai'i. Since no laws were enacted to rectify this situation, he sold the lots as having the 'rights to access and water' as guaranteed by the Kingdom of Hawai'i."

Easy Eddie "Hasn't anyone caught this error since then?"

Detective Aoki "I checked with the Attorney General (AG) on this, and, apparently, it fell through the law reviews. Everyone just forgot that Kahuku Sugar Company's land under lease even existed. I mean you can't blame them, the lease existed before the state of Hawai'i became part of the United States and before cars were invented."

Easy Eddie "Come on Detective, what about that road that weaves in and out of the valley? Someone must have paid enough attention to the real estate requirements to make that road."

Detective Aoki "You know I asked that very question to the AG. Do you know what he told me?"

Easy Eddie "What?"

Detective Aoki chuckling, "Eddie, he said that road was merely the remnants of the old Kahuku Sugar Company railroad right of way. The people who bought lots from this real estate broker just began using the area after the sugar company had the railroad tiles removed."

Easy Eddie surprised, "Are you kidding? That road was once a railroad."

Detective Aoki "Eddie, think about it. How did the sugar company remove the harvested cane? Eddie, there were no cars in the mid to late 1800s. They used railroad cars. So, they needed a railroad to move their sugar."

Easy Eddie still surprised, "But, it looks like a real road."

Detective Aoki "I know it does. There are two things to consider though: First, City & County roads are required to be forty-four feet wide; whereas, a railroad right of way is required only to be forty feet wide. This road is forty feet only. There is no stretch of that road that is in excess of forty feet. Second, if it is a City & County road servicing the house lots in the valley, then how come it isn't paved?"

Easy Eddie stops eating, "That's right! How come it is not paved?"

Detective Aoki nodding in agreement, "Yes, Eddie, how come it is not paved? The City & County must know it is there. They do surveys all the time."

Easy Eddie "If there is no City & County road out there, then how were all those house lots created? How did they get subdivision approval?"

Detective Aoki leaning forward to whisper, "Eddie, I hear for a reasonable campaign donation to the Democratic Party, i.e., the mayor, anything is possible. It's a political thing."

Easy Eddie "Do you mean to say the mayor allowed that whole valley to get all screwed up for a few campaign donations?"

Detective Aoki "Well, it's not all about real estate and campaign donations. Besides, these politicians are just that. They have no expertise in anything except bullshit. The mayor probably can't spell 'subdivision.'"

Easy Eddie asks for a break in the conversation while he requests more hot tea from the main waiter.

While they wait for the main waiter to return with the tea, they engage in small talk.

Detective Aoki "So, what did you do over the weekend, Eddie?"

Easy Eddie somewhat excited, "I'll have you know that I played my first round of golf at the Ala Wai Golf Course with a tee time on Sunday."

Detective Aoki surprised, "No shit! I haven't been able to get a tee time there in over six years. Congratulations!"

Easy Eddie smiling, "That's right! I finally got in."

The main waiter brings a hot pot of tea and leaves. Tea is provided in a little metal pot then self served.

Easy Eddie motions with his right hand for Detective Aoki to continue telling him the information about Punaluu.

Detective Aoki leans over the table to get closer to Easy Eddie and speaks softly, "Well, there's a major marijuana patch out there deep in Green Valley. One of the guys in Narcotics told me that they even grow some cocaine out there."

Easy Eddie "Why doesn't Narcotics bust these drug dealers?"

Detective Aoki "Eddie, I hate to tell you this but Police Chief Gomez lives in the valley. And, the drug dealers provide handsome campaign donations to the politicians out there. What's more is that the drug dealers fund the valley's wild community association with anonymous contributions."

Easy Eddie surprised, "Is Police Chief Gomez involved in this?"

Detective Aoki "No one has fingered him, but one thing is certain, he has to be aware of the illegal activity. I suspect that he is getting a payoff from the drug dealers to remain quiet, maybe even to provide them security. Besides, Eddie, I'm not one to be looking down on the Police Chief for being involved with drug dealers."

Easy Eddie laughs, "That's for sure!"

Detective Aoki "What I'm saying though is that Punaluu Valley is being kept in this pristine state in order to allow the drug dealers to operate undetected."

Easy Eddie "What about all those houses out there?"

Detective Aoki "They are either Mormons who know to keep to themselves or drug dealers."

Easy Eddie lowers his tea cup, "So, the drug dealers payoff everyone to keep the valley free from development, is that it?"

Detective Aoki "Well, it didn't start out that way. This real estate broker assisted them unknowingly by screwing up all the property. Once that was done, it turned into what can be considered as an administrative nightmare to correct even without the drug dealers. The drug dealers just added financial incentives to the bureaucrats, police and politicians to refrain from trying to rectify the situation."

Easy Eddie "A friend of mine mentioned that the Bishop Estate discovered over two miles of PVC piping out there in the valley. Did you know about that?"

Detective Aoki "No, I didn't; however, with that much PVC piping, you can imagine how large the marijuana patch must have been."

Both guys nod their heads as they sip tea. This was the major marijuana patch on the island of O'ahu.

Detective Aoki "Eddie just imagine how much marijuana they supplied to Honolulu. I hope you can appreciate now why we have to fly in marijuana from the Big Island every few weeks. We have customers in grave demand."

Easy Eddie "Was Fat Willie Wong involved in this marijuana patch in Punaluu?"

Detective Aoki "I can't say that he was directly involved, Eddie, but that was his territory. Undoubtedly, he received a portion of the proceeds. Fat Willie was the Big Boss on O'ahu."

Easy Eddie "What can you tell me about the potential for real estate development in the valley?"

Detective Aoki "Well, if the drug dealers have left the valley, then it is just a matter of clearing up the sales fiasco of the real estate broker. Those involved will be protective of themselves, so you should expect a rough go of it. Remember, anyone who approved these illegal subdivisions did so as a result of receiving illegal payments from drug dealers. If that knowledge were to be opened to the public, they would lose their careers. Since the heyday of the valley was a decade or so ago, the bureaucratic accomplices have been promoted into more senior positions, perhaps even totally unrelated to their past assignments."

Easy Eddie "Who would be likely to be involved?"

Detective Aoki after sipping some tea, "Well, certainly the surveyors would be involved. Someone had to submit bogus civil engineering surveys. There would be attorneys who attested to the documents. The Real Property Tax Office would be involved for assigning tax identification numbers to the bogus lots. The Department of Land Utilization (DLU) would have to approve the subdivisions. The Building Department would be involved for approving the building permits. The real estate brokerages are responsible for selling the lots. Let's not forget the Police Department for overlooking the drug trade in the valley. The local politicians would be crucified. The Environmental Department and Urban Planning would come under criticism for not catching the buildup of residential homes within the shoreline management area. That ridiculous community association out there would be discredited. The list goes on, Eddie. Oh, I almost forgot, the title company that insured those lots would be grievously affected, if it got out that all those lots were bogus."

Easy Eddie "This had to have major political support."

Detective Aoki "Eddie, drugs are big business on O'ahu."

Easy Eddie "This is big trouble, isn't it?"

Detective Aoki nodding his head, "Yes it is, Eddie. Bureaucrats, police and politicians protect drug dealers to cover up this mess. This mess is like dropping an A-Bomb on the state of Hawai'i. For the sake of making a few dollars, these idiots burdened the state of Hawai'i with an administrative nightmare."

Easy Eddie "Do you think our presence in the valley trying to push development could ease recovery from this mess?"

Detective Aoki "I would say it would take the utmost delicacy to be successful. Remember, a horde of careers is on the line here. I would say it is an uphill battle."

Easy Eddie, finishing his meal, pats his belly and says, "That was great! I'm glad you invited me here."

Detective Aoki smiles, "Do you know who sat in your seat not too long ago?"

Easy Eddie at a loss by the question, "No, who was it?"

Detective Aoki "Fat Willie Wong sat there the night they gunned him down."

Easy Eddie "Are you kidding?"

Detective Aoki "No, Eddie, I'm not. I saved that seat especially for you."

Easy Eddie getting nervous, "I'll be OK when I leave here, right?"

Detective Aoki "Relax, Eddie, I'm teasing you. But, I'll share this with you. If you divulge what we just talked about, next time, I may not be kidding."

Easy Eddie notices the serious intent in Detective Aoki's eyes. He means business. For the first time, Easy Eddie realizes that it was Detective Aoki that set up Fat Willie Wong. Today, Detective Aoki was just trading favors.

As they are about to leave, Detective Aoki asks, "Eddie, did you happen to see Hatsue anytime after you left her with Joshua?"

Easy Eddie "No, I haven't heard form her at all. Why?"

Detective Aoki "I was just checking. Frank hasn't seen her since, either. He's worried, you understand."

The two men exit Canton's smiling. As Easy Eddie steps to cross Maunekea Street, Detective Aoki pinches him and yells "Bang!" Easy Eddie nearly has heart attack. Detective Aoki just smiles at him, turns and walks toward his parked car on River Street.

Easy Eddie turns around from time to time to watch Detective Aoki walk to his car. This guy is dangerous, Easy Eddie thinks to himself. Today, he had some great information about the situation in Punaluu Valley. Easy Eddie decides to keep in close contact with Detective Aoki. Undoubtedly, he will continue to be a fountain of information.

As Easy Eddie enters his store's showroom, he is greeted with the usual verbal abuse from Jacob. Today, he is five minutes late. Jacob's hounding never seems to cease.

Once in the sanctuary of his little office, Easy Eddie calls Hans Hoffman to relay some of the information that he just received.

Easy Eddie after getting Hans on the phone, "Hans, I just found out that the road that runs perpendicular to Green Valley Road might be an old railroad right of way. It's not a road at all."

Hans "You know Erik suspects something is wrong with that roadway as well."

Easy Eddie "A good friend of mine told me that suitable access would require forty-four feet. He said that this road was only forty feet wide?"

Hans "Yes, it is only forty feet wide according to the tax map records. It will need to be widened to forty-four feet. It doesn't seem like too much to ask the adjoining landowners to give up four feet."

Easy Eddie "Some of those landowners might not want to part with four feet, because they have hidden agendas."

Hans "Well, those who don't want to assist in creating a roadway out there will be exposed by our company to the other agreeable landowners. I guess you could say when the time comes to discuss access we will be giving them an offer that they can't refuse. If they do refuse, the suspicion of being drug dealers will be too incriminating."

Easy Eddie laughs, "Yes, I can see your point. Their hidden interests will point to only one agenda. Did Erik think this up?"

Hans "Actually, I heard it was Erik's lawyer's idea to expose the drug dealers. By the way, have you found out anything about who these drug dealers might be?"

Easy Eddie "No, I haven't heard who they could be just yet, but I have some people working on it. Whoever they are though, they are well connected with the City & County."

Hans "Erik's lawyer felt the same way. How could the laying of two miles of PVC piping go unnoticed by all the agencies doing surveillance out there? Also, as nosy as that wild community association is out there, you know they had full knowledge of what was going on."

Easy Eddie in agreement, "Yes, I've heard bad reports about that community association. They seem to be involved in all sorts of illegal activity. What surprises me is all the support that they receive from the press and the local politicians. I always had the impression that they were legitimately trying to help the local farmers in the area. I never realized that about the only farming that took place in Punaluu Valley was marijuana cultivation."

Hans laughs, "You're right, Eddie, the only farming that I know of in Punaluu Valley is marijuana...well, and there's cocaine, too."

Easy Eddie "Well, on second thought, there is a *lilikoi* patch out there. And, I've run across a few banana trees being grown by some of the gentlemen farmers. So, I guess, it's not all marijuana. But, when you consider two miles of PVC piping, you could say that over 95% of the farming is in the cultivation of illegal drugs."

Hans "What about the politicians out there, don't they realize that these drug traffickers can ruin their careers?"

Easy Eddie "The way I am hearing it, they wouldn't be in office if it weren't for the drug dealers."

Hans "I see, it is that bad, is it?"

Easy Eddie "I'm afraid so"

Easy Eddie hears Jacob yelling for him to get in the showroom and help. He excuses himself from Hans, rests the headset in the cradle and makes his way into the showroom.

As Easy Eddie enters the showroom, he says, "Yes sir, who can I help?"

A large Hawai'ian looking character in bold Aloha shirt answers up, "Right here, you can help me."

Easy Eddie "What are you looking for, sir?"

The large Hawai'ian speaking softly, "Eddie, my name is Kahele. I spoke to you on the phone last week concerning Joshua."

Easy Eddie had seen Kahele before, but he could not remember where it was.

Easy Eddie "OK, I remember talking to you."

Kahele "Good, can we talk some place in private?"

Easy Eddie sensing trouble, "Sure, we can, but I can't leave the store. Let's go back to my office."

Kahele nods in agreement and follows Easy Eddie back to his office. Seeing Easy Eddie's office is too small for him to enter, Kahele suggests they speak in the back of the storeroom. Easy Eddie agrees.

Once in the far, back corner of the storeroom, Kahele still speaking softly says to Easy Eddie, "You remember that gal you brought to meet, Joshua, don't you?"

Easy Eddie nods, "Of course, I remember her. Why, does Joshua want to see her again?"

Kahele grimacing, "Eddie, Joshua had some trouble with her. He needs you to try to smooth things over with Frank for him. Do you think you could do that for him?"

Easy Eddie expresses a concerned look, "What kind of trouble are we talking about here?"

Kahele reluctant to say more, "It's big trouble, Eddie. Joshua is really concerned."

Easy Eddie "What happened? Did Joshua get in a fight with her and beat her up?"

Kahele nodding his head, "Yes, Eddie, Joshua got out of control with her. He wants to make it up to Frank."

Easy Eddie "OK, how badly beaten up is the girl?"

Kahele pauses, exhales a few breaths, "Eddie, Joshua killed her."

Easy Eddie furious, "What do you mean he killed her? I left her with Joshua just last week. What happened?"

Kahele "Eddie, I wasn't there. Apparently, the girl wanted Joshua to get rough with her. When he wasn't getting rough enough, she laughed at him. She said some degrading things about him. Joshua was on drugs and went crazy. He tied her up and cracked her head open."

Easy Eddie exhales deeply, "Frank isn't going to like this at all. He really liked that girl."

Kahele "Joshua says he is really sorry. He didn't realize her skull was so delicate."

Easy Eddie realizing this guy isn't right in the head, "OK, I'll see what I can do. Where's the girl's body now?"

Kahele pauses again, "Well, I heard Joshua dumped her body in a trash bin."

Easy Eddie in disbelief, "My God, the first thing we have to do is to get her out of the trash bin. We need to clean her up, so she is presentable for Frank."

Kahele in agreement, "I can take you to see Joshua. I don't know which trash bin they put the girl in."

Easy Eddie doesn't bother to tell Jacob he is leaving. He escorts Kahele out the back entrance of the storeroom. Once in the hallway, he scoots past the showroom entrance, so Jacob will not see him. Time is slowing down for Easy Eddie, as Kahele and he wait for the slowest elevator in Honolulu. His mind races between getting the girl presentable for Frank and having Jacob confront him before he can get into the elevator. Luckily, the elevator arrives before Jacob discovers Easy Eddie has departed.

In the underground garage, Easy Eddie tells Kahele to get in the passenger seat of his car. Within less than a minute they are out of the garage and on their way to Joshua's condo. The slaying of Hatsue disturbs Easy Eddie. He is certain now that Frank will have Joshua killed. He sees no way to turn this around. He thinks his best protection from Frank's wrath is to retrieve the body of Hatsue, get her cleaned up and return her to Frank.

After some reckless driving from Downtown Honolulu to Waikiki, they arrive at Joshua's condo. Kahele asks Easy Eddie to let him do the initial talking to Joshua. Joshua is armed and a little crazy right now, he tells Easy Eddie.

After one of Joshua's boys allows Kahele and Easy Eddie to enter the apartment, Easy Eddie can hear Joshua singing. Joshua obviously is out of his mind on drugs. As he and Kahele enter the room that Joshua is in, they see a number of cocaine lines on the table. Joshua has to squint to see them. He has a revolver in his hand. Another gang member near Joshua has to grab Joshua's arm to prevent him from shooting Easy Eddie and Kahele. Easy Eddie realizes that Joshua is out of his mind.

Kahele speaks gently to Joshua, "Boss, where's the girl?"

Joshua squinting and slobbering, "She's in the bathroom."

Kahele exhales a sigh of relief as he motions to Easy Eddie, "That's this way."

When Easy Eddie and Kahele make their way to the bathroom, they notice blood on the hallway carpet. There is a lot of blood. Easy Eddie notices that the blood trail must have come from this one room. He cracks the door open. A horrible stench greets him. Closing his nose with his hand, he notices that the bed sheets are soaked in blood. He quickly closes the door, firmly.

Kahele is first in the bathroom. There is no body in there, just blood trails and a horrible stench. As Easy Eddie enters the bathroom, he tells Kahele to pull back the shower curtain. Kahele does so and looks into the bathtub. The base of the inside of the bathtub is red. Kahele gasps, closes his nose and turns away.

Easy Eddie seeing Kahele's reaction asks, "What's wrong?"

As Kahele moves away from the bathtub, Easy Eddie moves closer to the tub and looks into it.

Easy Eddie "My God! What the hell happened here?"

There are two severed arms with the shoulder still attached in the bathtub.

Easy Eddie and Kahele are stunned as they walk back to the living room where Joshua is seated. As they enter the room, Kahele says, "Joshua, where's the rest of her?"

The gangster seated next to Joshua after he snorts one of the cocaine lines, "She's in the trash bin."

Kahele puzzled, "Why are her arms still in the bathtub?"

Gangster enjoying his cocaine high, "Well, we tried to get her into the trash shoot, but she wouldn't fit. So, we cut off her shoulders to get her in. Besides, Joshua likes choking his chicken with her hand."

Easy Eddie whispers to Kahele, "This guy is seriously mentally disturbed."

Kahele nods to Easy Eddie then turns to the gangster, "Has Joshua been doing that lately?"

Joshua breaks in laughing and stuttering, "Oh yeah, brah, as matter of fact, I'm going in there right now. I love her hands, brah."

Joshua tries to stand up, but collapses and falls to the floor.

Gangster "Hey guys, you should have seen Joshua skull screw that gal before he forced into the shoot. It was far out, brah!"

Easy Eddie to Kahele, "Let's get her out of the trash bin."

Kahele and Easy Eddie leave the apartment and make their way down into the parking garage to where the trash shoot empties into the trash bin. When they arrive, there is no body in the trash bin. Small drops of blood here and there cling onto discarded items.

Easy Eddie "Do you think someone got here before us?"

Kahele puzzled, "Well, it happened last week. When do they come around to empty this trash bin?"

Easy Eddie "If someone emptied this trash bin, they would have noticed the mutilated body, and there would not be this much blood. What's more, the police would be investigating. It would have been in the paper."

Kahele "You're right. Those guys are so drugged up they might have forgotten what they did with the body. It's probably still up in the room. Let's go back up and check?"

Easy Eddie and Kahele take the elevator back up to the 17th Floor apartment. The same gangster lets them in. Once inside, they commence to interrogate the occupants that are still somewhat conscious. They get the same responses. The girl was forced into the trash shoot. They all saw her body go into it.

Easy Eddie "Do you suppose she got stuck on the way down the shoot?"

Kahele "I suppose that is possible. We would have to check the trash shoot flappers on each floor."

Easy Eddie "Let's do it."

As they ride the elevator down to each floor, one of the residents mentions to them that there is a strange odor emanating from the 7th Floor. Another elevator rider mentions a similar putrid odor near the 8th Floor elevators. Easy Eddie and Kahele take the elevator to the 8th Floor. Sure enough, the stench is unmistakable. Easy Eddie, plugging his nose, opens the 8th Floor trash shoot flapper and sticks his head inside. Hatsue's torso has wedged itself in the trash shoot between the 7th and 8th Floors. The torso is covered with the weekend's trash. Easy Eddie asks for a mop fastened on the wall near the elevator. He uses the mop handle to dislodge Hatsue's torso. Once dislodged, he hears it fall into the trash bin below. Easy Eddie and Kahele take the elevator down to the parking garage and pour Hatsue's battered, bloodied and trash caked body into a black garbage bag and dump it in the trunk.

Easy Eddie to Kahele, "It's best if I take her body from here. I'll drop you off in town, so you can get your car. Just let me handle this, OK."

Kahele surprised and relieved, "Are you sure?"

Easy Eddie "Yes, I'm sure."

Kahele "What will we do about her two arms?"

Easy Eddie hands Kahele a garbage bag, "Why don't you go get them. I'll wait for you here."

Kahele leaves with the garbage bag. Easy Eddie, in jitters, just stands around with his mind running at light speed. He keeps repeating, "This is just too much!"

After some jittering about, Easy Eddie realizes that he needs to give his good friend downtown a heads-up that he is bringing in a package. He decides to close the car trunk and join Kahele. He makes his way back up to Joshua's apartment. As he exits the elevator on the 17th Floor, he notices two of the gangsters holding Joshua up on their shoulders, as they try to get him to walk down the hallway. Joshua has overdosed again and requires assistance to be revived.

The door to Joshua's apartment is still open. Easy Eddie just walks inside. He sees more cocaine lines on the coffee table and the same cartoon show on the television. Joshua enjoys cartoons. Shaking his head, Easy Eddie joins Kahele in the bathroom. Kahele has just finished placing the second arm in the garbage bag.

Easy Eddie to Kahele, "I thought I'd give you a hand."

Kahele surprised, "No thanks, I just loaded two hands into this garbage bag. I don't need another one."

The two men laugh. This is so gruesome that it provokes laughter. It is almost like a cartoon show played out in real life.

Easy Eddie smiling, "I need to make a phone call. Do you have all this under control?"

Kahele nodding, "Oh yes, I got it."

As Kahele is sealing the garbage bag, Easy Eddie calls his friend downtown. Easy Eddie meets up with Kahele in the living room, and they make their way to the car.

Once at the car, the garbage bag containing Hatsue's arms is loaded into the trunk. Easy Eddie delicately adjusts the bag so as not create any tear holes. He does not want Hatsue's blood or body parts to seep out into his trunk. Once the bag is stowed, Easy Eddie has Kahele take the passenger seat, as he gently and slowly weaves the vehicle through traffic to Downtown Honolulu.

Kahele tells Easy Eddie that his car is parked in the Nuuanu parking facility. Easy Eddie lets Kahele out of the car, as he stops for the Nuuanu overhead street light. Kahele just closes the passenger door and walks away briskly. Easy Eddie thinks it is best that he does not have anything to do with Kahele or Joshua for a while.

Nuuanu Street runs North-South and is located one block west of Cornish Street.

Instead of driving to his store, Easy Eddie, seeing Kahele get into his car in the parking facility, drives directly to his friend's place. His friend, a prominent businessman in Honolulu, is waiting for him to arrive with the package.

As Easy Eddie drives his car to the back entrance of his friend's old, two-story, red brick building, he notices two men in long, olive overalls standing around outside. One of the men motions for Easy Eddie to park the car next to a side entrance. As soon as Easy Eddie disembarks the vehicle, one of the men asks for the trunk key.

Easy Eddie hurried, "It's the two black garbage bags."

One of the men, "He's in two bags? What'd you do, Eddie, take time to carve him up?"

Easy Eddie stunned, "It's a long story."

The same man "Please, spare us."

The two bags are delicately removed and ushered into the building. Easy Eddie notices that neither bag is leaking, as they are removed and transported. He conducts a thorough check of the trunk and does not notice any blood in there either.

One of the men comes back out from the building, "Eddie, Albert is waiting for you upstairs."

Easy Eddie as he finishes checking his trunk area, "OK, I'll be right up there."

After Easy Eddie is convinced his trunk is clean, he makes his way to Albert's office. It is a familiar walk, although, it is usually done late at night. Albert handles all types of emergency packages for the wise guys. As Easy Eddie enters Albert's office, he is greeted with the usual chiding.

Albert is short, heavy set, Hawai'ian-Chinese gentleman that enjoys good living. He is always smiling, it seems. Easy Eddie always wondered why he smiled so much. It does not seem to go hand in hand with the demeanor of a person running a crematorium.

Albert smiling, "Hey, Eddie, I hear you're getting into the bizarre now."

Easy Eddie shrugging off the comment, "It's a long and crazy story, Albert."

Albert still smiling, "Hey, for something this bizarre, I'd love to hear it."

Easy Eddie nodding his head, "I don't think so, Albert."

Albert insisting, "Eddie, something like this could elevate Honolulu into the category of New York City for despicable crimes."

Albert offers Easy Eddie some glazed donuts. Easy Eddie declines. After a lengthy and chidingly-embarrassing interrogation period, one of the over-all-attired men enters the office and informs Albert that the body is ready. Albert escorts Easy Eddie down to the crematorium spaces.

In the preparation room, Albert gets a chance to look over the body. Though beaten, after it has been cleaned with water, the girl's face is still somewhat recognizable. Easy Eddie can tell that Albert recognizes the girl.

Albert surprised, "Eddie, is this who I think it is? Isn't this Kealoha's girl?"

Easy Eddie "Yeah, this is Frank's girl."

Albert admiring what is left to the girl's physique, "You won't be able to hide this from him. You know that, right?"

Easy Eddie nodding his head up and down, "I know, but I can't let Frank see her like this."

Upon seeing Hatsue's mutilated body, Easy Eddie realizes he has to have her cremated. He cannot allow Frank to see her mutilated body. Frank will never let something as horrible as this go unpunished.

There is a moment of silence in the preparation room. Everyone realizes that Frank will erupt into a fit of rage. Albert can expect to be busy for the next few weeks.

Albert interrupts the silence, "Eddie, did you ever do this girl?"

Easy Eddie saddened by the comment, "No, I never did."

Albert motions for the other man to leave the room, then he walks over to Eddie and says, "If you want, I can leave you alone for a while with her."

Easy Eddie forms a disgusted look on his face, "Do you think I'm that sick? This is Joshua's work. It's not mine! I'm just cleaning up after him, again!"

Albert embarrassed, "Sorry, Eddie, I didn't mean it that way."

Easy Eddie looks over at Albert disgusted, "Do what you have to do here? If someone asks, I made the call to have to girl cremated. That should keep you out of trouble with Frank's boys."

Albert sheepishly, "OK, Eddie, I'll take care of this."

Easy Eddie exhales deeply and leaves the crematorium. What a way to start the week!

After Albert is certain that Easy Eddie has left the crematorium, he asks his men to warm up Hatsue's body. Albert never had the pleasure with this gal before, either. So what if Hatsue waits a few more hours to be cremated?

CHAPTER 5

Tuesday Morning, Hawai'ian Plate Breakfast Wagon

Easy Eddie spent a sleepless night tossing about a number of scenarios he would utilize to convey to Frank Kealoha that Joshua Puna murdered his girlfriend. He decided on involving Billy. At least with Billy present, Frank and his boys would know that a shootout would be possible, if the situation got out of hand. Easy Eddie expected the situation to get out of hand sooner or later. His only hope was that it would get out of hand with Joshua and not with him. One of the sad facts of life in dealing with the Hawai'ian underworld is that they often shoot the messenger.

Billy is sipping some coffee at one of the outdoor tables when Easy Eddie drives into the parking area adjacent to the Hawai'ian Plate Breakfast Wagon. The Breakfast Wagon looks like it is an old, converted, recreational vehicle that has been gutted and fitted with hot plates, warmers, and refrigerators. Its dingy, white color conveys its lack of gourmet appeal. Billy never orders anything from the Wagon except coffee. And, he insists the coffee be served only black.

Easy Eddie is on his way to work. That is why he selected the Breakfast Wagon, since it is on his way. Billy did not mind the meeting place, since he was in the area last night gambling until dawn.

Easy Eddie walking briskly to Billy's outdoor table, "Good morning, Billy, I'm so glad you could meet me."

Billy sipping his hot coffee, "What's up Eddie? What's so urgent?"

Easy Eddie nervously says, "Billy, I need a big favor from you."

Billy smiles, "For a big favor, Eddie, you sure aren't impressing me with your choice of dining establishments."

Easy Eddie looks around and realizes how ridiculous it is to meet at this greasy dive.

Easy Eddie shrugs his shoulders, "Billy, it was a last minute thing. I needed to meet with you, immediately."

Billy smiles, "Relax, Eddie, what do you need?"

Easy Eddie nervously leans over and speaks softly into Billy's ear, "I need you to cover me when I tell Frank some bad news."

Billy forms a worried look on his face, "I take it we will both be packing heat when you tell Frank whatever you are going to tell him, is that right?"

Easy Eddie moves his head up and down, "That's right, Billy. We'll be packing."

Billy sips his coffee slowly and says, "Is there a good chance we'll be squeezing off some rounds as well?"

Easy Eddie once more does his head movement, "I think so, Billy."

Billy allows Easy Eddie's words to sink in. Easy Eddie and he go back a long way. It was not so long ago that Easy Eddie stood by Billy, so Billy is obligated to stand by him.

Billy sips some more coffee and looks beyond the Breakfast Wagon out to the Koolau Mountains and says, "OK, Eddie, what are friends for?"

Easy Eddie taps Billy on the biceps, "Thanks, Billy, I knew I could count on you. I plan to call Frank today to set a meeting. I'll try for tonight."

Billy "OK, I'll be waiting. Call me at my Waikiki number. Shall I bring a few more boys?"

Easy Eddie ponders the offer, "No, Billy, it's best if it is just you and me."

Billy sips his coffee, "Eddie, can you tell me just how bad this news is that you plan to tell Frank?"

Easy Eddie leans over and speaks softly again, "Frank offered his girlfriend to Joshua to smooth things over between the two of them. Joshua accepted Frank's offer, then he killed the girl."

Billy quickly sets his Styrofoam cup down on the table and shouts, "What?"

Easy Eddie puts his hand on Billy's shoulder, "Calm down, Billy, I don't want this getting around."

Billy with a worried look on his face, "Eddie, we are going to our deaths, if you intend to tell that to Frank tonight."

Easy Eddie nods in agreement, "Billy, you know I would never call on you for something unless it was dangerous."

Billy smiles, "Oh yeah, this is dangerous, Eddie. I guess you didn't let me down. Since we were kids, we always thought we'd go out in blaze of gunfire."

Easy Eddie laughs, "I had forgotten about that. You're right though. We did say that."

Billy stands up and pats Easy Eddie on the shoulder, "Call me tonight, Eddie. We'll go out together."

As Billy is about to leave, he turns and says, "By the way, Eddie, did you ever eat here?"

Easy Eddie looks over at the dingy Wagon, "Are you kidding? This is the worst toilet in Honolulu! I wouldn't take a crap here."

Billy "I guess I know why I didn't like their coffee."

Easy Eddie pointing at Billy's coffee cup on the outdoor table, "Did you buy that coffee here?"

Billy as they are walking to their cars, "Yeah, it was early. I needed something to wake me up."

Easy Eddie looks around, "Billy, I hate to tell you this, but do you see any water lines running to the Wagon?"

Billy looks over the Breakfast Wagon a few times, "You're right, Eddie, there aren't any water lines."

Easy Eddie with a disgusted look on his face, "Where do you suppose those Hawai'ians got the water to make that coffee."

Billy raises his hands palms up to this waist, "Rain runoff, do you think?"

Easy Eddie smiles, "I hope you were that lucky. It might be sewage or that polluted swamp in the rear of the Wagon."

Billy shrugs off the comment, settles in his car and drives off.

It takes a while for Easy Eddie to get back into his car. Easy Eddie has a luxury car. It is second hand. He prefers unpretentious second hand things. It has something to do with the Chinese concept of caution that in a nutshell proffers: The tallest nail is the one that gets hits first. Or, the pretty flower is the one that gets plucked first. Hence, Easy Eddie buys all his showcase items second hand. Given Easy Eddie's profession, following this Chinese adage is a wise choice, less he ends up like Fat Willie Wong.

This morning, Easy Eddie takes time to observe the scenery along the highway to Downtown Honolulu. For the first time, he identifies some of the names on the faces of the businesses abutting the roadway. He even manages to appreciate their strange, architectural designs. There is one that resembles a huge turtle being supported by what seems to be gothic buttresses. Easy Eddie laughs, because the building now acts as the main office for a used car lot. The impression that these used cars are so bad that they require buttressing just to remain upright is hard for him to shake out of his mind. This site gives new meaning to the comment: Buy a new car; push it home. A smile seems to freeze on his face for the rest of the drive to his store.

As usual, Jacob spouts a plethora of undignified comments concerning Easy Eddie's work performance, as he enters the showroom. Easy Eddie thinks that Jacob must stay up all night dreaming up these derogatory comments then gets to the store early just to barrage him with them. Easy Eddie just nods, as if repeating: I know, I know.

After a few broadsides of Jacob's choicest chidings, Jacob informs Easy Eddie that one his friends called him. He hands Easy Eddie a message the caller left. Easy Eddie looks over the message. It is in code: Need to set time for you to view old Mercury. In translation, the caller will be in on Wednesday afternoon to discuss the heist of the jewelry store that was talked about at the Chinese restaurant. Easy Eddie realizes that he needs to speak to the security guard for the building.

About mid-morning when the security guard tours the Third Floor, Easy Eddie asks him to check out the lock on the rear door of the store. There is little traffic around the rear door, so it makes for an ideal location to discuss their quiet business.

Easy Eddie as he and the security guard pretend to checkout the lock on the rear door, "There's a job going down this weekend, I need to borrow your extra set of keys to the jewelry repair shop in the basement."

Security Guard after accepting a one hundred dollar bill from Easy Eddie, "Sure thing, Eddie. Do you need any other keys?"

Easy Eddie cautiously insuring that no one is around to hear them conversing, "The key to the underground garage would be nice to have as well."

The security guard fiddles with his ring of keys. He selects the keys and hands them to Easy Eddie and says, "There you go, Eddie. Do you need any others?"

Easy Eddie palming the keys and placing them into his pants' pockets, "No, that should do it. I'll get these back to you next week Thursday morning. We'll meet back here at this lock, OK."

Security Guard "OK, Eddie, I hope you have good luck this weekend."

That was quick. It usually is. Easy Eddie and this security guard have done a lot of business over the years. The poor guy only gets the minimum wage, but thanks to Easy Eddie, he has been able to cash in on the fringe benefits. One hundred dollars here and there, tax-free, has done wonders for him and his family. To Easy Eddie, a hundred dollar bill is a small price for borrowing the access keys to a bounty of precious metals. Given the security guard's knowledge of Easy Eddie's business, he always duplicates every new key provided to him by the building management.

It is a requirement that all lessees provide the management company one set of keys for access to their area in the event of a fire. The management company duplicates the keys, so that the security force will have a set of keys for quick access. Since there is no way to control the duplication of keys, the security guard has another set of keys made.

It is not unusual for security personnel to be duplicating keys. As long as, the security guard has the keys duplicated by a locksmith other than the one being used by the management company, no one is the wiser. Most Chinatown locksmiths realize that key duplication for less than honorable intentions is a main stay of their business, so they are quite tightlipped about their activities.

This management company has not implemented the advanced, slanted and numerically-coded, key designs of the upper-class, office buildings. Hence, duplication can be done with anonymity. The fringe benefits of the Downtown Honolulu security guard profession far outweigh the mere salary remuneration. The fringe benefits have become a boon for this security guard.

The rest of the morning passes with Easy Eddie packaging items for shipment to outer-island customers. Just before lunchtime, he receives a call from Hans Hoffman. They agree to meet for lunch. Hans has a taste for Mexican food. Easy Eddie acquiesces to please Hans. Mexican food seems too spicy and starchy for Easy Eddie.

Just before noon, Easy Eddie makes his way to the agreed upon Mexican restaurant. Located a few blocks from Easy Eddie's building, this restaurant offers an excellent view of the Fort Street Mall area. During the lunch hour, the Mall is a beehive of activity. Acquiring a seat on the lanai of the restaurant allows the diners to witness the hustle and bustle of lunchtime city life in Honolulu. Easy Eddie knows this, so he arrives early in order to get one of those seating arrangements.

Hans arrives early as well, so like two surfers, both Easy Eddie and Hans get to watch the surf of office workers and students build up in the Mall. An occasional ocean-like spray of perfume greets them as they admire the Mall coming to life.

Hans "It's good to see you, Eddie. I hope all is well with you."

Easy Eddie smiling, "Well, I guess I can't complain. How's the project coming along?"

Hans "Well, I met with Erik and the lawyer yesterday. The lawyer says that there are some irregularities with the way our lot was subdivided."

Easy Eddie remembering Detective Aoki's report just listens to Hans, "Really? What kind of irregularities?"

Hans "According to the lawyer, somehow Kai Svensen and his partners got the Department of Land Utilization (DLU) to agree to allow our parcel to be split without specifying a particular access road suitable to City & County standards."

Easy Eddie pretending ignorance, "Can they do that?"

Hans grimacing, "Well, the lawyer doesn't see how they could have, but since they did, it must fall into some sort of exemption of which he is not aware."

Easy Eddie "Is that possible? He is a real estate legal specialist. He should know all the exemptions."

Hans grimacing even more, "Yes, I agree, but you know they make changes to the laws all the time. Anyway, the lawyer said that he would do some research into the matter. As it stands now, Kai Svensen could have sold us an unsubdivided lot."

Easy Eddie "If our lot is unsubdivided, what can we do about it?"

Hans "Erik says we can force Kai Svensen and his partners to properly subdivide the lot and provide a road that conforms to City & County standards. The lawyer even says that this is an option; however, the more likely option would be that Kai Svensen negates the sale. The lawyer mentions something in the statutes that an unsubdivided lot cannot be sold."

Easy Eddie "Kai Svensen is the principal broker for his real estate firm, how could he sell a lot that was not properly subdivided? He could lose his real estate license for something like that."

Hans "The lawyer did mention that this subdivision issue, if valid, would cause a lot of problems. He even went on to say that from his initial impression of the entire Punaluu Valley that if our lot is not properly subdivided, then there are quite a few more lots sharing our predicament, and all were sold by Kai Svensen Real Estate Company on behalf of the Blackwater Holdings."

Easy Eddie pondering, "I see, so we can expect some big trouble out there."

Hans nodding in agreement, "I would say so, Eddie."

The waiter disturbs the conversation to take out orders. The enchiladas rancheros is the favorite here. We both order that entrée.

After the waiter leaves, Hans asks, "Were you able to find out anything on the drug dealers out there?"

Easy Eddie "No, not yet, I have someone working on it though."

Hans leans over to speak softer, "Eddie, Erik got wind of the name Ollie Carter from someone high up in the Republican Party here. Apparently, this Ollie Carter character is the drug lord of the North Shore. Have you ever heard of him?"

Easy Eddie surprised, "No, I have never heard of this guy. What else do you know about him?"

Easy Eddie is stunned, because he truly never has heard of a drug lord named Ollie Carter.

Hans "I don't know anything about him. What Erik was told is that he is real trouble, if he is involved."

Easy Eddie "The only Carter that I've heard of is the Carter that runs the big title company, South Pacific Title."

Hans lowering his voice to almost a whisper, "Erik told me that this Ollie Carter is that South Pacific Title's Carter's brother."

Easy Eddie sets his cool drink on the table firmly, "Are you serious?"

Hans "According to Erik, the North Shore drug lord is the brother of the South Pacific Title President."

Easy Eddie pauses a moment then says, "David Carter is the President of South Pacific Title. I had to deal with him when a cousin of mine tried to get into Braddock Academy. David Carter is on the board of trustees of the school."

Braddock Academy is the premier, private, college-preparatory school in the state of Hawai'i.

Hans surprised, "Is that right? You know, Erik's lawyer mentioned once that Kai Svensen's lawyer is on the board of trustees for Braddock Academy as well."

Easy Eddie laughs, "This is going to be a really interesting project, once the link between drug trafficking and Braddock Academy gets publicized."

Hans "No one has established that connection yet, but I agree, it seems to be lurking under the surface of these shenanigans, waiting to be unearthed and exposed."

The waiter brings our enchiladas rancheros. We pause the conversation to apply generous amounts of sour cream to our entrée. Hans adds lots of taco sauce to his enchiladas. He enjoys them hot to the taste.

Easy Eddie manages to breathe out as he bites into his beef enchiladas, "I guess we won't have to ask from where all those anonymous grants came from to support Braddock Academy."

Hans stops forking his enchiladas, "You're right, Eddie. Where do those anonymous grants come from that are sponsored by the Board of Trustees of Braddock Academy?"

Easy Eddie enjoying his enchiladas mumbles, "One thing for sure, the graduates of Braddock Academy have lots of clout here in Hawai'i. It will be very difficult for us to get around them. They have graduates everywhere. If they start badmouthing us, we'll never get that property developed."

Hans nodding in agreement, "Let's just hope that they aren't drug traffickers."

Both men continue to devour their enchiladas. A silence seems to overcome the table. The faint sounds of mastication time like soft music.

Finally, Hans lays down his fork and says, "Wow, that hit the spot."

Easy Eddie just nods, as he rolls his enchiladas with his fork like someone preparing to eat spaghetti.

Hans "By the way, Eddie, did know that a police chief resides in Punaluu Valley."

Before Easy Eddie can restrain himself, he utters, "Gomez lives out there."

Hans surprised, "Did you know that already?"

Easy Eddie somewhat concerned about the error tries to recover, "Yes, he has a place in the adjoining *apuaha*. Gomez doesn't actually live in the same area as our project."

Hans emphasizing the surprise, "But did you know this police chief lived out there?"

Easy Eddie smiling, "Yes, I did, but I didn't think it was that important."

Hans with more emphasis, "Eddie, this valley could be the major drug harvesting area on O'ahu, and you didn't think it was important to tell me that a police chief lived in the valley, is that right?"

Easy Eddie realizes that he is caught says, "Well, I just didn't put the drugs and the police chief together. Besides, the police chief resides quite a ways from the drug area."

Hans concerned, "Eddie, the road out there goes right in front of the police chief's residence. In order for the drug traffickers to exit the valley away from a busy intersection, they have to pass right by his house. Eddie, you are the one connected with the underworld here. How could you miss this connection?"

Easy Eddie realizes that he has been snared. Hans knows him too well.

Easy Eddie nods in agreement, "Yes, I knew, but I didn't want to alert anyone that the drug traffickers could be the police until I knew that for certain."

Hans seeming reassured, "OK, I can buy that. You're right. There is no need spreading around that a police chief runs the drug trafficking on O'ahu until we are certain." Hans pauses a moment then says, "You know, Eddie, given the connection with the trustees of Braddock Academy developing, you have to admit, if the police chief is running things, it would make the trustees feel pretty safe."

Easy Eddie nods in agreement, "It sure would."

Easy Eddie sees the connection unfold before his eyes: the police, the trustees, the Carter family and that wild community association. That is a killer combination. They could make everything happen. Easy Eddie realizes now why it has been so difficult to uncover anything out there.

For the rest of the dining experience, Easy Eddie and Hans go over future scenarios for possible property purchases. A fifty-acre parcel, abutting the major highway that circles the island, has appeal to them. Though the parcel is situated well, it has the topological drawback of being six feet below sea level. Fortunately, the 99-acre parcel currently in their custody has a topological plenty of fill material. Situated some 400 to 1000 feet above sea level, it will require terracing in order to create spectacular views for the intended residential estates. Terracing will translate into an abundance of fill material that will need to be relocated. The fifty-acre parcel could become the recipient. Hans calculates that if some 500,000 cubic yards of fill material could be extracted from the 99-acre lot, then it could be used to raise the ground level of the fifty-acre parcel to sea level, making the fifty-acre parcel an attractive investment. As luck would bless them, a rough estimate of the potential fill material that could be available from the 99-acre parcel reaches the one-million-cubic-yard level.

Easy Eddie and Hans are gloating. They could: 1) finance the purchase of the undesirable and unusable fifty-acre parcel from the future proceeds of the sale of the extra fill material; 2) fill in the fifty-acre parcel to meet sea level requirements for subdivision; 3) either sell the fifty-acre parcel to another developer for five times its current worth, or subdivide the fifty-acre parcel themselves and sell the smaller lots for twenty times its current worth. The key is the fill material. As it turns out, that just happens to be an abundant commodity that they have inherited with the 99-acre parcel. Enchiladas never tasted so good!

After parting with Hans, Easy Eddie decides to make a quick trip over to the bank vault. He needs to pick up some heat for this evening's activities. The walk through the Fort Street Mall, as lunch hour is closing, is hectic. Everyone is scrambling to return to their work places. Easy Eddie, anticipating the usual wrath from Jacob for being tardy, just takes his time. He waits for the crosswalk lights to change rather than risk scrambling across Honolulu's main thoroughfare, King Street.

Once in the vault, he exchanges the usual greetings and requests access to Mr. Ed Sone's safe deposit boxes. He chooses a particularly large box in the rear of the vault and takes it to a secluded, private booth. Once securely in the booth, Easy Eddie opens the box and sifts through the contents. His hand moves aside the heavy caliber weapons until he locates the layer of .32 caliber Saturday night specials.

The snub nose .32 is the ideal weapon of choice for his meeting with Frank. It is a small, easily-concealed weapon. Its small snout creates a loud noise whenever the weapon expends a round. The loud noise is beneficial when scaring your opponent is desired. As a kill weapon, it is not a good choice. It has little stopping power for an attacker pumped with adrenaline. However, for surprise of someone at rest, it is ideal. Its six-bullet cylinder is sufficient. If an altercation ensues, Easy

Eddie does not expect to be able to empty the cylinder before he takes a round himself, anyway. He selects two .32 caliber weapons. One is for him, and the other is for Billy.

Rather than secure the two .32 caliber pistols in his waistband, he wraps the weapons in newspaper that was discarded by some prior user of the cubicle so as to hide their shape. As Easy Eddie is wrapping the weapons, he smiles from the thought that even if the weapons are detected, their small caliber will not alarm anyone. A .32 caliber pistol is considered a defensive weapon. Frank will assume Easy Eddie was acting with self-preservation in mind. Given the gravity of the bad news that Easy Eddie will be conveying to Frank, coming to see him packing heat will be understandable.

Frank is a smart guy, Easy Eddie thinks. After all, he is running for governor. He will appreciate Easy Eddie's situation. In a sense, it was Frank that asked Easy Eddie to try to talk with Joshua. Everyone knew how crazy Joshua was. That is why they opted to allow Easy Eddie to meet with Joshua. Joshua almost shot Easy Eddie. He pointed a gun at him twice in the two short meetings that he had with him. Joshua is crazy. Everybody knows that. Of course, Easy Eddie doubts that anyone suspects that Joshua is as crazy as he is. Easy Eddie is convinced that Joshua has lost all touch with reality now. Joshua lives in a cartoon world.

Easy Eddie replaces the safe deposit boxes and makes his way back to his store, carrying a large, newspaper wad. He takes his time returning. Jacob will be in a rage anyway. Besides, if Jacob gets to abusive, Easy Eddie smiles when he realizes that he is carrying two loaded .32 caliber revolvers that police experts have cleansed of any fingerprints.

That Evening

The showroom closes its doors at 5:00 PM sharp. Two of the partners have obligations right after work, so they need to scoot out immediately. Jacob and Easy Eddie often linger around the store for another thirty minutes or so. Jacob does so to catch those last minute jewelers who always seem to get caught up in traffic. Easy Eddie tells Jacob and the other partners that he feels obligated to put in the extra time to compensate for his tardiness and collateral endeavors. They chuckle at his representations, because they are well aware of his after-hours dealings. They just do not say anything.

Around 5:30 PM, as Jacob is leaving for the day, he reminds Easy Eddie to lock up before leaving. Easy Eddie just smiles in acknowledgment and busies himself with packaging items for shipment to the outer islands.

Just before 6:00 PM, he hears a familiar, faint knocking on the rear door. Sure enough, he opens the door to see Billy standing there all smiles.

Billy "Are you ready to do this, Eddie?"

Easy Eddie letting Billy inside, "For something like this, Billy, I was born ready."

Billy smiles, "Me too! Tonight, we get to appreciate life."

Potential gun battles have always had a special place in Billy's heart. The anxiety of anticipation feeds his deep desire for excitement. He would have made a great racecar driver or test pilot. Unfortunately, killing two guys at seventeen tarnished his resume.

Billy looking around the storeroom, "Looks like you've done some rearranging in here, Eddie."

Easy Eddie "I always keep busy in here."

Billy "Why haven't you become a wise guy? Why screw around with this nine to five work? You could be good, Eddie."

Easy Eddie shrugs his shoulders, "You know, Billy, it's a family thing. My mother got me into this."

Billy nods his head; pauses a moment to reflect on what he would have done; then says, "Hey, did you get us our six little friends?"

Easy Eddie quickly steps into his office, opens one of his desks draws, takes out the newspaper wad, and says, "I got them right here."

Easy Eddie makes his way to an open packaging table and unfolds the newspaper wad. Inside are two .32 caliber revolvers with six bullets each, sealed in plastic bags.

Billy looking them over, "Eddie, are these from the police department? They look like they came from the evidence locker."

Easy Eddie puts his index finger in front of his lips and breathes, "Sheeew! It's a secret."

Billy smiles, "OK, I got it."

Easy Eddie handing Billy a surgical glove says, "Put on the surgical glove, remove the gun from the bag, load it and put it where you want to hide it on your body. You should handle the gun only when you intend to shoot someone."

Billy putting on the surgical glove responds, "These are from the evidence locker, aren't they? You had these guns cleaned."

Easy Eddie just nods, "Remember not to handle the gun with your bare hands unless you intend to shoot."

Billy admiring Easy Eddie's planning, "You're OK, Eddie. I'm excited about this meeting tonight already."

Billy wears the gun inside his waistband under his Aloha shirt. That way, the gun is easy to get his hand on and easy to draw out. Easy Eddie follows Billy's lead and places his gun inside his waistband as well. After the men discard their surgical gloves, they recite a little Chinese prayer for men preparing to go into battle. This evening may be the last time they see each other alive. They cherish the moment together then make their way to Easy Eddie's car.

Frank Kealoha resides on Martin Avenue in the middle of the Waikiki jungle. It is a one-way street, but luckily it is easily accessible from the main thoroughfare in Waikiki and empties into Ala Wai Canal Drive, the main exit road of Waikiki. If trouble should start at Frank's address, quick exit is available.

Easy Eddie decides to park his vehicle halfway between Frank's condo complex and the Ala Wai Canal, removing the possibility of exit interference in the event of a shootout. Both Easy Eddie and Billy anticipate gunplay this evening. There is no way in their minds that Frank will handle the news of his girlfriend's murder lightly.

Easy Eddie turning off the ignition, "Here we are. Are you ready?"

Billy smiles, "Hey, Eddie, nobody lives forever. Let's do it."

Easy Eddie and Billy cross the avenue and ring the secret code to Frank's apartment. It takes a few rings to get a response.

A deep Hawai'ian voice finally answers, "Who is it?"

Easy Eddie "It's Eddie, I need to speak with Frank."

Deep Hawai'ian voice "He's busy right now; come back later."

Easy Eddie with a commanding voice, "I need to see Frank, right now. It's important."

Deep Hawai'ian voice "Listen, Frank hasn't got time for any Mickey Mouse nonsense. If you don't get lost, I'll come done there and kick your ass."

Easy Eddie "You tell Frank we aren't leaving until we speak to him."

Easy Eddie and Billy hear the Deep Voice turn the voice pager off.

Billy tapping Easy Eddie on the shoulder, "When he comes to the door, let him see you. You move backward a bit to let him come out. I'll shove my gun into his ribs, as he steps out."

Easy Eddie "That's a good idea."

A few minutes pass before Easy Eddie and Billy hear footsteps on the other side of the door. Suddenly, the door flings open. A huge, three-hundred-pound Hawai'ian fills the doorway.

Hawai'ian with a mean look on his face, "I thought I told you to get out of here, Chinaman!"

Easy Eddie steps backward to allow the huge Hawai'ian to pass through the doorway. It's a close fit, but the Hawai'ian manages to walk out the door. As he does so, Easy Eddie notices that there is little daylight between the body of the huge Hawai'ian and the door frame. This guy is huge! Easy Eddie begins to think the little .32 caliber revolvers that they brought might be inadequate. Easy Eddie realizes that he does not have a bazooka with him.

Billy lunges at the huge Hawai'ian, as he steps through the door, grappling him around the neck and thrusting his revolver into the huge Hawai'ian's back ribcage.

Billy says with emphasis, "Just cool your jets, Moke, or I'll empty this gun into your kidneys."

The huge Hawai'ian is stunned by the turn of events. He calms down quickly. Amazingly, he becomes quite accommodating to Easy Eddie and Billy. He agrees to take them up to the penthouse to meet Frank.

It is a tight fit into the elevator. Billy never puts his gun away the entire trip up the ten flights.

As they exit the elevator onto the penthouse level, Billy says, "OK, Moke, which way is it?"

Hawai'ian points to the corner unit, "It's that one."

Billy with his gun pointing at the Moke's back, "Well, announce us, Moke."

Hawai'ian "Listen guys, Frank won't like seeing that gun when we enter."

Billy jabbing the huge Hawai'ian in the back with the gun, "I bet he won't like me gunning you down in front of him either, will he?"

Hawai'ian nervous, "Hey, there's no need to get excited here. I'll cooperate. Just tell me what you want to talk to him about before I knock on his door. If I don't him tell what you want, he will start shooting."

Easy Eddie to the Hawai'ian, "Just tell Frank that we come in peace. We want to talk with him about Hatsue Yanage."

The huge Hawai'ian tries to turn around to face Easy Eddie, but Billy jabs him with the revolver again.

Billy "Just tell him, Moke, or you won't have to worry about Frank shooting through the door."

The huge Hawai'ian knocks on the door to Frank apartment. Someone behind the door says, "Who is it?"

Hawai'ian "It's me, Kimo."

Voice behind the door "Are you alone?"

Hawai'ian nervously, "No, I got that guy and a friend of his that rang us earlier. They want to talk to Frank about Hatsue."

Voice behind the door "Do they have news about Hatsue?"

Hawai'ian "Yes."

The door opens, and another huge Hawai'ian fills that doorway. Billy puts his gun away as the door is opening.

Second Hawai'ian "Who has the news on Hatsue?"

Easy Eddie steps to the door, "I do. Is Frank here?"

Second Hawai'ian steps aside and invites Easy Eddie and Billy inside. The apartment is full with six huge Hawai'ians. From the bulges on the waistbands, they are all packing, too.

Frank walks out of the kitchen. He has been making some Portuguese bean soup, a favorite in the islands. Frank is a six-foot, two-hundred-pound Hawai'ian with a receding hairline.

Frank notices Billy, "Billy, why didn't you say it was you?"

Frank walks over to Billy and embraces him. They exchange friendly gestures.

Frank to his gang, "Relax, brahs. I know this guy. This is Billy from River Street. He used to be Fat Willie Wong's main lieutenant."

After a few more pleasantries are exchanged, Frank inquires as to the reason for the visit.

Billy "Frank, this is Eddie. He's the guy you asked to make a parlay with Joshua. Hatsue went along to calm Joshua down."

Frank nodding, "Yes, I remember that detective asking if Hatsue could accompany some guy to meet Joshua. I haven't seen Hatsue though, since that meeting took place."

Billy "That's what we're here about, Frank."

Frank joking, "Joshua didn't kill her, did he? That crazy Moke just might have, as nuts as he is."

Easy Eddie clears his throat, "Frank, Joshua did kill Hatsue."

Frank tells the room to shut up.

Frank to Easy Eddie, "Come again?"

Easy Eddie looks over at Billy. This could be it.

Easy Eddie clears his throat, "Joshua killed Hatsue, Frank."

Frank smiles, "Are you serious? Joshua actually killed that worthless bitch."

Easy Eddie and Billy are taken back by Frank's bizarre response.

Frank to one of the Hawai'ians in the room, "Get me Vince on the phone, right now."

As the Hawai'ian dials the number for Vince Nene on the Big Island, Frank says to Easy Eddie and Billy, "Can I get you guys anything?"

Billy anticipating a gun drawn anytime now replies, "No, we're fine, Frank."

Easy Eddie shakes his head to decline Frank's hospitality.

Frank can tell the two men are very nervous.

The Hawai'ian has Vince Nene on the phone. He hands the phone to Frank.

Frank all smiles, "Hey, Big Guy, Joshua killed my woman."

Easy Eddie and Billy listen to Frank relay the news to Vince Nene. They are ready for anything after the phone is hung up. Yet, both men notice that the room is not affected at all by the news of Hatsue's death.

Frank closes the phone call with, "Remember now, Big Guy, you promised me, if Joshua killed that Jap bitch of mine, you'd back me for governor."

There is obvious pleasure in Frank's voice and mannerisms as he hangs up the phone.

Frank picks out two white pins from the kitchen counter and hands one to Billy and one to Easy Eddie, "Here are two pocket pins for you. Vote for me in November!"

Easy Eddie looks over the pocket pin. It has a picture of Frank on it with the words: "Vote Kealoha."

Frank to Billy, "That was a wager I had with Vince. Thanks to you two guys, I could tell Vince that I won the wager. I bet Vince that Joshua would kill my girlfriend. I didn't like that Jap bitch anyway. By the way, did Joshua do her up good?"

Easy Eddie in disbelief and relief, "Yes, he did, Frank."

Frank nodding, "Good, that little bitch had it coming. She would have embarrassed me as governor anyway. Are you sure I can't offer you some Portuguese bean soup?"

Billy "No, that's fine, Frank. We just stopped by to tell you about your girlfriend."

Frank smiling, "That's ex-girlfriend! What did you do with her body?"

Easy Eddie "I had her cremated, Frank."

Frank all smiles, "My God, I do like this guy, Billy."

Frank laughs and slaps his thigh.

Frank still laughing, "That lunatic Joshua must have really messed her up. That Joshua's crazier than an outhouse rat."

Billy tells Frank that he and Easy Eddie need to be going. Frank bids them farewell and reminds them to vote for him.

On the way to the car, Billy mentions, "Eddie, I got my fingerprints all over the gun."

Easy Eddie as they reach the car, "Yes, I know, when we get to my store, I'll take the gun from you."

The ride back to Easy Eddie's store is quite enjoyable for the two men. Easy Eddie relates over and over again how much he enjoyed seeing that huge Hawai'ian's face when Billy jabbed the revolver into his ribs.

Easy Eddie "Billy, you really need to consider an acting career. You were great with that Moke."

Billy with one of those post-soccer goal smiles, "Do you think so, Eddie? I could bring some real gangsterness to the big screen."

Easy Eddie slapping the steering wheel. "You sure convinced that Moke tonight."

Billy "Yeah, I thought he was going to crap in his pants there for a while."

Easy Eddie "He was scared. That's for sure."

They reach Easy Eddie's building. The entrance to the underground parking lot is locked after hours. Easy Eddie has to get out of the car to unlock the gate. It is a huge, eight-foot, heavy-iron gate. It sheer size deters anyone from thinking about trying to drive through it.

Billy looking over the gate, "Have they ever considered using one of those sliding, metal-screen gates that can be remotely controlled?"

Easy Eddie as he slides back into the driver seat, "I don't know. This works pretty well. I admit that it can be undesirable when it's raining."

Easy Eddie sizes up the jewelry repair shop in the underground garage, as he parks his car. His friends will hit that place this weekend.

Once in Easy Eddie's office, Easy Eddie puts on a surgical glove and extracts the gun from Billy's waistband. He wipes off Billy's gun then places it in a small plastic bag. He labels the bag: "Used." With his own gun, he just replaces it in a plastic bag. Both guns are stowed in Easy Eddie's desk safe.

Removing the surgical glove, Easy Eddie says, "That will do it. We did it, and we're still alive."

Billy "That we are, Eddie. That we are."

Billy pauses a moment and says, "By the way, Eddie, if you don't mind my asking: what do you do with these guns?"

Easy Eddie "Your gun will go back to my good friends. It needs to be thoroughly cleaned of your prints. My gun, on the other hand, will go to my safe."

Billy "Your good friends clean the guns for you, do they?"

Easy Eddie "Yes, I have an arrangement."

Billy "Detective Aoki is involved in this, isn't he?"

Easy Eddie hesitates to respond, "Well, can we just say I have some good friends?"

Billy smiles and pats Easy Eddie on the shoulder, "We sure can, Eddie."

Easy Eddie "Do you feel like eating?"

Billy pats his belly, "Yes, I do. Shall we go over to the Yantse Dream restaurant?"

Easy Eddie nods, "It's on me."

Easy Eddie locks up the store and the two men decide to walk over to the Yantse Dream. Since the restaurant remains open until midnight, they can reminisce their exciting evening. Easy Eddie remembers that Billy likes Almond Pudding dessert. That happens to be a specialty of the Yantse Dream.

CHAPTER 6

Wednesday Afternoon, Easy Eddie's Store

Easy Eddie has been waiting around for thirty minutes now. It is 1:30 PM already. His cat burglary friend has not arrived yet. Jacob left at 12:00 sharp today to be on time for his haircut appointment. Easy Eddie has to laugh at the thought of Jacob believing he needs to get a haircut. At sixty-seven years old, he barely has any hair left at all.

Suddenly, there is a hard slap on the rear door. After hours, all of Easy Eddie's special business is conducted via that door. Like mice sneaking through a portal to evade the cat, Easy Eddie's friends scurry into his storeroom.

Easy Eddie relieved, "It's good to see you could make it."

Friend "Traffic was rough, and I had to make a few stops."

Easy Eddie checks the hallway after he lets the friend inside the storeroom to see if there was anyone following him. The hallway is clear. There are just some sounds emanating from the beauty salon a few doors down.

Friend rubbing his hands together, "It's cold in here, Eddie."

Easy Eddie smiles, "Yes, we feel the building's central air conditioning the most on Wednesday afternoons when there are few people in the store. The building has to keep it running full blast for the benefit of the other tenants."

Friend joking, "Hey, if you want I can give the building management an offer they can't refuse to turn it down for you."

Easy Eddie shrugs off the comment, "Are you still set for this weekend?"

Friend "Yes, I cased the place again just before I got on the elevator. We're going to hit him this weekend. Did you get the things that we talked about?"

Easy Eddie walks over to one of the storeroom shelves and removes a cardboard box. He lays the box on one of the packaging tables and opens the flaps. Easy Eddie reaches inside the box and hands his friend two keys.

Easy Eddie "This skinny key unlocks the jewelry repair shop's front door. Once inside the store, you will encounter another door that leads into the office where he keeps his safe. I don't have a key to that door, but it is a normal bedroom door. You should be able to force it open easily."

Friend taking the first key, "The skinny key goes to the store. I got it."

Easy Eddie continuing, "As I recall during my last visit to the jewelry repair store, the office door is locked by a simple padlock attached to a L-shaped, hinged fastener. All you need is a screwdriver to remove the fastener. You can unscrew it, or pry it open."

Friend "OK, it sounds simple enough. What about the safe?"

Easy Eddie "Well, you can drill the hinges off, or take the whole safe with you."

Friend "We plan to pry it open. I hear it is too heavy to lug out of the store."

Easy Eddie running his index finger over his lower lip, "It should be quiet enough that early in the morning on a weekend."

Friend "We will have cops keeping the street area clear for us. So, we should be able to get that safe open with no problem."

Easy Eddie "Just in case, I think, you should plan on bringing a drill with you. Make sure you have a long extension cord as well."

Friend "That's good thinking, Eddie."

Easy Eddie handing the friend the second key, "The fat key is for the lock on the gate to the underground garage."

Friend taking the fat key, "Fat key goes to the gate."

Easy Eddie closes the flaps and replaces the box on the shelf.

Easy Eddie "Return the keys to me next Wednesday afternoon. We can meet at the same time, right here."

Friend placing both keys into his pocket, "OK, I'll be here. Did you still plan to fence some of this stuff for us?"

Easy Eddie "Let me look over what you get next Wednesday. I can tell you what I can handle, after I see the goods."

Friend smiles, "It sounds like a plan, Eddie."

Easy Eddie "I will take all the coins you get, for sure."

Friend "Our main objective is to take the coins."

Easy Eddie "Good! There's quick money in gold and silver coins. Besides I can have them melted down."

Friend looking at his watch, "I have to be going, Eddie. I told the group I'd meet them for some beers."

Easy Eddie and the friend shake hands.

Easy Eddie "Good luck!"

Easy Eddie lets the friend out the rear door.

As 3:00 PM approaches, Easy Eddie hurries to lock up the store. He promised Hans he would attend a meeting on site in Punaluu. The store consists of a number of smaller office spaces in tandem, so the lighting arrangement requires individual switches to control the lights in each office. Easy Eddie has to systematically go to the main switch in each of the former offices in order to turn the lights out. Business expansion has its little annoyances. To a newcomer in the store, finding the individual light switches is like an Easter egg hunt. The store partners arranged the wall display cases and gondolas without any regard to the location of the light switches. Hence, a few are located behind the display cases. Eventually, Easy Eddie flicks them all off and is on his way to the North Shore.

The drive across the Koolau Mountain Range is a wonderful experience. The cross-island highway has been carved out of the mountains. It resembles more of a water culvert that has been recessed into the land. About halfway though the mountain range, pine trees begin to wall the skyline above the roadway. For a moment, Easy Eddie is reminded of similar drives on the Mainland. The multitude of pine trees makes it hard to imagine that he is still in Hawai'i.

The pine tree forest takes Easy Eddie to the Pali that lays claim to being the most spectacular view in the world. From the Pali, the entire Kaneohe Bay with its sandbars lies before his eyes. The calm blue waters, dotted with golden and ivory sandbars, create a serene setting. To his left, as he descends the road from the Pali, are the thousand-foot, near-vertical cliffs of the Koolaus stretching into the clouds. A slight mist seems to be polishing the rich vegetation clinging to the cliffs and the terrain below. This is a breathtaking landscape. The drive over the Koolaus is worth it, even if Easy Eddie only got a glimpse of this site, and he has lived on beautiful O'ahu all his life.

From the Pali, Easy Eddie weaves his way along the coast road to Punaluu. The drive from the Pali takes about thirty minutes. The road is only one lane coming and going so gawking tourists slow the procession. Easy Eddie understands the need for tourists. The island economy depends upon them. Besides, as he follows the coast road, he cannot escape remembering all the great times he had as a kid at the various ocean settings along the way. Kahana Bay brings a particularly enjoyable memory for him.

Kahana Bay looks like someone pressed a thumb into a ripe papaya and created an indentation into the Koolau Mountain Range. To one side of the bay, is a little lagoon that weaves its way back into the valley. A scant bamboo forest shelters the lagoon. Glimpses of the lagoon can be seen from the road where the bamboo maze thins out. One glimpse offers a view of a little sandbar that seems to reach back into the early days of the native people. Easy Eddie can imagine a local fisherman tossing his net into the lagoon while his family cleans his catch on banana leaves along the shore behind him. Such a peaceful vision forces Easy Eddie to take in a deep breath and be thankful that he lives in Hawai'i.

Making his way around the edge of the Koolaus that resemble a pincer shaping the far side of the bay, Easy Eddie notices Hans talking with Erik on the porch of the local food store. They seem to be sipping orange juice. Easy Eddie suddenly gets a thirst for some apple juice. He pulls his car to the side of the store. Hans and Erik come over to greet him. After a few cordialities are exchanged, Easy Eddie excuses himself to get a bottle of cold apple juice.

The local food store is a converted home that caters to the local residents and the occasional tourists that frequent Punaluu Beach. Most of the items for sale are snack foods, hinting at the store's convenience for tourists taking a drive around the island. The refrigerators conveniently are located in the rear of the store, forcing thirsty tourists to wade through isles of snack foods before reaching them. The temptation works on Easy Eddie as well, as he grabs a bag of dried pineapple on his return to the cash register.

Outside the store, Easy Eddie joins Erik and Hans as they walk down the access road to Punaluu Valley. The road is tarred for about one hundred feet; thereafter, it turns into gravel the rest of the way into the valley. To the right of the access road is the fifty-acre parcel. Today, it is under water for the most part. Six-foot or better tall grass spouts up everywhere where the standing water is not visible. In the islands created by fill material along the roadway, three residential homes have been erected. To the left of the road are one house and a large taro plantation. None of the houses seem to have occupants today.

Erik is a 6' tall, slender-built, redheaded Caucasian, originally from California.

Erik pointing to the fifty-acre lot, "The reason that there is so much water on the lot is that years ago it served as a drainage canal for the land at higher elevations in the valley. If you compare the elevation of the land on the fifty-acre lot to elevation of the highway just behind us, you will notice the highway is constructed a few feet higher. That's because, this fifty-acre lot is a few feet below sea level. The highway actually doubles as a sea wall. For our purposes, that means we would have to fill in this fifty-acre lot before it could be considered for subdivision and future resale."

Easy Eddie acting surprised, "How can you tell that there is a drainage canal on the lot?"

Erik smiles, "I had a chance to look over some old maps of the valley and a map of this *apuaha* in particular. Actually, it is not one drainage canal but two. One drainage line starts in the far corner closest to this road, and the other commences at the opposite far corner of the fifty-acre lot. Both converge near the center of the lot; after which, the combined drainage canal runs diagonally to the corner nearest this road and the highway. Once at the corner of the highway, the drainage ditch connects with a culvert constructed under the highway and dumps into Punaluu Beach."

Hans "Does it really dump into Punaluu Beach?"

Erik "Shall I show you?"

Easy Eddie and Hans respond affirmatively, "Sure."

The group backtracks, crosses the highway and walks out on Punaluu Beach. Since it is low tide, they are able to walk about thirty feet upon the beach. The ocean is calm today. The waves massage the shoreline gently. The sand is soft below their shoes, as if it were sifted finely.

Once the group nears the furthest reach of the waves, they turn and look back at the highway. Erik points out the huge, rusty-brown, metal tube that protrudes out from below the highway. The way the tube is constructed reminds the group of an anus. Some water can be seen draining onto Punaluu Beach, as if it were an oozing genital…and not exactly the type that would cause anyone to salivate.

Erik pointing to the tube, "There it is."

Easy Eddie surprised, "Well, I'll be. There is a drainage tube under the highway. Looks disgusting, doesn't it?"

Erik laughs, "When it rains, water comes gushing out of that tube, so I'm told. All the water runoff from this part of the valley dumps right here onto Punaluu Beach."

Hans walks over for a closer inspection of the runoff draining from the culvert. He notices some mushy substance lying within the fan-shape of the runoff boundary.

Hans to Erik, "What do you make of this stuff?"

Erik forms a grimace, "I have no idea. Maybe it got caught up in the runoff and got deposited out here on the beach."

Hans noticing a few more similar patches, "Erik, there are a few more of these here. The seem to be composed of the same material but their colors have a slightly different shade to them."

Easy Eddie walks over to inspect one of the patches. He sticks his index finger into the closest patch to him then raises his index finger to his nose to sniff it.

Easy Eddie sniffing the substance exclaims, "It's shit!"

Erik in disbelief, "Are you serious?"

All three members of the group repeat Easy Eddie's experiment. They all concur that the substance lying within the fan of the runoff boundary is excrement. What is more, they are convinced that it is human excrement.

Hans to Erik, "We should report this."

Erik "Yes, I'll report it to the Environment Department."

Easy Eddie perplexed, "How could shit be out here on the beach?"

Erik "Let's fan out and see if we can find any other patches outside the runoff area."

After some ten minutes of searching the area, the three agree that the only location the human excrement can be found is within the fan of the runoff boundary. The human excrement, they conclude, is coming from the valley via the drainage ditch and culvert.

Erik to the group, "I need to report this. This is an environmental concern, for sure. I hate to think where this human excrement originated."

Hans to Erik, "The patches are different colors. That seems to indicate they came from different people who consumed different things."

Erik remembering his high school biology class chuckles, "You're right. This is not just the result of a few people crapping in the drainage ditch. There's more to this."

Erik takes notes of what they found, and the group continues their original plan to inspect the valley.

The group walks back down the access road to where another dirt road runs perpendicular and caps off access road, making a T-shape. From the T-shape intersection, there seems to be a road that runs up the valley, over another lot, to our 99-acre lot.

Erik pointing to the road going to our 99-acre lot, "The lawyer has submitted a proposal to the owner of this lot in front of us to allow us to use this access in order to get to our property. We haven't received a reply yet."

Hans "Our contract with the prior sellers of the 99-acres stipulates that they have to provide us with suitable access to City & County standards, isn't that right?"

Erik "Yes, it does. The lawyer felt he could expedite our access by approaching this adjoining landlord. Apparently, there is some bad blood between the prior owners of the 99-acres and this property owner."

Hans "Now, that's all we need."

Erik "Really, I suspected something was brewing when I first met the owner of this property. He seemed somewhat upset when I told him we were considering purchasing the lot behind him."

Easy Eddie sipping his apple juice and munching on some dried pineapple slices, "What's the name of this roadway that runs across the valley access road?"

Erik chuckles, "That's another problem, Eddie. This isn't a road, the best I can tell. It is described as a number of lots forty feet wide."

Hans "When did you discover this?"

Erik "The lawyer and I were looking over possible access routes to the 99-acres. When we looked over this roadway, we realized that it did not meet City & County standards for a roadway this far from a major highway. It has to be forty-four feet wide. With a little more research, we discovered the roadway that we are standing on was a series of lots forty-feet wide. Believe it, or not: when the lots forty-feet wide were connected, they contained a railroad. This roadway that we are standing on right now was once an old railroad right of way."

Easy Eddie pretends that this is all new to him. He seems to slowdown his pineapple slice munching though.

Erik continues, "The lawyer will research this anomaly and get back to me."

Hans looking over the roadway, "This place really is screwed up, isn't it?"

Erik nodding, "It sure is. What I'm beginning to sense is that we are only at the tip of the iceberg of the problems out here in the valley."

Hans "If this roadway is a series of lots that are forty feet wide, couldn't we just buy them?"

Erik pauses a moment then says, "I'll make that suggestion to the lawyer. I think we can buy them. We could take them in the name of the company."

Hans "That would be something: buying a road!"

Easy Eddie stops munching long enough to say, "What would happen to all these landowners out here who use this road for access?"

Erik "That's a good question, Eddie? Theoretically, we could block the road and deny them access over our road. We wouldn't do that, but we could."

Hans adds, "How could they have been granted building permits, if we could own the road? There is something terribly wrong here."

Easy Eddie "Well, you know the people who work at the DLU and the Real Property Tax Office aren't the brightest in the world. Actually, they are quite lazy and stupid. Anyone could have swept this right by them. And, let's face it, despite all the political talk, there's no one competent enough to check up on them. Something this screwed up has to be brought up by the landowners."

Hans to Eddie, "But, Eddie, at least one of these landowners must have suspected that this road did not meet City & County standards."

Easy Eddie trying to avoid the obvious, "Well, you know, these landowners are mostly Mormons. The Church sold them their properties via Blackwater Holdings, so they trust in the Church to do right by them."

Hans nodding, "That does make sense. Most of this property was owned by the Church or other Mormons, like Kai Svensen."

Erik interjects, "Speaking of Svensen, he's the one that owns most of these forty-foot wide lots that comprise this roadway. There are other incidental owners merely because their lots extend into this roadway."

Hans "Well, well, given our experiences with this guy already, it is no wonder this place is so screwed up."

Erik "What's more, it was his real estate company, Svensen Real Estate Company on behalf of Blackwater Holdings, that sold the house lots along this roadway."

Hans surprised, "Svensen is a real estate broker. He must have known about this roadway problem."

Erik "He sure must have, and that is what disturbs the lawyer the most. We could be dealing with fraud here. And, from the looks of all this mess, there could be multiple instances of fraud."

Easy Eddie puts away his dried pineapple and says, "How far does this roadway go into the valley?"

Erik pointing westward, "Along this route, it goes into the next *apuaha* and exits onto the Kamehameha Coast Highway." Turning around to face eastward, Erik says, "If you follow the roadway this way, you cross Punaluu Stream and make your way back into the three-thousand-acre forest reserve."

Easy Eddie "This is a long roadway. Is there a bridge or something to cross the stream?"

Erik "No, there used to be a bridge many years ago; however, during one of the heavy rains, it got washed away."

Easy Eddie "How do we cross the stream now?"

Erik "We can cross the stream with no problem in a four-wheel drive vehicle. My Jeep is perfect for the job."

Hans "Do people still go back there?"

Erik "As a matter of fact they do. I've noticed fresh tire tracks along the stream bank every time I go out there."

Hans "Do you think it is the marijuana gang?"

Erik clearing his throat, "That's exactly who I think it is."

Erik motions for the group to walk the old railroad westward. As the group makes their way down the road, Erik narrates some of the history of the lots that surround us on either side of the roadway.

Erik pointing to the fifty-acre parcel says, "A few years ago, Blackwater Holdings sold this lot to a Mainland, California company with the expressed understanding that they would construct a forty-four-foot wide road from the Kamehameha Coast Highway through this fifty-acre lot to the roadway that we are standing on. Given the problems that our lawyer has uncovered out here, it appears that this forty-four-foot wide road was the intended access solution for the valley."

Stopping along the old railroad, Erik points toward the ocean with his entire right arm and says, "The proposed forty-four-foot road would have come right through this portion of the fifty-acre lot and connected to the road we are standing on right about here."

The pathway that Erik has lined up on consists of dense, tropical vegetation. It looks a little swampy as well.

Erik continues, "Years ago, a dirt road existed here. It probably still exists, but since the drainage ditches on the fifty-acre parcel haven't been cleared in years, it is now underwater. It should not be hard to resurface the road, once the drainage ditches are cleared."

Hans "Who will incur that expense?"

Erik "According to our lawyer, the owner of the fifty-acre lot has to keep those drainage ditches clear. Since he's a Mainland owner, he hasn't been around to inspect his property in quite a while. And, for some reason, no one has complained to him about the status of the ditches."

Hans "Do we plan to complain?"

Erik "Yes, we do, but we won't complain just yet."

Erik points out an area on the forty-foot old railroad where two one-acre lots straddle the roadway.

Erik "One of the reasons that I brought you guys out here was to show you these two lots. Although their location is ideal because they lie on this roadway, there is a more attractive reason for us to consider purchasing them."

Erik walks the distance of the lots and says, "If we can establish that this is in fact a roadway, which should be easy, this roadway, passing through these lots, subdivides these two one-acre lots into six separate lots. Now, admitted that two of the lots are part of the roadway, the remaining four lots are suitable house lots. For the price of two agricultural lots, we acquire four, essentially, residential lots. We should be able to triple our investment."

Easy Eddie nodding his head up and down, "That's right! If this is a roadway, it automatically subdivides these two lots into six separate lots."

Hans obviously pleased, "We should purchase these lots."

Erik "The lawyer has assured me that once we purchase these lots, he can apply for separate tax key numbers for each of the six lots. It's a sweet deal."

Easy Eddie "It's a good thing you looked into this roadway and discovered these straddling lots."

Erik smiling, "Well, if you like the deal with these two one-acre lots, I've discovered a few more lots located within the boundaries of the fifty-acre lot with similar opportunities. There are four more lots out there that can be turned into ten lots. I estimate we would need about $250,000.00 to purchase all the lots. We make an easy $750,000.00 just by having the lawyer apply for separate tax key numbers."

Easy Eddie to Erik, "Do those other ten lots straddle a roadway as well?"

Erik "No, those other four lots are composed of what the old Kingdom of Hawai'i referred to as *kuleanas.* The lawyer's research has uncovered ten *kuleanas* within those four lots. Since the old Kingdom of Hawai'i created the lots, they remain as separate lots to this day. What's more is that they retain the right of access and water."

Erik indicates the approximate location of the four lots within the fifty-acre parcel. The fifty-ace parcel merely wraps around them. The three of us agree to create an investor group in the form of a limited partnership to purchase the lots.

Erik encourages Easy Eddie and Hans to walk down the old railroad a little further westward. As we make our way down the road, Erik identifies each of the house lots on the mountainside of the road that have improvements erected upon them. After passing some six house lots, we come upon a ditch dug across the roadway. Erik looks at his map and identifies the ditch as residing on the property of someone named Gomez.

Hans inquires, "Do you think he is planning on running an underground water line?"

Erik "No, the ditch runs the full length of his property, and it is about six feet deep and four feet wide. Besides, a waterline would run along a roadway for ease of maintenance. This ditch has been created for another reason."

Hans looking over the ugly ditch, "Well, it sure disrupts the road. Nobody could pass over this ditch without ruining their vehicle."

Easy Eddie trying not to disclose the ditch's true reason through his gestures says, "This sure is strange."

Erik to Hans, "You're right about that. This ditch isolates Gomez' property like an old castle moat."

Hans "He could be trying to impede traffic across his property so as not to create unknowingly a prescriptive easement."

Erik smiling, "That's most likely the reason. He wants to avoid creating an access easement over his property."

Easy Eddie smiling, "He sure goes to the extreme, doesn't he?"

The entire group laughs.

Hans "He probably got tired of telling people to stay off his property. This seems like a drastic measure."

Erik to the group, "OK, let's make our way back and check out the other portion of the old railroad."

The group begins walking back to where the valley access road meets up with the old railroad.

Easy Eddie resumes consuming dried pineapple slices. The sound of his masticating is just barely perceptible over the insect noise. Now and then, his pineapple chewing is interrupted with a swig from his apple juice bottle. Erik and Hans smile at the sound Easy Eddie makes after each swig. It reminds them of the noise cowboys, fresh in from a cattle drive, made in old western movies after gulping a shot of whiskey.

At the cross roads, Erik focuses the group's attention on a small triangular-shape of land that extends over the old railroad.

Erik pointing to the map, "This part of the roadway is owned by a guy named Hardin. His lot resembles a pyramid."

Erik points to Hardin's house and barn, "The rectangular base of the lot is located just past his barn. At about twenty feet from this roadway, the lot forms a slanted triangle that crosses this roadway and forms this little triangular-like-shape on the other side of the roadway. It doesn't seem like much, but we will need to purchase this little triangular-shaped lot in order to acquire suitable, forty-four-foot access to the 99-acre parcel."

As Erik describes the proposed access road to the 99-acre parcel, Hardin comes trailblazing up Punaluu Valley Road. A cloud of dirt quickly forms behind his truck as he approaches. Some distance behind him is an old two-ton truck carrying a half a dozen or so migrant workers. Hardin nearly runs our group over as he skids his truck into the yard of his neighbor. He hops out of his truck, slamming the driver's side door. The truck door bounces a few times against the door frame, but it remains open as it slowly dampens to a standstill. Hardin, obviously infuriated, stomps up his neighbor's steps and pounds his right fist on the neighbor's door.

Our group is recovering from almost being run over when the two-ton truck, carrying the migrant workers, parks in front of Hardin's house. As the migrant workers are disembarking, we can make out what appears to be a dead cow in the back of the truck. It appears that the migrant workers had been gutting the animal.

Erik to our group, "That looks like Hardin's cow."

Hardin commences screaming at a local Hawai'ian guy that comes to the front door of the neighbor's house, "You son of a bitch! Why did you kill my cow?"

Local Hawai'ian responds, "Hey, your animal wandered onto my property, so I shot it."

Hardin slams his fist against the neighbor's house, "You worthless drug addict, couldn't you tell it was my cow? You dumb shit!"

Erik mentions to our group, "Hardin's neighbor is a troublemaker named Manama. He's one of the valley's drug dealers."

Manama somewhat defensive, "Listen, that animal came on my property and crapped, so I shot it."

Hardin in disbelief, "Why do the migrant workers have my cow?"

Manama "Hey, I didn't want that carcass on my property, so I sold it to the migrant workers that till the taro patch."

Hardin still upset, "Didn't that drug addicted brain of yours realize that it was my cow?"

Manama staggering a bit in the doorway, "Tell you the truth, Mr. Hardin, when I shot it, I had no idea what it was. It was just crapping on my property."

Hardin sternly to Manama, "Moke, I catch you on my property, and I'm going to shoot you, you worthless drug addict."

Manama smiles, "I bet you'd really do that too. That's really cool man. I better make sure I don't wander on your property."

Hardin stomps slowly down Manama's steps, "You better make damn sure you don't come on my property, or those migrant workers will be gutting you as they drive down the coast road."

Easy Eddie to Erik, "It's probably not a good idea to ask Hardin if he wants to sell that little triangular-shaped lot, right now."

Erik chuckles, "I guess not. Can you believe this guy Manama? He shot Hardin's cow, because it wandered on his property and crapped."

Hans shakes his head side to side, "This valley has some real lunatics."

Easy Eddie to Hans, "It's the drugs. These Mokes get so hooked on it, they eventually lose their minds."

Hans in disbelief, "I can't believe the guy would shoot a neighbor's cow like that."

Easy Eddie remembering Joshua Puna's ordeal with Hatsue exhales, "Trust me, these Mokes do much worse than that. They live in a cartoon world."

Erik exhales, "Well, I think we've seen enough for today. We should be getting back to Honolulu, before it starts getting dark."

Hans "I agree. If we stay out here too long that lunatic might shoot us."

Erik "Yes, the three of us together might make him think we are a cow."

Hans laughs, "We might be safe as long as we don't take a crap."

The group breaks out in laughter as they walk down the Punaluu Valley Access Road to their cars.

Easy Eddie needs to hurry back to Inter-Island Air Terminal. Detective Aoki is waiting for him there. Tomorrow morning is the scheduled marijuana flight from the Big Island. He has time to catch the last flight out to Kona. In order to allow him even more time, he decides to drive on the scenic H-3 loop that recently opened in Kaneohe.

The new H-3 loop connects Kaneohe with H-1 near Pearl Harbor. Once in the Pearl Harbor area, it is only a few miles to the Inter-Island Air Terminal. The view from the thousand-foot-elevated H-3 loop is as spectacular as the one from the Pali. The loop stands almost even with the mountain peaks of the Koolaus. At times, the drive includes passing through thin, cumulus clouds that often envelop the upper portion of the mountains. Easy Eddie has heard pilots describing the driving experience through this cumulus as akin to flying a small propeller plane in cloud formations.

Since it is quitting time in Honolulu, most of the traffic will be in the oncoming lane. Easy Eddie should be able to enjoy a pleasant trip over the Koolaus. His mind wanders back to the railroad right of way. He realizes that many heads will roll once the word gets out how poorly that whole section of the island has been managed by the bureaucrats. That means trouble for anyone trying to develop in the valley. He knows that. Accordingly, it is unlikely that he, or for that matter anyone involved in these land projects, would realize any profits from the undertakings. Perhaps, his only avenue to make any money out of this is to play both sides.

Easy Eddie grew up in the islands where the culture does not seem to support playing fairly. It is second nature for him to sell out his friends. Avoidance of civil duties, including income taxes, is a social trait. Whereas, trying to obtain the maximum benefits from the government, even if through fraudulent means, is an acceptable and socially-praised endeavor. He will investigate to discover the identities of those bureaucrats and interested parties that created this mess. Blackmail becomes an attractive, dark alley to explore.

Deep in his thoughts of fast money schemes, Easy Eddie notices the Inter-Island Air Terminal banner on the roadside. That was fast. Time sure does fly by when making money is pondered. As he drives down the access road to the Inter-Island Air Terminal, he sees Detective Aoki in the distance pacing back and forth along the side his car, as he smokes a cigarette. Easy Eddie realizes that Detective Aoki is nervous. Well, Easy Eddie did cut it close to the departure time.

Detective Aoki upon seeing Easy Eddie motions him to park in a reserved slot beside his car. Easy Eddie follows Detective Aoki instructions.

Easy Eddie to Detective Aoki as he parks the car, "How's it?"

Detective Aoki tossing his cigarette to the ground, "I was beginning to think that you weren't coming."

Easy Eddie as he turns off the ignition, "Hey, would I let you down? Relax, Detective, we have plenty of time."

Detective Aoki looks at his watch as Easy Eddie disembarks the car, "Eddie, you have twenty minutes to board that plane."

Easy Eddie locking his car door, "Well, let's get going then."

The two men walk briskly to the ticket counter. The receptionists smiles and has Easy Eddie's plane ticket already processed. Easy Eddie realizes that his tardiness did make the group here a little nervous.

Detective Aoki flashes his badge and accompanies Easy Eddie to the ramp of the airplane, "You have a safe trip now. I'll meet you here tomorrow morning."

Easy Eddie nods, "I'll be here."

Detective Aoki watches Easy Eddie climb the ramp and enter the plane. In less than ten minutes, the plane is airborne on its way to Kona, Hawai'i.

CHAPTER 7

West Waianae Resort

The worst of all possible scenarios seems to be unfolding, Easy Eddie thinks to himself, as he disembarks the helicopter at the West Waianae Resort helipad. This marijuana run is getting to be routine. Everyone in Kona acknowledges him as the escort. During this last trip, no one, not even Ralph, even bothered to ask him if he liked the work. They just assumed that he did. Easy Eddie realizes that he will never be able to get out of this business.

Detective Aoki greets Easy Eddie; "I hope you had a good stay in Kona, Eddie?"

Easy Eddie forcing a smile, "It was OK."

Quickly the cargo is taken off the helicopter and loaded into other vehicles. Easy Eddie notices that this time there are more vehicles.

Detective Aoki motioning to get in his car, "I'll take you to the Inter-Island Air Terminal to get your car."

Easy Eddie quickly settles into the detective's car. As they leave the West Waianae Resort complex, Detective Aoki informs Easy Eddie that he has uncovered some more information on Punaluu Valley.

Detective Aoki "Eddie, do you know who those drug dealers are that are operating in Punaluu Valley?"

Easy Eddie "No, I don't. The last time we talked, you mentioned that a police chief was involved."

Detective Aoki "Well, the police chief is involved to the level that we discussed. His role is passive. Are you aware of the title company that underwrites the lots out there?"

Easy Eddie "I think I saw South Pacific Title's name on a few of the mortgages."

Detective Aoki nods his head in agreement, "Yes, South Pacific Title underwrites the real property titles in Punaluu Valley. The Carter family runs South Pacific Title."

Easy Eddie recognizes this line of discovery. Hans mentioned the same connection to him at the Mexican restaurant.

Easy Eddie faking surprise, "OK, I'm familiar with South Pacific Title."

Detective Aoki "That's good. The Carter family has three sons. Two of the sons now run the company; whereas, the third son, Ollie, seems to have arisen as the North Shore drug lord. Ollie Carter is the guy behind the drug operations in Punaluu Valley."

Easy Eddie still faking, "This Ollie Carter must be a powerful guy."

Detective Aoki nodding in agreement, "Yes, Eddie, he is. The quiet word in the police department is that he makes regular payoffs. He has good connections in the department. Also, he spreads his money all around town. I suspect his money is the reason your friends are having so much trouble discovering anything about the valley."

Easy Eddie "Did you know that at least one of the Carter brothers is a trustees for Braddock Academy?"

Detective Aoki "Like I said, Eddie, Ollie Carter spreads his money all around Honolulu."

Easy Eddie sensing the magnitude of the problem exhales, "I see."

Detective Aoki "That's good. So now you know not to go around sniffing up trouble about the valley."

Easy Eddie "I can see it's not a wise idea."

Detective Aoki chuckles, "Who would have thought that the best way to control access to a valley was to own a title company? Think of it, Eddie, without proper title, no one can get a loan to purchase property. South Pacific Title insures that only select buyers can purchase land out there."

Easy Eddie "There are other title companies."

Detective Aoki "Yes, there are other title companies; however, South Pacific Title informs the other title companies that they are investigating the title problems in the valley, alerting the other companies to impending litigation. Since title companies have to foot the bill for any litigation, they are dissuaded persuasively from underwriting any properties in the valley. Hence, no one can purchase property in Punaluu Valley without first being screened by South Pacific Title...Ollie Carter."

Easy Eddie "How did we get to purchase our property in the valley?"

Detective Aoki "I suspect no one felt the location of your property would effect their business out there. Or, your friends were being suckered into a land sale that they could never use and eventually would give up on. Once your *hui* realized that they could never utilize or profit from the purchase of the 99-acre parcel, they would be unwilling to continue to carry a huge mortgage on the property. It would be tempting for them to just default on the mortgage and walk away from the deal. Besides, doesn't your *hui* have an agreement of sale with the vendors?"

Hui is the Hawai'ian word for group.

Easy Eddie "I think it is an agreement of sale arrangement."

Detective Aoki "Correct me if I'm wrong but doesn't an agreement of sale require that the title to the property remain with the seller until such time as certain conditions are met?"

Easy Eddie "That's correct; however, I believe the *hui*'s arrangement is a purchase money mortgage which transfers the title to the buyer. So, our *hui* has the title to the 99-acre parcel. The *hui* is just waiting for the access, suitable to City & County standards, to be provided in order to completely consummate the sale."

Detective Aoki "I see, OK, so your *hui* would have recourse to remedy against the title company."

Easy Eddie changing the focus, "Do you think the real estate broker is in with the drug dealers?"

Detective Aoki "You never know, Eddie. One thing is certain, if the real estate broker is familiar with the valley, then he certainly is aware of the title problems and the drug trafficking."

Easy Eddie "We have a disclosure problem then with the real estate broker, don't we?"

Detective Aoki "That you do, Eddie. That you do. The real estate broker has to know the Carter family very well."

Easy Eddie "Do you think the other two brothers are in cahoots with Ollie?"

Detective Aoki "Well, it would be hard to prove, but, I suspect, at least one of the other brothers has to be involved. The system is greased too well."

A moment of silence passes as Easy Eddie contemplates the magnitude of the problem.

Detective Aoki drives into the Inter-Island Air Terminal's special lot where Easy Eddie's car is parked.

Detective Aoki stopping the car, "Here you go, Eddie. See you in a couple weeks."

Easy Eddie's Store

Easy Eddie is in the store early this morning. He even beats Jacob. When Jacob arrives, the shock of seeing Easy Eddie busy at work is too much for him to take. Jacob pretends to be friendly. It is so unusual for Easy Eddie to witness Jacob in this manner that the sheer pleasure of the experience is a reward in itself for Easy Eddie.

Jacob is suspicious but smiling, "It's so good to see that you have finally come around, Eddie. For a while there, I thought you were doomed to a life of crime. Congratulations!"

Easy Eddie smiles, "Well, yes, I have thought about the way my life was going for some time now. I realize that my only salvation is too attend to our business here."

Jacob patting Easy Eddie on the back, "Good for you, Eddie. I'm proud of you."

Easy Eddie realizes just how little his Uncle Jacob has a grip on reality. If he only knew what Easy Eddie has gone through over the last ten days?

As Jacob is about to leave to go to his desk area, he says, "Did you hear about the funeral service for one of that Kealoha gangster's friends?"

Easy Eddie nervously responds, "No, I didn't. When is this happening?"

Jacob thinks a moment, "I'm not sure. I'll find out at lunchtime. It's supposed to be a big event. My friends were talking about it yesterday afternoon. They said the service was going to be held in the funeral parlor down the street."

Easy Eddie puzzled, "No, I haven't heard a word."

Jacob chuckles, "I guess when you run for governor, you have to acquire popularity anyway you can."

Easy Eddie "That's right, Kealoha is running for governor."

Easy Eddie remembers the pocket pin Frank gave him. He wonders if the funeral service is for Hatsue Yanage. If the funeral service is for Hatsue, then that would be a nice touch by Frank. Easy Eddie feels obligated to attend, if it is.

The store was hectic all morning. Easy Eddie doubts that he will have time to go to lunch, because he acquired four special orders that require a lot of paperwork. He decides to remain in the store and get those orders in the mail.

About 12:30 PM, Easy Eddie hears a familiar knock on the rear door. He answers the knock. It is his cat burglar friend, the one that is planning the heist in the basement jewelry store this weekend.

Friend rubbing his hands together, "Eddie, I waited for you downstairs. When you didn't come down, I thought you might be working through lunch?"

Easy Eddie "What's wrong? Are you still on for this weekend?"

Friend "Yes, we are. Nothing is wrong. What I came to tell you was that we're planning a cowboy hit on the funeral parlor down the street."

Easy Eddie stunned, "You're going to hit a funeral parlor. Is that what you are saying?"

Friend smiling, "Yeah, Eddie, we're going to hit it Saturday morning. There's a big crowd that's going to be there. I understand some real rich guys will attend. There will be lots of jewelry."

Easy Eddie sits down slowly, "Is this the Kealoha funeral?"

Friend "No, it's some Jap. They got people from all over the world attending the funeral service! You know how them Japs like to doll up with jewelry."

Easy Eddie realizes that this guy is losing it. Robbing a funeral! Tell me that will not be bad press. Easy Eddie begins to wonder how he got involved with these kooks.

Friend "I wanted you to be ready to fence some more jewelry for us."

Easy Eddie "OK, I'll see what you got when you bring it. We can do this as scheduled next Wednesday afternoon."

The friend taps Easy Eddie on the biceps then makes his way out of the store.

Saturday Noontime, Nishimoto Funeral Parlor

The streets are overflowing with lines of parked cars around the Vineyard Circle, located just six blocks mountainside of Easy Eddie's store. Both the nearby city parking facilities are full. It gets like that when an important person passes away. Like a popular beach during a surfing event, people from all walks of life descend upon Nishimoto Funeral Parlor.

Today, a beautiful day in paradise, the family of Hatsue Yanage and her relatives gather to pay their last respects. Since her prosperous family members from Japan are in attendance, many social climber-types have gathered as well to rub shoulders with them, including Frank Kealoha and a few of his political staff.

Nishimoto Funeral Parlor is the largest and most conveniently located funeral parlor in the city. Its façade displays an ancient Japanese design. At first glance, one would imagine oneself in 19th Century Japan immersed into a *Shinto* establishment. The funeral parlor has a large, 200-person-plus viewing room, adjacent to the service room. Double doors provide easy access to and exit from the viewing room. From the viewing room, a wide driveway stretches out to the main roadway. Surrounding the funeral parlor is an ample parking area with easy access to the main thoroughfare and a side street.

As Frank introduces his staff to a prominent businessman from Tokyo, the rear end of a rusty, old van bursts through the double doors of the viewing room. Like marines disembarking a landing craft, five, armed, hooded goons emerge. One of the goons fires a shotgun into the ceiling of the viewing room.

Female voiced goon "This is a stickup! Put your hands in the air."

A sterner male goon takes a position next to the female voiced goon's side, "Y'all face the wall and take out all your valuables!"

Two of the other goons take positions on either side of the viewing room. All five have shotguns. A sixth goon comes out of the passenger side of the van with two large garbage bags. He hands one of the bags to the female voiced goon, and they begin to separate the patrons from their valuables: money, wallets, watches, jewelry, ear rings, wedding rings, necklaces, etc. They even collect a few guns.

One Japanese gentleman is unable to converse in English.

Japanese person "*Wakarimasen.*" ("I do not understand" in Japanese)

Collection goon "Hey, brah, you speak English in America. Now give me, your damn money!"

The female voiced goon walks over to the Japanese person and says "*Okane.*" ("Money" in Japanese)

Japanese person understands, "*Choto mate.*" ("One moment" in Japanese)

The Japanese person reaches into his pocket and hands the female voiced goon his wallet.

In the far rear corner, once the collection goons have passed them, Frank whispers to a buddy, "Can you believe these guys? This is a damn funeral parlor!"

Frank's buddy "They got my high school ring, those assholes."

Frank "We'll get our stuff back. I think I know their fence."

Frank's buddy relieved, "Thank God for that."

Frank "I guess Hatsue is still tormenting me from the grave. That bitch!"

One of the male goons as the van is about to pull away, "You all have a wonderful day in paradise now. Aloha!"

The van speeds away, scrapping some of the paint off the double doors. Shocked beyond belief, the mourners begin cackling like chickens in coup.

Frank says to his staff, "See, this is why I am running for governor. I'll put an end to this cowboy shit. Right now, there is no respect for the law in Honolulu."

Frank is overheard by some of the guests who promise him campaign donations to clean up Honolulu. The Japanese in attendance are stunned. Nothing so vile could happen in Japan. Nobody, I mean, nobody, robs a funeral parlor. To them, is there nothing sacred in the United States of America?

The robbery was fast. It took less than ten minutes to clean out over two hundred mourners. Frank believes that has to be a record.

As Hatsue's mother makes her last farewell to her, she notices that the robbers even took Hatsue's favorite pendant that was wrapped around her urn. The goons even robbed the urn!

Fumes seem to be emanating from the heads of Frank and his staff, as they walk out of the viewing room into the wide driveway. One of the staff offers Frank a cigarette.

As Frank exhales cigarette smoke, he says, "Did anyone of you identify any of these cowboys?"

The larger staff member responds, "The skinny one collecting money from the patrons resembles a drug addict from the back alley in Chinatown."

Frank to the larger staff member, "Do you know this guy?"

The larger staff member shakes his head "No. Sometimes I see him hanging around the Bobby's Cocktail Lounge. He's a loser."

Frank to the rest of the group, "Anybody recognize any of the cowboys?"

The group shakes their heads side to side.

Frank "OK, let's have the boys shakedown this drug addict. The nerve of these assholes! They robbed a funeral parlor."

Just as Frank curses the robbers, a TV crew drives up the wide driveway in one of their on-scene mini-vans. Out pops one of Honolulu's most recognizable TV news figures.

Frank curses the cowboys again.

The TV newscaster walks directly up to Frank and sticks a microphone near his mouth, "Mr. Kealoha, what can you tell us about the robbery?"

Frank faking a smile, "It all happened so fast. Six or seven, armed, hooded men burst through the funeral parlor door in an old van. They confronted us with shotguns and robbed everyone."

TV newscaster "Isn't this an odd occurrence for you?"

Frank, feeling the tip of the dagger to the question, sidesteps, "Yes, it is. It's the first time I've ever heard of a funeral parlor being robbed."

TV newscaster just smiles, "Do you think we can expect copycat robberies in the future?"

Frank sensing the newscaster's intention to stab the dragger deeper, "I doubt it. This robbery was the work of some pretty sick individuals. When I am governor, I intend to eliminate this type of behavior from the streets of Honolulu."

TV newscaster chuckles, "I'm sure you have a persuasive course of action in which to do so. Thank you."

The TV newscaster walks around getting interviews from the victims. Since she speaks Japanese, she even interviews Hatsue's relatives from Tokyo.

Frank senses a large knot forming in his belly. For the first time, he realizes how his checkered past will be exploited by the news media in the upcoming campaign for governor. This TV newscaster just about implied that the robbery was his doing. How will he convince the electorate that his intentions are benevolent when his name is the household word rife with connotations connected to the criminal elements of Honolulu?

Frank motions for he and his staff to exit the area quickly. The funeral parlor robbery merely heightens the public's awareness of his underworld connection. Being interviewed by the most popular TV newscaster ensures his face will be on the 6:00 PM news. He can envision the 6:00 PM TV news headlines: The Collector Squeezed at Funeral Parlor! Or, Crooks Fleece Crime Boss at Funeral Parlor!

By the time Frank and his staff are driving their vehicles out of the parking lot, the police have still not arrived on scene. The staff car driver suggests to Frank that the police must have been in on the robbery.

Frank nodding his head in agreement, "You're probably right. How does the TV news get on scene twenty minutes ahead of the police?"

Car driver "Frank, the police station is only six blocks away. They would have had time to walk down to the funeral parlor."

Frank shaking his head, "Honolulu really needs my help. These cops need to be fired. How more corrupt can these worthless boys in blue become?"

Car driver "Do you think that the police acted as lookouts for the robbery?"

Frank "It sure looks that way. The streets were too quiet during the robbery, and the cowboys had a clear getaway."

Car driver "Maybe you should offer those comments to the TV newscaster. That would be one way to deflect criticism about your business activities."

Frank "That's a good idea but let's wait a while before we expose the police's involvement in criminal activity. I don't want to give them time to damage us with a few snap-draw arrests for publicity."

Car driver as they proceed onto the main thoroughfare, "You're right. The police would respond in that way. They have a knack of making ridiculous arrests just to embarrass someone."

Frank "Yes, they are the real crooks in Hawai'i. They're just a bunch of uniformed thugs."

Car driver "When do you plan to get our stuff back, Frank?"

Frank "We'll stop in on Easy Eddie next week. That asswipe weasel could be a relative to these demented cowboys."

Car driver laughs, "Do you think that crazy Chinaman planned this caper?"

Frank "Who else would think up something crazy like this? Remember, he was nuts enough to meet Joshua for us."

Car driver as they enter the exit ramp for Waikiki, "What's Joshua up to nowadays?"

Frank laughs, "Joshua? I heard he axed his old girlfriend in the sugar cane fields over the weekend."

Another passenger in the car, "Do you mean he abandoned her in a cane field, Frank? God, she was a good looking *wahine*."

Frank turns to respond to the passenger in the back seat, "No, Joshua chopped a fire axe into her head and dumped her in the cane fields."

Back seat passenger "Say it ain't true, Frank!"

Frank "That's right. Joshua heard she squealed on him to the cops, so he did her in."

Back seat passenger "WOW! I knew that *wahine* in junior high. She was great until she got involved with drugs. She gave great blowjobs, too. In junior high, we would sneak her into the boys' room. She really could perform a number on you, like a monkey with a hundred feet of grapevine, for a joint. Suck the chrome off a bumper."

Frank "Well, Joshua must have thought so too. I heard he made love to her all the way to the cane fields. I heard he had one of his lieutenants chop the axe into her head as she was giving him a blowjob."

Car driver chuckles, "No shit! That Joshua really is crazy."

The car arrives at Frank's Martin Street address. The occupants file out laughing their heads off at Joshua's antics.

Former back seat passenger to Frank, "What are the cops doing about Joshua?"

Frank chuckles, "Are you kidding? The cops are more afraid of Joshua than we are. I think they are waiting for us to kill him."

Former back seat passenger, "We should, you know, Frank."

Frank "Yes, it would be good for the people of Honolulu to see us take corrective action and rid the city of this madman."

Former back seat passenger "He's killing to many good looking women, Frank."

Frank "Well, they are all drug addicts and prostitutes. Some people might think Joshua is an avenging angel sent to rid society of worthless women."

Former back seat passenger "Well, Joshua should turn his attention to the sluts of the Democratic Party then."

The entire group laughs.

Monday Morning Underground Parking Garage

Chinatown is quiet at 3:00 AM. The Magnificent Seven, as they call themselves, have the police posted as lookouts in Fort Street Mall and the entranceway to the underground parking garage. The leader, Kiko, is fumbling through his keys to find the one to the jewelry repair shop door. Under constant urging from his accomplices, he locates the key and four of the seven enter the shop. With no one around, they turn on the lights to appraise the obstacles ahead of them. First, the entrance door leads them into an empty area where the shop staff receives jewelry in need of repair. The area is separated from the rest of the shop by a locked door and three, solid, wood, frame walls. The locked door leads into the repair area of the shop.

As Easy Eddie described, the inner door is hinged-locked. Attempts to unscrew the hinge fail. One of the group leaves to get a crowbar. A number of tries with a large screwdriver fail to dislodge the hinge. After some cursing amongst the remaining burglars, they decide to use a huge crowbar. One lever motion with the crowbar is enough to rip the hinge out of the solid, wood frame door.

Once inside the repair area, the burglars scope out the repair tables. There is nothing of value left on the tables or in the table drawers. Kiko is confronted by another hinge lock. He makes quick use of the crowbar to remove the lock. Though the removal of the hinged locks generates some noise, there is no one around to hear it. Kiko is puzzled as to how Easy Eddie missed seeing these huge hinges fastened securely into solid wood frames? These were supposed to easy to remove hinges.

At last, the burglars confront the safe. It is an early-design, thick metal, combination-lock unit. At first glance, the crowbar seems inadequate to do the job. After twenty or so attempts, the burglars agree that the crowbar will not work. A runner is sent to get a power drill from their fully equipped, special tool bag. The group gives up on using this device after ten minutes of only wearing out the drill bit. Finally, the burglars select a blowtorch to cut their way through the metal doors. The safe's door's three hinges are cut in about thirty minutes. It was a small torch, so the cutting was tedious and long. With the hinges cut, the burglars pry the door ajar with the crowbar. It is a jackpot! The safe is loaded with silver coins. One, small, upper shelf contains a few stacks of twenty-dollar gold pieces. It takes the burglars three trips each to unload the safe of all its gold and silver coins. A few other items are taken as well. There are two, solid-gold Rolex watches, twenty-five thick, eighteen-karat gold necklaces, and two gold, diamond rings. All totaled, the burglars have relieved the jewelry repair store of over $100,000.00 in precious metals and jewelry. By 4:30 PM, they are locking up the entrance gate to the underground parking garage.

As they drive out away from the entrance gate, they signal the police lookout that they are done. The entire group clears out of the Chinatown area.

Back at Frank's Apartment, Monday

Frank's staff is busy organizing his first fund raising rally over a few beers and cold pizza from the night before. In the background, a popular cartoon is playing on the TV distracting a few of the younger Hawai'ians. From time to time, Frank has to caution the group to keep focused on the proposed rally.

Suddenly, a slender, out-of-shape *wahine* enters the apartment and informs the group that she overheard someone talking about the funeral parlor caper in Chinatown.

Kimo, the huge doorman, "Where did you hear this?"

Wahine bumming a cigarette from one of the cartoon addicts, "I heard it in the parking lot near the fishing piers downtown."

Kimo "Are you sure about this?"

Wahine "Hey, Kimo, the guy said he was in on the heist. And, he tipped me good for a short time. This guy was easy with his bread, too."

Kimo "What did this guy look like?"

Wahine "He was dirty. I could tell he was on something pretty good. He was really out, brah."

Kimo getting upset with the *wahine*, "No, no, I mean. What did he look like? Was he Hawai'ian looking?"

Wahine sensing Kimo's insistence on a direct answer, "Oh, yeah, brah. He was a Moke. He was slender, like someone on heroin. The skin on his face was pulled tight against his bones. He hadn't had a haircut in quite a while. He was dirty looking with a scraggly beard."

One of the younger, cartoon addicts laughs, "How big was his *chocho*, titah?"

Wahine "Hey, brah, I'm going to wash your mouth out with soap, if you ask me that again?"

Kimo touches the *wahine* on the arm to regain her attention, "How tall was he?"

Wahine recovering from the sprite's improper question, "Let me see, he was shorter than you Kimo. I think he was about 5'6""

Frank interjects, "Kimo, that description does fit one of the guys that covered the wall near us at the funeral parlor."

Kimo "It sure does, doesn't it."

Frank taps his fingers on the table, "Kimo, take one of the guys and check this out."

Kimo nods, "Sure thing, boss."

Kimo points to one of the carton addicts, "You, get the car ready. We're going to Chinatown."

Cartoon addict pointing to the cartoon on the TV, "Hey, someone tape this for me."

Chinatown, Pier Parking Lot

Kimo and the cartoon addict make their way through the alleyways of Chinatown to the pier parking lot. They seem out of place in their bright Aloha shirts and slacks. Their dark sunglasses announce them as wise guys.

About ten men of various age groups are haggling over the price of quick sex with three prostitutes. Most of the men are fishermen from the nearby moored vessels. This parking lot is a favorite release spot for foreign fishermen. Fishermen of all nationalities learn quickly were the easy catches are. There are two locals amidst the group. They probably work in the sweatshops that teem in the upper floors of the surrounding 19th Century buildings.

Kimo approaches one of the prostitutes, "Hey, sista, have you seen one stoned-out, slender, local guy about 5'6" tall?"

Prostitute pauses, "There was a Moke who looked like that here earlier."

The prostitute looks around the parking lot and points away from the piers to an alley that disappears into the maze of plywood barriers leading further into Chinatown.

Prostitute "One of the sistas took the Moke into that alley. He's probably still there. He was so gone that I refused to do him."

Kimo handing the sista a $20.00 bill, "Thanks."

Motioning to the cartoon addict, Kimo leads the way to the alley. As they peak around behind the green-painted, plywood barriers, Kimo notices a body resembling their Moke lying in a puddle of urine. He appears to be passed out.

Kimo walks over to the body and kicks it, "Hey, asshole, wake up."

The body absorbs the kick like a huge glob of jelly being jarred.

The Moke rolls over in the urine pool, "Leave me alone."

Kimo kicks the body harder, "Get up, asshole. We need to talk."

The Moke struggles to regain consciousness a few times but fails. Finally, Kimo grabs the puny Moke by the shoulders and props him up against the plywood barrier. Seeing the Moke is still in a stupor, Kimo slaps him around a bit.

Kimo angry, "Wake up, asshole."

Moke slobbering, "What do you want?"

Kimo sensing some form of consciousness asks, "Were you in on the heist at the funeral parlor, Saturday?"

Moke laughs spewing some spit on Kimo's shirt, "Hey, screw you."

Kimo thrusting his fist into the Moke's abdomen, "What did you say?"

Moke gasping for air, "I said 'screw you.'"

Kimo thrust his fists into the Moke's groin. The Moke collapses in pain into the urine pool on the pavement.

Cartoon addict to Kimo, "Kimo, this guy is too far gone."

Kimo steaming with determination, "He'll start talking soon."

Kimo drags the urine-marinated Moke up and props him against the plywood barrier again, "Are you ready to talk now, asshole?"

Moke obviously scared, but still somewhat high on drugs, "Yeah, man, what do you want to know?"

Kimo pointing his index finger into the Moke's face, "One more time, asshole, were you in on the heist at the funeral parlor, Saturday?"

The Moke begins to teeter. Kimo has to prop the Moke up with his hands pressing the Moke's shoulder against the plywood barrier.

Moke teeters a bit more like he might throw up, "No, brah, I don't know what you are talking about."

Kimo grabs the Moke by the neck, "Are you lying to me?"

Moke beginning to slide down the plywood barrier sideways slobbers out, "Wait, did you say, Saturday?"

Kimo bashes his open hand against the plywood barrier. A loud bang propagates out of the alley.

Cartoon addict to Kimo, "We need to be quiet, Kimo."

Kimo shrugs off the sprite's comment.

Kimo grabs the Moke, "Yes, asshole, Saturday. That was two days ago in your drug addicted mind."

Moke "Oh yeah, we had a good time on Saturday."

Kimo frustrated steps back and releases the Moke, "What happened Saturday?"

The Moke teeters a bit then catches his fall. He seems to be gaining control of his leg muscles when Kimo and the cartoon addict observe the Moke unzip his fly and urinate on Kimo's shoes. Kimo and the cartoon addict are in total disbelief.

Kimo hurriedly takes his pocket knife out of his pant's pocket, opens the knife, grabs the Moke's skinny face in his left hand just like a coconut, presses the head firmly against the plywood barrier and cuts off the tip of the his nose. The cartoon addict is shocked. The Moke comes to his senses quickly, as he tries to cover his bleeding nose with both his hands.

Kimo says to the Moke, "OK, asshole, I'm going to ask you one more time. If you don't give me a straight answer, I'm going to cut your cock off. Do you understand me, asshole?"

Moke in terrible pain and shock, "OK, OK, Saturday...I didn't do anything. I was just along for the ride."

Kimo "Who else was involved?"

The Moke names those in the group that he knows. He confirms that someone will fence the loot this week. It becomes obvious that the Moke doesn't know much more. Even when Kimo places the tip of the knife blade under the Moke's private parts, he does not reveal any new information. He was truly just along for the ride.

Kimo thrust his left fist into the Moke's abdomen and allows him to slowly collapse down the plywood barrier.

As the cartoon addict and Kimo are leaving the alley on the way to their car, the cartoon addict says, "Don't you think you were a bit rough with that guy?"

Kimo wiping the knife blade on the cartoon addict's Aloha shirt, "No, the Moke was making me upset. I hate drug addicts."

Cartoon addict shocked to see the blood on his shirt, "Why did you do that? Why not wipe the blood off on your shirt?"

Kimo as he slides into the driver seat of the car, "It wouldn't look right for the future governor's public relations man to have blood on his shirt, now would it?"

Cartoon addict sensing his cue to shut up, "Sure thing, Kimo, you have an image to project."

Kimo smiles, "There you go. You're learning."

Frank's Apartment

When Kimo and the cartoon addict arrive, they find Frank's gubernatorial staff munching on a series of pineapple extravaganza pizzas, sipping beers and laughing at cartoons. At first glance, Frank's living room seems too small. However, when your eyes adjust to the six 300-pound Hawai'ians in the room, the room normalizes. Two of these huge beasts can sit comfortably on a sofa meant for three people.

Kimo laughing, "I see we didn't miss much."

Group of Hawai'ians "How's it, brah. We got some pizza while you were out."

The meeting encourages the friendly Hawai'ian *chaka* gesture with the hands to communicate: taking it easy. The *chaka* sign is made by curling the index, middle and ring fingers while extending the thumb and little finger and twisting the wrist back and forth quickly a few times.

Frank emerges from the bathroom, "What did you find out, Kimo?"

Kimo's enormous bulk stressing a seat at the lunch counter, "We got a few names. They're all Chinatown hoodlums. It'll be easy to track them down. The guy didn't know who the fence was or where the goods were."

Frank "Did you make it known to him that we didn't like getting hit?"

Cartoon addict slobbering some pizza interrupts, "Oh yeah, Frank, Kimo cut his nose off."

Kimo turns his head and gives the cartoon addict a nasty stare indicating his displeasure with the interruption.

Frank forms a grimace, "That must have hurt like hell, Kimo."

Kimo shrugs his shoulders, "He was so high on drugs that he probably won't realize his nose is missing for a few days."

Frank nodding, "Yes, drugs, I have to do something about that when I am governor."

Cartoon addict interrupts again, "Hey, Frank, we can cut off the noses of all the drug addicts."

Kimo turns and slaps the cartoon addict along side the head, "Shut up. Frank and I are discussing serious business."

Frank laughing, "I bet that would curb drug use quite a bit, wouldn't it?"

Kimo laughs, "It sure would."

Frank "OK, enough of that, let's get back to the goods. Since most of the cowboys are from Chinatown, my guess is that the fence is our friend, Eddie."

Kimo nodding his head up and down, "That's what I think, too."

Frank smiles, "Don't you have a score to settle with his friend, Billy? We could kill two birds with one visit."

Kimo smiles, "That we could, Frank, but I doubt Billy had anything to do with this."

Frank "You're right. Billy's a triggerman."

Kimo "The way these cowboys burst through the funeral parlor door, I doubt Eddie had much to do with the caper either. He's probably just fencing."

Frank points his index finger at Kimo, "You're right, again. Eddie has more class than that circus act we saw at the funeral parlor. OK, we'll just go roust Eddie up later this week. Let's give the cowboys time to move the goods to Eddie."

Cartoon addict to the other Mokes watching TV, "Hey, did you guys tape the cartoons I wanted to watch."

Far corner Hawai'ian "No, we didn't. Just eat your pizza and shut up. We're trying to watch TV."

Cartoon addict "Can we watch some other cartoons? I hate this haole farmer."

Nearest Hawai'ian slaps a slice of pizza into the cartoon addict's face, "Shut up and eat."

Frank chuckles, "What are you going to do with this sprite, Kimo?"

Kimo looks the cartoon addict over slowly, "I don't know. He's got so much pizza on his face, I can't find his nose to cut it off."

Frank laughs, "Cut his whole face off, then."

Kimo looks over at Frank, nods with a wide smile, then turns to the group, "Hey, guys, Frank thinks we should cut the sprite's face off. What do you think?"

The cartoon addict is too busy removing pizza from all over his face to overhear what is being said about him. The nearest Hawai'ian grabs his hands while another Hawai'ian slips a plastic bag over his head and drags him to the floor. Once on the floor, the group watches the sprite, as he gasps for air inside the plastic bag. Kimo looks over at Frank. Frank gestures to let him up.

As the sprite coughs and inhales deeply, thankful to be alive, Kimo says to him, "Never interrupt Frank when he's talking. Do you understand?"

Cartoon addict still sucking in air, "Yes, sir, Kimo."

Kimo taps him on the shoulder, "Good. Now, have some pizza, and shut up."

CHAPTER 8

Svensen Real Estate Company Office, King Street

The intersection of Bishop and King Streets is Honolulu's business center. At the far end of the intersection, seaside, King Street block, Svensen Real Estate Company located their principal office. It is a short walk from Easy Eddie's store, since Cornish Street forms the far boundary of the intersecting King Street block.

Easy Eddie has been summoned for an emergency 10:00 AM meeting at the Svensen Real Estate Company office. The summons puzzles him, as he is not a real estate salesperson with Svensen Real Estate Company. Nonetheless, around 9:50 AM he whisks away to cover the two-block distance between his store and the realty office. Monday is always a nice day to escape and enjoy the peacefulness of Honolulu in the morning. Walking past the Old Tavern brings a smile to his face. Some of those same sorry Mokes that he encountered earlier will be sipping their lives away inside. What a waste of life! Another smiles forms on his face as he passes the locksmith's establishment. This two-block stretch contains history for Easy Eddie.

Waiting for the streetlight to change, Easy Eddie looks over at the façade of the Svensen Real Estate Company principal office. The dark marble stands out against the rain-weathered paint of the surrounding buildings. Money! That is what the dark marble communicates to Easy Eddie.

Entering the realty office, he is greeted by the receptionist. She is a shapely, local haole about twenty-five years old. There is no wedding ring on her finger. Easy Eddie smiles at the thought of this gal being some senior broker's mistress. The receptionist leads him into a luxurious room in the back of the office. Kai Svensen and two other gentlemen are sipping coffee.

Kai smiling, "Here's our man now!"

Easy Eddie surprised by the friendliness, "I hope I'm not late."

Kai introduces the other two gentlemen as Eliot Warren, head of Blackwater Holdings, and Malcolm Chide, legal counsel for Blackwater Holdings. Easy Eddie has never met either of them. Eliot Warren is a 5'10", average-built Caucasian with dark hair. Malcolm Chide is a slender, non-athletic, 6'0" Caucasian with sandy blonde hair. From their general appearance and mannerisms, they both appear to be Mormons.

Kai "Eddie, we called you here, because we have a problem developing that, we were told, you can help us out with. We have been informed by reliable sources that you are discreet and offer special services."

Easy Eddie somewhat apprehensive, "I'm not sure what you mean."

Kai smiles, "Do you know a Detective Aoki?"

Easy Eddie "Yes, I do."

Kai nodding his head as a gesture to the other two gentlemen, "OK, Detective Aoki informs us that a service that we desire you can provide."

Easy Eddie begins to get the picture, "What service are you asking about?"

Kai leaning forward, "Eddie, we are having a problem with your partner, Erik Collins. We would like that problem to go away."

Easy Eddie puzzled, "Do you want me to talk to him?"

Kai pauses a moment, "Eddie, are you aware of the access problems in Punaluu Valley?"

Easy Eddie thinks a moment, "If you mean the roadways, then, yes, I have been informed that there might be a problem out there."

The other two members lean forward as well.

Kai "Yes, we are talking about those problems. Well, it just so happens that a number of our associates are getting nervous about all of Erik's sniffing around. We'd like Erik to stop."

Easy Eddie "OK, I can talk to him."

Eliot Warren leans over closer to Easy Eddie, "Eddie, we've talked to him a lot over the last few years. Erik seems to need some extra prodding to get him to back off."

Easy Eddie leans back in his chair, "I see."

There is a pause in the conversation as Easy Eddie begins to appreciate exactly which special services they require from him. He takes his time sizing up the three men at the table. It would be important that Easy Eddie could rely on their secrecy, if he decided to have Erik persuaded vigorously.

Easy Eddie breaks the silence as he leans forward, "Is there something special that you had in mind?"

Malcolm Chide answers, "Eddie, Erik has uncovered too much about our business out there in the valley. If his sniffing got publicized, too many important people would be embarrassed. I'm sure you can appreciate our position."

Easy Eddie after a short silence, "I can't have this done for free. Do you understand?"

Kai smiling, "We understand."

Malcolm Chide adds, "What about this Hans character, can we deal with him?"

Easy Eddie "Oh yes, Erik and Hans are like night and day. Erik is too bull-headed. Everything has to be right with him. There is no room for little errors."

Kai nodding, "OK, we want Erik to go away."

Easy Eddie "Let me talk to Erik, first. Maybe I can get him to back off. Also, I will need to feel Hans out on this proposal."

The group "OK, get back to us as soon as you can."

Easy Eddie "I should have something before the end of the week. My friends will prefer cash…small bills…do you understand?"

The group nods in approval.

Kai smiling, "Don't worry, Eddie, we can get the cash."

Easy Eddie "You just want Erik to go away, is that it?"

Kai "Yes, Eddie, just make him go away. People are getting nervous whenever he starts sniffing."

Easy Eddie "What about his participation in the land project that he has out there in the valley?"

Kai "We prefer that Erik is gone altogether. His very presence in the valley makes people nervous."

Easy Eddie with a little anxiety creeping into his voice, "I see. That may take a bit more money."

Kai "We understand. Just quote us a price."

Easy Eddie pondering a moment, "Let me check on what my friends want. I'll get back to you."

The conversation is interrupted by the shapely, haole secretary as she enters the boardroom, "Here you go, Eddie. I was told you liked apple juice."

Easy Eddie surprised she even spoke to him, "Thank you very much."

The shapely, haole secretary pats Easy Eddie on top of the shoulder, "Enjoy."

After the secretary leaves the room and closes the door, Kai whispers to Easy Eddie, "She's great in bed! Do you like her?"

Easy Eddie nodding as his sips some apple juice, "No kidding! Yes, I like her a lot."

Kai touching Easy Eddie's shoulder and smiling, "Do this for us, and we'll let you test drive her."

Easy Eddie's face forms a wide smile, "It's a deal!"

After leaving the Svensen Real Estate Company office, Easy Eddie hurries on down King Street to the River Street pool hall. Billy should be there holding court. The River Street pool hall is where all the local wise guys hang out. Billy is the headman in the River Street area; more so, now that Fat Willie Wong has departed to his final resting place. Billy now has the entire Chinatown area to himself. It was a gift from Frank.

Turning the corner onto River Street that familiar polluted canal stench greets Easy Eddie. The canal is supposed to be a huge rain runoff gutter. Instead, it serves as a latrine for the local drug addicts and homeless. In the dry season, like now, there is little water flow in the canal. Like a toilet bowl, unflushed for weeks, the canal provides the right atmosphere for the slimeballs of the underworld. Topologically speaking, River Street forms the low point and far boundary of Chinatown. It is interesting how the low point of the land attracts the low point of society.

The stores that line the east side of River Street have not been worked on since the 19th Century. A paint job, in dark and dreary colors, is the only facelift these establishments ever have seen. It is as if Chinatown created a repository for its refuse here and coated it with appropriate colors.

The first person Easy Eddie passes is bleeding from the belly. It looks like a stab wound. Since the person is a homeless-looking drug addict, he will probably bleed to death in one of the alleys. Easy Eddie shrugs his shoulders satisfied that the drug addict would be one less welfare and subsistence recipient in Chinatown.

The pool hall is packed today. It usually only gets that way on welfare paydays. Easy Eddie thinks it is his lucky day. The bums all have money in their pocket, so they will not try to roust him. He hears Billy laughing away in the rear of the establishment. As Easy Eddie walks into the pool hall, he can sense a hundred or so eyes follow him. Like hungry tigers observing a slab of raw meat passing in front of their cage, they keep their eyes locked onto him. Easy Eddie is used to it. He realizes that he looks too good to be in a place like this. But, under his Aloha shirt, he carries his five little friends.

Easy Eddie as Billy notices him approaching, "Hey, Billy, how's it?"

Billy surprised, "What's up? I never expected to see you come in here. You could get mugged."

Easy Eddie smiles, "I didn't see any Democrat politicians in this place. Who would mug me?"

Billy chuckles, "That's my Eddie, always joking. What's up?"

Easy Eddie in low voice, "Billy, I need to talk to you in private."

Billy "OK, Eddie."

Billy turns to his associates, a group of ex-cons, "Guys, I'm going to go outback with Eddie. If you hear any shooting, call 911."

The group laughs. Even though, today, Billy is making a joke, on another day there must have been a shooting. For Billy's joke to be as funny as it was to these goons, there must have been a shooting outback.

Billy escorts Easy Eddie into a sleazy, blind alleyway. New species must be spawning on the slime-caked walls of the 19th Century buildings in the alley. The alleyway is cold and damp. Easy Eddie would hate to die in a place like this.

Billy closing the door, "OK, Eddie, what is it? We can talk here. It's safe."

Easy Eddie in a low voice, "Billy, some important businessmen have asked me to rub out one of my partners. They want to know how much money it will cost."

Billy smiles, "Well, the store is open for business, Eddie. I'd offer you the best seat in my office here, but I'm afraid the medical bills to remove the gifts you received in this place would overwhelm you. Who's the guy they want to ice?"

Easy Eddie "It's the main partner in our land *hui*."

Billy "Is this the North Shore *hui* that you are involved in?"

Easy Eddie "Yes, that's the one."

Billy "It's the redheaded fellow, right?"

Easy Eddie "How did you know?"

Billy smiles, "The guy's an asshole. He doesn't like locals at all. I see him walking up and down Maunakea and Pauahi Streets all the time."

Easy Eddie "Well, he doesn't seem friendly, at first."

Billy "Eddie, he's got that look in his eye that most white people have when they see locals. I hate that look."

Easy Eddie trying to redirect the conversation, "So, what do you think? Would you like the job?"

Billy surprised, "Of course, I want the job, Eddie. Come on, I'd lose my reputation if I didn't kill at least one haole every now and then. Besides, my boys need the work."

Easy Eddie nods, "Yes, when I came into the pool hall, I could tell that they were desperate."

Billy "Could you tell that? That's good!"

Easy Eddie "So, how much do you want for the job, Billy?"

Billy ponders the amount for a while and says, "Did they have a preference on how they wanted this done? Do they want him gun downed?"

Easy Eddie "Well, this guy has caused a lot of trouble. If you gun him down, it will look like he was assassinated. They would want something more subtle."

Billy lifting his right arm quickly, "I know we could run him over with a truck."

Easy Eddie smiling, "Billy, that's fantastic! Yes, that's it. Getting run over by a truck would look like a regular traffic accident."

Billy "We could do it right here in Chinatown, as he is walking to work. We could catch him crossing the street."

Easy Eddie obviously elated with the idea, "The traffic here in the back streets is heavy enough. You could stage the whole affair in these back streets. There are no streetlights here, so it would be perfect. I love it."

Billy "Do you? Good, let's do it then."

Easy Eddie "OK, how much do you want?"

Billy thinks a moment as he calculates the team he needs, "For this unimportant haole, tell them $25,000.00 in cash, and stick a little something in there for yourself, Eddie."

Easy Eddie smiles, "I'll do that."

Easy Eddie leaves Billy with his pool hall goons and hustles back to his store. As ever, Jacob grills him upon his return.

Jacob obviously angry, "Where have you been, Eddie?"

Easy Eddie trying to escape Jacob's interrogation, "I went to the post office."

Jacob puts his hands on his hips, "Really? So, where's the mail?"

Easy Eddie "When I got to the box, I realized that I had forgotten the key."

Jacob "Eddie, you left three hours ago!"

Easy Eddie "Well, on the way back, I stopped for lunch."

Jacob with a frown on his face, "Eddie, do you mean to tell me you took a two hour lunch break?"

Easy Eddie "Listen, it wasn't that long. Besides, it's not 1:00 PM yet."

Jacob "You know, Eddie, we expect you to work here like the rest of us."

Easy Eddie acquiescing, "I know."

Jacob stomps his foot and walks away mumbling, "Jiminy Christmas."

Jacob suddenly turns, "Oh, by the way, you had a call while you were out. I put the message on your desk."

Easy Eddie thanks Jacob then walks to his desk. The message is from Detective Aoki. He wants Easy Eddie to call him as soon as he gets in.

Easy Eddie calls the number. Detective Aoki answers.

Detective Aoki "Eddie, what color hair does that partner of yours have in the Punaluu Valley *hui*?"

Easy Eddie thinks of Hans, "He has black hair, why?"

Detective Aoki breathes into the phone, "That's good. Someone dropped the dead body of redheaded gal on your *hui's* property."

Easy Eddie "Wait! The main partner has red hair."

Detective Aoki "Well, I would say your redheaded partner has upset the local hoodlums. The way the body was dumped gives the impression it was a warning to you guys."

Easy Eddie "How do you know?"

Detective Aoki "She had her throat slit."

Easy Eddie "Do you know anything about this girl?"

Detective Aoki "She's a teenage prostitute from Waikiki."

Easy Eddie "Maybe it is just a coincidence."

Detective Aoki "No way, Eddie, if they just wanted to kill her they would have dumped her body closer to Waikiki. No, these guys took the girl's body all the way out to Punaluu for a reason. You better tell your redheaded partner to watch out."

Easy Eddie thanks Detective Aoki for the heads up. After he sets the handset in the cradle, he realizes that Erik has kicked up a lot of dust. It is unlikely that too many people will miss Erik, if he should succumb suddenly in a traffic accident. My God! Slitting a teenager's throat to warn someone, these goons are crazy. They watch too many cartoons. Maybe Joshua Puna is not the exception but the rule!

Easy Eddie says to himself, "My God! It's only Monday!" This must be Death Week. He decides to risk a quick walk over to the Svensen Real Estate Company Office. Easy Eddie waits until Jacob is busy with a customer then acts like he is going to the men's room. The elevator is just to the right of the men's room. A quick step to the right and Easy Eddie is on his way down the elevator.

Not one block from his office, a police officer reminds him of a Hawai'ian bracelet that Easy Eddie promised. The officer is a little irate, since Easy Eddie is three months overdue. It just slipped his mind. Actually, he has to run over to the bank to sift through his loot to find an appropriate bracelet. This officer is a good friend, too. He performs lookout services during Easy Eddie's burglaries. It is important that he take good care of this police officer.

Entering the Svensen Real Estate Company office, the shapely haole greets Easy Eddie with her usual seductive manner. Easy Eddie likes her. From her gestures, he suspects that she has been informed of their eventual meeting.

Kai emerging from his office, "Eddie, what a surprise!"

Easy Eddie smiles, "I just stopped by to tell you what I found out on that matter that we were discussing earlier."

Kai gesturing towards his office, "OK, let's go into my office."

Kai to the shapely haole, "I'll be busy for about ten minutes. Hold all my calls. No one is to disturb us."

The shapely haole smiles at Easy Eddie, "Sure thing, Mr. Svensen."

Kai closes his office door and walks briskly to his chair. It is a plush office. Teak paneling covers the walls. Kai's desk seems to be made of solid *koa* wood.

Kai anxiously leaning forward, "What've you got, Eddie?"

Easy Eddie "I spoke to my man. He says he'll do it. He wants $50,000.00 in cash. I'm to deliver it, personally."

Kai leans back in his leather, executive chair, "$50,000.00 in cash."

Kai mulls over the amount a while and says, "OK, we can handle that. I'll need a few days to put it together."

Easy Eddie "Shall I tell my man it's a go?"

Kai leans forward, "Absolutely, tell him it is a go. By the way, your man will be prudent, right?"

Easy Eddie "Yes, he will be prudent. It will look like an accident,"

Kai pressing his lips together, "That's real good. I was concerned about that."

Easy Eddie getting up to leave, "I have to be getting back to my store."

Kai "I understand. I'll call you when I have the cash together."

Kai sees Easy Eddie out of the office.

As Easy Eddie passes the secretary's desk, she says, "Please come back soon, Eddie."

Easy Eddie struggling to control himself, "I will. I promise."

As he clears the realty office door, Easy Eddie says to himself, "Well, Billy did say to add a little in the price for myself."

Easy Eddie smiling to himself, "I don't think $25,000.00 is too much to add."

Easy Eddie considers making a quick run to the bank vault but decides against it. He needs to show Jacob and the other partners that he is committed to working. In a few years, they will all retire. The store will be his then, and he can come and go as he pleases.

As he crosses the street to the next block, he notices the policeman that he spoke to earlier. Easy Eddie makes a right turn on a side street to avoid the policeman. Easy Eddie is a master at avoiding people. In his business, it is a requirement. Regrettably, as he emerges from the side street, he runs into the distraught owner of the jewelry repair shop.

Owner in tears, "Eddie, they robbed me, destroyed my store and stole all my life's collection of silver coins. What am I going to do?"

Easy Eddie acting surprised, "What? What are you talking about?"

Owner "My store, Eddie, I got robbed over the weekend."

Easy Eddie placing a hand on the owner's shoulder, "That's terrible. How much did you lose?"

Owner "I lost all my coins. $250,000.00 in all, I think."

Easy Eddie, realizing the owner is Chinese, knows he is exaggerating. Nonetheless, he consoles the owner a while then hurries back to his store.

Upon reentering the store, Jacob unleashes a broadside of abusive comments at Easy Eddie.

Easy Eddie sensing Jacob's wrath abating, "Listen, I had to make a delivery. I promised the jeweler on Fort Street Mall that I would get this watch that I repaired to him. If you don't believe me, then you call him."

Jacob moves his head up and down, "OK, OK, you remember that we expect you to be here. You need to start checking out with one of us whenever you leave the store."

Easy Eddie "OK, I will tell one of you guys when I am going out on deliveries."

A silence overcomes the store. It is as if a hurricane just passed through, and the survivors are examining the wreckage.

Jacob breaks the silence, "Eddie, did you hear the guy downstairs got robbed?"

Easy Eddie "Yes, I ran into him before I came up the elevator."

Jacob shaking his head, "Can you imagine him losing $200,000.00 in coins?"

Easy Eddie mumbles, "It was $250,000.00 a few minutes ago. I guess he realized that the insurance coverage for robbery has a deductible."

Jacob "What was that, Eddie? I couldn't hear you."

Easy Eddie "I was saying to myself how terrible it was to lose $200,000.00 in coins."

Jacob "That's two robberies over one weekend within a few blocks of each other. Times are becoming desperate in Honolulu. We could be next!"

Easy Eddie "No one is going to rob us."

One of the partners mumbles, "Of course we won't get robbed. Eddie's involved in all these capers."

Easy Eddie pretends not to hear the comment. As he begins to walk into the storeroom area, the other partner informs him that he has a phone call. Easy Eddie decides to take the call in his office. It turns out to be Hans.

Hans somewhat excited, "Eddie, I'm glad I caught you. Erik just told me that the police stopped by to see him about a body that was found on our property over the weekend."

Easy Eddie acting surprised, "Really? Did Erik know the person?"

Hans thinks for a moment, "You know I didn't ask him, if he knew the person. I just assumed that he didn't."

Easy Eddie laughs, "Why's that? He is a pretty strange guy, you know."

Hans stutters a bit, "I suppose you're right."

Easy Eddie just laughs.

Hans after a moment of silence, "Erik also told me that he signed a DROA on behalf of the partnership for that roadway that we discussed."

DROA is an acronym for Deposit, Receipt, Offer, and Acceptance form. It is an instrument used to make an offer for real property in the state of Hawai'i.

Easy Eddie elated, "Now, that's good news."

Hans "I think so."

Easy Eddie "Hans, how well do you know Erik?"

Hans "I don't know him too well. We served together on an assignment a few years back. That's about it. We are not close friends. We are business associates."

Easy Eddie "So, you are not close to him, is that it?"

Hans "No, I'm not close to him at all. I think we had dinner together only once in the entire time that I've known him. He doesn't drink or play sports, so we have little in common."

Easy Eddie "OK, was there anything else you need to talk to me about?"

Hans "No, that was it."

What a Monday! Easy Eddie thinks to himself that days seem to fill up automatically as you get older. In his early years, he worked hard, but he always had time for surfing and nightclubbing. Now, he doesn't seem to work as hard, but he never seems to have time to devote to anything. When was the last time he even went to the movies? He used to be so carefree. Now, he carries a revolver almost every place he goes. He used to talk tough to discourage Mainlanders. Now, he plots to have them assassinated. He used to work hard buying and selling jewelry. Now, he organizes gangs to steal it. He used to have a family. It was four families to be exact. Now, he has mistresses. He used to wonder about his future. Now, he wonders if he will live past tomorrow, and sometimes he has concern about the next hour. For the remainder of the afternoon, Easy Eddie's mind follows, like clouds combining and dispersing, thoughts such as these.

Just before closing time, an old friend of Easy Eddie's walks into the showroom. Easy Eddie is glad to see him, because he has a favor to ask of him.

Easy Eddie "Good Afternoon, sir. You look like you've been working out."

Friend smiles, "Good to see you too, Eddie. Now, if I didn't already know that you wanted something, that comment would alert me right away that you wanted something."

The two men laugh. Whenever Easy Eddie wants something, his first comments are praises.

Easy Eddie escorts his friend into the storeroom.

Easy Eddie "Listen, are you still connected with the real estate exams?"

Friend "Yes, I am. I monitor the exam in progress, and I oversee that the completed exams are prepared correctly for shipment to New Jersey. Why do you ask?"

Easy Eddie "I have a favor to ask?"

Friend "What are friends for, Eddie, if not for granting favors?"

Easy Eddie "I need to get someone a real estate salesman's license. He has taken the exam a few times and failed."

Friend "Is he willing to pay to insure a passing grade?"

Easy Eddie "Of course, he is."

Friend "How much are we talking?"

Easy Eddie "He'll pay $1000.00 and a golf membership to the Ala Wai Golf Course."

Friend laughs, "Eddie, there are no golf memberships to the Ala Wai."

Easy Eddie touches the friend on the shoulder, "Trust me, there are memberships. They are secret, and they guaranty a tee time."

Friend obviously surprised, "Are you kidding? The Ala Wai is always booked."

Easy Eddie "With this membership, the Ala Wai is always open to you."

Friend "Are you sure about this membership?"

Easy Eddie "I'm real sure."

Friend "OK, Eddie, I'll need the guy's name and personal data. The money comes upfront when I receive his data. I'll deal with you only. Next exam the guy registers for I will insure he passes."

Easy Eddie "Thanks."

Wednesday Afternoon Easy Eddie's Building

Something is strange about Wednesday afternoons in Honolulu. Walk-in traffic at the retail stores seems to slow down. The streets seem empty. It is as if all of Chinatown took a siesta.

Although Kimo and the cartoon addict have taken a thirty-minute-limit parking slot on Cornish Street, the near absence of pedestrians allows their stakeout to go undisturbed. Kimo selected a parking slot with a vantage view of all the entrances to Easy Eddie's building. That way, it will be easy to spot the funeral parlor cowboys, if they try to fence their loot with Easy Eddie.

Within twenty-five minutes of their stakeout, two suspicious skid row types, toting a sack resembling one of those used to collect valuables from the funeral parlor robbery, enter Easy Eddie's building.

Cartoon addict nervously spilling some of his chocolate malt, "Kimo, that's them."

Kimo patting the cartoon addict's thigh, "Now, calm down. Let's let them get into the building."

Cartoon addict vehemently sucks on the straw to his chocolate malt. The cavitation sound of the air as he bottoms the contents of the container annoys Kimo, as they watch the two goons case out the underground garage entrance to the building.

Kimo extends a disparaging stare at the cartoon addict.

Cartoon addict looking back at Kimo, "What?"

Once the two goons have entered the building, Kimo tells the cartoon addict to get out of the car and go over to the coffee shop located two streets back and inform Frank that the goods have arrived. Kimo has to remind the cartoon addict that he should leave the empty chocolate malt container in the car.

Within minutes, Frank and two other Mokes appear at the passenger window of Kimo's car.

Frank to Kimo, "They still in there, brah?"

Kimo "Yeah boss, I never saw them come out."

Frank tapping the fender, "Good, let's do it. Kimo, you and your buddy enter through the same way that those guys did. We'll go in through the front."

Kimo "OK, boss."

Kimo exits the car and begins to lock it.

Frank gestures with his hand, "No need to lock it, Kimo, we may need to get out of here quickly if something goes down."

Kimo and the cartoon addict make their way into the underground parking garage. Kimo tells the cartoon addict to wipe the chocolate malt off of his shirt.

Kimo "Brah, wipe that malt off your shirt. In case you get hit today, you don't want the cops seeing chocolate malt on your shirt."

Cartoon addict as he uses his sleeve to wipe off the malt, "If I got killed, my mom would be able to see I enjoyed my last meal. She knows I like chocolate malts."

Kimo extends another disparaging look at the cartoon addict, "Check your piece. Make sure you can take it out easily."

As the cartoon addict checks his waist piece, a small rubber dinosaur falls onto the pavement of the underground parking garage.

Kimo seeing the toy on the pavement, "Are you kidding me? What's that?"

Cartoon addict picking up the toy, "They gave away a free toy, if you bought the malt with your burger and fries."

Kimo in disbelief, "Lovely!"

They take the elevator to the third floor.

As they exit the elevator on the third floor, Frank and one of the Mokes are waiting for them.

Frank "Did you see anyone in the basement, Kimo?"

Kimo "No, boss, the basement was empty."

Frank "Good, when our man gets back, we can move in on them."

Just as Frank is finishing speaking, the other Moke comes from up the hallway. He seems excited.

Moke "Boss, it's them. I overheard them talking about the stolen jewelry through the door. The stolen jewelry was in the bag that they were carrying."

Frank smiles, "This is good news. You guys check your pieces. Let's go."

The five Mokes walk toward the back entrance to Easy Eddie's store. As they approach, on Frank's cue, they begin removing their revolvers from their waistbands. Frank, Kimo, and two of the Mokes surround Easy Eddie's back door. The cartoon addict is told to watch the front entrance. Since the front entrance is only fifty or so feet down the hallway, Kimo believes the cartoon addict can handle it.

Frank gestures to Kimo to knock on the door.

Kimo nodding his acknowledgment, as he raps on the back door, "Eddie, open up, it's The Collector."

The four men overhear hurried sounds from within Easy Eddie's store. The inner inhabitants appear quite nervous. They would be more nervous, if they knew four guns were drawn to persuade them to open the door.

After a few minutes, the noise within Easy Eddie's store abates.

Easy Eddie in a soft voice, "Hold on, I'll be right there."

Easy Eddie opens the door slightly to see who is in the hallway. As he does so, 300-pound Kimo bursts the door wide open, pushing Easy Eddie back into the center of the storeroom. Suddenly, Easy Eddie sees four revolvers pointing at him.

Easy Eddie anxiously whispers, "Are you sure you guys got the right office? I don't owe you any money."

Kimo chuckles and turns to one of the Mokes, "Check the number on the door."

The Moke does, "Kimo, it reads 'asshole.'"

Kimo looks back at Easy Eddie, "Yup, Eddie, we got the right room number."

Frank "Cut the nonsense, Eddie, where's the stolen jewelry."

Easy Eddie acting confused, "What are you talking about?"

Suddenly, two gunshots are heard from the showroom area. As Kimo keeps Easy Eddie in check, Frank and the two Mokes enter the showroom to check out the gunshots. Upon entering the showroom, they find two men on the floor with belly gunshot wounds. Apparently, the two cowboys tried to slip out the front. As they did so, the cartoon addict shot them.

Frank to the cartoon addict who is still in the doorway, "Hey, kid, you're supposed to say, 'Stop or I'll shoot,' or something."

Cartoon addict "Sorry, Boss, it all happened so fast."

Frank tells one of the two Mokes to pick up the stolen jewelry bag.

Rushing quickly into the storeroom, Frank says to Kimo, "We got what we came for. Let's get out of here."

Kimo to Easy Eddie, "Thanks for your cooperation, Eddie."

Frank to Easy Eddie, "Eddie, you might want to clean this place up. Your friends are bleeding all over your floor."

As Kimo walks out of the back door, he says to Easy Eddie, "Good seeing you again, Eddie."

Easy Eddie allows his breathing to regain a natural rhythm. He walks into the showroom to find his two cowboys moaning in pain from the gunshot wounds. Blood oozes out covering every square inch of the showroom floor. How does he explain this? Two skid row goons bleeding all over his floor. It is difficult for Easy Eddie to think with all their moaning. He decides to frisk the two goons. They both have handguns on them. In a stroke of Hawai'ian brilliance, Easy Eddie dons surgical gloves, removes their two guns and shoots each goon in the heart with the other's gun. Then, he pulls up a chair and waits for the goons to bleed to death. As he watches them die, he decides on the obvious, four goons broke into the store to rob him. During the robbery, a scuffle broke out amongst the robbers, and the four robbers began shooting each other. The other two robbers ran away. With bullets flying everywhere, Easy Eddie survived. Heroism never felt better for Easy Eddie.

Cornish Street

Frank and his Mokes, toting the bag of loot, exit Easy Eddie's building from the Cornish Street entrance. The street looks deserted, like there was a hurricane about to hit. A slight breeze from the harbor carries discarded napkins and loose dust down the street. The Mokes feel their bodies shrink a little from the effects of the coolness of the breeze.

Frank to Kimo, "Where'd you leave the car?"

Kimo looks at the parking spot where he thought he left the car. It is empty. He makes a quick check up and down the street. The car is nowhere to be seen.

Kimo to Frank, "Boss, I think someone stole our car."

Frank exhales, "This just isn't our day, is it?"

Kimo frantically looking up an down the street for the car, "Who'd be dumb enough to steal our car?"

Suddenly, a taxi comes down the street. Frank tells Kimo to flag it down. Kimo stops the taxi.

Taxi driver, "Sorry guys, I'm on a call."

Frank to the driver, "Cancel it, we're getting in."

Taxi driver "I can't do that. My boss will kill me."

Kimo flashes the revolver on his waist to the taxi driver, "Your boss will never get the opportunity."

Taxi driver stunned, "Oh!"

The five Mokes try to get inside the taxi, but it is too small for all five. Frank tells Kimo and the cartoon addict to catch the next taxi while he and the two Mokes with the loot bag leave in this taxi.

Taxi driver as the taxi pulls away from the curb, "I normally charge extra for baggage."

Frank "Just drive to Waikiki. We got you covered."

Taxi driver "Aren't you Frank Kealoha? Aren't you running for governor?"

Frank "Yes, I am."

Taxi driver "I thought it was you. Were you out campaigning?"

Frank smiles, "Yes, we were."

The other Mokes laugh at the taxi driver's comment.

Taxi driver misses the humor, "Is that bag full of handouts for your campaign?"

One of the Mokes leans over and whispers to the taxi driver, "It's full of campaign donations."

From the sound of the Moke's voice and the intensity of his stare, the taxi driver realizes that he had better just drive these guys quickly to Waikiki.

Watching Frank drive off in the taxi, Kimo says to the cartoon addict, "Come on let's get out of here."

They begin walking toward the harbor where there is a better chance to catch a taxi. The harbor drive teems with taxis this time of day. As they reach the harbor drive, they notice Frank's car coming down the road. There are two Mokes in the front seat. Kimo does not recognize either of them. They are drinking beer and blasting the radio. Kimo tries to wave the car down. As he does so, the passenger tosses a small disc at him. The small disc hits the cartoon addict in the chest and falls to the street. The car zooms on by Kimo and the cartoon addict. Kimo picks up the small disc. It looks familiar. Sure enough, it is a "Vote Kealoha" campaign pin. Kimo and the carton addict watch Frank's car as it travels down the road. Now and then, the passenger tosses a small disc at pedestrians.

Cartoon addict to Kimo, "Frank isn't going to like this, is he?"

Kimo exhales, "Unbelievable, this is absolutely unbelievable!"

Cartoon addict "Shall we catch a taxi and go after them?"

Kimo "No, let's just get back to Waikiki. We don't need any attention right now. Besides, Frank is getting some free publicity. The cops will catch up with those two crazy Mokes soon enough."

Cartoon addict "Think we've got time to stop at a drive-in on the way? I left my malt in Frank's car."

Kimo just stares at the cartoon addict, nods his head up and down a few times and then turns to flag down a taxi.

After a few minutes of whining in the taxi by the cartoon addict, Kimo acquiesces to making a stop for malt. He tells the taxi driver to keep the meter running while the cartoon addict gets his malt. The taxi driver selects the first malt drive-in on the way to Waikiki. It is FS Drive-in.

FS Drive-in was established by Fjord and Svensen, hence the FS in the name. Svensen is none other than the family name of Kai Svensen, the owners of Svensen Real Estate Company. Fjord was a real estate partner of Kai's dad who went to prison for real estate fraud.

As the taxi enters the parking lot of FS Drive-in, Kimo notices Frank's car. The Mokes stopped off here for lunch and left the car in the lot. Kimo hands the taxi driver a $50 bill, tells him to keep the change and get out there. Kimo and the cartoon addict hurry over to Frank's car. It has been hot-wired.

Kimo to the cartoon addict, "You wait here. I'm going inside to find these guys. If they come out here first, don't shoot them, OK. Just hold them here at gunpoint, if you have to."

Cartoon addict "Sure thing, Kimo, I got it."

Kimo makes his way into FS Drive-in.

In the old days, FS Drive-in was just that...a drive-in. You drove your car into a parking stand where a waitress roller skated out to serve you. As the years progressed, the roller skates were removed and individual radio communication boxes were installed with each driving stand. You ordered via the radio box, and a waitress brought your order out on a tray that mounted on the top of your door sill when the window was rolled down. Today, some of the remnants of the old stands remain, but all ordering and service are conducted inside the restaurant.

Kimo enters the restaurant dining area. He scans the room for the two Mokes. They have taken the third of eight cushioned booths on the right. He decides to join them for burgers and fries. The two Mokes do not notice Kimo, as he approaches. He walks right up to the table, says nothing to them and sits down next to one of them. His 300-pound frame causes the wooden backrest to make a crinkling sound as he sits down.

First Moke "Hey, brah, that seat is reserved."

The other Moke just slows down sampling his French fries, as he sizes up Kimo's huge size.

Kimo "How ya doin' boys?"

First Moke "Listen, we aren't interested in your religion, so get out of here and leave us alone."

Kimo "I want to vote for Kealoha. You tossed me one of these pins a while ago."

Kimo lays a "Vote Kealoha" pin on the booth's table.

First Moke "Hey, brah, can't you see we are eating. We'll talk some other time."

Kimo slowly removes his revolver and keeping it under the table, he presses it into the French fry Moke's side sitting next to him.

Kimo moves his face close to the French fry Moke's face, "I want to talk about Kealoha right now."

First Moke "Listen, if you don't leave, I'll call the management."

French-fry Moke to his buddy, "I think he means business, brah. I think he really means business."

First Moke notices the fear on his buddy's face and the serious look on the huge visitor's face.

First Moke "OK, OK, brah, what do you want?"

Kimo "The three of us are going to get up and walk out of here nice and slow. We're going to take a ride in Kealoha's car."

Kimo tossing $20.00 on the table with his free hand, "Now, nice and easy, let's get up and walk out of here."

Without a disturbance, the three Mokes leave the FS Drive-in restaurant dining area. Kimo has one of the Mokes hot-wire Frank's car. They drive to a secluded area in the rear of the Ala Wai Canal. Kimo orders the Mokes out of the car.

Kimo to the cartoon addict, "Frisk that one. I'll check this one out."

Cartoon addict to French fry Moke, "Do you know that you stole Frank Kealoha's car?"

French-fry Moke "No, we just took any car, brah. We were bored, so we thought we'd go for a ride. Is he the Hawai'ian gangster who is running for governor?"

Kimo is frisking his Moke when he hears, "Shit! BANG!"

Kimo looks over at the cartoon addict, the cartoon addict has shot his Moke in the back of the head.

Kimo to cartoon addict, "What happened?"

Cartoon addict "I forgot how to frisk. I got nervous, and my gun went off."

Kimo and the other Moke are in disbelief.

Kimo exhales as he turns the other Moke around to face him, "This doesn't look too good for you, brah."

Moke "Don't shoot me. I swear to you I won't say anything."

The Moke begins to stutter, "I'll vote for Kealoha, I promise."

Kimo stunned, "What?"

Moke still stuttering, "I promise you I will vote for Kealoha."

Cartoon addict yells, "He's lying, Kimo. He's a lying Moke."

The cartoon addict runs over to the Moke, jabs his revolver into his cheek and pulls the trigger.

BANG!

The Moke stiffens, his face contorts and the left side of the Moke's face explodes onto the hood of Frank's car. The Moke collapses to the ground.

Kimo steps back and observes the half-head body of the Moke, as it oozes blood onto the gravel bank of the Ala Wai Canal.

Cartoon addict fires another shot into the body of the Moke, "I hate lying Mokes!"

Kimo just stares in disbelief at the cartoon addict.

Kimo as the cartoon addict is about to expend another round into the Moke, "He's dead, kid."

Cartoon addict "Kimo, I hate lying Mokes. He was never going to vote for Frank."

Kimo pats the cartoon addict on the shoulder, "OK, OK, kid, let's get out of here."

With the car engine still running, Kimo puts the car in gear and drives back onto the street in the direction of Waikiki.

With the Ala Wai Canal scene a distance behind them, the cartoon addict says, "Kimo, can we stop for that malt now? I could sure use a chocolate malt right now."

Kimo with a Moke's blood, facial bone and flesh all over the hood of the car pulls into a fast food restaurant parking lot, "Go get your malt, kid."

As the cartoon addict runs for his malt, Kimo just sits behind the steering wheel and rubs his index finger back and forth across his lips.

CHAPTER 9

Thursday Afternoon, Easy Eddie's Store

Hans enters the showroom at just about quitting time. He has a puzzled look on his face, as he sees Easy Eddie nervously moving about the showroom stowing merchandise.

Hans "Eddie, I thought I'd stop by. I heard the news on the radio about the robbery here yesterday. Are you OK?"

Easy Eddie nervously responds, "I'm fine. I can't talk about this, right here. Let's go into my office."

As Easy Eddie leaves the showroom, Jacob asks if he will be OK. Jacob even seems overtaken by the events of two dead bodies on the showroom floor. Hans notices how daintily Jacob sidesteps the faint markings on the floor where the dead bodies were located. Though the police had completed their investigation, shades of the dead body markers remained. To the police, this was an open-shut case of a bungled robbery. Undoubtedly, Easy Eddie's clandestine association with the police department hastened an extremely speedy conclusion to the investigation.

Hans as he and Easy Eddie enter the office partition, "What happened, Eddie?"

Easy Eddie "After the store had closed, I was working late restocking the showroom when four locals burst into the store and demanded money and jewelry. When I told them we didn't stock jewelry, two of the men started arguing. All of a sudden, one of the men shot one of the others. Before I could figure out what was happening, all four men were shooting each other. Two of them fell on the floor. The other two fired shots into the downed men and then fled. I was left lying on the floor scared out of my mind."

Hans "Are you OK now?"

Easy Eddie shakes his head, "No, I just had a near death experience. I think they would have shot me, if I had said anything during the shootout. Why they didn't shoot me, I have no idea? I was just lucky, I guess."

Hans "Well, I'm so glad that you survived."

Easy Eddie exhales, "So am I."

Hans "Did you recognize any of the robbers?"

Easy Eddie "No, I didn't. I may have seen one or two of them around, but I didn't know them."

Hans changing the subject, "Listen, Erik informed me that the lawyer recommended that we sue Svensen and his partners for the access mess out there in Punaluu Valley. According to Erik, Svensen caused all that mess out there in the valley. Besides, Erik thinks we are better off forcing Svensen to clean up that mess rather than us poking our noses around out there with all that drug trade going on."

Easy Eddie "When does the attorney plan to file suit?"

Hans "I think the lawyer is having the sheriff serve the complaints as we speak."

Easy Eddie realizing the reason for Svensen's urgency to eliminate Erik, "That's fast. I guess Erik's lawyer means business."

Hans "According to Erik, the lawyer sees this suit as an open and shut argument. Svensen messed that place up. Erik says it was negligence on the part of both Svensen and his partners."

Easy Eddie "Do you know Svensen's lawyer's name?"

Hans thinks a moment, "Yes, his name is Chide. He's with Byrd and Mason law firm. Malcolm Chide is his full name."

Easy Eddie realizes why the money to eliminate Erik was so easy to come by, "Tell me, Hans, do you agree with Erik's lawyer about suing these people?"

Hans "Well, if they created the mess Erik's lawyer says that they did, we might be better off negotiating an amicable resolution. After all, these guys are in the deep *kimche*. But, if we move toward a resolution, Erik's lawyer doesn't make as much money."

Kimche is a spicy-hot, mouth-burning, marinated cabbage popular with the Koreans in Hawai'i.

Easy Eddie "Do you think the lawyer made the suit recommendation in order to acquire legal fees from us?"

Hans "Yes, I do. He must know that Punaluu Valley is an administrative nightmare that no one wants exposed. If he files suit, he can make enough on the legal fees to send his kids though one of the Ivy League colleges."

Easy Eddie settling back into his chair, "Why doesn't Erik choose this resolution option?"

Hans "I'm not sure. If he follows his lawyer's advice, then he can't be faulted. I think he is concerned primarily about his fiduciary responsibilities to the partners."

Easy Eddie "I can see his point. If he sues, he lets the lawyer cover his responsibilities."

Hans "That's how I see it, too."

Easy Eddie "I take it you would not sue Svensen."

Hans shakes his head, "No, Svensen is in a lot of trouble. We could help him out and be so much better off. Svensen has projects everywhere. His family has been around here since the 19th Century. This is an opportunity to wedge us into the real estate industry here. It is much better to play along."

Easy Eddie "I see. What about the partners?"

Hans "We bring them along with us, as we carve ourselves out a piece of the industry. Besides, if we back out of this deal, they get their money back. The lawyer route means they spend more money on legal fees. If we are successful in the suit, which we should be, there is a big payday down the road. But, we have not improved our position in the real estate business."

Easy Eddie "That's good to know you feel that way. Listen, it's quitting time, I want to get out of here. Do you feel like grabbing something to eat?"

Hans smiling, "Hey, Eddie, when it comes to eating, the only time I say 'No' is when they ask me if I've had enough."

Easy Eddie pats Hans on the shoulder, "Good, let's get of here. I have too many memories of dead bodies in here."

Hans as Easy Eddie closes up the store, "You seem to have dead bodies dropping all around you lately, don't you?"

Easy Eddie shakes off the comment. If Hans only knew how many dead bodies!

As they exit the elevator into the underground garage area, the jewelry repair shop, Chinese owner greets Easy Eddie and Hans, "Eddie, I'm so glad I caught you. I wanted to thank you for killing those two crooks."

Easy Eddie modestly responds, "I didn't kill them. They killed each other."

Chinese owner "No matter, Eddie, they're dead. Those dirty bums! They stole over $300,000.00 from me. Those dirty bums!"

Easy Eddie to himself, "Just the other day it was $250,000.00 they stole from this guy. Every time I see this guy the amount goes up $50,000.00. By next week, it will be over one million dollars."

Easy Eddie consoles the Chinese owner, as he and Hans make their way to Easy Eddie's car. Easy Eddie has to push the Chinese owner away to close his car door.

Hans puzzled, "Was there another robbery in the building?"

Easy Eddie nods as he backs the car out of its parking stall, "Yes, he got hit over the weekend."

Easy Eddie points to the Chinese guy's store, as he drives out of the underground garage.

Hans "Do you think it was the same guys who tried to rob your store?"

Easy Eddie squeezes his shoulders up, "I don't know. They could be the same guys. If they were the same guys, their robbing days are done."

Hans as Easy Eddie navigates the one-way streets of Downtown Honolulu, "Eddie, I stopped by for another reason, this afternoon."

Easy Eddie "What was that?"

Hans "This cop is giving my wife a hard time. He's been coming on to her."

Easy Eddie "Is this a local cop?"

Hans "No, my wife says he's a white guy."

Easy Eddie "He's probably an ex-army guy that joined the force when his tour of duty was up."

Hans "From her description, he sounds like that type of guy."

Easy Eddie as he parks the car a block from the Chinese restaurant, "Is your wife worried about this guy?"

Hans "Yes, she is. She says he's a little crazy. She thinks he does cocaine."

Easy Eddie "He might be a tough guy to get off her back."

Hans "He seems like the type who would frame her with some crime just to get into her pants."

Easy Eddie as they disembark the car, "I know the type. He could be dangerous. Do you have a gun?"

Hans "Yes, I do. I have a .357 Magnum revolver."

Easy Eddie as they walk to the restaurant, "Tell you what I'll do, I can get you a clean gun. If this guy comes around your house, or you catch him inside your house, you can use this gun on him. You have to keep this quiet though."

Easy Eddie holds up from going into the Chinese restaurant. Hans and he discuss this matter in a dark area outside the restaurant.

Hans "Can you really do that for me?"

Easy Eddie patting Hans on the shoulder, "Hey, what are friends for, right?"

Hans nods, "OK."

Easy Eddie "In the meantime, tell me this guy's name, and I will have a friend of mine on the police force talk to him. We might be able to resolve this without any trouble."

The two men talk a while longer in the dark.

Easy Eddie after some ten minutes, "You stop by the store next week, Wednesday afternoon, and I'll take care of you."

Hans smiling, "Thanks, Eddie. Shall we get something to eat?"

Easy Eddie looks over at the restaurant. He is not really hungry. He just needed to make some distance between him and the slain body markers on his showroom floor.

Friday Lunchtime, Easy Eddie's Store

It has been a busy morning. Friday mornings usually are not that busy, yet this morning, the partners could barely keep up with the walk-in traffic. Jacob believes that people are coming in just to get a look at the store's new celebrity, Easy Eddie.

At just about high noon, Detective Aoki enters the showroom, looking for Easy Eddie. Jacob directs him to the rear storeroom.

Easy Eddie glad to see Detective Aoki, "Hey stranger, am I glad to see you."

Detective Aoki smiles, "Yes, I've been reading reports about all the commotion that went on here a few days ago. Are you OK?"

Easy Eddie motioning Detective Aoki to follow him into his office, "Yes, I'll survive."

Detective Aoki as he squeezes into Easy Eddie's client chair, "You know, Eddie, I'm beginning to get concerned about all the dead bodies dropping down around you, lately."

Easy Eddie breathes heavily, "I'm getting worried, too. Maybe the Good Lord is giving me a message to go clean."

Detective Aoki laughs, "Now, that will never happen! The Good Lord is wasting His time."

Easy Eddie whispering, "How bad does this all look for me?"

Detective Aoki leans forward and whispers, "Don't worry, Eddie, I got your back. There are some homicide detectives that doubt your story, but they are junior in the division. I got you covered. The case is closed."

Easy Eddie leans back in his chair and exhales, "That's so good to hear."

Detective Aoki, "Listen, Eddie, I need you to do me a favor. I've got this gun that I want you to hold for me. You have to keep it out of sight."

Easy Eddie shrugs his shoulders, "Sure, I can do that."

Detective Aoki hands Easy Eddie a canvas bank deposit bag, and says, "Just keep this out of sight. No one is to know you have this. Do you understand?"

Easy Eddie "OK, I can keep this quiet."

Detective Aoki staring into Easy Eddie eyes, "You are to tell no one about this package. Do you understand?"

Easy Eddie nods his head in understanding, "Yes, I got it. I will tell no one."

Detective Aoki "It might be a good idea to put this package in your vault as soon as you get a chance."

Easy Eddie begins to look into the canvas bag when Detective Aoki places his hand on the bag, "It's best that you don't see what is inside the bag."

Easy Eddie "This must be pretty sensitive, if you are being this cautious."

Detective Aoki "It is, Eddie. It is. The least you know the better it will be for you."

Easy Eddie "OK, I understand."

Easy Eddie puts the canvas deposit bag in his desk safe and locks it.

Detective Aoki gets up to leave, "Thanks, Eddie."

Easy Eddie motions for Detective Aoki to remain in his office, "Listen, I have a favor for a friend to ask of you."

Detective Aoki settles back into the client chair, "OK, what is it?"

Easy Eddie relates his friend Hans' predicament with this Romeo police officer. Detective Aoki laughs and tells him not to worry. He will have the officer's supervisor tell him to cool his jewels or face suspension.

Detective Aoki "You need to be unseen for a few weeks, Eddie, until all this mess dies down. Remember, we have people counting on us on the Big Island. We can't acquire a high profile. There is too much money to be made here."

Easy Eddie "Do you think the police will have me tailed?"

Detective Aoki "I'm working like hell to make sure that they don't. I'll be informed, if a tail is assigned to you. If there is a tail assigned, you won't be able to make any runs to the Big Island. So, Eddie, don't kill anymore people for a while, OK."

Easy Eddie laughs, "OK, I promise. I won't kill anyone."

Detective Aoki "By the way, do you know anything about the execution of two locals near the Ala Wai Canal?"

Easy Eddie puzzled, "No, I never even heard of any killings out that way. Are people connecting me with that, too?"

Detective Aoki laughs, "No, no one has mentioned your name, yet. These two Mokes were both shot in the head. From your *modus operandi*, you shoot people in the chest or slit their throats."

Easy Eddie retorts immediately, "You know I had nothing to do with that teenage whore on the North Shore."

Detective Aoki "Like I said, Eddie, keep a low profile; otherwise, every goon and slut that meets their demise by suspicious means will be identified with you. By the way, I had to squash an investigation into your involvement with the mutilation death of Hatsue Yanagi. The word was making the rounds that you retrieved her armless body from a trash dumpster."

Easy Eddie deflates in his chair, "My God! I forgot all about that fiasco. You know that was Joshua, don't you?"

Detective Aoki chuckles, "Yes, I'm quite well versed in Joshua's bizarre affairs. I spoke with our man Albert already. Do you know he complained to me that there was semen in the girl's mouth?"

Easy Eddie disgusted, "How did he know that? Did he do an autopsy on her?"

Detective Aoki smiles, "Well, Eddie, I wouldn't classify what that demented pervert does as an autopsy."

Easy Eddie thoroughly disgusted, "He didn't really do her dead body, did he?"

Detective Aoki shakes his head in disgust, "That guy is one sick Moke. If I die, I sure in hell don't plan on being cycled though his operation."

The two men talk a few more minutes about the sick practices of Albert, the Cremator, before Detective Aoki has to get back to the station.

Soon after Detective Aoki leaves the store, the phone rings. It is Kai Svensen's sexy secretary. She is relaying the message that Easy Eddie can stop by principal office of Svensen Real Estate Company at his convenience to pick up a package. Easy Eddie realizes that Billy and he are in business. He also realizes that he had better get over there quickly in order to safely stow his portion of the take in the vault before he delivers the package to Billy. Quickly, Easy Eddie gallops out of the store, mentioning his departure to the lone partner sipping *saimin* for lunch, down the elevator and out into the street level entrance to the building.

As he enters Svensen Real Estate Company, the secretary extends him a very sensuous greeting. He knows he has to have this woman. God, she is gorgeous!

Secretary pointing to Kai's office, "Just go right in. He's expecting you."

Kai upon seeing Easy Eddie appear at his doorway, "Eddie, I'm so glad to see you. Come in. Sit right down. Close the door behind you."

Easy Eddie closes the door and plops into the first chair in front of Kai's desk.

Kai after Easy Eddie sits down reaches into his large, desk drawer and removes a medium-size, thick, brown paper bag. It looks like one of those bags the barbecued rib places hand out for take-out orders.

Easy Eddie "It looks huge."

Kai chuckles as he pats the bag, "It does look huge, doesn't it?"

Easy Eddie "Is it all there?"

Kai smiles, "Yes, $50,000.00 just like you asked for. It took us a while, because we drew the money from different banks in smaller amounts so as not to call attention that we were making a large withdrawal. The bills are in denominations from $20.00 to $100.00. But, it's all there, if you want to count it."

Easy Eddie rifles through the bag. The contents seem to be right. If there isn't $50,000.00 inside this bag, there is close to it. He is satisfied.

Kai as Easy Eddie checks the contents of the bag, "I hadn't realized this, but you can transfer a million dollars by check or wire-transfer without so much as raising an eyebrow, but you ask of anything over $10,000.00 in cash and every eye in the bank is upon you."

Easy Eddie satisfied with the contents of the bag says, "Great!"

Kai "Now, before you leave, you have to assure me that this transaction will be handled professionally and discreetly."

Easy Eddie "You have my word on it. These boys are professionals."

Kai nervously smiles, "OK then, good luck! I'll trust all the rest with you."

Kai shakes hands with Easy Eddie. Easy Eddie departs the Svensen Real Estate Office and heads immediately to the bank vault less than a city block away.

As Easy Eddie enters the vault area, the vault clerk on duty, a friend of Easy Eddie's, "Are you planning on having your lunch down here, Eddie, as you count your millions?"

Easy Eddie just laughs off the comment, as he signs in as Ed Sone.

Once the vault cubicle is locked, Easy Eddie thoroughly counts the money in the bag twice. The amount is correct: $50,000.00. He places $20,000.00 in $100.00 bills in his safe deposit box. The remaining $30,000.00 he places back in the bag. Even though, Billy asked for only $25,000.00, it will look good to bring $30,000.00 and tell Billy that the extra $5,000.00 was Easy Eddie's addition for himself. Easy Eddie understands how Billy thinks. While he has his safe deposit box there in the cubicle, Easy Eddie takes out the remaining clean guns from the box and places them neatly inside the bag. He knows Billy will ask for clean guns just in case the unexpected comes up. There are four guns. That should be plenty for the job Billy has in mind.

As Easy Eddie checks out of the vault, the clerk complains that Easy Eddie never even bothered to offer him a rib. Easy Eddie tells the clerk that he is too fat already, and the extra barbecued rib would raise the clerk's blood pressure. They both laugh.

Easy Eddie makes his way down King Street to River Street to meet up with Billy. Billy should be holding court in the rear of the pool hall at this time of day. It does bother Easy Eddie to be carrying $30,000.00 in cash and four clean guns into the anus of Downtown Honolulu.

The familiar stench of the sewer canal offends Easy Eddie's nostrils, as he turns the corner onto River Street. The street is lined with drug addicts and winos. One filthy local, wearing a torn, green bowling shirt and 1960s-era, brown, corduroy pants is slouched down against a cement wall urinating on the sidewalk and himself. The bum asks Easy Eddie for a cigarette. Easy Eddie just ignores him like he was just another discarded piece of trash littering the street.

As Easy Eddie approaches the pool hall, one of Billy's goons yells, "Eddie, you brought my ribs!"

Easy Eddie smiles, "How's it! Is Billy in the back?"

Goon "Oh yeah, he's back there. Go on in. Save me some ribs now."

Easy Eddie makes his way to the rear of the establishment. Once again, he feels the cold stares of desperate ex-cons. Each one would slit his throat, if they knew what he carried in the bag. Most of these creeps have slit throats for the change in a victim's pockets. Drug addiction makes them that way.

Billy sees Easy Eddie coming, "Hey, look who comes to see me today! Is that my lunch?"

After Easy Eddie and Billy exchange local greetings, Easy Eddie says, "Can we go some place and talk in private?"

Billy "We can talk here. These are my boys. It's safe here."

Easy Eddie gesturing to the bag, "Maybe, it's not so safe."

Billy nods, "I see. Well, OK, if you insist, we can step into my office."

Easy Eddie "Let's do that."

Billy escorts Easy Eddie to the same slime-caked alley. After Billy closes the back alley door behind them, Easy Eddie opens the bag and allows Billy to inspect the contents.

Billy surprised, "How much is in here?"

Easy Eddie "$30,000.00."

Billy looks strangely at Easy Eddie, "I thought we agreed on only $25,000.00."

Easy Eddie "You wanted me to add something in for myself, so I asked for $5,000.00 more for me. I kept it in the bag, so you would know I was being straight with you."

Billy pats Easy Eddie on the shoulder, "That's OK, Eddie. You know I trust you."

Billy counts out a few stack of bills and hands them to Easy Eddie, "Here's your $5,000.00."

Easy Eddie tucks his Aloha shirt into his waist and neatly places the stacks of bills inside his shirt. Billy has given Easy Eddie big bills, so the stacks are small and barely noticeable as they rest along his waistline.

Billy rifling through the contents of the bag, "I see you have four guns in here. Are these guns all clean?"

Easy Eddie "Yes, all the guns are clean."

Billy "Good, they might come in handy, if anything goes wrong."

Easy Eddie "The client expressed concern about anything going wrong."

Billy smiling, "Did he, now? Well, tell him not to worry. We will take care of this matter in style."

Easy Eddie "He'll be glad to hear that."

Billy chuckles, "Speaking of hits, I heard you had some action up at your place the other day."

Easy Eddie snickers, "Oh that, yeah, some crazy Mokes tried to rob the store and shot each other."

Billy laughs, "They shot each other, did they?"

Easy Eddie "Well, you know, these Mokes were really crazy."

Billy smiles, "Yeah, I know, Eddie. Mokes get really crazy when they do drugs. Look at how crazy Joshua gets."

Easy Eddie "Billy, let's not talk about Joshua, OK. He's beyond crazy."

Billy "You know, Eddie, I shouldn't say this, but aren't a lot of dead people turning up around you lately?"

Easy Eddie somewhat embarrassed looks down at the slimy pavement and exhales, "Yeah, I've been real lucky lately."

Billy nodding his head, "Yes, Eddie, you have. You might want to consider retiring from this line of work. I don't want to see you on a cold slab. Hearing about the two dead Mokes in your store, if I were you, I'd stay clear of Mokeland."

Easy Eddie "I haven't been to Mokeland, since they put up that sign: 'Haole, don't let the sun go down on you in Waimanalo.'"

Billy "That's good advice anytime, Eddie. But, it is better advice now that you've had a few Mokes expire in your store. When you combine the sovereignty movement with drugs and cartoons, these Mokes are becoming quite dangerous. You know their brains were eaten away already by the white man's syphilis."

Easy Eddie "You're right, Billy, I need to lay low for a while."

Billy "You're damn right, I'm right. You need to lay low. Those two Mokes had families that are probably crazier than them. And, you know, those Mokes aren't going to believe their relatives shot each other in your store. You can expect trouble, Eddie. But, I guess if you're going to walk around town with a bag full of guns, you should be fine."

Easy Eddie just laughs.

Billy tucking the bag under his left arm, "Come on, let's get you out of here. Just leave this matter with me, OK. I'll see that it gets taken care of personally."

Easy Eddie's Store

Upon returning to the showroom, Jacob greets Easy Eddie with his usually rhetorical barrage about taking too much time for lunch. However, this time, Easy Eddie senses a strain of levity in Jacob's voice. Jacob's voice takes on that air when business is good. Happy Jacob, that is what the other partners call him. When Jacob's happy, everyone is happy in the store. Apparently, Easy Eddie's after-hours affairs have created a boon to the business. Easy Eddie is content to be appreciated for once. It does not happen often, so he figures he will relish the popularity while it lasts.

This Friday is busier than most Easy Eddie can recall. Constantly, he is going into the storeroom to get items that have been depleted on the showroom shelves. He realizes that a huge order will be required soon in order to replenish the storeroom. There have been so many sales since the incident that Easy Eddie actually can move about the storeroom unimpeded by impromptu storage stacks. The vacancies communicate success.

Easy Eddie plans on a quiet weekend with Patricia. He promised her a trip to one of the secluded beaches on the North Shore. Patricia loves the beach. She could have been a swimsuit model. Regrettably, she met the wrong Moke earlier in her life. It is such a pity how the island boys deflower and discard the local girls in their teens. Patricia seems to have survived the affair. Her early lover is serving a ten-year stretch in a Mainland prison for raping and killing some underage girl. Hopefully, in ten years, the Moke will have ridded his system of the cornucopia of drugs that marinated his brain.

Will it be a beach on the far west shore or one where the body surfing is spectacular? The body surfing beaches are too close to Waimanalo. Easy Eddie figures, if he is noticed, his body might be riding the surf for a long time before it washes up on some remote beach in the South Pacific Ocean. Easy Eddie decides on a far west coast beach of O'ahu. On those beaches, Patricia and he can enjoy the waves without the constant harassment of the surfers. The waves break close to the shore on those beaches, making them unsuitable for surfing. He dreams of a picnic on pristine white sands, secluded from the rest of the beachgoers…a sanctuary from the current ongoings in Honolulu.

CHAPTER 10

Billy and His River Street Rats

Billy waited until Easy Eddie had left the premises a few minutes, before he informed the trusted members of his crew they had been given a job. They are mostly ex-cons who have served over two years in a federal penitentiary for capital crimes. These men can be trusted to carry out a job. Like a slaughterhouse crew, these men perform like automatons during a hit. They live off hurting and killing people. Life seems to have dealt them these cards.

Billy's most trusted lieutenant is a guy named: Edward. Edward is a slender built, 6' tall, Chinese-Filipino local. His forte in Billy's crew is that he is also an undercover detective for the Honolulu Police Department's Narcotics Division. He has an outstanding rapport with the beat cops and blue and white patrol cars, enabling him to muster their cooperation for any of Billy's endeavors.

The River Street Rats are a muscle gang. They do handle some prostitution, some gambling, and some drug trafficking, but their prime importance is to enforce the will of organized crime in Downtown Honolulu. There are a few Mokes in the group, but this is a mainly Chinese-American gang. Rumors abound of their relationship with the Triads of China. But, it is just a rumor. There is little Triad influence in Honolulu, other than the connection between the satellite office of the infamous Hong Kong's Noble House and legitimate businesses. Billy does not travel in that company. His boys are all locals. There are no "passing through" mercenaries with Billy. About Billy's only interface with the Triads is the local human smuggling operation that entices young girls to travel further west in search of higher paying hostess employment. But then, his part in the white slave trade ends at the Honolulu International Airport.

Billy gives the signal to clear the rear of the pool hall for business. Two of his goons clear out stragglers and stand guard so no one can happen in on Billy's meeting. There are three men with Billy, huddled around a worn pool table. Edward always stands closest to Billy. He is Billy's closest confidant. Turtle stands across from Billy. He is a somewhat heavy-set Chinese local, about 5'5" tall with a noticeable goatee beard. To Turtle's left is Spider. Spider is a lanky, local Chinese about 5'10" tall. Spider has arms and legs that appear too long in proportion to his trunk. His specialty is knife fighting.

Billy passes the bag that Easy Eddie left around the pool table, so the three men can examine the contents. After Billy senses from their smiles that they are satisfied, he commences, "We got a job. We have been asked to hit some haole."

Turtle "Are we popping his head, Billy?"

"Popping his head" is a Hawai'ian underworld phrase for killing someone with a gun.

Billy "No, they want this to look like an accident, so we have to plan it. One thought was that we would run him over with a truck."

Spider "We can do that."

Billy leans forward into the group, "What I hear is that this haole walks to his office everyday down Maunakea Street and turns up Pauahi Street. We can hit him when he crosses Maunakea to go onto Pauahi. It's perfect. There is no streetlight at that intersection, and there is not really a stop sign. The set up is perfect, if we sit on Maunakea Street and allow him to pass by us. We can park near the lookout for the gambling house. If the haole notices our vehicle, he will think we are picking up one of the gamblers. When the haole crosses the street, we will be coming from his rear."

Billy sketches his idea with table ornaments on a pool table.

Edward "If we do this in the morning, we will have the sun at our backs, as well. He will have difficulty making out what is happening, as he will be staring into the sun."

Spider nods his head up and down, "That's right, Billy. The sun this time of year in the morning can be quite blinding."

Turtle "I agree, Billy. Waiting until the haole walks by us on Maunakea Street will give us a number of advantages."

Billy "OK, here's what we will do. We watch this guy for a week while he makes his way to work each morning. We get his timing down, so we know exactly when to hit him. Is everyone agreed?"

The group nods in agreement.

Billy turns to Edward, "Your boys in blue can help us. We need the intersection at Maunakea and Pauahi Streets clear of police."

Edward "I can have a patrol car sweep the area first then have the car post at our exit to insure we get a clean getaway."

Billy gestures with his finger that he acknowledges Edward.

Billy "Remember, this has to look like an accident."

The group nods in agreement again.

Billy "OK then, let's go in the back and split this stuff up. I got us four clean guns, too."

The group smiles and makes their way to the back alley.

In the back alley, Billy's private office and sanctuary, Billy metes out the payment. Each of the men gets one of the clean guns. The feel of the stacks of money in the men's hands excites them. It has been a while since they got to handle a stack of bills. Turtle and Spider flick their thumbs across the short edge of the bills a few times to hear their sonorous fluttering. Smiles are plenty in the alley. Even the vermin that slithers about the slime-caked walls of the alley appears happy. Like a recently flushed commode, the alley seems to reflect the good fortune of Billy's men.

Billy "We start next week. Spend some money this weekend. First thing Monday, we will start tracking this haole. I want to be able to complete this job the following week."

Turtle "You got it, Billy. I'll be on Maunakea Street at 5:30 AM Monday and every other day of next week. We'll have this haole's routine down pat by next weekend."

Billy "OK, that's good, Turtle."

Billy turns toward Spider, "How do you feel about driving the truck, Spider?"

Spider "I can do that, Billy."

Edward "I'll prep the blue and white that patrols this area."

Billy to Edward, "We need a truck for this. Can you get one?"

Edward "I'll talk to the guy over at impound."

Spider interjects, "Billy, maybe we should just jack a truck off the street."

Billy "If we jack one, we run the risk of the cops accidentally stumbling onto the vehicle while we have it parked on the street."

Edward "Billy, I'll have the blue and white patrol car under control. They won't perform any police work while the hit is on. The truck won't be discovered until long after the hit."

Spider to Billy, "It's much cleaner if we just jack a truck. If we use an impound vehicle, eventually someone will notice the vehicle missing."

Edward to Billy, "We can make the records disappear at impound. We could get around this, but Spider is right. It's much cleaner if we jack a truck early that morning."

Billy "OK, we can jack a truck, but we need to case the truck ahead of time to insure we have one ready."

Spider "I'll case three or four, so we can choose from a variety. I'll have a truck there when we need one, Billy."

Billy nods his head in agreement, "OK, we'll jack a truck."

Billy to Turtle, "We will need a reserve parking space, as well. Get one of the gang to park a vehicle on Maunakea Street in the precise space that we will use for the hit. We should have the spot locked up right after midnight on the day we decide to do this."

Edward to Billy, "If someone takes our preferred spot, I can have the blue and white patrol car have them towed."

Billy smiling, "Don't you just admire our police at work?"

The group laughs at Billy's comment.

Billy "Lastly, keep the guns in their plastic bags. We will take them out only just before the hit goes down. That way, we keep the guns as clean as possible. If you don't have to handle the guns, don't handle them. These guns are clean. We don't expect to shoot anyone. The guns are for the unforeseen circumstances. Do you understand?"

The group responds positively.

Billy "Good, we have a plan. Shall we enjoy some of this money?"

Smiling overwhelms the group, as they respond affirmatively with enthusiasm. The group decides on going to see the naked dancers at a skin house near Waikiki. Spider spews on about some weird, Moke gal that can smoke a cigar with her vagina.

Later that evening after having taken the time to stow the guns and the cash, the four men meet up at the River Street pool hall. They decide to travel to the Waikiki naked dancer club recommended by Spider. Since Spider made the recommendation, the group imposes upon him to be their chauffer. Spider has an old jeep that has experienced the damp, rough weather of the North Shore. As the men climb aboard, they comment on the decadent decorum of the vehicle.

Turtle disgusted, "Spider, do you always have to feed the latrine lizards that inhabit this jalopy?"

Spider laughs, "Hey, I cleaned it up for you guys, before I came down here."

Edward looking over the back seat, "Spider, that's impossible! What did you do, toss out the dead bodies?"

Spider "It's not that bad, Edward. Just get in. There's nothing dangerous living back there."

Turtle and Edward tenderly adjust themselves into the backseat. Both men check the seat covering under them to insure that nothing that slithers is taking a siesta. Billy gets the shotgun seat. As the men drive off from the pool hall, one fluorescent decal can be distinguished from the rest of the debris on the rear fender. The decal reads: Hawai'ian Mafia Staff Car. Spider has a sense of humor.

It is a short trip into Waikiki, this time of night. The openness of the jeep provides a cool sanctuary from the island's humidity. Spider jacks his jaws all the way about the lovely, performing *wahines*. To hear Spider's description, the men are headed for the Playboy Mansion. Those impressions fade quickly as Spider steers the jeep into the parking area behind the establishment. Establishment hell, it looks more like an ill-designed shack that lost control of its expansion. In the dark parking areas, Billy can distinguish figures exchanging cash for drugs. There are a lot of dark areas. This is a Moke entertainment time.

At the horse blanket entrance, four, drug-addicted Mokes pretend to be security. Billy recognizes one of them.

Billy "Hey, brah, how's it?"

The exchange *chaka* signs and smiles.

The brah "Long time no see, Billy. Good to have someone like you visit our place. You need anything, you call me, OK."

Billy slips a twenty-dollar bill into the Moke's hand, "This is for you."

The brah turns to a stoned Moke, "These are my good friends, get them a good seat."

The stoned Moke escorts Billy and the boys into the nightclub. As they enter, their ears are bombarded with music so loud the lyrics are incomprehensible. The sudden feel of flimsy plywood under their feet makes the men walk gingerly as they follow the stoned Moke. The interior consists of six pool tables adorned with two, semi-naked, twenty-year-old dancers each. Most of the dancers performing now are Mokes. There are two haoles dancing on one of the far tables.

The walls are made of hastily nailed up sheets of a potpourri of paneling. No two consecutive panels are the same type, and there is no reason or rhyme to the pattern. Some four, randomly-erected stanchions hold up the uneven roof. From the construction, it appears that some four shacks were tacked together to create this place.

As the men walk past the bar, Billy notices a strange advertisement on a huge, pickle bottle filled with eggs that reads: Chicken Dinner Ten Cents. The bar seats six comfortably. It has an open area in the center where the hostesses draw drinks.

About a half-dozen, bikini-clad hostesses wander about the establishment taking orders for drinks.

As the men take their seats in a prime, leather-cushioned, U-shaped booth to watch the haole table dancers, a buzzer sounds, indicating a change of dancers. The hostesses remove their tops and climb on the pool tables and commence dancing to the next record while the six dancers being relieved don bras and tops and commence serving drinks to the customers.

Turtle immediately sees an opening at one of the pool tables, so he hurries over and commandeers the open seat. He takes a stack of one-dollar bills out of his pocket and begins tempting one of the Moke dancers to come closer to him. He whispers something to her that makes her smile. She says something to her co-dancer and takes off her thong. She sits right in front of Turtle and spreads her legs. As she slowly moves her rump muscles, Turtle blows air onto her exposed vagina. As the other three men look on, it becomes obvious that the dancer is good at this. She lifts her hips toward Turtle each time he hands her a few dollars. Her vagina comes so close to Turtle's face that her moisture begins to appear on his nose.

Edward shaking his head, "That Turtle is one weird guy."

Spider "He sure is. When he gets done with that seat, I plan to slip right in there myself."

Billy and Edward look at each other and shake their heads.

One of the bouncers comes over and asks Billy and Edward if they want a blowjob from one of the dancers. They decline but tell the bouncer to bring a girl for Turtle. Billy and Edward agree that Turtle is about ready for a blowjob. Spider interjects with his order for blowjob from one of the haole dancers. The bouncer walks away to get the haole, as Spider slips further into the U-shaped booth and unzips his fly.

A hostess brings four bottles of beer to the table. As the hostess is collecting the money for the drinks, the haole dancer makes her way under the table on her hands and knees and begins servicing Spider. The money exchange for the beers and conversation with the hostess goes on as routinely as if they were paying for a pizza. Spider's entertainment unfolds without comment from anyone. It is as if Spider were sampling a salad bar. Every now and then the rhythmic sound of slobbering, pumping from under the table, is broken by a gasp resembling the experience of having bitten into a jalapeno pepper.

After the hostess leaves the table, Billy and Edward light up a cigarette and enjoy the show. Now and then they have to calm their beers from trembling after

Spider's legs vibrate the table. The haole dancer is going to the suck the chrome off Spider's bumper.

Edward "Billy, I think this gal enjoys here work."

Billy "It's the motto of this place: Customers Come First."

Edward tapping his beer bottle against Billy's, "Here, here, to that."

Billy smiles, "It's good to get out of Chinatown for a while, isn't it. We need to do this more often."

Edward checking out the haole twisting her head back and forth under the table, "It sure is, Billy. We need more jobs like this."

Billy "Don't you have to make a bust now and then to keep up with your real job?"

Edward "I suppose I should, but I'm assigned into deep cover. That means I have a few years to get established as an underworld figure."

Billy surprised, "A few years! And, do they pay you the whole time?"

Edward surprisingly looks at Billy, "Of course, they pay me, Billy. How do you think the cops get their kids through college? Guys like me in deep cover inform them of big deals, so they can squeeze the dealers and players for money."

Billy "Do you mean you never bust the dealers?"

Edward "We bust dealers when they are invading territory under the protection of the department." Edward pauses "...unless of course, they show us the right gratitude and respect."

Billy "They pay you off, right?"

Edward "Exactly, they pay us off."

Billy "Our tax dollars pay for you to live like a criminal, so the police can extort drug dealers, is that it?"

Edward "That's it. Don't get me wrong; we do some good. Like, take this poor haole slut slobbering away on Spider. I give her work."

Billy laughs, "You give her work, do you?"

Edward "Sure, I do. If she weren't slobbering over Spider, she'd be eating out of a trashcan looking for her next fix. This way, she earns a few dollars to buy enough dope to make her forget all the blowjobs she's given, then she can dine at whatever trashcan she desires."

Billy smiles, "I never looked at it that way."

Suddenly, Spider exhales "My God, that was wonderful."

The haole dancer pops her head up from under the table and slides up into the seat next to Spider. She busies herself with a dingy face cloth wiping her chin and lips.

Edward to haole dancer, "I see you enjoy your work."

Haole dancer stops wiping her lips, "Well, it's kind of a suck ass job, if you ask me."

Now, there is a career statement!

Edward "Where are you from?"

Haole dancer putting her face cloth away, "I just spent a few years overseas as a hostess in Hong Kong."

Edward "Wow, I hear you can make lots of money doing that."

Haole dancer frowns, "Yes, I did, but the worm got to me, and I blew it all."

Spider to haole, "You were great. What's your name, by the way?"

Haole dancer "Lips. Be sure to ask for me next time you come."

Spider to Billy and Edward, "Lips! Now, there's a name I'll never forget."

The haole dancer smiles at Spider and slides out of the booth.

Spider slowly reaches for his beer and grasps it like he had been dying of thirst on a deserted island. Placing the bottle to his lips, he raises it high noon above his head and lets the contents gurgle into his mouth…West Texas style. Without so much as a slight choke, he lowers the empty bottle onto the table. He burps.

Spider spews, "Damn that was good! Nothing like a blowjob and a beer!"

Billy and Edward laugh out loud.

Spider "Billy, what did Lips mean when she said 'the worm got to me?'"

Billy leans toward Spiders and whispers, "Heroin."

Edward to Billy, "You would think the gals would learn to stay clean of heroin."

Billy smiles, "The boys overseas slowly slip the drug into the girls. The idea is to get them hooked, so they can use them to their full potential. Once they are hooked, the boys squeeze the girls for all their money and get them to really turn tricks for them. When they are done with them, they recycle them through places like these. It's a great business."

Spider "Damn, she was good! I need another beer."

Billy pointing toward Spider, "See, we are providing a satisfying service."

Spider to Billy, "Amen to that! We need to cycle through a hundred more Lips."

Billy exhales, "God knows we are trying, Spider."

After a few more rounds of beer, Turtle finally relinquishes his seat. From the look on his private dancer's face, she is pooped out from thrusting her hips into his nose. Turtle returns to the booth smiling.

Edward "Did you wear her out, Turtle?"

Spider exists the booth to allow Turtle to slide in. Before allowing Turtle to settle in his seat, Spider uses a drink napkin to air out Turtle's face.

Spider fanning Turtle's nose, "You're the champ, man. You're the champ, man."

Turtle slides far back into the U-shaped seat, "That was fun, guys. We have to come here more often."

Edward to Turtle, "Did you get her number?"

Turtle "No, she said she'd meet me Wednesday for lunch in Chinatown. I thought I'd take her to the Canton's."

Billy chuckles, "Now, there's an uptown spot for you."

Turtle "She said she hadn't been in Honolulu for some time, Billy. She wanted to see old Chinatown."

Billy leans toward Turtle, "Turtle, she's looking for a hook up for the worm. That's why she wants to see Chinatown."

Turtle puzzled, "The worm? We can fix her up with that."

Billy smiles, "Be sure you mention that to her when you see her Wednesday. Better yet, if you like her, go tell her that right now."

Turtle "She's a hardcore junky, is she?"

Billy "She sure is. We cycled her through here about four years ago in the hostess program."

Edward "How can you remember her, Billy?"

Billy pauses a moment before he responds, "Fat Willie Wong liked her. He tried his best to persuade her not to travel to Guam. She wanted to see the world. Fat Willie knew she would come back like this."

Edward "Why didn't Fat Willie tell her what she would be getting into overseas?"

Billy pauses a few moments, "If Fat Willie told her, she might tell the other girls. If that happened, Fat Willie would be dead meat with the Triads. I guess he should have told her. Fat Willie ended up that way all the same."

Edward "Did you know her, Billy?"

Billy shaking his head side to side once, "The only time we talked was when she was waiting for Fat Willie, one time. She smoked a cigarette and said a few words to me. That was all. Remember, four years ago I was doing time in Yuma Prison."

Turtle to Billy, "How do you remember her so well?"

Billy "I don't actually. I remember how much Fat Willie liked her. He was hurt when he watched her plane take off for Guam."

Turtle "Is she a local girl?"

Billy thinks a moment before he answers, "I think she is originally from the Oakland area. She joined the hostess express in San Francisco where she worked tables at a Market Street nightclub. Her folks were from Maui, I think."

Turtle surprised, "You know quite a bit about her, Billy."

Billy "Fat Willie talked about her a lot when we were just waiting around. Like I said, I only talked with her once, briefly."

Turtle decides to wait until Wednesday to tell her that he can hook her up. The rest of the evening, the group exchanges buying rounds of beer. Spider succumbs to the urge for another blowjob while the others cheer him on. Spider's irises really float the second time. Draining the lizard took on new meaning. The men agree to do this again sometime after the job. It is good to get out, now and then, to relax and spurt some semen.

Around 2:00 AM, as they get up to leave, Billy, Turtle and Edward notice that Spider is moving slowly and deliberately.

Billy to Spider, "Are you OK, Spider?"

Spider nodding his head up and down and inhaling deeply, "Yes, my legs feel like rubber that's all. I need time to adjust them."

Billy patting Spider on the back, "I guess that haole dancer gave you your money's worth, didn't she?"

Spider just inhales again and smiles. It is a million dollar smile!

Monday Morning Maunakea Street

This part of Honolulu still experiences some traffic this time of the morning. A few cars with inebriated passengers bark offers to female impersonators sashaying their way around the River-Beretania-Maunakea-Pauahi block. Turtle settles deep into the driver's seat, feigning sleep, in order to avoid the little taps on his passenger window followed by soft, but too deep, voices offering sexual satisfaction. From his parking location on a westside high point of Maunakea Street, he has an excellent view of the hoale's condominium and the entire block to the Pauahi Street intersection.

The breeze from the harbor deposits news of the latest disco crazes on Turtle's windshield. He marvels at the imaginative names of the troupes and the establishments that permit them to express themselves. Turtle never got the chance to experience this part of life. By the end of his sophomore year in high school, he was already on the street forging for a living. As he sits waiting for the haole they intend to hit, he reminisces the trying times of his late teens. How his life could have been different, if he had grown up around different friends? How his life could have been different, if his folks ensured he went to school and did his homework? They were too busy drinking and carousing to care. He and his brothers and sisters fended for themselves. His older brother was dead before he was eighteen, killed in a gunfight with rivaling drug dealers. His two sisters make their living as prostitutes in Waikiki when they are not serving time in prison.

Just as the rays from the sunrise behind him begin to slowly fan across the dashboard, the haole emerges from the high rise. Turtle marks the time: 6:30 AM. Turtle's eyes follow the haole as he walks down Maunakea Street. He walks the west side of the street until just before he reaches Pauahi, whereupon he checks traffic in both directions, crosses Maunakea Street and walks eastward up Pauahi Street. The only people on Maunakea Street are two female impersonators who are preoccupied with potential clients in cars. The lookout for the gambling house has not taken up his seat on the sidewalk, yet. He should be out there, unless the gamblers broke the game earlier. Turtle assesses that the only sure eyes on the street at this hour would be those of the gambling house lookout. And, guys like that, usually ex-cons, never admit to seeing anything.

In his mind, Turtle replays the haole's trek down Maunakea Street. The crucial point is when he crossed Maunakea Street to walk up Pauahi Street. The haole waits at the intersection and checks traffic. Turtle makes a note that the haole looks toward the harbor first, then to the mountains before he crosses the street. The ideal location for the truck would be to be parked on the west side of Maunakea Street a few stalls from the intersection. With the sunrise bearing down on the intersection from the mountain direction, it will help mask the movement of the truck. Turtle theorizes that the time to move on the haole would be after he has made his mountainside check before crossing the street. When he looks mountainside, the sunlight will squint his eyes. At that time, the truck engine can be started. The haole will only check the street traffic. The squinting action of his eyes will muffle his sensitivity to the engine starting in a stall. As he steps into the street, the truck can be shifted into gear quickly and torpedoed into the intersection. By 6:35 AM to the latest 6:40 AM, the whole affair would be over. The lookout will duck into the gambling house to alert the players. The female impersonators will scatter. The truck will drive two blocks then escape onto the boulevard. The haole will be left bleeding in the intersection. By 7:00 AM, the haole will have bleed to death. The entire affair should take only twenty minutes.

Turtle jots down his notes. He will compare these notes each day this week, as he maps the haole's every move down Maunakea Street. By the weekend, a concrete game plan to do in the haole will have been cemented.

Turtle shifts his car into gear and pulls away from the curb.

Following a week of observances, Turtle has the haole mapped out. Each morning the haole emerges from his condominium at just about 6:30 AM. He walks leisurely, but without stopping, down Maunakea Street. With the exception of one "good morning," on one morning, to the gambling house lookout, he speaks to no one. By 6:35 AM, the haole is standing at the intersection of Maunakea and Pauahi Streets, checks traffic in both directions and crosses the street using the pedestrian lane. The haole is an automaton. This will be an easy hit.

Friday evening, Turtle relates his surveillance report to Billy, Edward and Spider at the pool hall. Billy thinks over Turtle's report. He has Turtle run back through the haole's trek down Maunakea Street a few more times. Once Billy is satisfied that he has the mental image of the haole's movements, he asks Turtle for his recommendations on the hit.

Turtle "We torpedo the haole from a parked vehicle waiting in a stall on the west side of Maunakea Street."

Billy acknowledges, "Yes, we proposed that last week, and it does seem like a good idea."

Edward interjects, "We should insure the parking stall we want is available. Maybe we should use two vehicles. One vehicle parked before the stall. One vehicle parked after the stall but encroaching into the stall we want to insure no one else can park in that stall. Remember, we plan on using a lifted vehicle. There is a chance someone could park in our stall."

Billy to Edward, "That's a good point. A better idea would be to use three vehicles. We could have a vehicle in the stall we want, reserving it, so to speak, until the lifted vehicle arrives."

Turtle "What if we had the vehicle reserving the stall leave as the haole starts down Maunakea Street, then have the lifted vehicle pull into the empty stall vacated by the reserving vehicle?"

Edward "That's a good idea, Turtle. That way, the lifted vehicle still would have the engine running when the haole reached the intersection."

Turtle "Yes, the engine would be still running, and the haole would discount the vehicle attempting to park. When the haole checks the traffic, he will see the vehicle backing into the stall. It would just be a matter of changing gears to move forward into the intersection. The haole, even if he heard the gear shift and engine revving, would discount the noise as a vehicle attempting to adjust to the parking stall."

Billy "I like this! This is brilliant. Since it is parallel parking, the vehicle will be aimed at the center of the intersection, and the haole will not be alerted. Didn't you say the sun would be in his eyes as well when he looked mountainside on Maunakea Street, Turtle?"

Turtle "That's right, Billy. He'd have the sun in his eyes."

Billy "So, even if he looked in the direction of the noise, the sunlight would disable his ability to sense the direction and speed of the vehicle's motion."

Turtle, seeing the plan unfold, appreciates the mental capacity of his gang members. They have the ability to concoct such brilliant hit scenarios, yet they are all high school dropouts. Here, high school dropouts are plotting to kill someone who finished high school. Perhaps an education system would rethink their penchant to discard failing students, if they were aware of the ends to which these students would be directed. High school dropouts just don't disappear from the face of the earth. They make do as they can. If they cannot get good paying jobs, then they get involved in good paying crime. High school dropouts are the assassins, burglars, drug dealers, human smugglers, prostitutes, etc., of society. They make do. Seeing the creativity of his gang members in plotting to kill someone makes Turtle realize that these guys could have become someone important. They could be living successful lives as professionals in some trade or industry, if they had just been given a better chance.

Billy settles on Wednesday morning for the hit. On that morning, the gambling house lookout did not take his post until after the haole had crossed the intersection. Street traffic was slow that morning as well. It will be Wednesday!

Early Wednesday Morning

Spider and Turtle are cruising the streets where Spider had designated likely vehicles to be used for the hit were located. Up in Pearl Harbor Heights on poorly lit back street, Spider spotted a yellow truck that he felt would be ideal for the job. As the men drive up to the yellow truck, Turtle notices that it is a cheap Chevy S-10 with a two-to-three-person cab and a loading area in the rear.

Spider pulls his vehicle up alongside the yellow truck. He is prepared to boost the truck. He tells Turtle to take the driver seat and move their vehicle back a few stalls to observe anyone coming into their field of view. Spider disembarks his vehicle with a special booster bar, flathead screwdriver, and stripping pliers.

Looking in all directions as he slides up alongside the driver's seat door of the yellow truck, Spider quickly places the booster bar against the rear part of the driver's window. With a sudden downward thrust of the booster bar, the door lock pops open. He removes the booster bar and quickly slides into the driver's seat. Crouching down, he checks the likely location for an extra set of keys. Sure enough, the owner has a set of keys stashed in the left, front, wheel-well compartment. Spider lays his tools on the passenger seat and starts the ignition. The truck purrs up nicely. He checks all the indications. They are fine. He notices that he has a half tank of gas. That is plenty. Spider motions with his hand for Turtle to follow him. The two men drive off with Turtle following closely behind the yellow truck.

It is still early. They have two hours to wait before the haole appears. Nevertheless, Spider and Turtle make their way to Maunakea Street. There is a dark, blind alley, located a block mountainside from the haole's condominium, where Spider can hide the yellow truck until it is needed. Spider drives the yellow truck into the blind alley. Turtle parks his vehicle behind the truck to obstruct any view of the yellow truck from Maunakea Street.

As the two men wait for the hour to arrive to take up positions along Maunakea Street for the hit, they decide on having a morning coffee. Rather than drive to the all-night convenience store a few blocks away, Turtle decides that he will walk.

Honolulu is calm around 5:00 AM. There are few bird sounds. The breeze from the harbor is comforting. Since the temperature always gravitates about 85 degrees Fahrenheit, there is little need for anything other than an Aloha shirt for comfort. Turtle admires the walk. When he arrives at the convenience store, only the cashier is inside. He notices that she is doing her homework behind the checkout counter. She must be a student at one of the universities. Taking these early morning shifts is ideal for students working their way through college. Turtle could see himself so engaged.

He selects hazelnut coffee for himself and vanilla for Spider. Medium size cups will do for the short time that they will be waiting. The temptation of fresh donuts on the checkout counter overcomes Turtle, and he picks up two sugar-coated, jelly donuts. The cashier is shy and pays him little attention. She makes no eye contact. He hands her a ten-dollar bill. She makes change without conversation. Turtle notices the book from which she is doing her homework is a Physics book. She must be an engineering student. Turtle laughs to think whether or not she could assist Spider in determining the right angle with which to aim the truck to torpedo the haole in the intersection. That is probably not a homework question this convenience store clerk would ever receive as an assignment. In less than two hours, Spider and he will be conducting an exercise in applied physics.

The feel of the warm coffee and the soft, jelly donuts in his hands causes Turtle's mouth to water. He cannot wait to return to the vehicle. He imagines he could be doing this same thing night after night, if he were a detective. He reasons it would be too boring, if he had to do it all the time. But, once in a while for a big payoff is exciting. As he approaches the vehicle, Spider opens the door to let him in. Turtle stops to hand Spider his coffee and one of the jelly donuts. Spider's face lights up upon feeling the jelly donut in his hand.

Spider "Fantastic! I was getting a little hungry."

Turtle "Well, there's breakfast. I got you vanilla. Is that OK?"

Spider "Vanilla, sure, I'm in for vanilla, this morning."

The two men settle into the car and await 6:00 AM. Between munches into the donuts and the sips of hot coffee, the latest feats of the professional football teams are exchanged. Life is exciting this morning. It must be the rush of adrenaline that makes this form of life exciting. If they were cops, a stakeout would be tiresome. But, a hit makes you feel alive. One has to wonder whether life should be lived with this intensity of excitement, or is life intended to be boring like a cow meandering about a meadow munching here and there. For Spider and Turtle, this is what life is all about. It is boredom interspersed with times of intense excitement and sharing hot coffee and jelly donuts just before a thrill session.

Spider breaks the pleasure of the moment, "What time do you have, Turtle?"

Turtle looks at his watch, "It's a few minutes before 6:00 AM."

Spider takes the last sip of his coffee and exhales, "That coffee sure hit the spot this morning."

Spider crimples the cup and tosses it into the alley. Turtle does likewise. It is showtime!

Spider disembarks the vehicle, as Turtle backs his vehicle out of the alley. Turtle proceeds up Maunakea Street to the selected, west side, parking stall. As planned, Billy's goons have placed vehicles in the forward and rear parking stalls. Turtle slides his vehicle into the designated stall. Spider backs the yellow truck out of the alley and waits a block away, mountainside on Maunakea Street. Spider will wait until the haole emerges from his building to drive up Maunakea Street. Turtle, minding his rearview mirror, will take his cue to vacate the parking stall when he sees the yellow truck moving up Maunakea Street.

By 6:15 AM, everyone is in position. Edward has a blue and white cruiser cleanse the street then take up a position a few blocks away protecting the escape route to the boulevard. If anything unusual happens, the blue and white will be the first on scene to conduct damage control.

At 6:30 AM sharp, the haole emerges from his building. There is nothing like punctuality during a hit. It makes things unfold effortlessly. Spider identifies the haole and commences his drive up Maunakea Street. Turtle's reconnaissance was correct, the gambling house lookout has not taken up his seat yet. Spider notices

Turtle's vehicle moving back and forth to exit from the parking stall. Spider eases the yellow truck two truck lengths behind Turtle's vehicle, allowing him ample space to maneuver out of the stall. The haole does not notice the movement of the vehicles. It is amazing how routine activities pass below our threshold of perception.

Turtle's vehicle exits the stall and makes its way through the intersection of Maunakea and Pauahi Streets. The yellow truck moves abreast of the forward parking stall and begins slowly backing into the designated stall, as the haole walks leisurely past the designated stall. Timing is perfect. Spider takes his time backing into the stall. Just as the haole reaches the intersection, Spider stops the truck. The haole looks towards the harbor then towards the mountains. As he looks towards the mountains, Spider notices the haole's eyes squint as they react to the sunlight. Spider shifts the truck's gear from reverse to forward. As the haole steps into the street, Spider floors the gas pedal and speeds into the intersection. In a split second, the haole retreats back to the sidewalk. The yellow truck clips his foot and spins him to the pavement. Spider, realizing that he did not hit the haole squarely, speeds the truck down Maunakea Street and exits onto the boulevard.

The haole lies on the sidewalk pavement holding his ankle. From the grimace on his face, his ankle may be broken. The haole does not try to stand. He just remains on the sidewalk holding his ankle firmly. Pain overcomes him, as tears form in his eyes.

By 6:45 AM, the haole is still lying on the pavement. It appears that he is unable to stand. He has managed to remove the shoe from the effected ankle. There is no blood on his socks. He begins to cry out for help.

Suddenly, the gambling house lookout emerges. He bends over to take his seat. Noticing the screaming haole on the pavement at the intersection, the lookout retreats quickly back into the gambling house to alert the players. Soon Maunakea Street experiences an outpouring of gamblers, like someone finally relieving himself after a long wait. None of the gamblers rend any assistance to the haole. They just make their way out of the area as quickly as possible.

By 7:00 AM, the blue and white patrols through the area. The Moke policeman driving the patrol car notices the haole on the pavement and stops to investigate.

Policeman "Are you OK?"

Erik in pain, "No, someone tried to run me over. I think they broke my ankle."

The policeman calls for an ambulance.

Policeman "OK, hold on now, the ambulance is on its way."

Policeman leans over and checks Erik's ankle, "Did you get look at who did this?"

Erik "It was a yellow truck. That's all I know. There was only one person in the cab."

Policeman "Did you recognize this person?"

Erik "No, I couldn't make out his face. The sun was in my eyes."

Policeman "Did you get the license number of the truck?"

Erik "No, it happened too fast."

Policeman "Has anyone threatened you lately?"

Erik "No."

Policeman "Any idea who would want to try to run you over?"

Erik thinks a moment and responds, "Maybe some drug dealers on the North Shore."

Policeman "Do you have any names in particular?"

Erik "No."

Policeman as the ambulance arrives, "OK, we'll look into this."

Before the medics take Erik into the ambulance, the policeman gets his address, phone number, place of employment and social security number.

The policeman returns to the blue and white and writes in his notepad: Caucasian male, about 40 years old, incoherent, stumbled off the sidewalk and turned his ankle. Subject is probably on drugs and makes false claims of being hit by a vehicle. This is a routine self-inflicted injury. No further inquiry is required.

CHAPTER 11

Wednesday Afternoon, Easy Eddie Store

Jacob and Easy Eddie are assisting the typical, closing-bell customers when Hans enters the store all pooped out.

Hans exclaims, "Thank God, I made it."

Jacob gives Easy Eddie a demeaning look, "You better attend to your friend."

Jacob takes charge of the remaining customers as Easy Eddie escorts Hans into the storeroom.

Hans "Sorry, I wasn't able to get free last Wednesday in time to meet you."

Easy Eddie puzzled, "Were we supposed to meet last Wednesday?"

Hans still trying to catch his breath, "Yes, remember, you told me to stop by to pick up a gun."

Easy Eddie realizing what Hans just said, quickly turns to him and whispers, "You need to keep your voice down."

Hans nods and whispers back, "OK."

Easy Eddie realizes that in the excitement of the two previous weeks he gave his remaining clean guns to Billy. Then, he remembers he received a gun from Detective Aoki. It is still in his desk.

After Easy Eddie settles into his office area, he begins searching his desk drawers. His hand feels the canvas bank bag that contains the gun. He has to bend over and reach far back into the side drawer to get a good grip on the bank bag to remove it from the drawer.

Easy Eddie removing the bank bag, "Here it is. I knew I kept one for you in here."

Easy Eddie hands the rolled up bank bag to Hans. Hans slowly unrolls the bank bag on Easy Eddie's desk. Sure enough, as Hans allows the contents of the bank bag to empty on the desk, a sealed plastic bag containing a revolver with some bullets slides out onto the table.

Hans whispering, "Wow, you even have the gun sealed up."

Easy Eddie realizes that this gun is from the police evidence locker and was being stowed as evidence.

Easy Eddie speaking softly, "Hey, just like I told you. The gun is clean. If you keep it in the bag until you need it, it will be clean."

Hans admires the gun.

Easy Eddie smiles, "It's police certified clean. You can't get a gun better than that."

Hans places the plastic bag containing the gun and bullets back in the bank bag. He rolls the bank bag up and places it gently into his valise.

Easy Eddie "Now, don't get caught with that gun. You'll get into big time trouble. Keep it hidden away until you intend to use it."

Hans very appreciative, "OK, I got it."

Easy Eddie repeats, "Do not get caught with that gun. Policemen will know that there is only one place where you could have gotten it. You'll be in big trouble."

Hans nods to the repeated caution, "I got it, Eddie. You can trust me."

Easy Eddie "The gun is perfect for your cop problem, if you catch him around your wife. Only a cop could have that gun on him."

Hans realizing what Easy Eddie is saying, "That's right, Eddie. This is a great gift, isn't it?"

Easy Eddie smiles, "You bet your life it is. You better take good care of it."

Hans shakes Easy Eddie hand, "Thanks, Eddie."

Easy Eddie "I have to get back into the showroom and help finish up with these last minute customers. They know we close early on Wednesday, so they come in here at closing time to hold us up. Sometimes, I think they come in just to piss us off."

Hans "OK, Eddie, I'll take off. I can wait, if you want to get some lunch."

Easy Eddie shakes his head, "No, I promised one of the jewelers I would meet him at his shop to fix something. I'm already late as it is."

Easy Eddie knows if he mentions a prior business engagement, then his inability to have lunch with Hans will not be questioned.

Hans shakes Easy Eddie's hand again. Easy Eddie lets Hans out the back door. After Hans leaves, Easy Eddie realizes that Patricia is waiting for him in the Chinese restaurant for lunch. She will be upset with him again for being late.

Entering the Chinese restaurant, Easy Eddie spots Patricia sitting alone at a four-seat window booth. She seems occupied watching some kids playing in the street. Easy Eddie knows she is upset with him. Patricia looks especially pleasing to the eyes today, although, big breasts always have been pleasing to Easy Eddie's eyes.

Easy Eddie as he strolls up to the table, "Sorry, I'm late. Last minute customers swooped down on us."

Patricia doesn't smile, "I'm hungry, Eddie. Let's order right away, OK."

Easy Eddie gestures for the waiter.

Easy Eddie to Patricia, "You look lovely today."

Patricia just stares at Easy Eddie. It is one of those cold stares that convey the words: Don't push your luck.

Easy Eddie as the waiter approaches, "The lady will have Mongolian Beef with noodles. I'll have the boneless chicken."

Waiter jots down the order and asks if he could get them anything else. Easy Eddie shakes his head to indicate that will be fine.

As Easy Eddie recommences charming Patricia, Edward comes over to the table.

Easy Eddie surprised to see him, "Edward, I haven't seen you in here before."

Edward somewhat nervous, "Eddie, could I speak with you for a second?"

Easy Eddie looks over at Patricia. She gives Easy Eddie her usual "What is it now" stare.

Easy looks back at Edward, "Is this important?"

Edward "Billy asked me to find you."

Easy Eddie looks back over at Patricia, "This won't take long, honey. I'll be right back."

Patricia exhales, "I understand."

Easy Eddie hates to leave her like that. She is already upset with him for being late. Nonetheless, Edward and he leave the booth area.

Edward as they walk outside the restaurant, "Eddie, Billy wanted me to tell you that we tried to hit the haole this morning. We weren't able to do him in. We may have broken his ankle."

Easy Eddie disappointed, "How bad is he?"

Edward "Like I said, we may have broken his ankle. He moved out of the way instinctively before we could make solid contact with the truck. He must have some seventh sense, that haole."

Easy Eddie "Do you think he got the message that someone is upset with him?"

Edward "Oh yeah, he got that message real clear."

Easy Eddie "Well, let's hope that will be enough."

Edward "Billy said he would be in the pool hall, if you wanted to talk to him."

Easy Eddie "No, tell him that I'll will talk to the interested parties, first, and find out if more needs to be done. Is the haole's leg hurt pretty bad?"

Edward "Yes, he couldn't walk when the police left him with the ambulance crew. He needed to be sedated. The truck whacked his ankle pretty good."

Easy Eddie "OK, thanks for the information. Tell Billy I will get back to him."

Edward "OK, sorry to interrupt your lunch."

Easy Eddie leaves Edward and returns to a fuming Patricia inside the restaurant. By the time Easy Eddie returns, the food is steaming on the table. Patricia has not touched her food. She just sat there and waited for Easy Eddie to return.

Easy Eddie as he slides into the booth, "Sorry, I had to take that short meeting."

Patricia "I understand, Eddie. You know Eddie, one day, a guy like that is going to ask you outside, and all I am going to hear is a gunshot."

Easy Eddie sensing concern from Patricia, "Don't worry, honey, Edward is my good friend."

Patricia "Eddie, it will be a good friend that shoots you. Given the type of good friends you have, it probably will be a firing squad waiting for you."

Easy Eddie realizes that despite Patricia's demeaning remarks about his good friends, she could be right. It would be that easy. He just walked outside with Edward, just now. If Billy knew that he pocketed $20,000.00 of the money before he made the arrangements for the hit, Billy could have been waiting out there to shoot him.

Easy Eddie "You worry too much. Let's eat. It sure smells good, doesn't it?"

Patricia does not respond; she just starts mouthing the Mongolian Beef with her chopsticks. Easy Eddie, sensing her preoccupation with the food, realizes that she is starved. He pours Patricia and himself a cup of hot Chinese tea and smoothes his wooden chopsticks. He decides to enjoy the meal in silence. Patricia is happy when she eats. He will let her savor the happiness of the moment.

Erik's Office in Waikiki

The North Shore Land *hui* allocated a portion of their funding to support an office. Erik selected a condominium zoned for joint residential and business activities. This way, he could overnight at the office when he was stuck downtown.

The office design resembles a one-bedroom apartment with a spectacular view of the entrance to Waikiki from Honolulu. The one-bedroom is a split design that offers an office area separated by a wall from a residential area. The residential portion of the office is fully furnished with wall-to-wall carpeting, refrigerator, central air conditioning, sink with garbage disposal and full bath accommodations. The office area consists of a work desk equipped with an automatic typewriter, a drawing board, a comfortable three-seat sofa for meetings and two executive chairs. The sofa converts into a pullout bed. The office workspace is crowded with furniture but comfortable. One person can navigate the workspace quite easily. With two people working, as long as one is typing and the other drafting, the space is tolerable. Meetings of five persons or less are comfortable. Four-person meetings are ideal.

Erik is occupying one of the work desk chairs with his ankle propped up on the work desk when Hans arrives.

Hans seeing Erik's leg in a cast, "What happened to you?"

Erik in obvious pain, "Someone hit me in a crosswalk."

Hans "Is your leg OK?"

Erik "Yes, I think so. The anklebones are badly bruised. The doctor recommended the ankle remain in a cast while the bones healed."

Hans relieved, "Nothing is broken inside that cast, I take it?"

Erik "The doctor said he took a full round of X-rays. They revealed nothing broken."

Hans "How did this happen?"

Erik "I was crossing the street on my way to the lawyer's office. All of a sudden, out of nowhere this yellow truck comes barrel-assing through the intersection. I just caught a glimpse of the truck in the corner of my eye. It was a good thing, too. Had I taken another step, I would be dead. I am sure of it."

Hans "How did he hit your ankle?"

Erik pauses a moment, "I must have turned instinctively to run back to the sidewalk. The truck must have hit my ankle, as I ran to the curb."

Hans "What happened to the truck driver?"

Erik moves his shoulders up, "I don't know. All I saw was the back of the yellow truck briefly as it turned onto the boulevard."

Hans "Was this a hit and run?"

Erik "He hit me, and he drove off. I doubt that the truck ever slowed down, after he hit me."

Hans "Did you get an ID on the truck? Like, a license plate number?"

Erik "No, it all happened so fast. I saw the truck. He hit me, and he just drove off. Before I realized anything, I was on the curb in terrible pain."

Hans "Did the police show up?"

Erik adjusts his leg gingerly, "It took the longest time, but the police finally arrived on scene. I told them what I could, but I doubt I was much help to them."

Hans "You would think the truck driver would have stopped and rendered assistance, wouldn't you?"

Erik "That's why I called you here, Hans. I think I was being set up to have a traffic accident."

Hans "It sure seems that way. Do you always take that route when you walk to town?"

Erik adjust his leg again, "I sure do. From now on, I intend to alternate my routes."

Hans "That sounds like an excellent idea."

Erik "Why I called you here, Hans, was to alert you to be careful as well. The real estate company, the title company and the prior owners of the *hui*'s land were served earlier this week with our lawsuit. This hit and run accident could have been their response. According to our lawyer, from the shenanigans that he has uncovered in Punaluu Valley, the owners and the title company may want us to disappear in any manner possible. The lawyer estimates the potential damages to be in the hundreds of millions of dollars."

Hans surprised, "Can the damage really be a hundred million dollars?"

Erik "No, the lawyer estimates the damage to be more than five hundred million dollars. It could be more. So, we need to be careful. I can't say this hit and run was an attempt on my life, but it sure felt like it was. You need to be careful, Hans."

Hans sits down on the couch and exhales, "I guess I better be careful. Do you think the drug dealers could be involved as well?"

Erik exhaling, "They are a possibility, as well. We did dig up over two miles of their PVC piping."

The two men go over and over the possible enemies that would try to eliminate Erik via a hit and run.

After some forty-five minutes of brainstorming the possible culprits, Erik concludes that it was either the drug dealers or those people who messed up the subdivision status in Punaluu Valley. Both groups either lost a tremendous amount of money or will lose a bankroll attempting to recover from the problems.

Erik "The more I contemplate this hit and run incident, the more I believe that it was a disguised assassination attempt on my life. If the culprits wanted to kill me, they could have. Yet, in this case, they tried to make it look like an accident. To me, that seems to negate the drug dealers as the possible assassins. They would just kill me. They would not try to make it look like an accident."

Hans "Could this hit and run just be a coincidence?"

Erik pauses a moment, "I suppose it could, but something alerted me when I walked by the yellow truck, as it was attempting to park. Something caused the hairs on my upper spine to stand up. My body sensed danger. That's why I was extra cautious when I stepped off the curb into the Maunakea Street crosswalk. It was like my body anticipated the assassination attempt. I know how that must sound, but it is true. My body was warning me."

Hans "I've had those spinal sensations, as well, when I am in a strange port. I listen to them and stay clear of any area that tingles my spine."

Erik "Don't you find it amazing how our bodies sense danger, despite how far removed we are from the days when we lived according to our sense impressions in the wilds?"

Hans "Yes, our bodies are still as keenly aware of danger today as they were in the caveman days. We should learn to listen to our bodies more."

Erik "I wonder what other sensations we receive that we may be ignoring because of our acclimatization to social settings."

Hans "I bet there are many signals coming in that we ignore completely."

Erik "Well, I'm glad I listened to that spinal sensation on Maunakea Street."

Hans "Will the cops get back to you on the hit and run?"

Erik "I suspect that they will. It shouldn't take them too much time to connect the yellow truck with someone. How many yellow trucks are there in Honolulu?"

Hans "I've never seen a yellow truck in Honolulu."

Erik "I never have either, come to think of it."

A few minutes pass before Hans says, "You are thinking the title company or the guys who sold our *hui* the land are responsible for the hit and run, aren't you?"

Erik "Yes, I do. Who else would try to make it look like an accident?"

Hans "I can see your point."

Erik "I think the key to this caper lies with the damage our involvement in Punaluu Valley will cause the guilty parties."

Hans "Well, the number of bogus subdivisions is alarming."

Erik pauses, "That's true, but I think the bogus sewer line running along Kamehameha Coast Highway may be the worst fraud. Without proper sewage, none of those bogus subdivisions could have been created."

Hans "The real estate company made that error."

Erik "No, actually, the lawyer for the Blackwater Holdings made the error by entering in the deeds that there was a sewer line that ran along Kamehameha Coast Highway. That may be the critical fraud that contributed to all the problems in the valley. Realization that the sewer line was fictitious would devastate Blackwater Holdings. I bet that's what triggered this hit and run."

Hans "Why would they come all the way into Honolulu to hit you, Erik? Why wouldn't they do it out there in the valley where they have strength in numbers?"

Erik "That's the beauty of the hit and run. It was professionally contracted."

Hans in awe, "Wow, this is serious. Do you think that they hired professional hitmen to do this to you?"

Erik "Yes, that is the conclusion to which I am inclined to believe."

Lawyer's Office Downtown Honolulu

The lawyer's office is located in the Old Territorial Building on the corner of the Nimitz Highway and Bishop Street. A remnant of the days when Hawai'i was still a territory of the United States, the Territorial Building served as the territorial seat of government. Entrance is via columned archways that open up into a huge open-spaced vestibule. In the territorial days, the open space was a gathering area. Two, wide stairwells provided access to the upper administrative offices. Today, the two stairwells are augmented with three elevators.

The open-area vestibule today is littered with little, outdoor-style, table & chair settings, providing a cozy atmosphere for the lunchtime crowd of the surrounding skyscrapers. A small New York-style deli lines the mountainside wall of the vestibule. At lunchtime, this deli experiences a continuous stream of office personnel. Most patrons select half-sandwiches and a cold drink. The sandwiches are prepared right in front of patrons, preserving the New York deli freshness.

The lawyer's office is a three-room complex at the far end of the third floor facing the ocean. A walk down the wood-paneled hallway provides a glimpse of what it must have been like to do business in the early 20th Century. The thick, floor carpeting muffles the foot traffic in the building. Walking down the hallway resembles a quiet, serene walk in the woods. A pastiche of memories streams into Hans' mind, resembling those that reminded him of ancient battle sites.

The office doors are reminiscent of those offices still in existence in the older sections of large Mainland cities. Three-quarter length, opaque-glass with identification labels adorns each of the doors. Old, artistic-designed, turn knobs with skeleton key locks encourage delicate opening and closing of the doors.

Entering the lawyer's office, the vestibule expresses the cramped nature of the legal profession. Boxes of case files line the rear and the oceanside walls. The lone reception sofa seems like the only sanctuary from the office overflow. Beyond the vestibule rear wall is the legal secretary's office. From the looks of her inbox, more than six months of legal documents await her attention. The lawyer's office is beyond the oceanside, box-lined wall of the vestibule.

The legal secretary greets Hans, as he enters the vestibule. She invites Hans to take a seat on the sofa while she announces his arrival to the attorney. Within a few minutes, she emerges from the lawyer's private office area and informs Hans that he can just go right in.

The lawyer's office is carpeted with boxes of case files stacked up against all the four walls. An old, work desk with a sliding, slotted-wood, arch cover embellishes the center of the room. From the look of the private office, the attorney has a huge caseload.

The attorney offers Hans a seat in the lone client chair. It is a simple, wooden Captain's chair. The private office does not offer a view of the ocean. It has one lone window peering out above the stacks of case files on the rear wall. The only view is the reflection of the glass plates of the skyscraper across the walkway from the Old Territorial Building. Daydreaming is not encouraged in this office.

Lawyer "Erik asked me to fill you in on the upcoming litigation, Hans. As you know, Erik will be immobile for the next few weeks."

The lawyer is 6'2" tall, slender, Caucasian in his mid-forties. From his mannerisms, the legal practice has worn him down mentally. Enthusiasm is not one of his best traits.

Hans settling into his seat, "Yes, I spoke with Erik yesterday. His ankle looks pretty bad."

Lawyer "OK, let's get started. First, I have sent out the written interrogatories. The defendants will have thirty days in which to respond. Hopefully, reading the interrogatories will enlighten them to the hopelessness of their position. Their responses will educate them to the fact that many properties were sold by their agent that were improperly subdivided, amongst a plethora of other professional improprieties. It is my hope that we can settle this affair quickly rather than drag their names through the mud."

Hans "Do you think that they will concede quickly?"

Lawyer "Well, you never know. On our side is the fact that they were negligent in many professional procedures. What is going against us is that they have screwed up, so much, that they may need to fight us in order to stave off complete financial loss. How they envision their liabilities will determine whether or not they will settle with us."

Hans "I understand that their errors are many in the valley."

Lawyer "Unfortunately, it is not just Punaluu Valley. Their incompetence extends to the entire North Shore. I have identified over one thousand lots with similar troubles as ours. We are dealing with total professional incompetence on the part of a principal broker for a large real estate firm. What is more, he has implicated a title company and the state bureaucracy in his weird dealings. Many people will have their careers on the line here."

Hans "I see. So, we have a delicate matter with which to contend with here, don't we?"

Lawyer "I think delicate is a proper word for this fiasco. Whatever the outcome, it is hard for me to envision this principal broker ever being trusted in Hawai'i again. He is finished."

Hans "Somehow, I don't see him just rolling over for us."

Lawyer "That's why Erik wanted me to apprise you of the litigation we are undertaking."

Hans "OK, first, we await the responses from the written interrogatories. Is that right?"

Lawyer "Yes, in the meantime, I am preparing the oral depositions. We will bring in the principals of the real estate firm, the title company and the county bureaucrats that allowed these illegal subdivisions to be created."

Hans "Oral depositions are where the people come in person to answer interrogatories, is that right?"

Lawyer "Yes, they will have to appear. They will all have their lawyers attempting to obstruct our discovery into their culpability. These depositions will become lively affairs."

Hans "When do we go to trial?"

Lawyer pauses and looks to the ceiling "Let me see, I think, the earliest court date will be a year from now. It is a matter of case backlog. In the interim, we are allowed to continue discovery. We will use the time wisely to encourage their submission."

Hans "Trial should be in our favor. I would think they would want to avoid it."

Lawyer "Well, it is in our favor; however, having practiced law in Honolulu for over ten years now, I can tell you that trials are crapshoots. First, trial by jury means twelve individuals decide your fate. Those twelve individuals are less than equipped to understand a complex case like this. So, presenting the case requires us to provide the facts in a manner understandable by the jury. That might be hard to do if the defense engages in half-truths and misleading lines of inquiry."

Hans concerned, "I see."

Lawyer "It is a fact of life that juries are chosen from the common people of Hawai'i. By common, I mean regular laborers. They have no training in real estate. Most of the testimony provided in the trial will escape them completely. The defense, knowing their weaknesses, will try to steer the trial into making your *hui*, Erik in particular, look like crooks."

Hans "Can they do that?"

Lawyer "Well, it is like this. In trials, there are three avenues of defense. First, there is the law. If you have the law behind you, then you stick to that. We have the law behind us. Second, if you don't have the law behind you, then you use procedure to win. Procedure refers to technicalities that derail the plaintiff's efforts to acquire a decision. That means we have to follow administrative procedures. The nice thing about procedures is that if you miss one, you just have to go back through the wicket, so to speak, to resume your complaint. We have procedure behind us. Lastly, if you don't have law or procedure available to you, then you attack the person. Essentially, you make the argument that even if the plaintiff is right, he is such a bad person that he should not win. That defense has merit if they create the image that Erik is a bad person. They don't have to prove Erik is a bad person; they just need to create the impression that he is."

Hans "I see, so we can expect a lot of mudslinging."

Lawyer "Yes, they will go out of their way to show Erik is a bad guy. Knowing this group, they will even fabricate scenarios to show this. These are dishonorable people. I will warn ahead you of time, Hans. The *hui* will come under attack by these people. They will do whatever it takes to intimidate the *hui* to drop the lawsuit."

Hans "Should we be concerned about the judges?"

Lawyer "Well, some judges are more competent than others. For me to identify any one of them as dishonest would jeopardize my license, so I will just state that as in the rest of life's professions, some people are more competent than others."

Hans "Do we have a say in jury selection?"

Lawyer "We do, but the pool is generally of a poor quality. And, the loyalties of the jury members have to be a concern as well. Some may well be affiliated in some way with the defendants. It would be next to impossible for us to determine that. We could be going in against a stacked deck."

Hans concerned, "Have you ever heard of anything like that happening?"

Lawyer "Well, there is nothing that I would go through in an effort to prove something like that; however, I would have to say that it happens all the time. There are too many open-shut cases that have gone the other way. Some are so questionable that one wonders if the jury listen to the trial at all. In civil court, you do not need an unanimous decision to prevail. You just need a majority to win. These are poor people on these juries. Some people stand jury duty, because it is the only job that they have. You can imagine their vulnerability to bribery or other enticements."

Hans "I never realized the poor quality of justice."

Lawyer "It is a fact of life. People above such temptation generally get excused from jury duty. The courts are left with what remains. We do with what we have. It is a sad affair, but we make do. So, in conclusion, trials are crapshoots."

Hans "Won't a trial expose the errors of the defendants?"

Lawyer "Yes, the trial will; however, if the defendant is about to lose his shirt if he concedes before trial, then he is better off crapshooting. He just might win!"

Hans "I see your point."

Fort Street Mall

On the way from the lawyer's office, Hans decides to walk down Fort Street Mall and catch a quick snack for lunch. The usual lunchtime crowd of office workers and college students keeps the Mall traffic bustling. Ukulele players strum away tunes of the old Hawai'ian cowboys. The Mall comes alive at lunchtime. It is probably the only time of the day on O'ahu when the Mall coeds outnumber the Waikiki beach bunnies.

As Hans is deciding between a submarine sandwich and a Mexican plate, he notices Easy Eddie engaged in a lively conversation outside a jewelry store. Hans decides to greet Easy Eddie. As he approaches the conversation, it appears that a short, unshaven, slovenly-dressed local is scolding Easy Eddie about some failed transaction. Easy Eddie tries furiously to calm the ranting local.

Hans as he approaches Easy Eddie, "Eddie, good to see you. Am I interrupting something here?"

A large crowd has begun to form in the vicinity of the altercation between Easy Eddie and the local. Rubbernecks, pretending to be secret agents eavesdropping on the conversation, are a plenty on the Mall.

Easy Eddie turns toward Hans quickly, "Oh, hi there! No, it's just a misunderstanding. He was just leaving anyway."

Local angry, "No, I wasn't just leaving, Eddie. Where's our money?"

Easy Eddie to the local, "Can we discuss this another time? Why don't you stop by my store after work, and we can talk this over then, OK?"

Local raises his fist in a threatening gesture, "OK, Eddie, I'll stop by after work, but you had better have our money."

The local walks a few steps away from Easy Eddie, turns and says, "You had better have our money ready, Eddie."

Hans after the local has distanced himself sufficiently, "What was that all about, Eddie?"

Easy Eddie exhales, "It's some deal that went sour. I tried to explain it to him, but he is in withdrawal pains from some drug he is on. I will have trouble with him, if he doesn't get a fix before the end of the day."

Hans "Maybe you should call the police?"

Easy Eddie laughs, "No, that won't be necessary. Besides, he is family, so I can't get him in trouble."

Hans remains quiet realizing the strange relationships that exist within these local families.

As the two men stand there in a moment of silence, the jewelry repair shop owner walks by and says, "There's my hero, Eddie. Thanks again for killing those two crooks."

Easy Eddie to the jewelry repair shop owner, "How's it?"

Jewelry repair shop owner, "It's good, Eddie. Hey, did I tell you I'm sending my daughter off to a private college on the east coast?"

Easy Eddie surprised, "No, you didn't. Aren't those colleges expensive?"

Jewelry repair shop owner, "Yes, but I figured, since I will get about $400,000.00 back from the insurance claim for the robbery, I might as well spend the money on my children."

Easy Eddie locks his jaw to prevent from laughing. He has to force his jaw to remain locked while the jewelry repair shop owner is present. The temptation to laugh is overwhelming.

Jewelry repair shop owner, "Well, I have to run, Eddie. Good seeing you!"

Hans whispers to Easy Eddie as the jewelry repair shop owner departs, "Didn't this guy tell us just the other day, he got hit for only $300,000.00."

Easy Eddie still keeping his jaw shut just stares at Hans and shakes his head. This Chinaman is making out better than the robbers and Easy Eddie. The Chinaman actually revels in the fact that he got robbed. He is making a profit on the robbery.

Easy Eddie shakes his head form side to side, "Can you believe that guy? He's putting his daughter though college on the robbery."

Hans "Eddie, maybe somebody should rob you."

Easy Eddie laughs, "Now, there's an idea."

Both men laugh.

Easy Eddie "What brings you into town, today?"

Hans "I had to stop in on the lawyer. Oh, I almost forgot to tell you! Erik got hit by a truck the other day."

Easy Eddie speaks before he can catch himself, "I know."

Hans surprised, "How did you find out? It just happened on Wednesday. Did Erik call you?"

Easy Eddie realizing that he is on the spot, "I heard about it on the street. Let's face it, there are a few people who don't like Erik."

Hans "I can believe that. Erik thinks someone tried to have him assassinated."

Easy Eddie "Like I said, there are a few people who don't like Erik."

Hans "Erik thinks it might be the owners of the property we bought."

Easy Eddie looks at Hans with a serious look on his face, "Does he now?"

Hans "It does make sense."

Easy Eddie "I bet it does."

Hans sensing Easy Eddie knows more than he is letting on, asks, "Eddie, did you have anything to do with this?"

Easy Eddie pauses for a moment then says, "Confidentially, now, OK, yes, I knew people were going to hit Erik. There are many people who desire for you to take over the land company, Hans, OK."

Hans surprised by the response, "Really?"

Easy Eddie nodding his head up and down, "Yes, many people in the valley prefer you to be running the *hui*."

Hans "Why is that?"

Easy Eddie "Erik is too stubborn. And, he gets really vindictive when people ignore him. Those people in the valley want to be left alone."

Hans "Most of them are engaged in the drug trade out there."

Easy Eddie "That's true, but they don't like Erik broadcasting it to everyone."

Hans "Do they think that I will be more tolerant of their drug operations?"

Easy Eddie "I have assured them that you would be easier to work with."

Hans pauses a moment, "Eddie, you were involved in this hit with Erik, weren't you?"

Easy Eddie waits a while to respond then says, "Yes, I was. Erik has to be out of the picture, if the *hui* is going to get any place out there in the valley. The people out there don't feel comfortable with Erik."

Hans shocked, "This is incredible. How were you involved?"

Easy Eddie "This is confidential, right?"

Hans "Right."

Easy Eddie "The Blackwater Holdings' lawyer paid $25,000.00 to have Erik taken out of the picture."

Hans "What? Is that right?"

Easy Eddie "That's right. That's how bad they want Erik to be out of the picture. Erik scares them. He knows too much, and he will expose them to hundreds of millions of dollars in liability. So, they felt it was easier to get rid of him."

Hans "There has to be some really bad things going out there that they are trying to hide."

Easy Eddie "Well, now you know. They want Erik gone."

Hans recovering from the revelation, "Shall we grab some lunch, Eddie?"

Easy Eddie "I'd love to, but I have to go to the bank first. Walk with me, and then we can go to lunch, if you like."

Easy Eddie comments often on the shapeliness of the young coeds parading Fort Street Mall, as Hans and he make their way to the bank.

Hans "Eddie, how did this arrangement to hit Erik go down?"

Easy Eddie just keeps commenting on the pretty things walking all around him.

Hans getting irritated with Easy Eddie evasiveness, "OK, OK, if you don't want to tell me. That's fine."

Easy Eddie "Golly look at that one!"

Easy Eddie eventually turns to look at Hans, "What were you asking me?"

Hans "The hit on Erik, how did it go down?"

Easy Eddie as they stop walking to wait for the street light to change, "The lawyer for the Blackwater Holdings wanted him out of the picture."

Hans "How do you know that guy?"

Easy Eddie "I don't. Kai Svensen got us all together."

Hans "Was Svensen involved in all this as well?"

Easy Eddie "He was the bagman. It was the Blackwater Holdings' manager and the lawyer that wanted it done. Svensen just provided the service, me."

Hans "Doesn't this bother you at all? Erik is our partner."

Easy Eddie "He's your partner not mine. And, besides, it was just business."

The light changes and Easy Eddie hurries across the street. Hans has to walk briskly to catch up.

Hans "Slow down, Eddie. What's your hurry?"

Easy Eddie "I can't take too much time off for lunch. I'm in a hurry. I'm sorry."

Hans "Should I leave you, then?"

Easy Eddie as they approach the elevator to the vault, "It's probably best, I need to get going and get back to the store."

Easy Eddie and Hans shake hands. The elevator doors open, and Easy Eddie steps into the elevator.

Hans recovering from the conversation decides to call Erik immediately. There are stanchions affixed with standup pay phones near the entrance to the bank elevators. Hans fumbles through his valise furiously to find the correct change. The phone rings a few times before Erik answers. The news shocks Erik.

Erik excited, "Are you sure Eddie said it was Blackwater Holdings' lawyer that paid to have me hit?"

Hans "I'm positive, Erik. I even asked him twice."

Erik "Don't mention to Eddie that you told me this. It is very important. What I will do is subpoena Eddie to appear for an oral deposition."

Hans "I doubt Eddie will repeat any of this at an oral deposition. Erik, Eddie would be implicating himself in conspiracy to commit murder."

Erik chuckles, "Then, I'll ask him real nice."

Hans "This is really bizarre when people try to have you murdered. Are you sure you want to pursue this?"

Erik "Oh yeah, if someone pays someone to have me killed, I want to get them for sure."

Hans "When will you subpoena Eddie?"

Erik "I have to check with our lawyer. By the way, did you meet with our lawyer today?"

Hans "Yes, I spent a few hours with him going over the proposed strategy for the lawsuit. I met Eddie on Fort Street Mall, after I had left the lawyer's office."

Erik "Let me get back to you on this, OK."

After Erik hangs up, Hans realizes that this legal fiasco will engage both the civil and the criminal courts. He envisions having to testify and be cross-examined forever.

Saturday Morning, Easy Eddie's Store

Saturdays are half days for Easy Eddie's store. This day services those clients too busy during the normal workweek to come in for supplies. Jacob and his partners split Wednesday and Saturday in order to maintain a 40-hour workweek. Hence, Wednesday and Saturday afternoons are free time for the store's staff.

This morning, Easy Eddie is able to park his car in the underground garage, come up the elevator and walk down the hallway without so much as one person saying "good morning" to him. The silence amuses him, but he enjoys the serenity of it.

As Easy Eddie enters the showroom, Jacob is all smiles. The other two partners bellow out a warm "good morning" to him. Since Easy Eddie realizes that he is at least a half an hour late, this warm welcome troubles him.

Jacob grinning ear to ear, "Eddie, did you get a chance to read the morning newspaper?"

Easy Eddie shakes his heads indicating negatively, "No, I had to drop my son off at the Chinese School."

Easy Eddie realizes that was the poorest excuse he has ever given Jacob. Easy Eddie only can see his son one weekend a month. Even then, he only takes advantage of his visitation rights a few times a year, if that often.

Jacob still smiling, "OK, I put a copy of the paper on your desk. There's an article on the front page that you might find interesting."

Easy Eddie somewhat apprehensive, "OK, I'll take a look at it."

Jacob before Easy Eddie can enter the storeroom: "There were some phone calls for you as well. One was from your detective friend. I put the messages on your desk."

Easy Eddie as he enters the storeroom, "OK, thanks."

The other two partners have not taken their eyes off Easy Eddie, since he entered the showroom. This puzzles Easy Eddie. He makes his way into the storeroom. Only stopping to place his lunch bag in the fridge, he anxiously enters his cubicle. Sure enough, there is a copy of the Saturday newspaper folded up neatly on his desk. He scans the front page. The main article comments on the carnival of characters competing in the governor's race. Suddenly, he notices the bold letters blazing across the upper portion of the front page: "EASY EDDIE IDENTIFIED AS MASTERMIND OF JEWELRY STORE ROBBERIES."

Easy Eddie's heart stops beating. The rhythm of his breath is interrupted as he gasps a huge inhale. An eternity seems to pass between each breath as his eyes follow the words of the article: "Police have obtained confessions from members of a cowboy-style robbery gang that Easy Eddie masterminded some seven jewelry store robberies." The identities of the stores that were robbed are listed. Fortunately, the jewelry repair shop in the underground garage is not among those listed. Regrettably, the funeral parlor stick up is listed in great detail. The article goes on to describe the seven robberies in some detail. Easy Eddie realizes that the information squealed in this article had to come from members of the gang. Now, he realizes why the local who was supposed to meet him last evening, after work, never showed up. He must have been arrested. As Easy Eddie reads on, the article mentions that only a small portion of the loot was recovered. Easy Eddie smiles acknowledging that the robbers held out on him and got caught with the stolen goods.

Easy Eddie slowly lays the newspaper on his desk. He looks over the phone messages. There is none from Detective Aoki. Easy Eddie feels an emptiness rise in his tummy when he sees a message from a Criminal Investigation Detective, requesting his immediate response. The message beneath the detective's message is from a criminal trial lawyer advertising his services. Easy Eddie smiles at how fast these lawyers respond to leads. From the time listed on the message, this guy must have been waiting at the drop off site for the morning paper and made the call to the store from a street pay phone.

Easy Eddie decides to make the call to the lawyer first.

As Easy Eddie suspected, the lawyer has a phone message service. He opts to emergency page the lawyer. Amazingly, Easy Eddie has no sooner rested his phone handset in its cradle, and his phone rings. It is the lawyer!

Easy Eddie "Yes sir, I'm responding to your phone message."

Lawyer "Have you made any statements to the police yet?"

Easy Eddie "No, your number was the first one that I dialed."

Lawyer "That's good. I checked into your file, and as of yet, you have not been charged with any crime. However, there is a felony charge being processed."

Easy Eddie somewhat nervous, "I haven't heard anything."

Lawyer "You won't hear anything until they come to arrest you. If you desire to employ my services, I can meet with you today and discuss my fees."

Easy Eddie "Well, I have a message here to call a detective."

Lawyer "Before you make that call, you should employ me to represent you. I, then, can make that call for you. I suspect the detective will want you to come down to the main station to answer some questions. There is a good chance he will arrest you at the main station."

Easy Eddie "When can you meet me? Or, can you explain your services over the phone?"

Lawyer "There is a contract you have to sign in order for me to represent you. Without that contract in place, I can't represent you."

Easy Eddie "OK, can you come to my store in Honolulu?"

Lawyer "Yes, I'm calling from Fort Street Mall. I can be there in five minutes."

Easy Eddie relieved, "Please, come right up."

After Easy Eddie hangs up the phone, the thought begins to form in his mind that he could actually go to prison. The idea of being incarcerated scares him. With all the shenanigans that he has pulled in his life, there are a number of inmates quivering with anticipation to get him cornered inside. Easy Eddie realizes that he cannot go to prison.

Easy Eddie hears Jacob's voice from the showroom, "Eddie, there's someone here to see you."

Easy Eddie breathes deeply and slowly. He hopes it is the attorney and not the police coming to arrest him. He utters a sigh of relief when he enters the showroom to see a tall, haole gentleman in a three-piece suit carrying a briefcase.

Easy Eddie "Are you the lawyer I just spoke with?"

Lawyer "Yes, I'm Derek Gleeson, Attorney at Law."

Lawyer presents Easy Eddie his business card.

Easy Eddie overlooks the business card, as he escorts the lawyer into his office area.

After the two have settled into Easy Eddie's office, the lawyer remarks, "Do you do quite a bit of business here?"

Easy Eddie "We used to do quite a bit. There's competition now, so our volume has diminished."

Lawyer leans forward and opens his briefcase, "OK, let's get right to this. You will be facing a felony charge that carries with it a term of up to ten years in prison. I can slow that process down and possibly frustrate the prosecution for a few years. They might just drop the case, if they see a conviction will be costly to them."

Easy Eddie "OK, it sure looks like I can use your help."

Lawyer "I don't come cheap. I will want a $10,000.00 retainer fee to be paid before I can commence any representation for you. The fee will be used to cover billable hours to keep you out of custody."

Easy Eddie exhales, "Did you say $10,000.00 retainer fee?"

Lawyer "Yes, for felony charges, $10,000.00 is a standard in the industry. The amount of work I will have to put in to file documents with the court and represent you during your interviews with the police will amount to that much. If I don't get that in advance, there is little likelihood I will be able to get any reimbursement, if you are convicted."

Easy Eddie "I don't have $10,000.00 on me. I could get it in a few days,"

Lawyer "It is actually easier than that, you just need to sign a lien on your property. That way, I can foreclose on your property, if you can't pay me. I have the form right here."

The lawyer places the lien form on Easy Eddie's desk. Easy Eddie reads over the document quickly. He thinks it over a moment.

Easy Eddie "OK, can I sign this, and you'll represent me?"

Lawyer "Yes, you just need to sign on the line indicated for your signature. I am a notary, so I can seal the document."

As Easy Eddie signs the document, the lawyer produces another document for Easy Eddie to sign. It is a duplicate of the first document, so Easy Eddie will have a copy.

After Easy Eddie has signed both documents, the lawyer says, "Do you have that phone message from the detective?"

Easy Eddie hands the message to the lawyer. The lawyer immediately phones the detective and informs him that he is representing Easy Eddie. The lawyer informs the detective that all communication henceforth must go through him.

The lawyer hangs up the phone and says, "You don't need to call the detective now. Remember, you are to make no statements unless I am present. If anyone contacts you, then you refer him or her to me. I'll take care of anything now."

Easy Eddie breathes a sign of relief, as he escorts the lawyer out of the store.

The disapproving stares of Easy Eddie's partners, as he returns to his office area, speak volumes about the headline article in the newspaper. This could mean he might lose his partnership rights. He remembers a clause in the partnership agreement that refers to bringing discredit upon the goodwill of the business. If he is convicted, the partnership will mean nothing. He will lose everything anyway. Easy Eddie realizes that he has to check that clause. If being arrested or this negative headline could be interpreted as degrading the goodwill of the business, his partners could oust him. Then, what would he do? It is not like he can just start over. He is in his late forties. If he gets ousted from this business, this headline article will scuttle his chances for another jewelry store position. Easy Eddie concludes that he cannot be convicted.

Exhaling deeply as sits in his office chair, Easy Eddie begins to read over the newspaper. In the lower right hand column, he notices another article of interest. The article mentions Albert, the crematorium operator. The front-page portion of the article is only a few paragraphs. When he turns to the sixth page, the article seems to cover the entire page. Easy Eddie reads the article with keen interest. Apparently, Albert was arrested for arranging a jewelry robbery. The article says that he hired some drug addict brother of an undercover detective to steal a five-carat diamond ring off the finger of a wealthy jeweler's wife. The robbery was bungled when the ring would not come off the woman's finger, so the drug-addict robber improvised and cut off her finger. The woman was then beaten and left to bleed to death. The drug addict was apprehended, after he gave the ring to Albert. During the arrest-search of the drug addict, the woman's finger was found in one of his coat pockets. The drug addict confessed under interrogation to the robbery, mutilation and murder when his detective brother pleaded with him to come clean. In his confession, the drug addict implicated Albert, as the person who conceived of the plan to steal the five-carat diamond ring. The drug addict told the police that Albert was going to pay him $5,000.00 for the ring. The money was going to be used to feed his heroin habit.

Easy Eddie leans back in his chair and realizes that Albert may have been the one that put the finger on him. Where would Albert go to fence the five-carat diamond ring? He would come to Easy Eddie. If Albert mentioned that to the drug addict, then the drug addict would have told his detective brother. Easy Eddie realizes that is probably the reason he has not been arrested, yet. The police have not put enough of his fencing operation together. Albert must be connected to the local goons doing the jewelry store robberies for Easy Eddie, as well. Easy Eddie begins to see how this headline article got printed. Suddenly, Easy Eddie realizes that the reason for the detective's phone message was to arrange an interview where they could trap him during an interview. Right now, at best, the police have a hearsay statement from a heroin addict and possibly statements from a motley band of locals. Since none of the remaining, local burglars ever actually met with Easy Eddie to fence anything, the police have hearsay information at best. Easy Eddie thinks he could be off the hook, as long as he remains silent. Thank God that he retained that lawyer.

A smile forms on Easy Eddie's face, and he breathes a sigh of relief.

CHAPTER 12

Monday Morning, Easy Eddie's Store

Monday mornings are always slow in the store. It has to do with the ordering cycle of the retail stores. The weekends are generally the busiest days for the retail stores. Saturday and Sunday, the retail stores' salespeople make sales and take orders. On Monday morning, the retail store managers look over the orders and draft a list of supplies that they will need to fill those orders. For the most part, Easy Eddie and his partners await the retail store managers' call to fill these orders. By noon, the orders start coming in, and they never stop coming in until Friday.

This morning, Jacob announces to Easy Eddie that he has company. Before Easy Eddie can exit his office area, Jacob has escorted a sheriff into the storeroom. Jacob points out Easy Eddie to the sheriff.

The sheriff is a tall, half-haole, Chinese guy of slender build. His business, Aloha attire gives Easy Eddie the impression that he is an insurance salesman.

Sheriff "Are you Eddie?"

Easy Eddie "Yes, I am. What's the problem?"

Easy Eddie is confused. The police would never send a sheriff to arrest him. Sheriffs serve subpoenas. Easy Eddie wonders if he has any outstanding bench warrants for illegal parking. He acquiesces that if an audit were to be done on his parking violation file, he would have the hundred or so violations that would warrant an arrest.

Sheriff hands Easy Eddie a subpoena, "Here you go this subpoena is for you."

Easy Eddie looks over the subpoena, "What's this for?"

Sheriff shrugs his shoulders, "I don't know. I don't read them. I just deliver them."

Sheriff points to a line on a service form and tells Easy Eddie to sign for receipt of the subpoena. In Honolulu, most sheriffs get paid per subpoena served. They have no set salary. Their income is derived from the serving of subpoenas. The going rate is $35.00 per subpoena.

As Easy Eddie reads over the subpoena, the sheriff makes his way out of the storeroom into the showroom. The subpoena is from Erik's lawyer. It requests Easy Eddie's presence for an oral deposition on this Wednesday. Easy Eddie is totally puzzled as to the reason for this oral deposition. He shrugs it off as a fishing expedition into his relationship with the vendors of the property.

Jacob bursts into the storeroom and disrupts Easy Eddie's reading of the subpoena, "Eddie, why was that guy here to see you?"

Easy Eddie "I've been subpoenaed for an oral deposition."

Jacob concerned, "Is this over the jewelry robberies?"

Easy Eddie "No, this has nothing to do with the article in the paper. This has to do with my land deal on the North Shore."

Jacob relieved, "OK, that's good to hear. All day Sunday, I was fending off calls about the newspaper article. How bad is this article?"

Easy Eddie "Well, I retained an attorney on Saturday. Apparently, some guys were arrested for the jewelry store robberies, and they gave the police my name. There is no truth to my involvement with these guys."

Jacob "How did they get your name?"

Easy Eddie "Well, I suppose, they saw me with some of my childhood friends that have spent time in prison. They assumed a business connection existed between us. That's all I can figure. Anyway, the lawyer will be handling it for me. As soon as I hear anything, I'll let you know."

Jacob pats Easy Eddie on the shoulder, "That's good to hear. Remember, we are all behind you here, OK."

Easy Eddie "OK, thanks. I'll keep you posted."

Before Easy Eddie can make his way back to his desk, he hears one of the partners yell that he has a phone call. Easy Eddie can only imagine who could want to speak with him now.

Easy Eddie picking up the phone in his office, "Eddie, here."

Mr. Lau "Eddie, I see you name in paper. I know bad time to call you, but I had to tell you my son, he pass real estate exam. I get you membership in Ala Wai Golf Course, OK."

Easy Eddie wonders what this guy is talking about, "Who is this again?"

Mr. Lau "Eddie, this Mr. Lau, Silver Teal Jewelry. You help my son get real estate exam. Do you remember?"

Easy Eddie "Oh yes, Mr. Lau, how are you?"

Mr. Lau "I fine, thank you. I remember you with membership, OK."

It takes a while for Easy Eddie to recall what he did for this guy, because his use of English is so broken up.

Easy Eddie finally smiles, "Thank you so much, Mr. Lau."

Mr. Lau "OK, I know you busy, Eddie. Thank you."

Easy Eddie settles back in his office chair and smiles. It is good to know that something right has happened. And, if he does not end up in prison, he will get to play golf whenever he chooses at the Ala Wai Golf Course.

Suddenly a voice startles Easy Eddie. He looks in the storeroom and sees Billy walking towards him.

Billy "I must admit, Eddie. With the latest newspaper headlines, I didn't expect to see you smiling. You're cool, brah."

Easy Eddie smiles even more, "It's good to see you, Billy. What's up?"

Billy taking a seat in Easy Eddie's office, "I was just in the neighborhood, and I thought I'd stop in on the latest celebrity."

Easy Eddie chuckles, "Well, it's not exactly the kind of notoriety I had in mind, but hey, if it sells newspapers."

Billy "So, Eddie, what's this all about in the papers?"

Easy Eddie looks at Billy a while before he speaks. Easy Eddie wonders if Billy knows already or is he just inquisitive?

Easy Eddie leans toward Billy and says, "Well, I guess there are a few too many canaries in the docks."

Billy whispers, "Are you on the spot with these guys?"

Easy Eddie whispers back, "I don't think so. I already retained a lawyer. To the best of my knowledge, it just some guys who mentioned my name. I've never dealt with any one of them, as best I can tell."

Billy nodding his head, "Since the police hadn't arrested you prior to the newspaper release, it is a sure sign they don't have enough to prosecute you."

Easy Eddie "Yes, I thought it was strange that they didn't arrest me. The newspaper article took me by surprise."

Billy "The newspaper article is meant to embarrass your store. It may curtail some of your business. I suspect the cops are sending you a message. Don't you deal with some of those cops, privately?"

The way Billy stresses the word "privately" makes Easy Eddie realize that Billy knows that he sells stolen jewelry to the cops, and the cops know the goods are stolen.

Easy Eddie just nods his head up and down.

Billy whispers, "The newspaper article is all that will happen. They may have to bring you in for show, but I bet they will just go through the motions."

Easy Eddie "The lawyer said they were preparing a felony charge against me."

Billy surprised, "Did he, now? Someone must be upset with you, Eddie. Do you think the Jewelry Association is upset with you?"

Easy Eddie thinks a moment, "They might be. Our store has not renewed our membership for a few years, and we haven't donated to their fund drive in quite a few years. That would be the only reason that they would be upset with us. But, we are a wholesaler, and the Jewelry Association in Honolulu is for retailers only. We actually do not qualify for full membership."

Billy "It's probably not them then. Someone is pushing your conviction though, if they are preparing a felony charge against you."

Easy Eddie "Let's hope I have some good friends in the police department."

Billy "Yes, they will save you more than the lawyer."

Easy Eddie changes the subject, "How did we do on the Maunakea project?"

Billy "That's the other reason I stopped by to see you. We didn't do as well as we had planned. Reflexes are what saved the guy. But, our on-scene man reported that the guy was really shaken up. We might have broken his leg. He will think twice before he hassles your clients."

Easy Eddie smiles, "That's good to hear. I'll pass that on."

Billy taps the desk lightly with his fist, "Well, that's why I came by. Hope all goes well with you. If you need some help, just call me, OK. I'll be glad to persuade someone for you."

Easy Eddie chuckles, "OK, Billy, thanks for stopping by."

As Billy leaves through the back door, Easy Eddie realizes how good of a friend Billy is. Every time Easy Eddie has been in trouble, Billy comes to his rescue. It is good that he has a friend like that. Easy Eddie cherishes the moment a while. Life is measured in true friendships.

About midmorning after Easy Eddie had finished stocking away a shipment of gift boxes from the Mainland, Detective Aoki stopped by to see him.

Detective Aoki entering the storeroom and seeing Easy Eddie sweating, "Hey there stranger, how you doing?"

Easy Eddie stops stowing boxes, "Oh, hi there, Detective, what can I do for you?"

Detective Aoki jabs Easy Eddie in the shoulder gently with his left fist and takes on a boxing stance, "What can you do for me? Now, there's a laugh. Looks like you're getting popular down at the station, Eddie."

Easy Eddie takes on a semi-boxing stance in response, "Really? How come I'm so popular all of a sudden?"

Detective Aoki shadow jabs at Easy Eddie a few more times, "It beats me, Eddie. Maybe it's all the dead bodies showing up around you lately? What do you think?"

Easy Eddie smiles, "What dead bodies?"

Both men bellow out in laughter.

Easy Eddie continues, "There's no more than usual, Detective."

Detective Aoki whispers, "I actually just stopped by to tell you not to worry about flying to the Big Island on Wednesday. With all the heat on you right now, the police will have people tailing you. We can't afford to let them in on our little business, now can we? Besides, I have enough partners already. All I would need is a crew of homicide and robbery cops to tip each month."

Easy Eddie smiling, "You're right, Detective. You don't need to make your life anymore complicated than it already is."

Detective Aoki steps back, "Eddie, I'm so glad you see it my way."

Easy Eddie just smiles and shadow jabs a few times.

Detective Aoki "By the way, what did you make of Albert preserving that Jap bitch?"

Easy Eddie shocked, "What?"

Detective Aoki surprised, "Oh, you didn't hear? Albert from the crematorium was keeping that Jap girlfriend of Kealoha's preserved."

Easy Eddie with a puzzled look on his face, "He wasn't doing her, was he?"

Detective Aoki chuckles, "Oh yeah, Eddie, that's why he was preserving her body."

Easy Eddie exclaims, "Her arms had been chopped off!"

Detective Aoki "Eddie, Albert sewed them back on. He even had a warmer pad under her crotch."

Easy Eddie puts his hand over his mouth and gasps, "He is one sick son of a bitch!"

Detective Aoki "Eddie, Homicide tells me in one of the interviews with the guy who cut the jeweler's wife's finger off that Albert was suckling one of the Japs' nipples during one of their meetings to plan the diamond ring robbery."

Easy Eddie "You know, Detective, I'm glad they will be putting that sicko away. He needs to be incarcerated."

Detective Aoki jabs Easy Eddie's shoulder once as he laughs, "Hey, maybe I can arrange to have you share a cell with Albert. You can wake up in the middle of the night to feel Albert suckling on one of your nipples...or worse!"

Easy Eddie tightening his face, "I'd kill that sicko."

Detective Aoki looking around the room, "Easy now, Eddie, there are enough bodies dropping dead around you already."

Easy Eddie takes a few moments to calm down. The thought of Albert preserving the body of Hatsue for his sick amusement seems to have driven Easy Eddie off the deep end. She deserved better than that. If Kealoha finds this out, he will be even more upset.

Detective Aoki continues, "Now, calm down, Eddie. The girl's body has been cremated. I know whose girl she was, so I made sure it was kept quiet. But, Eddie, Albert is going down. Whatever business you had with that freak, end it, right now. He's gone. You won't see Albert alive on the outside of a prison again."

Easy Eddie thanks Detective Aoki. They chit chat a bit longer on unimportant items, then Detective Aoki bids him good luck and leaves through the rear exit.

Easy Eddie gets a few free moments to ponder the chaotic condition of his life before lunchtime. Since his name made the headlines, he is leery about walking around town. Some of his usual jewelry deliveries will be tense situations, as those were some of the stores identified in the newspaper that he allegedly masterminded the robberies. He has to make those deliveries; otherwise, the owners will condemn him. He has to show up, if for anything, to exhibit his innocence. That is the right approach, he thinks. He has to remain calm under pressure. It is a small price to pay for the loot he took from the jewelers.

He decides to stay in the store for lunch. A few pieces of apple pie are leftover in the fridge from last Friday. Cold apple juice and apple pie will sate him just nicely. As he munches away on a generous piece of apple pie, he reflects on how his life has turned out. He wonders how different it would have been if he had stayed in the Navy. He entered the Navy through the reserve program, meaning he only had to serve two years. Fortunately, the local reserve center assigned him to duty in Hawai'i. For two years, he wandered about the docks at Pearl Harbor Naval Station. As a seaman, his daily routine was limited to sweeping piers and swabbing the decks of buildings. He never served aboard a naval vessel. Perhaps, if he had done so, he might have looked more favorably upon a career in the military.

In comparison, here he is now at forty-seven, a partner in a wholesale jewelry store waiting for retirement from social security at age 62. If he had taken to military service, he would have retired at age thirty-nine and free to choose whatever line of work suited him.

Military service allows retirement after twenty years of service. Since Easy Eddie entered the reserve program at age nineteen, he could have retired twenty years later at age thirty-nine with full medical benefits.

The thought of retiring so early disparages Easy Eddie. However, when he realizes that he would have to endure a number of long deployments at sea and away from Honolulu during those twenty years of service, the line of work he eventually chose does not seem so meaningless. At least in his line of work, he got to see the land of his birth almost every single day. He kept up with his childhood friends. Had he left for the military service, he would have missed large portions of the lives of his friends. That would be hard to imagine. Leaving one day while life as usual goes on in Honolulu, then returning three years later to catch up on what he missed. Easy Eddie recalls how others who did make the military choice coped with the absence.

In particular, he remembers a soldier who got stationed in Germany for three years. It was at a Christmas party that Easy Eddie remembers how when the soldier asked what happened while he was away, the soldier's friends could only come up with three things for the entire three years of the soldier's absence. Easy Eddie recalls one of those three things was a movie. The other two things did not even happen to any of the friends.

Smiling to himself, Easy Eddie knows that more than three things of note happened in his life, and to him, over the past few weeks. But, it is so true that we take life so much for granted that we stop living it. Our time is precious. We have to live every minute of it, because a time comes when it is over. Easy Eddie pities those friends of the soldier that only have three things of note to remember over a three years period. Easy Eddie concludes that military service is too big a price to pay for early retirement.

Swigging the remaining droplets of the apple juice from its aluminum container, Easy Eddie is content with his life of excitement. That slice of apple pie was enough to carry him through the rest of the day. It seems strange to him, but this lunchtime spent in reflection was far more enjoyable that all those he spent with company in the restaurants. He needs to do more of these. It is time to go back to work.

Wednesday Afternoon, Deposition Room, Old Territorial Building

The lawyer has the floor boardroom reserved for a series of depositions concerning the subdivision status of the *hui*'s lot. The boardroom essentially is an office that all renters on the floor share. The usual entrance vestibule has been left open in the boardroom to give the appearance of a huge, open area. The board table in the center of the room seats twelve comfortably. There are plenty of electrical outlets conveniently located to source any form of electrical equipment. A pull-down, projection screen is mounted against the far wall of the room.

Starting at 10:00 AM going straight through to 3:00 PM, the vendors' and their agents, adjoining landowners, and selected bureaucrats were cycled through the depositions. Most sessions were only thirty minutes in duration. The lawyer merely intended to get a feel for the opposition.

Conveniently, last on the deposition list was Easy Eddie. When Easy Eddie enters the room, the lawyer introduces himself, Erik and the deposition recorder. After swearing in Easy Eddie, the lawyer excuses himself and turns the deposition over to Erik. The lawyer explains that Easy Eddie might feel more comfortable answering the upcoming line of questioning, if the lawyer were not in the room. Easy Eddie graciously agrees.

Erik "Eddie, do you know why we asked you to come in for this deposition?"

Easy Eddie "No, I just figured it had to do with my involvement with the *hui*'s formation and my knowledge of the valley."

Erik "Actually, Eddie, our reason for calling you to testify has little to do with that. I wanted you here to discuss your relationship with Kai Svensen, the Blackwater Holdings' manager and their attorney."

Easy Eddie still calm, "I have met them. As you know, Kai Svensen is the principal broker for Svensen Real Estate Company, so I have met him more often."

Erik smiles, "I understand you met with all three of them recently."

Easy Eddie "I may have. They have some lots they want to sell that are located around Kamehameha Coast Highway."

Erik leans forward, "No, I mean even more recent than that. I mean like in the last two weeks in which a sum of money in cash was transferred to your care."

Easy Eddie feels his jaw tighten, "What do you mean?"

Erik "I think you know exactly what I mean, Eddie. I believe, you might say, it is the reason my ankle is in a cast."

Easy Eddie leans back, exhales and smiles, "Hey, Erik, I can't talk about that. I have a reputation to uphold."

Erik "Eddie, the vendors tried to kill me. Doesn't that bother you?"

Easy Eddie "Erik, it wasn't personal. It was just business. Besides, you're alive."

Erik sternly, "Eddie, did you accept money to have me killed?"

Easy Eddie laughs aloud, "You don't actually expect me to answer that, do you?"

Erik "Tell me, Eddie, how much money was it?"

Easy Eddie "Erik, I have a reputation to uphold. I can't be divulging private affairs like this. You have to understand that."

Erik "Do you admit to meeting Kai Svensen, the Blackwater Holdings' manager and their attorney in the last two weeks?"

Easy Eddie thinks over the response a few minutes then says, "Yes, I met them."

Erik "Did they give you any money?"

Easy Eddie "Yes."

Erik "What was the purpose of the money?"

Easy Eddie "Like I said, Erik, I have a reputation to uphold. I refuse to answer that question or any other questions at this meeting."

Erik signals to the deposition recorder to stop typing. From the look on the deposition recorder's face, he wants to get out of that room, immediately.

Erik to Easy Eddie, "OK, Eddie, I stopped the recorder. This is off the record, now. Did Kai Svensen hire you to have me killed?"

Easy Eddie "Like I told you, Erik, I have a reputation to uphold."

Erik "Eddie, there are guys out there trying to kill me. Can you understand why I am asking you these questions?"

Easy Eddie leans forward, "OK, Erik, for the *hui*, yes, certain people want you to go away. They don't really want to kill you. They just want you to back off."

Erik "They tried to run me over on Maunakea Street, Eddie."

Easy Eddie smiles, "They didn't though, now, did they?"

Erik exhales, "It was only through the grace of God that I am alive."

Easy Eddie "Well, maybe you should be thanking God for His mercy."

The deposition recorder has heard enough and says, "Are we finished here?"

Erik looks at the deposition recorder, "Yes, we are finished."

Easy Eddie just gets up and walks out of the boardroom.

The deposition recorder says to Erik as he is packing up his transcriber, "There is a lot more going on here than just a land dispute, isn't there?"

Erik nods his head up and down, "You bet there is."

Lawyer's Office

After the deposition recorder leaves, Erik assembles all the notes taken during the depositions and makes his way toward the lawyer's office down the hall. He has to curl his arms around the stacks of notes.

Entering the lawyer's office, Erik hears the lawyer ask how things went.

Erik "He said 'he had a reputation to protect.' But, he did confirm that he met with Kai Svensen, and that Kai Svensen gave him money."

Lawyer "When your associate responded that 'He had a reputation to protect' was the deposition recorder typing it down?"

Erik "His name is Eddie."

Lawyer nods, "Eddie is his name, OK."

Erik "Yes, I got at least one of those statements on the record."

Lawyer "That's real good. I can get the attorney general involved in this now. Did you get the impression that he, in fact, was hired to have you killed?"

Erik "From his mannerism and responses off the record, there was no question in my mind that he was hired to have me killed. I believe the deposition recorder would agree."

Lawyer "Was the deposition recorder in the room the whole time?"

Erik "Yes, he was present for all of it. He was there for Eddie's statement that there were people that wanted me out of the way."

Lawyer "Did Eddie say that in the presence of the deposition recorder?"

Erik "It was off the record, but, yes, Eddie said that."

Lawyer "And, did the deposition recorder hear that statement?"

Erik "I'm certain that he did, because he commented to me, after Eddie left, to the effect that there was more going on here than a land dispute."

Lawyer leans quickly forward seemingly licking his lips like a hungry wolf, "This is dynamite!"

Erik "I don't have that statement on the record."

Lawyer "Erik, you have a court certified witness in the room who overheard it. That's as good as it gets. You have a guy essentially admitting to conspiracy to commit murder for hire. This is a hell of a case."

Erik smiling at the lawyer's sudden exuberance over the case, "I thought it was a great case all along."

The lawyer regaining his composure leans back in his chair, "So did I, but now, it seems so exciting."

Erik "Let me change the subject. How did the other depositions look?"

Lawyer begins going through each person deposed, making comments on their testimony. In summary, he concludes that most of the people in the valley are aware of the subdivision problems and the requirements for access. Most of them, however, trust in the Mormon Church to make good on the access requirements. The lawyer relates that the other property owners in the valley recall a forty-four-foot road reserved in the deed to the fifty-acre parcel that will connect to the railroad right of way to provide the needed access to the Kamehameha Coast Highway.

Erik interjects, "Aren't they aware that Blackwater Holdings allowed that proposed, forty-four-foot roadway to be removed from the deed of the fifty-acres in one of their most recent negotiations?"

Lawyer "I didn't inform them of that. That's a revelation that can wait for trial, so I can show how underhanded the agents for Blackwater Holdings have been in their dealings."

Erik "What about the drugs?"

Lawyer "Few of those deposed were willing to venture into that discussion. Apparently, there is a reason for fear in divulging anything about the drug trade in the valley."

Erik "OK, I can appreciate that. What about our access to the 99-acre lot? Did you get anything from the vendors when you deposed them?"

Lawyer "The vendors seem convinced that the sixteen-foot driveway that they proposed will suffice. I tried to inform them that sixteen-foot driveways could only be granted when they connect to a City & County approved street. I even pointed out to them that neither the railroad right of way nor the Green Valley road was an approved City & Country street. What's more, I even mentioned that the ¾ mile distance between the only approved City & Country street, Kamehameha Coast Highway, and the 99-acre lot requires a forty-four-foot access road, since it far exceeds the 350-foot maximum distance from a City & County street for driveways. And, despite all that, two real estate brokers, who also happen to be land developers, were unmoved by my mention of the regulations for access, driveways and subdivisions. Erik, I would have to suspect that they are relying on political connections to outmaneuver us in court. They are obviously in error. They are too accomplished to think otherwise."

Erik "Well, we know they are connected well politically. They make their large, campaign donations to the Democratic Party."

Lawyer "They seem too unmoved by their ridiculous position. It is a basic state law in the Hawai'i Revised Statutes that all property must have suitable access. There are no exceptions. And, here in Punaluu Valley, we are confronted with a myriad of improperly accessed lots of record. All these lots were subdivided improperly by Svensen Real Estate Company on behalf of Blackwater Holdings. Their position is untenable. Yet, they sit boldface when confronted with the law."

Erik "Do you think they have the judges bought?"

Lawyer "This would be too difficult a case in which to buy a decision. Even if they got passed the state circuit civil court on some nonsense, the state supreme or appellate court would have to review the matter. The state of Hawai'i would be humiliated if either one of those higher courts went along with this Punaluu Valley nonsense. Cases would pile up claiming precedence for similar adventures in lunacy."

Erik "We have them tied up then, I take it?"

Lawyer "Erik, to the best of my knowledge from my twenty years of experience in real property law, I would say that we do. So, that leaves them with procedure and coming after you. This murder attempt will look bad on them when it gets out. It will show their desperation. I'd be careful, if I were you from here on out. More so, now, that you have deposed Eddie."

Erik "I sure will be careful."

Lawyer "On another matter, I subpoenaed a real estate law expert from the Law School up at the university to testify on our behalf. I interviewed him earlier this week. He is quite knowledgeable in these subdivision affairs. In his legal opinion, the *hui*'s property was never legally subdivided in the history of the property."

Erik surprised, "What about the engineering surveys on the property? They seem pretty official to me. I thought our problem was the access not being adequate."

Lawyer "That's what I thought as well. To me, this was simply a matter of pointing out how the proposed access was inadequate to comply with City & County regulations. That is not the case, according to this expert. He says that the engineering surveys are flawed. Whoever did those surveys did not know what they were doing."

Erik grimaces, "The engineering surveys were done by one of the most respected civil engineering firm in the state. Ask anyone down at the Lands Department, they will attest to that firm's credentials."

Lawyer leaning closer to Erik, "Erik, the people down at the Lands Department say those things about that firm, because that firm makes large political, campaign contributions to the Democratic Party in the state. In return, the City & County awards them many contracts. It is not that they are competent in their work that gets them all their notoriety; it is that they are politically connected. In this case, the expert says they screwed up real bad."

The lawyer removes a small, tax key map of the area and lays it on his desk in plain view of both Erik and him.

Lawyer pointing to the map, "The expert points out three trouble areas in the engineering survey: First, there is the point."

The lawyer uses his pencil to direct Erik's attention to the point on the map. Truly, a huge parcel forms a triangle on the map with the sides culminating in a single point.

Lawyer "This point, according to the engineering firm, forms a distinct boundary with this other semi-rectangular-shaped lot. According to the expert, a single, apex point like this cannot form a boundary in the middle of another lot's side boundary. It would be OK at the two ends of a side boundary but not somewhere along the side boundary in between the two ends. Just look over the entire plat map. You won't see any other similar instance."

Erik peruses the small tax map until the lawyer interrupts him by overlaying a larger, plat map over the smaller, tax key map. Erik takes some time looking over the plat map.

Erik "OK, I can see where this triangular point is an anomaly."

Lawyer as removes the plat map, "That's one. Second, the expert states that the northern boundary of the *hui*'s property, the man-made ditch, is not an approved land boundary, since the ditch can be moved. According to the expert, it is a common rule in surveying that non-permanent items cannot serve as boundaries."

Punaluu is on the North coast of O'ahu. Hence, the 99-acre lot's lower boundary would face north. The top of Koolau Mountain Range would face South.

The lawyer traces how the northern boundary of the property runs exactly along the course of the man-made ditch. The lawyer points out other properties in the valley that straddle the ditch. He also points out that only those properties sold as individual lots by Svensen Real Estate Company on behalf of Blackwater Holdings have the ditch as a boundary.

Erik "Wouldn't the engineering firm have known that this was an improper boundary?"

Lawyer "That response is precisely the expert's point. He says that the only way this could have passed scrutiny is by political interference. This is too common of an error. The expert believes that the engineering firm made these surveys according to the direction of the landowners. The expert even bets that when the surveys were done, there was no mention of any subdivision of the property to the engineering firm. The surveys were done for the sole purpose of establishing tracks of land for some specific farming need. These surveys were never intended for anything else."

Erik "How did they get registered in the tax office as individual lots?"

Lawyer "The expert believes the lots were registered, unbeknownst to the engineering firm, in return for political campaign contributions. Given the corrupt nature of the Democratic Party to interfere with everything in return for campaign donations, the expert bets that is how the *hui*'s lot and other lots were created."

Erik nodding his head up and down, "This was deceit all the way, wasn't it?"

Lawyer "Yes, it was. We are dealing with some terribly, unethical individuals. They use people as they need then set them up."

Erik "You mentioned a third reason."

Lawyer "Yes, the expert says that the lack of access in the valley is a result of this deception in creating the land boundaries."

Erik "Well, this makes sense now."

Lawyer "It sure does make sense. Erik, we are dealing with crooks."

Erik asks to see the plat map again. The lawyer places the plat map over the desk.

A few moments pass and Erik says, "I bet these improperly subdivided lots were created when Kahuku Sugar Company began to retract their operations from the pressure of increased land taxes."

Lawyer "That is entirely possible."

Erik pointing toward the plat map, "Notice how the lots in question for the most part have their northern most boundary as the ditch."

Erik traces with his pen the entire length of the ditch from where it emerges from Punaluu Stream to where it wanders off into the western most *apuaha*.

Lawyer following Erik's pen, "Yes, you are right. That could mean that the ditch selection originally was predicated on the intended agricultural use of the property. The lands below the ditch were kept in cultivation; whereas, the upper ditch lands were not cultivated."

Erik "That's it! The difference in land use determined the tax rate of the land. The original use of the ditch was for tax purposes only. That is why the original metes and bounds of these lots were recorded at the tax office."

Lawyer "Yes, I believe you are right, Erik."

Erik pointing with his pen to some of the smaller lots, "These smaller lots must have been created by Kai Svensen via the campaign donation method in return for subdivision grants. These four smaller lots must have been one solid lot at one time. Kai Svensen subdivided it into four lots and sold the lots to members of the Mormon Church."

Lawyer "I recall the date of those sales. I thought it coincided well with the sale of the lower fifty-acre parcel in which Blackwater Holdings insisted on the buyer creating a forty-four-foot road that would connect these four, smaller lots to Kamehameha Coast Highway."

Erik "Yes, I remember that road construction as a condition of sale in the deed of the fifty-acre lot, as well."

Lawyer quickly sits up straight, "We can use this against the vendors, since they sold the fifty-acre lot as well. The fact that they insisted that a forty-four-foot roadway be created through fifty-acre lot, then they must have acknowledged the requirement for access suitable to City & County standards for the interior, four, smaller lots."

Erik tapping his pen on the plat map, "You are right. They must have known about the requirements for access."

Lawyer "Yes, at that early point in their grandiose plan to sell off the valley into small lots, they knew the valley had access problems. They knew it!"

Erik grimacing, "Those dirty buggers! They knew it all along."

Lawyer "Yes, they knew it. They surely did know it. This is incredible. To avoid responsibility for the access, they found some Mainland pigeons to buy the fifty-acre lot and made it a condition of sale for those people to create the road. Then, the vendors sold the remaining lots in the valley with the promise of a forty-four-foot access road connecting to the railroad right of way. If the Mainland pigeons failed, then the vendors could point to the Mainland pigeons as the guilty parties. All the liability would fall on the breach of contractual obligation by the Mainland pigeons. This is a sweet, yet deceptive deal."

Erik "Wouldn't the interior, smaller lot buyers still have recourse against the vendors?"

Lawyer "Erik, my boy, that is where the large, political campaign contributions come into play. They buy their amnesty and immunity from the courts with campaign donations. That is why that they were so cocky when I deposed them."

Erik "Can the courts turn their back on something this screwed up? There must be twenty people wronged by the vendors."

Lawyer "That is the beauty of it. The vendors have implicated the institutions that oversee shenanigans like these. And, most of the buyers are Mormons, so they will trust in the Church to insists that Blackwater Holdings make things right."

Erik leaning back in his chair and exhales, "I see your point. The land use agencies of the City & County and state are implicated in wrongful oversight in the creation of all these illegal lots."

Lawyer "That is right! If the court decides against the vendors, the vendors have claims against the City & County and state for approving these lots in the first place. What is more, such a decision would embarrass the Democratic Party by pointing out their gross ineptitude in land management and oversight."

Erik "So, in a sense, we are right, but no one will listen to us. Is that what you are saying?"

Lawyer "That's my conclusion. The valley has been so screwed up that all the guilty parties will band together to maintain the image of the Democratic Party."

There is a short pause as both men think over the implications.

Lawyer leans closer to Erik, "What's more is that all the sitting judges were appointed by the Democratic Party. Now, off the record, generally, the type of lawyer that gets appointed to be a judge is one that is not very successful as a lawyer. The pay is not that good as a judge, but it beats a poor legal practice, if you know what I mean? Consequently, it is unlikely for one of these state judges to give a decision that would be contrary to the wishes of the Democratic Party. This mess in Punaluu Valley is one of those 'silver bullets' they talk about that clears away all obstructions."

Erik chuckles "In other words, they are so screwed up, the judge can't decide against them. Is that it?"

Lawyer nodding in acknowledgment and leans back in his chair, "It's something like that, yes."

Erik "Is there any other place we can go if the courts stall us?"

Lawyer "Well, if we get caught up on a technicality in the courts, we can appeal to the Zoning Board. Although, in reality, the Zoning Board would be our best venue to overcome a court technicality, the members of the Board are volunteers, mostly hand-picked by the Democratic Party. Hence, the same problem we encounter with the judges repeats itself with the Zoning Board."

Erik "The vendors essentially have us in a box with their faithful lined up on all sides, is that it?"

Lawyer "Well, with the Zoning Board, there are five members; although, only three need attend a hearing. Chances of a successful plea with the Zoning Board are a little better than with a lone, state civil court judge. Since the Zoning Board consists of volunteers, they are not as indebted to the Democratic Party as the judges. We could fare better with the Zoning Board."

Erik "How would we be directed to the Zoning Board?"

Lawyer "If in the opinion of the civil court judge there is a sense that we have not exhausted the administrative remedies, then he can direct us to the Zoning Board for a recommendation. You see in our case, we are claiming an improper subdivision. Since subdivisions come under the jurisdiction of the Zoning Board, the civil court judge could direct us to seek their opinion on the matter. In which case, we basically present our argument to the Zoning Board who, in turn, makes a decision as to the subdivision status of the *hui*'s property. If the Zoning Board sides with our position, we, then, take that decision back to the civil court for a legal decision."

Erik "That sounds fantastic! Why haven't we done that already?"

Lawyer "Erik, when I said the Zoning Board was made up of volunteers, I meant volunteers from all walks of life. Of the five board members, one may be a realtor or a lawyer, the rest are common bureaucrats or business people looking to make points for their resume of community service. We wouldn't be explaining our position to people versed in real estate law. The hardest thing to accept would be a decision against us from the Zoning Board in which the only knowledgeable member voted in our favor. That could happen."

Erik "I see your point. If the majority of the members of the Zoning board were birds of a feather with the vendors, we could be up against a stacked deck."

Lawyer "Well, it would be no more stacked against us than the courts."

Erik "Do you think we should go to the Zoning Board?"

Lawyer "If we have to go to them, then we have to go. But, I am of the opinion that it would be a waste of time."

Erik "It sure seems like a short cut to me."

Lawyer "Another issue comes to mind. Now, that you have mentioned a 'short cut.' Another pitfall, given the strength of our case, is that the civil court and the Zoning Board could play ping pong with us."

Erik "Ping pong?"

Lawyer "Yes, the civil court can send us to the Zoning Board to avoid making a decision against the Democratic Party. When we get to the Zoning Board, they can likewise send us back to the civil court, because they feel the 'obvious' decision goes against the Democratic Party, as well. It's a way for the Democratic Party to keep us in limbo forever. By citing case law, both the civil court and the Zoning Board can frustrate us by endlessly cycling us back and forth between them."

Erik "Have they ever done that?"

Lawyer "Yes, they have. One group with a similar subdivision problem as ours presented their case to the Zoning Board, after being referred to them by the circuit civil court. The Zoning Board took testimony for over a month on the matter. During the entire session, only four members were present. The absent member was the girlfriend of the mayor's son and was off on vacation in Europe.

Two of the members were bureaucrats with the administration of the state. The other two members were a lawyer and a real estate broker. Now, upon conclusion of the hearing, the lawyer and the real estate broker voted for the party claiming lack of subdivision like our case. The other two members refused to vote 'for' or 'against.' Instead, they voted to refer the case back to the circuit civil court. So, the party claiming lack of subdivision had a 2-0 vote in their favor. Since a Zoning Board decision requires three votes, they received no decision for the Zoning Board."

Erik "Can they do that?"

Lawyer "Technically, they can; however, it is in bad faith to allow the pleadings to go on for over a month and then decide to refer them to another authority. It was an obvious 'ping pong' game that the Democratic Party was playing to avoid responsibility for the lack of subdivision."

Erik "Aren't there criminal sanctions against this kind of behavior?"

Lawyer "There certainly are; however, once again, who will enforce them? The grieving party will have to seek redress with the same Democratic Party, so the redress effort will encounter similar resistances. The Democratic Party has established itself above the law in the state of Hawai'i."

Erik "What about redress to the US Supreme Court?"

Lawyer "You will get a fair hearing there, usually. In this case, however, the state of Hawai'i has a powerful senator in Congress. He is quite adept at political interference. If he deems our case to be detrimental to the Democratic Party and the image of the state of Hawai'i, he can interfere with the judicial process in return for a favor. That's how his 'low key' managerial style works. He's a compromiser."

Erik surprised as the reality of the situation sinks in, "WOW, we could be screwed all the way."

Lawyer "Well, remember, my job, as the *hui*'s attorney, is to point out all the pitfalls, Erik. On the bright side is the fact that this valley has been so screwed up that sooner or later the Democratic Party will have to face the sad music of cleaning it all up. Right now, they have the vendors, the title company and Blackwater Holdings on the hook for it. I find it unlikely that they would let them slip away and dump this mess on the taxpayers at a later date."

Erik smiles, "You're right! They would never allow this mess to become a burden on the taxpayer. If they did, it would doom their political leadership of the state."

Lawyer smiles "Now, that is something they would fight hard to retain."

Chapter 13

Easy Eddie's Store

One of the partners hurries into the storeroom to get Easy Eddie. Easy Eddie has been demonstrating the operation of a centrifugal molding device to a professional caster. The device spins around with a mold of a desired item attached to its furthest extension. Molten silver or gold is fed into a center crucible where it is directed by centrifugal force via metal tubing to the mold attached to the outer extension.

Partner "Eddie, your friend, the detective, is here to see you. He says that it is very important. I'll take over here for you."

Easy Eddie takes off his protective eye goggles and says to his partner, "OK, the centrifuge just has a few more minutes left on rotation, before you can shut down the machine, open the mold and inspect the item."

Partner, donning the eye protection, relieves Easy Eddie.

Easy Eddie somewhat surprised by the interruption. For Detective Aoki to barge in like this means that there is some serious trouble brewing.

Easy Eddie as he enters the showroom, "Yes sir, Detective, what can I do for you?"

Detective Aoki lowers his eyes and walks to the edge of the showroom away from eavesdroppers, "Eddie, I need to talk to you in private."

Easy Eddie checks the showroom and realizes that there is no place to talk. His partner is exhibiting in the storeroom near his office area, so that location is unavailable as well.

Easy Eddie after some thought, "We can talk in the stairwell of the fire escape."

Easy Eddie motions Detective Aoki to follow him, as he exits the showroom and walks down the hallway to the far, fire escape door. Once inside the stairwell

Easy Eddie checks for anyone lingering around on the floor above and the floor below.

Easy Eddie breathing heavily from the quick stair climbing, "OK, what is it?"

Detective Aoki "Are you sure it is safe to talk here?"

Easy Eddie "Yes, it is safe, if we speak softly."

Detective Aoki leaning close to Easy Eddie, "Eddie, I just overhead some homicide detectives discussing a contract murder case, and your name came up as the facilitator. Tell me there's nothing to this?"

Easy Eddie pauses a moment, "News sure seems to travel quickly, doesn't it?"

Detective Aoki exhales, "Are you involved in a contract murder, Eddie?"

Easy Eddie nods his head up and down, "Yes, I arranged for some haole to get hit, but they only broke his ankle."

Detective Aoki "Eddie, that could mean a twenty-year rap, if they convict you. This jewelry robbery nonsense will be minor compared to the pressure they will put on you for a contract murder. They take contract murder seriously, Eddie. That's no small price."

Easy Eddie breathing rapidly, "Are they going to arrest me?"

Detective Aoki "No, I just overheard them discussing the case. The policeman that evaluated the crime scene is doing a good job discouraging the homicide detectives. He says the haole is a crackpot. Tell me, Eddie, this policeman, was he involved as well?"

Easy Eddie "Yes, I think so. He's a friend of Edward's."

Detective Aoki "Is this the Edward that runs with Billy?"

Easy Eddie "Yes."

Detective Aoki "OK, if the policeman can hold his story, you should be in the clear then."

Easy Eddie breathes a sigh of relief, "That's good."

Detective Aoki "There is another item I wanted to tip you off about. Your lawyer is requesting a polygraph to determine your innocence in the jewelry robberies. He has got the robbery detectives to agree to drop the charges being processed against you, if you pass the polygraph. Do you think you can pass the polygraph?"

Easy Eddie "I don't know. Can you beat those things?"

Detective Aoki "The hush-hush word is to never take a polygraph if you are lying, because those things are really accurate."

Easy Eddie "Is that right, because I read all the time how inaccurate those things are?"

Detective Aoki "What you read are the pleas of defense counsels pointing the ability of individuals who have spent years mastering their body to defeat the polygraph machine. Without specific, long-term training, no one beats a polygraph."

Easy Eddie shaking his head, "That's terrible news. My lawyer never talked to me about any of this."

Detective Aoki "Eddie, he thinks you are innocent. Did you confess to him that you were involved in the jewelry robberies?"

Easy Eddie laughs, "No, I told him I never met those guys."

Detective Aoki "See what I mean, he believes you. The polygraph is the best way out for you though. Unfortunately, it is unlikely that you will be able to pass it, but you will have to take it. If you balk now, it will indicate your guilt. The robbery detectives will arrest you for sure, if you balk on the polygraph."

Easy Eddie "If I take the polygraph, I will fail and be arrested anyway."

Detective Aoki "That's not necessarily true. You won't be taking the polygraph to declare your innocence; you'll be taking it to disprove your involvement. The probably result will be 'inconclusive.' See, truth is determined by a score above five. If you fail to score above five, the results will be recorded as 'inconclusive.' It won't say that you are lying. Your lawyer is making a smart move here."

Easy Eddie "I have to take the polygraph then, I take it?"

Detective Aoki "Yes, if your lawyer sets it up, you have to take it. Eddie, I know this sounds strange, but you should have told your lawyer that you were guilty. That way, he would never have moved for a polygraph to clear you."

Easy Eddie smiles, "I could never tell a stranger I was guilty."

Detective Aoki reacting to the sound of the stairwell door opening on the floor above, "Keep that thought, Eddie."

Both men remain quiet. Two gals on the floor above are taking a smoke break in the stairwell. The men decided to end their conversation and return to the store.

Detective Aoki as they walk down the hallway, "Eddie, collect up all our guns. I don't want anything popping up to implicate the department in your misfortunes."

Easy Eddie "OK, I'll have them all together by the end of the week."

Detective Aoki "Do it faster if you can. We need to circle our wagons until this heat cools off. We won't be making any Big Island runs either for a while. Call me as soon as you get the guns together. I'll come over and pick them up. I need to get them back into the evidence locker."

Easy Eddie thanks Detective Aoki for the heads up and assures him that all will be in order as soon as possible this week. Easy Eddie returns to the store while Detective Aoki takes the elevator out of the building.

Easy Eddie makes his way directly to the storeroom to see how his partner is doing with the demonstration of the centrifugal molding device. As he enters the storeroom, he witnesses the partner finishing writing up a sales slip for a purchase of the device by the customer. A sense of satisfaction overcomes Easy Eddie. It is a wonderful feeling to sell a new-line, big sticker item in the store. As this customer uses the device, he will tell others and soon the store will be processing many orders for these items. That is the ticket to success for Easy Eddie's store.

Easy Eddie pats the partner on the back, as he passes en route to his office area. There is a momentary exchange of smiles between the two partners.

Remembering Detective Aoki's request about the guns, Easy Eddie realizes that he will need to make a run down to River Street to see Billy. On his way, he also needs to stop in on Kai Svensen. For some reason, he has not been able to reach Kai Svensen on the phone since the hit went down. Looking at the wall clock, Easy Eddie sees that it is close enough to lunchtime for him to step out. Jacob should have no reason to complain, as one of the partners and he just sold a big sticker item.

Easy Eddie slips out the rear door and decides to see Billy first. He can check on Svensen Real Estate Company on the way to the vault, if Billy has the guns readily available.

The walk down Pauahi Street to River Street is peaceful. Easy Eddie extends a half smile to the streetwalkers, hustling to feed their drug habits. During the daytime, Pauahi Street turns into a runway for these creatures, since the police seldom patrol the area. It is as if there is an unwritten agreement between the police and the pimps that Pauahi Street is reserved for prostitution during the workday. Few people use Pauahi Street anyway. It merely acts as a conduit between Fort Street Mall and the Honolulu Canal Area next to River Street. In the early days of the 20th Century, it was popular with the folks who ran most of the commercial enterprises in Honolulu. However, since World War II when servicemen overran the lower River Street brothels, Pauahi Street has lost its former charm.

In between cars parked in the mountainside Pauahi Street parking lot, Easy Eddie can see a few teenage prostitutes bobbing their head in the service of their clients. He shakes his head in disgust, as he realizes how much these young girls needed to stay in school. Some Moke, probably one of his associates even, persuaded the teenager with drugs to leave her classmates for empty promises. In the end, she ends up a sex toy on Pauahi Street during the daytime and in Waikiki or, worse, Maunakea Street at night. It is such a disgusting life, as derelict scumbags prey on the youth of Hawai'i. Easy Eddie thinks if only the police and politicians were not so corrupt they could put an end to all this. As he turns onto River Street, he concludes that the world needs a fresh supply of prostitutes anyway.

The usual street ruffians greet Easy Eddie, as he approaches the pool hall. In the space between the pool hall and the Vietnamese clothing store next door, he glimpses one of the street urchins sexually violating what appears to be an elementary school girl.

One of the street ruffians smiling, "Hey brah, do you want some of that? We can fix you right up, brah. This little gal, she can suck a banana out its peel."

Easy Eddie just shakes his head to indicate "no" and walks into the pool hall. As he enters, Billy is quick to greet him.

Billy "Hey stranger, how's it?"

Easy Eddie looks around the room, "Can we talk privately?"

Billy sensing the urgency, "Sure, come back here with me."

Billy stops short of entering the back alley. He and Easy Eddie take positions in the rear of the pool hall.

Billy "What's up?"

Easy Eddie "I have to get the guns I brought for you guys back. There is too much heat coming down, and my good friends are getting nervous."

Billy "OK, we never had to use them. I'll bring them to your store after-hours today. Is that OK?"

Easy Eddie "OK, I'll wait for you tonight, after the store closes."

Billy "How does 6:00 PM sound?"

Easy Eddie "Try to come a little before 6:00 PM. They security guy locks the front door at 6:00 PM sharp now."

Billy "I'll be there with all four guns at 5:30 PM, how does that sound?"

Easy Eddie "That sounds great."

As Easy Eddie is about to leave, the street urchin from the alley is bringing the little schoolgirl into the pool hall. Easy Eddie can tell she does not appreciate the urchin ordering her around.

Easy Eddie turns to Billy, "Do you know this goon with the young girl?"

Billy shakes his head, "I know him somewhat. He just got out of the slammer. Spider has got him running some girls for us."

Easy Eddie "Isn't that girl with him a little young?"

Billy "Hey, Eddie, some clients want them that young."

Easy Eddie "Billy, the police will come down hard on you for having girls that young."

Billy "Are you kidding, Eddie, Edward got her from a police holding area. She's a runaway."

Easy Eddie "Billy, I tell you, girls that young will be big trouble for you."

Billy patting Easy Eddie on the shoulder, "Eddie, we just have to pay the cops a little more money to look the other way. The cops are cool. They know we need to service a variety of customers. Besides, I give them free samples."

Easy Eddie exhales, "OK, OK, you know your business better than I do. I just hate to see girls that young get involved in this business."

Billy "That's what I like about you, Eddie. You have a conscience. The world needs people like you to save it. Think of it this way, Eddie, whatever the charges I would receive for running young girls, they would be far less than those I would get in my main line of business, murder. Eddie, running young girls is a small price."

Easy Eddie laughs and shakes his head, "I see your point, Billy."

As Easy Eddie walks out of the establishment, he can hear the street urchin hawking the young girl's talents to the deviates in the pool hall. Easy Eddie just looks forward and exits the establishment. Just as he walks out the door, he notices for the first time a sign on the lower section of the pool hall's front, glass wall. It reads, "The House of the Rising Sun."

Easy Eddie mumbles to himself, "Amen!"

The walk up King Street to the Svensen Real Estate Company office is pleasant. Honolulu is such a peaceful city in the daytime. Tourists prowl the Chinatown markets for bargains, as open-air shopkeepers taut their wares. Even the fish market is bustling with Mainland tourists today.

Easy Eddie shakes his head in disbelief as his nostrils revolt to the smell of stinky fish. It is beyond Easy Eddie's comprehension why someone from Nebraska would get excited over pallet after pallet of freshly caught tuna carcasses. The very scent of fresh fish repels Easy Eddie in a quick walk past the market. Another tourist attraction is the live eels squirming about in a fish tank in the window of a Chinese restaurant. How anyone can even eat one of those greasy-looking critters amazes Easy Eddie? The customers even pick the live eel they desire to eat, as the Pearl River backwater cook grasps the creature with a pair of tongs. Some Asians even eat the squirming eel live. Easy Eddie has watched some Hong Kongese drip lemon juice on freshly sliced up eel parts to make them wriggle, then take the moving piece of eel with their chopsticks and devour them. He even has witnessed the satisfying smile on a patron, as she swallowed the squirming eel. Easy Eddie first heard the Chinese expression: *way dow ha jee la* (delicious), from one of these Hong Kongese, after she swallowed a piece of squirming eel.

It takes two blocks of walking to liberate Easy Eddie's nostrils from the stench of fresh fish. How he hates that smell? He thanks God that he was never forced into the fish business.

On arriving at the Svensen Real Estate Company office, Easy Eddie notices that the office looks deserted. Nonetheless, he tries the door. To his surprise, it opens. The sexy secretary is quick to greet him.

Secretary in a louder than normal voice, "Eddie, what a pleasant surprise, what can I do for you?"

Easy Eddie somewhat taken back by the secretary's friendliness, "Is Mr. Svensen in?"

Secretary "No, Eddie, he's on the Mainland on business. Can I take a message for him?"

Easy Eddie noticing the nervousness of the secretary, "Well, I've been trying to reach him for some time now."

Secretary "Yes, I know. He hasn't called in from his trip. It's some big land project in South America, I understand. I can give him a message when he does call, if you would like to leave one?"

Easy Eddie sensing that there is something wrong, "Just leave a note that I stopped in to see him. Have him call me as soon as he gets back, please."

Secretary jots down Easy Eddie's note, "OK, I'll see to it that he gets your message the moment he gets back in his office. Is there anything else I can help you with?"

Easy Eddie senses that despite her friendliness, the secretary is too nervous in his presence. She wants him out of there as soon as possible. There is something wrong. Easy Eddie wonders if Kai Svensen has heard about his deposition. If he has, then he probably will choose to distance himself from Easy Eddie. This is probably what has happened.

Easy Eddie "Well, I need to get going. Give Mr. Svensen my best."

Secretary walks around her desk to escort Easy Eddie out of the office. She opens the door to let Easy Eddie out.

Secretary whispers to Easy Eddie as he steps out of the office, "Eddie, don't come around here anymore, the police were here talking to Kai about something really serious. I overheard them mention your name, and Kai really got scared."

Easy Eddie struggles to maintain his composure, "Thanks."

Easy Eddie steps onto the sidewalk and walks away quickly toward the vault. The secretary closes the door behind him. After a few steps toward the vault, he remembers that he does not have the guns. He changes directions and decides to walk back to his store.

Times will be tense, it seems. The thought of the prominent real estate brokers being involved in a murder for hire scam really will shake them up. He hopes they just can deny their involvement. With the kind of lawyers that slither about these guys, Easy Eddie concludes, they should be able to hamper any police work against them. Anyway, Easy Eddie thinks it might be too much wishful thinking to ask if that secretary will still be part of the deal with Kai Svensen. She had one stinky fish he did not mind sniffing.

If it were not for bad luck lately, Easy Eddie would not have any luck at all. The Chinese call it: *jos*. To the Chinese, life is a series of good and bad *jos*. It appears Easy Eddie is experiencing a run of bad *jos*. He just has to be patient and soon his fortunes will change.

As he approaches the building housing his store, the jewelry repair shop owner sees Easy Eddie. The jewelry repair shop owner quickly cowers his head, turns and walks in the opposite direction. Easy Eddie experiences a bitter sweetness in the jewelry shop owner's actions. On the one hand, it means the jewelry repair shop owner suspects Easy Eddie masterminded the robbery of his store. But, on the other hand, it means Easy Eddie will not have to hear the latest inflated figure the robbers stole from the jewelry repair shop owner's store. Easy Eddie relishes not hearing the inflated figure more than the owner's negative suspicions. Benefits come in strange packages. This could be a sign that some good *jos* is coming his way.

Easy Eddie's Store

The afternoon is uneventful in Easy Eddie's store. The walk-in traffic is slower that usual. Jacob comments on the decrease in special orders. Though no one mentions anything in particular as a reason for the slowdown in business, all the partners suspect Easy Eddie's making the front page in the newspaper as the major contributing factor. Easy Eddie tries to shake it off, but the disappointing stares from the partners are hard to evade.

It is strange how something so exciting at one time can become so depressing at another time. At least, Easy Eddie lived in the fast lane for a while; whereas, his partners, typical prodding Chinese, tiptoed through life. Easy Eddie would not have changed a thing. Life should be lived and not avoided. As for respect, probably in the churchgoers' eyes, Easy Eddie has diminished, but oh how he has been elevated in the wise guys' eyes. In whose eyes does Easy Eddie want to be admired most? It is in the eyes of his peers, the wise guys. The disparaging stares of the partners are a small price.

Jacob interrupts Easy Eddie's thoughts and busy work in the storeroom, "Eddie, your lawyer is on the phone."

Easy Eddie as he checks the wall clock. It is after 4:00 PM. This is a late call for an attorney.

Easy Eddie responds to Jacob, "OK, thanks."

Easy Eddie takes the call at his desk, "Yes, sir."

Lawyer "Eddie, I just finished talking with the robbery detectives. They said they would drop the charges pending against you, if you volunteered to take a polygraph. They will set one up, if you agree. What do you think?"

Easy Eddie without hesitation, "That sounds great! When can I take it?"

Lawyer "I just needed to respond to them. They will set it up for a later date."

Easy Eddie sensing the lawyer's pleasure with his quick response, "OK, I'll wait to hear from you."

Lawyer "This case looks good, Eddie. The robbery detectives have doubts about the credibility of the guys trying to implicate you. This volunteer polygraph will close the case pending against you for them."

Easy Eddie "Well, I'm glad to hear that."

Easy Eddie commends the lawyer on his initiative and support then returns to his busy work in the storeroom.

Shortly after 5:00 PM, Jacob informs Easy Eddie that he is locking up the store. The other partners left at 5:00 PM sharp, as usual. Easy Eddie recalls he has to wait around for Billy to bring him the guns.

Sure enough, there is a light tapping on the rear door at 5:30 PM. Billy is right on time.

Easy Eddie opens the rear door and greets Billy, "You are right on time, Billy. There is nothing like punctuality in this world."

Billy with a heavy-looking paper bag cradled under his arm, "Some appointments, Eddie, have to be kept. I want you to know I passed up shagging this haole tourist to make it on time."

Easy Eddie surprised, "Where did you meet this haole tourist?"

Billy "She was hanging around the Chinese martial arts school, looking to see a real Chinese martial artist. And, Edward and I just happened to be sparring in the exercise room."

Easy Eddie exhales, "No kidding!"

Billy setting the heavy bag on Easy Eddie's desk, "As God is my witness, Eddie, the gal wanted to shag a Chinese martial artist."

Easy Eddie "What did you do with her?"

Billy raising both his arms out with palms up in gesture offering an embrace, "Eddie, what could I do? I promised you I would be here."

Easy Eddie "You didn't just leave her there, did you?"

Billy "Eddie, I couldn't do that. She was so fine, too. I introduced her to Edward. Edward took her to the Chinese restaurant across the street from the martial arts school."

Easy Eddie "That place is a dive. There are better looking places on the wharves in Hong Kong."

Billy "Eddie, think of it this way. She will be experiencing Chinese all the way."

Easy Eddie shakes his head, "Is she really fine?"

Billy "Oh yes, Eddie, she's a looker. She's young. She's blonde and from some place in Northern California."

Easy Eddie as he inspect the contents of the bag, "I see the guns are still in their sealed plastic bags."

Billy "We never had to use them, Eddie."

Easy Eddie "That's good. This way, they will be easier to return."

Billy "You have quite a little arrangement going with the cops, don't you?"

Easy Eddie "Well, we do favors for one another."

Billy "Getting them to clean your guns is a big favor, Eddie. I hope you realize that if someday the heat gets near them, they will do you in."

Easy Eddie, realizing how true what Billy is saying, stutters, "I know, Billy, I know."

Billy "You be careful with the boys in blue. They can get as nasty as Frank and his Mokes. And, trust me, they are not as loyal as Frank."

Easy Eddie realizing just how shaky his bond with the police could be, "I know. Sometimes, you have to make strange alliances."

Billy "Don't I know that, Eddie."

There is a short pause as Easy Eddie's mind floods with negative connotations from Billy's cautions.

Billy "Eddie, I hate to just run off, but I can't keep a lady waiting. If you know what I mean?"

Easy Eddie just laughs, "Go on, and get out of here. Give her a pump for me."

Billy sees his own way out of the storeroom.

Easy Eddie places the bag securely in his side drawer and locks it. Suddenly, he realizes he should call Hans to get the last gun back. Easy Eddie thumbs through his rolodex for Hans' number. The phone rings a few times before Hans' wife answers.

Hans' wife "*Yoboseo.*" ("Hello" in Korean)

Easy Eddie "Is Hans at home?"

Hans' wife "Sorry, Eddie, Hans is on deployment."

Easy Eddie surprised, "Where did he go?"

Hans' wife "He's underwater, Eddie."

Easy Eddie "How long will be gone?"

Hans' wife thinks for a moment, "Um, I think a month. This is a short trip."

Easy Eddie thanks Hans' wife and hangs up the phone. He settles into his chair. If Hans is gone for a month, he will not be around for anyone to interview or subpoena him. I guess the only gun left will be secure. Easy Eddie feels he has securely buttoned up the gun business.

It is after 6:00 PM now. Easy Eddie contemplates going home to see Patricia; however, he feels that his mind is too unsettled just yet. What he needs, he thinks, is a few hands of poker. It has been a while since he visited the beauty salon on the floor below. Usually, he drops in on the game down there during the lunch hour. Yes, why not stop in before he goes home?

Easy Eddie quickly checks the lock up of the store, shuts off the lights and makes his way down the stairwell to the beauty salon. Sure enough, the game is still going strong.

Easy Eddie quick to announce his intention to play, "How's it? Can I sneak in a few hands with you guys?"

The group of five responds, "Sure thing, Eddie, we need your money. Grab a seat."

There are two seats open. Easy Eddie selects the one nearest to the entrance doorway. They call that seat the dead man's seat, because when you are in it you cannot see a new person entering the gambling house. Some players made up the name in reference to Wild Bill, the western cowboy who was assassinated while paying poker with a poker hand of two black aces and two black eights.

The group is multi-ethnic. Joe, to Easy Eddie's immediate left, is a Chinese-hoale businessman. Frank, next in the serving direction, is a Hawai'ian cook. Gail owns a brothel on River Street. Son Tok is a Korean appliance repairman. Russell is a Japanese lawyer.

Easy Eddie "What are we playing?"

Gail begins dealing, "This is Atomic Bomb, Eddie. Put your ante up."

Atomic Bomb is high-low, multiple, wild card game in which each player receives two initial cards. Three cards are placed face up, one at a time with subsequent bidding, in the center of the table. After each card is turned up in the center, the players are allowed to exchange one of the cards in their hand. Bidding occurs after each center card is turned up and after each hand card is exchanged. The game involves limit bidding with a maximum of three raises per bid.

As the bidding unfolds, Easy Eddie realizes that *jos* is not with him this evening. After two hands, accompanied by some reckless and incompetent play, Easy Eddie bids the group farewell. His wallet is lighter, and he has expunged enough unsettling angst to venture home to Patricia. Gambling has a cleansing effect on Easy Eddie, especially, when he loses. Eddie gets cleansed more often than he cares to admit.

As Easy Eddie is about the leave the table, Frank says, "Bring more money next time, Eddie."

Easy Eddie just chuckles and moves his chair away from the table.

Russell chides, "You could think of hitting a few more jewelry stores before you sit down to play, Eddie."

Easy Eddie contorts his face, stops short of professing his innocence and leaves the room. On the way down the elevator to the underground garage, Easy Eddie realizes that the comment was made in jest. He cannot help thinking how many non-vocal comments are made that are not in jest. How many of those types of comments are made with conviction? That newspaper headline could have ruined his business.

Exiting the elevator, Easy Eddie walks briskly to his car. As he approaches, he notices the left rear tire is flat. Upon closer inspection, a nail is found imbedded into the tire. Someone hammered a nail into his tire. It was probably done around 5:00 PM. That way, the tire would not be noticed and would leak air as he drove the car. He would probably be on the highway when the tire went flat. This is a popular trick with the college pranksters when someone steals their parking spot. The funny part is, if you discover the nail beforehand and remove it, then the tire just goes flat, as you listen to air gush out.

Easy Eddie opens the trunk and takes out his extra tire and car jack. It will take some getting use to the benefits of his new popularity. Undoubtedly, the jewelry repair shop owner did this. He is the cowardly, backstabbing type anyway. Easy Eddie gets to work changing his tire while the sun eases slowly below the horizon. Hurried bird sounds serenade Easy Eddie, as he toils with the jack and struggles with the tire. At least it is warm and a small price to pay for the looting and popularity.

CHAPTER 14

Hui's Lawyer Office

The *hui*'s lawyer and Erik are meeting over the recent briefs that have been submitted and argued in court. The lawyer recounts the points raised in his delivery to the circuit civil court judge, as Erik reads through the pleadings.

Lawyer "You know, Erik, when I mentioned which side of the fence the 'No Trespassing' signs were on, the judge seemed genuinely startled. This was in reference to the proposed forty-four-foot roadway through the fifty-acre parcel."

Erik "I was just reading the transcript where you asked if the vendors felt the cows, enclosed by that fence, could read. It does give the impression that the opposition's pleadings are frivolous."

Lawyer "It sure does give that impression. I don't think this judge is too pleased to hear this case. It seems to unnerve him. There is something more to this case. At some points in the proceedings, the judge actually scowled at the opposition's attorneys."

Erik "Really? That does seem strange. Do you think that this judge is somehow connected to this case?"

Lawyer "I'm getting that impression. Sometime in the past, it seems, this judge encountered this material. He seems way too familiar with the valley."

Erik "Maybe it is just the brief his clerk provided him on the case."

Lawyer "I doubt it. Although the clerks do provide the judges with an input on the relevant case law, the judges seldom read it all. They are just too overloaded. They skim through the brief, at best, to acquire the clerk's conclusion. No, this judge knows this valley."

Erik "Maybe, the judge just overheard a similar case."

Lawyer "That's a distinct possibility. If that is true, then he is scowling at the opposition's attorneys for suppressing the information that we are presenting."

Erik "Now, that makes sense. I see here where you point out how the opposition's lawyers are intentionally half-quoting case law to support their position; whereas, the actual full-quote of the same case law would be detrimental to their pleadings."

Lawyer "Yes, the opposition's lawyers intentionally have been misleading the court."

Erik "Isn't that in violation of the Hawai'i Revised Statues for courtroom procedure?"

Lawyer "It sure is a violation; however, the courts nowadays are run so loosely that no one reports any violations. The judges are near incompetent as lawyers. Hence, the courts are running amok with shoddy pleadings. As an example, just the other day, a hot shot graduate from the local law school pleaded for legal fees in case that his firm lost. And, the judge actually allowed the case to be heard. He should have disbarred the imbecile right on the spot for being so stupid."

Erik "Is it really that bad in the Hawai'i courtrooms?"

Lawyer "You're damn right, it is. This is like some weird fantasy where the court is in a dream state of free thinking. Lawyers go into the court and plead total nonsense, and the court, none the wiser, takes serious issue in their motions. Look at our case, a basic understating of the subdivision law tells you that a City & County roadway is required to be forty-four-feet in width and no lot can be considered separate and unique in the state of Hawai'i unless it has access. The *hui*'s lot lacks both. We should be winning hands down. This would be summary judgment material in any other state in the Union."

Erik "How do the vendors' lawyers prolong this nonsense?"

Lawyer "There is something more to this. Somehow, I suspect this judge was implicated in some way with the manner in which this valley got so screwed up."

Erik "Once, when I mentioned this circuit civil court judge's name to an associate high up in the Republican Party here in Hawai'i, she told me this judge used to be the head of the tax office here in Hawai'i."

Lawyer sitting up abruptly, "Did she really say that? My God! He might have been the one responsible for issuing the tax key numbers to all these unsubdivided lots. That's why the judge is scowling at the vendors' attorneys. The vendors set him up when he headed the tax office."

Erik shocked, "WOW! This is a revelation. How did he become a judge?"

Lawyer "I guess he couldn't hack it as senior bureaucrat, so they made him a judge to give him a job. Besides, it appears the Democratic Party knew he would come in handy someday."

Erik "Doesn't a judge require some formal training in law to be appointed?"

Lawyer "Well, I suspect he may have matriculated through some law school at some time. Or, worse yet, the powers-that-be just may have fabricated his credentials."

Erik "Would someone make up a law degree for this guy?"

Lawyer "Erik, trust me, I've seen worse. Besides, when you look at the caliber of the oversight group, you could process anything through these guys. Erik, we just had a surgeon who was banned from practicing medicine in three states operate on some poor soul and stick a screwdriver blade, that he purchased at Wal-Mart, into the patient's spine to lock his vertebrae together. A Wal-Mart screwdriver, Erik! The oversight group let this physician's banned credentials pass right through and allowed him to acquire affiliation with one of our largest medical hospitals. Erik, we had some Frankenstein-like-freak performing surgery. The nurses on the operating staff, under fear for their jobs, reported the ghoul."

Erik "When you make that example, I guess, the courts aren't so bad."

Lawyer "Well, the courts are incompetent, but the oversight is worse. The Hawai'i judicial system is a rudderless ship in the high seas. Sooner or later, it will flounder. Right now, we can sense the water lapping over the gunwales. It will take a lot of effort to get this ship ready to sail again. It will take more effort than most lawyers in the state are willing to expend. That's why the courts don't get fixed. We just sail until we run aground."

Erik "This is so sad, because so many innocent people get screwed in the meantime."

Lawyer "That's right. When fantasy pleadings become the norm, it only takes a few bribes to send the judicial system into utter chaos...like we find ourselves now."

Erik "Did you uncover anything concerning those political contributions allegations?"

Lawyer "The main lawyers for the opposition are from a law firm that has a history of being well-connected to the Democratic Party. As a matter of fact, the head partner of the law firm is under investigation for precisely what concerns us. Did you know he was the City Finance Director?"

Erik "No, I never thought even to ask who the head lawyer was for that law firm. Has he ever pleaded in one of our appearances?"

Lawyer "No, he spends most of his time dealing with the affairs of the City Finance Department. The Feds believe that he is the bagman for the Democratic Party in the City & County. Just to let you know, I tried to subpoena him, but the sheriff came back and told me that he could not find him."

Erik "How's that possible? If he is the City Finance Director, he should be readily available."

Lawyer "That's what I am saying, Erik. The man is so powerful, the sheriffs refuse to serve him."

Erik "This could mess up the entire legal process, if we have people in the state that no one can serve. How can he subvert the law like that?"

Lawyer "Speaking of the law, the word has it that when his tour as City Finance Director is up, he will be appointed as a judge in recognition of his superior service to the community."

Erik "Do you mean to say that a person who openly evades legal service is being considered for a judgeship?"

Lawyer "Well, he was being considered prior to his evading of service. I doubt the approval committee can overlook such a travesty of judicial procedure. If they did, it would tarnish their competence. You could say our attempt at service on this guy guillotined his aspiration of judgeship."

Erik chuckles, "Whoopee! Something we have done has brought about a change in the way these Democrats do business."

Lawyer "I suspect before we are done, the Democratic Party will change a lot of the ways that they do business."

Erik "What about the head of the Land Department did we get him deposed?"

Lawyer "Yes, actually, the opposition's attorneys went to great lengths to defend him at the deposition. Their lawyers brought up every conceivable objection to derail my line of questioning. Obviously, this guy is a weak link in their defense. The gist of his deposition was that he felt he could make decisions however he chose irrespective of the land regulations, because he was in charge."

Erik "That's an incredible response! Isn't he sworn to uphold the regulations as condition of his appointment as the head the Land Department?"

Lawyer "That he is. What we have here is a numb-nuts, political animal pretending to be a bureaucrat. This guy has no clue as to what it takes to run a department. After hearing his testimony, I wouldn't hire this guy to serve coffee at a fast food outlet."

Erik "How does a person like this rise to such lofty heights in the administration?"

Lawyer "Like I said, he's a political animal. He demonstrates strong loyalties to the powers-that-be in the Democratic Party. They can trust him to act in accordance with their wishes regardless of the situation. To tell you my honest opinion, this guy probably does not suspect the problems that he is creating by allowing all these improperly subdivided and sewaged lots. Erik, this guy, like most of the political animals appointed to similar statures, is clueless as to the regulations that he has been entrusted to enforce."

Erik "How does he get buy, if he is clueless?"

Lawyer raises his hands palms up, "Just like he did in his oral deposition, the opposition's attorneys defend him with stall tactics."

Erik "Aren't the attorneys in violation of the statutes by employing these tactics?"

Lawyer "They sure are, Erik, but to whom is anyone going to complain? The same kinds of people operate the legal oversight group. One set of numb-nuts is not going to chastise another set of numb-nuts. They are a brotherhood of morons. As Ben Franklin said after the decision was made by the colonies to split from the English Crown: 'If we don't hang together in this, we can be certain that we will all hang separately.' That statement rings true for any clandestine endeavor. That could be the motto of the state's corrupt Democratic Party."

Erik "Did Franklin really say that?"

Lawyer "He sure did. You could say he was the spokesperson for all political animals."

Erik "There must be some limit to what the head of the Land Department will tolerate, isn't there?"

Lawyer leans toward Erik, "Erik, this numb-nut wasn't moved even when I showed him the civil engineering report that the vendors' proposed, sixteen-foot-access easement to the *hui*'s property was so steep that a US Army tank could not traverse it. Now, you have to be pretty stupid not to acknowledge unsuitability, if a tank can't use it. Well, this guy is that stupid."

Erik "This is incredible!"

Lawyer "This is a measure of how bad things get when a mob of morons takes control of the administration of the state. The civil engineering report on the unsuitability of the proposed access route should be slam-dunk criteria for summary judgment. It's not. The circuit civil court judge even overlooks it."

Erik "Do these people realize how bad this makes the judiciary look when shenanigans like this get publicized?"

Lawyer "No editor in Honolulu will print anything like this. If they did, they would be 'hanging separately' for sure. The newspapers are politically-censured, if you haven't already figured that out."

Erik surprised, "I hadn't realized how closed the state of Hawai'i was."

Lawyer "Welcome to paradise!"

Erik stunned by the revelation that the press was not as free as he believed that it was. American institutions seem valueless all of a sudden.

Erik looking through the notes, “What does the title company have to say about all this?”

Lawyer “Now, there is an interesting question. Their response is mixed. In one aspect, they acknowledge responsibility for the correctness of the property rights; however, when confronted with this humongous mess, they circle the wagons in defense. They realize, correctly, that they may be held liable for all these illegally subdivided lots. When you consider that some one thousand lots could have title problems, the financial damages hit them like an atomic bomb. They would be devastated. Accordingly, it is not hard for me to appreciate their reluctance to cooperate. If we should prevail, then they become liable for all these screw-ups by the agents of the Blackwater Holdings.”

Erik “You don’t think they will take responsibility for all this, do you?”

Lawyer “Erik, this is too big. This could bankrupt the state of Hawai’i not to mention the title company. Just think, Erik, they have to pay the premiums and/ or right the problems. The premium on the *hui*’s property is $1.5 Million. Most lots are smaller than the *hui*’s lot, but nonetheless they would draw as a mean of some $400,000.00 per lot. Now, multiply $400,000.00 per lot by 1000 lots and you get $400 Million in just premium payouts. In order for the title company to use the property, they would need to bring each lot to City & County standards. That means proper subdivisions with proper access, water, and sewage. You can see the development costs rising to over a billion dollars. That would be money spent that they would have little chance of recouping from the sale proceeds. Remember, the title company premiums were set on bases that all these lots met City & County standards. Hence, the effort to develop them properly would not materialize in much added value to the lots. The roads, sewage and water lines would not be recouped in the resale prices. The title company could be looking at a $400-$600 Million loss. Erik, they can’t allow us to prevail.”

Erik “Can’t the title company cross-claim against the City & County for approving all these bogus lots?”

Lawyer “The City & County expects them to do just that. That’s another reason why the City & County will team up with the title company and the vendors against us. They are all on the hook for this fiasco.”

Erik “There must be some light at the end of the tunnel for us. We are right!”

Lawyer “I know, Erik. I know we are right, but they are so wrong it would be like falling into an abyss of debt for the City & County. They could never recover. So, they will use whatever means available to defeat us. They will fabricate scenarios to beat us. We can expect a horde of bad faith affidavits on surveys, testimonials, etc. We will be deluged with falsehoods and trickery.”

Erik shaking his head, "This isn't the country that I defended when I served in the military."

Lawyer exhaling loudly, "I know, I know. This is the product of one political party holding onto power too long and getting complacent in their duties."

Erik "Why weren't there any checks and balances on these bogus subdivisions?"

Lawyer "Most oversight agencies are staffed by political appointees who see their jobs as compensation for their political duties. They know and do little except keep track of their pay. With respect to our matter, they are incompetent, as are most of the bureaucrats that oversee these subdivisions. If the high boss gives his consent to the project, the minions under him just follow suit without question. The atrocities of bureaucracy run amok are what we are witnessing."

Erik "Do you think we are lost, legally, because of all this mess?"

Lawyer leaning back in his chair, "Well, Erik, as your attorney, I shouldn't answer that question."

Erik "Just be honest with me, off the record. Is it too late for us to back out now?"

Lawyer pressing his lips together, "OK, in the state circuit civil court, I feel the opposition will have too much influence. However, when this case is reviewed by the appellate or state supreme court, it will be another matter. At the state supreme court level, the justices will be required to make a ruling that will effect all other cases in the future. It will not be so easy to evade the facts here. Remember, any future case can reference the case law in the state supreme court's decision. These fantasized subdivision boundaries will not be able to stand up in the state supreme court."

Erik "Would you recommend a strategy that prepares the case for the state supreme court?"

Lawyer "Yes, that was, in fact, my intention. I will submit all the data in my pleadings to the circuit civil court in order for them to be reviewed in the appellate or supreme court."

Erik chuckles, "This was your strategy all along, wasn't it?"

Lawyer smiles, "Yes, I felt I should prepare for the higher courts. Once I appreciated the complexity of the mess ups out their in the valley, I realized the opposition would muster all the political support that they could to derail us, including steering our case to a politically-correct circuit civil court judge. Now that you have revealed to me the connection between this judge that was selected to adjudicate our case and the tax office, I realize that we are being set up. This judge can't decide against us without slinging mud on his administration of the tax office for issuing the bogus tax key numbers on all these unsubdivided lots."

Erik "Politics is a dirty business, isn't it?"

Lawyer "It sure is. That is why I never got involved in it. I knew that one day I would have to take a fall just like this judge is doing to cover some scoundrel's tracks. See, this circuit civil court judge knows his career and reputation for proper judgments are finished after this case. I'm not the only genius in town that will figure out why he made such a poor decision. He will be removed from the circuit civil court, once the appellate or supreme court reviews this case."

Erik "I hadn't realized it would go so bad on him."

Lawyer "The appellate or supreme court will support him, but they will recommend that he be removed at an appropriate time in the future."

Erik "Do you think the appellate or supreme court would decide against us to protect this judge?"

Lawyer "It will be harder for them to do so. But, if they can salvage the reputation of the judiciary on some technicality, they will do so. Keep in mind that any decision by the supreme court will empower all other pleadings to reference that decision. Hence, an error in their judgment will continue to spawn more erroneous decisions until it festers into discreditation of the judiciary. The supreme court of Hawai'i cannot allow that to happen. That would lead to complete disgrace for the state of Hawai'i."

Erik "We have a chance then in the supreme court, don't we?"

Lawyer "I think we have a good chance in the supreme court. This mess is too encompassing with too many severe ramifications to overlook."

Erik "Do you really think this circuit civil court judge would be politically biased as to overlook our findings?"

Lawyer "Erik, some time ago, a prominent lawyer drew this circuit civil court judge in a case. He came to the same conclusions that we have. In an attempt to embarrass the judge, the lawyer dropped on his knees, in the courtroom, and pleaded with the judge to give him a fair trial."

Erik shocked, "Are you serious? He dropped on his knees right in the courtroom!"

Lawyer "He dropped right on his knees in the courtroom and pleaded for a fair trial. This circuit civil court judge demanded the attorney take back what he said. When the attorney refused, the judge had him arrested for contempt of court. The attorney spent a few days in jail, before he came back into court and apologized for what he said."

Erik "WOW, they must have roughed him up in jail."

Lawyer "I never heard what they did to the guy in jail, but as soon as the trial was over, he left the state of Hawai'i for good. And, Erik, he was a prominent lawyer in town. The political powers in the state were sending all the rest of us lawyers a message not to question their judges. These are serious people we are dealing with. We should never forget that. They choose to enforce the laws, as they please."

Erik "This sounds like organized crime."

Lawyer "They are just a bunch of political cronies who have been in power too long. I wouldn't go so far as to say organized. Look at this mess in the valley. It is hard to imagine anything-organized going on here. They are just a bunch of numb-nuts trying to cover their errors."

Erik chuckles, "I see your point."

Lawyer "The point here is to keep our cool, especially in the courtroom."

The legal secretary interrupts the lawyer concerning another pressing legal matter. While the lawyer and the secretary discuss the proper wording of motion that needs to be filed in court later today, Erik continues to look over the notes of the depositions. He notices the large number of valley residents that have bought the illegal-designed septic tank. Erik has to chuckle when he reads the lawyer's report that few of these residents have ever seen the septic tank pumping truck in over five years. The lawyer assigned the affectionate term "honey dipper" to this vehicle. This is an environmental holocaust!

After reading the lawyer's notebook, Erik seriously considers if he wants the *hui* involved in this fiasco. If the *hui* continues to pursue this 99-acre property, they will be continually in the face of corrupt and incompetent City & County bureaucrats and managers. From the quick read of these notes, it is only too obvious that no one has been in charge in City & County for a few decades. The state has been a rudderless ship, cruising along on the good graces of its dwindling resources. Erik concludes that Punaluu Valley will be a continuous legal nightmare. There are enough screw-ups out here to discredit the entire Democratic Party forever.

The secretary thanks the lawyer for the input on the document and closes the door behind her, as she leaves the room. The lawyer takes a few moments to reorganize his thinking.

Lawyer rearranging his tie, "Sorry about that, she needed some right words for a motion."

Erik "Having the right words is important."

Lawyer exhaling, "It sure is important. With these judges, you have to have all the right buzzwords to get them to understand your case. It's sad, but I doubt most of these judges understand the motions being presented. They rely on first year law clerks to explain the cases to them. Now, tell me, what does a first year clerk at anything know about anything…even good sex."

The two men laugh out loud.

Erik after he regains his composure, "I've been mulling over the disaster this valley is in. I'm not so sure the *hui* would want to try to develop out here. It might take decades to resolve even this remediation issue."

Lawyer "Well, I appreciate your point. I believe the best recourse here is to claim against the title company for the property and investment loss due to inadequate subdivision. Since this eventually will be adjudicated as willful negligence…even malicious with your recent experience on Maunakea Street…we should be able to acquire treble damages or more. I would opt for that route in this litigation process. Taking the property just guarantees you a few more days in court."

Erik "I approve of that course of action. Let's just go for damages. I don't want this property after reading all your findings."

Lawyer "Yes, I was appalled myself, as I recorded the data. This is really a terrible situation for the state of Hawai'i to have to reconcile. Lots of taxpayer money will be forfeited over this mess up."

Erik "Why won't Blackwater Holdings have to rectify this?"

Lawyer "Blackwater Holdings has many strong, financial supporters who can become overwhelmingly generous when the time comes. They will buy their way out of this and persuade the City & County to accept, at taxpayers' expense, the liability for cleaning up this mess. Or, they will use their financial influence to buy a decision against us."

The room falls silent after the lawyer's last sentence.

Erik eventually manages to speak, "That's what Blackwater Holdings will do, isn't it?"

Lawyer nodding his head up and down, "That's why I am preparing for the appellate or supreme court."

Erik "When you put this Punaluu Valley mess in financial-liability terms, it is easy to visualize the course of action the opposition will take."

Lawyer "It's kind of like having X-ray vision, isn't it?"

Erik chuckles, "Yes, it is."

New York Deli, Old Territorial Building

The meeting concludes with a clear plan of action to go for the damages rather than attempt to keep the property and develop it. Erik hobbles his way down the hallway with an ankle cast that stretches up to just below his knee. The ankle is still tender, but he is able to ambulate with a minimum of grimacing.

Upon exiting the elevator, Erik decides to grab a snack before he treks his way back to his condo. As he files through the line of the New York style deli, he notices the afternoon headlines about an ongoing murder trial. After selecting his sandwich and a small bottle of orange juice, he adds a copy of the afternoon newspaper to his tab.

It is a cool afternoon. A slight breeze is coming up from the harbor tunneling its way through the open area in the Old Territorial Building. Erik has to place the orange juice bottle on a part of the open newspaper to keep it from flapping back and forth.

The headline reads: Police Lose Murder Weapon. Erik reads with interests how a murder weapon, stored in the police evidence locker, was misplaced. The prosecutor demanded an explanation from the supervisor of the police evidence locker, as to how something like that could happen. Apparently, the murder weapon was the key item in the prosecution's case against the defendant. Without the murder weapon, the defendant will prevail. The paper details the procedure for accountability of police evidence. Somehow, this particular item was misplaced in the evidence locker. Despite a thorough search of the entire evidence locker, the missing item was not found. From the words quoted of the prosecutor's reaction, he was livid over the misplacement of the evidence by the police. The article ended with the presiding criminal court judge dismissing the case against the defendant. This was a contract murder case.

Erik realizes that contract murder is the worst type of crime. It is passionless. A cold-hearted killer takes money to do someone in. Contract murderers have to be taken out of society. There is no excuse for that type of behavior. Erik has to read the article again to fathom the severity of the error by the police. He appreciates the anger displayed by the prosecutor. The prosecutor had this cold-blooded killer dead to rights. Somehow, the police dropped the ball and misplaced the murder weapon. Erik surmises that it had to be an inside job. Someone with access to the evidence locker went in and took the murder weapon out without telling anyone. That someone had to have free access to the evidence locker. How else could he remove such an important item without being detected? Corruption is dug in deep in Hawai'i.

Finishing off his sandwich and orange juice, he drops the newspaper into a trash receptacle. All the way back to his condo, he ponders the implications of a breach of the police evidence locker. If the crooks can breach the evidence locker, then they can distort just about anything the police are doing. Erik pictures his own situation. The same kind of cops that removed this crucial evidence could be involved in his hit-and-run case. If that is in fact the case, then he has no chance of bringing the culprits who tried to kill him to justice. It is a disturbing thought that the average citizen is at the mercy of these demented crooks. Erik concludes that the police cannot be trusted.

This afternoon, it is a long walk for Erik to his condo. His mind continually plays over and over how many groups are stacked against him and his *hui*. The utter hopelessness of the endeavor discourages him. The thought that he could be requested to attend a settlement meeting that is merely a pre-arranged hit on him in disguise unnerves him tremendously. How could he possibly know? This is gangster mentality. This is prison block mentality. He is a babe in the woods in this environment. His reflexes will not always be able to save him, as they did on Maunakea Street. Sooner or later, his luck will run out.

By the time he reaches the front, security door to his condo, his ankle is throbbing. It was a longer walk then he anticipated. At least he made it alive. Since the cops might be implicated, these culprits might feel that it is open season on him and try to do him in again. All of a sudden, Maunakea Street seems so unfriendly. Danger could pop out of any one of the crawl alleys that separate the old buildings lining the street. Erik decides definitely to avoid the intersection of Maunakea and Pauahi Streets. One brush with death was enough for him at that intersection.

What a day! How his ankle hurts from the walking. All he can think of as he takes the elevator up to his floor is raising his ankle to reduce the swelling. He will make himself a hot cup of tea, watch the news and rest his ankle all evening, as the street sounds and police sirens serenade him.

Entering his condo, he nearly collapses from the sudden immersion in air conditioning. He forgot to turn off the air conditioner before he left, so the room has cooled all day. It pleases him to feel his skin tighten to the colder temperature of the room. Settling into his chair, he forgets all about the hot tea. He closes his eyes, raises his ankle onto the back of another chair so it is well above his heart, and exclaims, "What a day!"

The sound of a sudden police siren disturbs his contemplation. Erik wonders if the police are responding to a genuine call for assistance or another police-involved hit. He always will ask that question from here on out. He cannot trust the motivation of the police anymore. How can he trust anyone in authority in the state of Hawai'i?

[illegible]ILOGUE

The real li[illegible] has never been convicted of any crime. He eventually was forced to se[illegible] his business soon after the other partners retired. Currently, he is retired and enjoys reminiscing with the remaining wise guys about the old days and their shenanigans.

The real life Albert, the Crematorium Operator, received a life sentence for his involvement in the murder for hire hit described in the novel. He is serving time in prison today.

The real life Frank Kealoha failed in his bid to become Governor of the State of Hawaii.

The real life Joshua Puna is serving a life sentence in prison for the murder of his girlfriend in the O'ahu sugar cane fields.

The real life Billy joins Easy Eddie regularly to reminisce the good old days. He has escaped prosecution to this date.

The *hui* lost the court battle against the real life Kai Svensen on the subdivision issue and were forced to forfeit the 99-acre lot. The investors in the *hui* lost all their investment. Kai Svensen subsequently resold the lot and won a second decision over subdivision status of the 99-acre lot against the new owners who purchased the property at the civil court auction. The real life Kai Svensen sold all his assets in the state of Hawai'i and moved to the Mainland.

The 99-acre lot remains unsubdivided to this date. The access, water, and sewage problems in Green/Punaluu/Waiono Valley remain unresolved to this date. Upon the author's last inspection, the Green Valley "access road" and the railroad right of way remained unpaved.

The majority of the real life politicians from the Punaluu electorate have been imprisoned.

After a gun battle between drug traffickers and the real life Bishop Estate personnel, the Drug Enforcement Agency (DEA) sealed off Green/Punaluu/Waiono Valley for 24 hours, resulting in tremendous reduction in the drug trade from the valley.

The real life Bishop Estate personnel removed over two miles of PVC piping from Green/Punaluu/Waiono Valley that redirected water from Punaluu Stream. The persons who laid those two miles of PVC piping remain unknown.

No drug traffickers from the Green/Punaluu/Waiono Valley area have ever been prosecuted.

Neither the real life Kai Svensen nor the real life Blackwater Holdings has ever been held accountable for the real estate and environmental disaster that they created in the Green/Punaluu/Waiono Valley.

The State Circuit Civil Court judges who adjudicate the problems in Green/ Punaluu/Waiono Valley in favor of the real life Kai Svensen and the real life Blackwater Holdings have either "resigned" or been "transferred out" of the State Civil Court System.

The law firm that defended the real life Kai Svensen and the real life Blackwater Holdings disintegrated as a result of their pleadings and shenanigans in the State Circuit Civil Court.

The Big Island underground marijuana plantation was discovered and shutdown by the DEA. The main operator of the plantation was sentenced to serve five years in prison.

The real life Detective Aoki and the real life Undercover Detective Edward were removed from the police force. Neither individual spent any time in prison.

The remaining gun that was removed from the Honolulu Police Department's Evidence Locker remains outstanding. ***The author offers a $100 bill to the first FBI or ATF Agent that appears on his doorstep with a property receipt form to take possession of the firearm.***

Abbreviations/Terms

AG	Attorney General
Apuaha	Hawai'ian word for tract of land from mountaintop to seashore
Brah	Local Hawaii'ian slang for man
Bishop Estate	Estate of Princess Bernice Pauahi Bishop
Big Island	Affectionate name for the island of Hawai'i
Breakfast wagon	Converted vehicle that serves plate lunches
Burning money	Hawai'ian underworld phrase for marijuana trafficking
DLU	Department of Land Utilization
DROA	Deposit, Receipt, Offer and Acceptance form. A form used for real estate transactions
4 Cs	Carat, clarity, color and cut in grading diamonds
carat (ct.)	100 points in one carat, diamond size measure
Chaka	gesture made with little finger and thumb of hand: Take it easy
Chinatown	a six-block by three-block area west of Downtown Honolulu
City & County	City & County of Honolulu (island of O'ahu)
Chocho	Hawai'ian slang word for male appendage
choto mate	Japanese for "one moment, please"
GIA	Gemologist Institute of America

H-1	Inter-island highway running east-west on O'ahu: Honolulu towards Waianae
H-2	Inter-island highway running south-north in Central O'ahu: Runs between the Koolau and the Waianae Mountain Ranges
H-3	Inter-island highway running south-north in the center of O'ahu: Pearl Harbor through the Koolau Mountain Range to Kaneohe
Haole	Hawai'ian word for foreigner–usually refers to white person
Hui	Hawai'ian word for group or company
Kamehameha Highway	Main roadway that circles the island of O'ahu
Karat (Kt.)	Gold measure of purity: 24 Kt. as 100% pure gold
Kimchee	spicy-hot, marinated Korean cabbage
Kingdom f Hawai'i	Hawai'i was a kingdom before it was annex to the United States
Koa	Tropical timber native to the Hawai'ian Islands
Koolau Mountains	Mountain range running the long length of the island of O'ahu
Kuleana	Hawai'ian word for a lot created by the Kingdom of Hawai'i
Lilikoi	tropical fruit that makes Guava
Louvre	Famous French art museum in Paris
Mercury	Code word for Wednesday from Mercury-day = French: Mecredi
Mahou	Hawai'ian word for female impersonator
Moke	Derogatory term for Hawai'ian male
Mokeland	Derogatory term for the Hawai'ian Homestead (Reservation) areas: Waimanalo and areas along the Waianae Coast
Okane	Japanese for "money"
Oral deposition	statements made under oath in person during an interview
Pigeons	slang term for gullible individuals easily taken advantage of

Plate lunch	meal on a paper plate consisting of an entrée, rice, and a vegetable
Popping his head	Hawai'ian underworld phrase for killing someone
PVC	Hard plastic like substance used to make piping materials
Saimin	Japanese noodle soup with spices
Sayonara	Japanese for "see you again"
Shinto	Japanese religion that stresses cleanliness and spirit worlds
Tita	Hawa'ian derogatory term for a masculine woman (tomboy)
Ukulele	small Hawai'ian guitar
VS	very slightly included clarity grade for diamond
VVS	very, very slightly included clarity grade for diamonds
Wahine	Hawai'ian word for female
Waianae Range	Mountain range running along the Waianae (West) Coast of O'ahu
Wakarimasen	Japanese for "I don't understand"
Waimanalo	Hawai'ian Homestead (Reservation) in Eastern O'ahu
Way dow ha jee la	Chinese for "delicious"
Worm	underworld slang term for heroin
Written	
Interrogatories	statements made under oath in writing
Yoboseo	Korean for "hello

0-595-30774-4